MAKIN' MY WAY

JOHN MUD

ARK ESSENTIALS PUBLISHING

CONTENTS

Ark Essentials Publishing

Ashton, Idaho 83420

Library of Congress Control Number: 2021914688

Makin' My Way

© 2021 Ark Essentials Publishing

All Rights Reserved

Hard cover ISBN: 978-0-9669280-4-4
Trade paperback ISBN: 978-0-9669280-2-0
Ebook ISBN: 978-0-9669280-3-7

Vers. 210923

A special thanks to:
Lila Martindale
Duane and Linda Kerbs
Dave and Julie Jacobson
And
My best friend who always believed in me
Vickie Smith

Here I go again. I'm off and running. I'd say I was moving about as fast as humanly possible. I might even be breaking some land speed records—for someone my size, that is. There is nothing like a dose of fear to stimulate the adrenaline output and get some serious g-forces working. If I could just find a way to bottle the stuff, I could make a fortune. Then maybe I could hire some bodyguards. With a couple of bodyguards carefully selected for their ability to inflict massive hemorrhages, compound fractures, and ruptured spleens, things would be different. Then maybe Clive Ashton and his three brothers, who live down the street in a dilapidated turn-of-the-century Victorian, and their assorted scuzzbucket friends, who laid claim to the neighborhood, and the hoods at school who bullied me since moving here in the fifth grade, after my dad left for greener pastures—and I mustn't forget, those less-than-attractive big mean dudes who are often found hanging out at the B&M Market on the corner of Burnside and 18th just two blocks north of my flat who make it hard for a guy with a slight gland problem to get his daily fix of Three Musketeers and cream sodas—would all get what's coming to them.

In 1965, being chased, beat up, or at the very least, picked on, which includes being made fun of, ridiculed, badgered, etc, for me, was pretty much a daily occurrence. Danger seemed to be around every corner. My life had flashed before my eyes so many times that I didn't even pay it any mind anymore. Not much of a life to keep reviewing anyway. It's kind of like an old rerun of a bad TV show you've seen a hundred times.

My name is John. I was born in California as the oldest of the youngest batch of children. Cindy—or actually, her real name is Cindra—is the youngest and the most protected and nurtured. Then there's Curt, my younger brother. He was a wanderer and a bit of a con. We never knew where he was and often had to send out search parties only to find him over at someone's house having dinner and watching TV. Cindy and Curt weren't bad as far as little brothers and sisters go. However, Curt would often get me in trouble with some of our local terrorists.

You see, Curt and I looked a lot alike. Even though he is a full twenty months younger, I would often be mistaken for him. This was not a good thing since Curt liked to rile up the bullies and tuff guys who roamed the streets of our neighborhood. He would often, without provocation, call them names directed toward their heritage and legitimacy and of course flip them off, usually from the safety of our front porch. Naturally I would come walking down the street minding my own business after one of Curt's motivational speeches and get thumped.

The oldest of my siblings is my sister Karen, who always had her nose in a book and frankly, that's about all I remember of her during our youth. However, I'll never forget when she went through a singing period that's still to this day indelibly etched into my mind's ear. I also remember her being very independent. She got a job as soon as she was of legal age and helped support our family during the tough transition times. She moved out on her own once the dust settled.

The second in the pecking order was Laurel. Mom named her after a bush. Everyone except family, of course, calls her Laurie. She was nice enough as sisters go and helped during the tough times as well. She too however removed herself from our family just as soon as she could find a suitable husband, which she did.

Next in line was my big brother, Scott. He's about six years older than me, and the youngest of the oldest batch of kids. He was the coolest guy I knew. It wasn't just his flat top with wings and the big D.A. greased back with a quarter cube of margarine or the black loafers, white socks, high-water Levi's and Sir jacket. No, he had cool running all through him. At least, it seemed so to a young dud like me. He was big and strong and played football at Parkrose High School. He also had the benefit of having a dad for most of his formative years, unlike me and my younger brother and sister.

Scott has often recounted the time when bullies were picking on him. We had just moved to Parkrose, a new suburb community of Portland, from Southern California. Some of the guys thought Scott's hair was not acceptable, since all of them were still sporting butches. They beat him up and told him if he didn't get a haircut, he would get more of the same.

Well, Scott did what most well-adjusted all-American kids do when they get in trouble. He went and told Dad. Dads are handy to have around. They know just what to do, and our dad was no different.

Our old man gathered his eldest son beneath his wing and said "Scott" in a very firm and confident manner, a manner that convinces one of his vast knowledge and wisdom gained from years of fighting through hard times and coming out the victor. "You are a big strong young man. What you need to do is stand up to these $#^&#@$" (Dad always had a way with words) "one at a time. The very next time you see one of them alone, go right up to him and let him have it, right in the gut, just as hard as you can. I guarantee you that those boys will leave you alone." So Scott did just that and the boys left him alone. I wish it were that easy for me.

My problem is, I can't make my feet stay put when the heat gets turned on. Before I have time to formulate a plan, I'm already halfway home. That is, if I don't get caught first. Then you'll find me under some pile of adolescent machismo getting what's coming to me, a fat kid who's rather vulnerable due to a lack of self-esteem and confidence.

But life wasn't all good. We moved from our nice new home in the suburbs, where everything was great and the future looked bright, where I had friends and did well in school, to a poor section of Portland. We had to rent a flat in a crummy neighborhood and accept assistance from the government until Mom was able to finish nursing school. Curt, Cindy, and I started attending Buckman Elementary, known for its troubled student body.

My dad was off doing his thing in the French Foreign Legion. Well, that's what I called it after hearing my mom say something about my dad's French Canadian girlfriend. My older sisters soon moved away, and Scott joined the Marine Corps. So, it was just my mom, Curt, Cindy, and me, a new school, new home, and new enemies. But I did make a friend.

Steven Hale was not your typical twelve-year-old boy. He was dirty. I mean, *really dirty*. Not just roll in the mud, have a good time kind of dirty that young boys often engage in. No, he was stinky dirty; never take a bath kind of dirty. He wore old second-or third—or even fourth-hand clothes—rags, really. His pants were always old baggy slacks that someone's grandpa had probably worn, maybe even died in. Steve would tug his belt tight to keep them from falling down, which only helped to accentuate his large behind. It was a rather wide, bulbous one that attracted a lot of attention, especially from bullies and most everyone else who had a need to express an unkind word or to play a joke to elevate themselves in some sick way.

But it wasn't just his dirty, ill-fitting clothing or his big rear end or his less than handsome features or his scraggly fly-away blonde hair that drew the attention of bullies, for Steve did indeed attract the attention of all bullies. It was the fact that he was a moving target that really riled them up. They couldn't catch him. Steve was very fast. I cannot say that I remember anyone ever catching Steve. In fact, I don't think he took all that many beatings. He was always on his guard, and at the first hint of trouble, he was gone!

Even though you had to stand upwind from Steve to remain in his company, he turned out to be a good friend. He liked all the same things that regular boys liked. He looked a little different, but if the other guys would have just given him a chance, they would have discovered that Steve possessed many highly prized qualities. For one, he was very adventurous. Many a night, Steve and I would sneak out and roam the neighborhood. We would hide from the cops and door shakers (security guards) as they made their rounds. We had secret hideouts under porches, in alleys, behind bushes, between buildings, on top of roofs—all over. If we wanted to disappear, we'd disappear—no one could find us.

Steve was also pretty daring. There was this very steep dirt bank over by the freeway. It was about a hundred feet high— almost a cliff in the air. One day, Steve just took off running and flung himself over the edge, landing about twenty feet below on the steeply inclined side of the bank, and then tumbled most of the way to the bottom. It seemed scary, but the dirt was soft and made for great landings. Before you knew it, we were both flying way out into space and falling down the face of the bank far below.

Another cool thing about Steve was his home. His father and mother were country people. My mom used to call them "hillbillies" because they were different and because they were from Hillsboro. Hillsboro is a suburb on the west side of the Portland metro area that's not the same as the hills of Kentucky or Tennessee, but it made little difference to my mom.

Anyhow, Steve's house was an old farm-type house with no paint. I'm sure it must have been painted at one time, but it had been awhile. It was pretty humble, possibly needing to be condemned, but it was put to good use. It had a full basement, where Steve's dad stored tons of newspapers to sell to the recyclers. Steve and I would spend hours making forts and wading around and through them. Upstairs on the main level were hardwood floors stripped of all varnish and color from years of use, and the walls had not seen a fresh coat of paint in decades. There were two bedrooms on the main floor, one for Steve's parents and one for Grandma. There was a front room, a kitchen, and a dining room. The dining room had a piano and was used as a music room by Steve's mother. She taught piano and trumpet lessons to supplement their income.

Upstairs was Steve's bedroom in an unfinished attic crammed full of junk, including a pool table. This pool table was a great distraction for me and Steve on many a dark winter night. There was just one problem. You had to go through Steve's grandmother's room to get to the stairs that led to the attic. She had some kind of bladder problem and constantly wet herself and her bed, and as far as I know, she rarely got clean bedding or under things. We would make a game of holding our breath while we dashed through her room and up the stairs.

Though the Hales were different and maybe a bit simple, they were good people. Granger, the dad, was a hard worker. He cleaned up at a local restaurant at night and did odd jobs, hauling junk and garbage, recycling stuff and the like during the day. I loved trips to the dump with a load of rubbish on Granger's old flatbed.

Like I said, Steve was a fun guy. He was just a little different.

So, there we were in the fifth grade. I was chubby, low self-esteem, no confidence, a product of a broken home, and Steve was . . . well, just Steve. It was like we had targets on our backs. We were irresistible, and that explains why I'm running at this very moment, and unlike Steve, I was not all that fast. I could and usually did, get caught.

CHAPTER ONE

"Uncle! Uncle!" I whimpered. There was no way anyone could hear my offer of surrender with three hundred and fifty pounds' of fifth and sixth graders crushing my face into the hard-packed path that led from the grassy combination football and baseball field to the upper level where the blacktop playground resided.

I was trying an alternate route that day, thinking that I just might slip by them unmolested. Of course, I mean the cool guys of the fifth and sixth grade. I liked to rotate my routes and keep them off balance, but unbeknownst to me, they were sneaking smokes in the doorway that led to our indoor swimming pool. Buckman is the only, K through 8, elementary school in all of Portland that has an indoor swimming pool. The doorway was completely isolated from the rest of the school, making it a great place for some of the more advanced kids on the social scale to smoke or make out undetected. Anyhow, I walked by as several of them were getting ready to fire up their cigarettes, and that was all it took. I gave it a good go, but there's only so much speed a kid weighed down with years of 3 Musketeers and cream sodas can generate.

After giving me the thrashing they must've figured I deserved, they left me in a heap for more enticing activities. Bunny Carlson, the most gorgeous woman in the entire fifth grade, just happened to stroll by with some of her friends, snickering as they saw my humiliating and painful plight. What was so funny? The joke escaped me.

"Hey Steve," I greeted my friend somberly as I panted up the steep hill where we often rode our skateboards halfway down before flying into space and skinning our knees, elbows, and heads. Our skateboards in those days were nothing like the high-tech coasting machines that modern baggy-pants type kids ride today. No, they were just boards with cheap metal roller-skate wheels attached to the bottom. When you got one of those babies going too fast, they would wobble like crazy, eventually sending the rider head over heels. It was painful, but exciting.

"Hey," Steve returned, looking me over questioningly. "What happened?"

I was rather rumpled and my shirt was torn and I had dirt and grass stains all over it, not to mention the blood running from my lip and nose.

"You don't know? What do you think happened?" I was beginning to get mad, and Steve was the one who was going to pay. Steve always paid. Even me, his best friend, would sometimes bully and abuse him.

"Let's shoot pool," Steve suggested.

"Okay," I agreed, letting the anger slip away. Getting mad didn't do any good. I would do something that I would regret, and then Steve and I wouldn't hang around with each other for a week or two. Eventually, though, we would be drawn back together like we were the only two people on a deserted island. There just wasn't anyone else. This time, I didn't feel like going to the trouble of clobbering him and all the other stuff.

"Yeah, let's shoot some pool," I said. "I'm going clean your clock."

"Yeah, you think you will, but you don't know who you're dealing with," Steve replied, getting cocky as we strolled toward his house, which was just about directly across the street from where we usually bit the dust on our skateboards. We called it "the point of no return."

"So, who're you? Minnesota Fats?" I asked, sizing up his large bulbous rear end. ("Minnesota Fats" was a famous pool hustler of the times.) "You got the butt for it—I'll give you that."

Steve ignored the rear end crack and we quickly climbed the rickety wooden steps that led to the front porch. He swung the door open and hollered to his mom, who was in the back part of the house somewhere, as we made our way through the small foyer and living room. We held our breaths as we ran through Grandma's pee-soaked room and up the steep attic stairs to Steve's designated living quarters and the pool table.

Steve was a good pool player, and who wouldn't be with a full-sized pool table in their bedroom? He would generally beat me two out of three times. This evening was no different. It didn't take long before I was tired of the beatings. I said my goodbyes to Steve's mom, who was busy getting dinner ready in the kitchen, and to Steve's dad, Granger, who was sitting on the couch watching TV and shaking salt into a bottle of beer.

"I'm home," I hollered as I flung open the front door of our apartment. We lived in a two-bedroom, one-bath apartment in an old pre-twentieth century fourplex two blocks off the infamous Burnside Street.

Everyone in town was familiar with Burnside and Skid Row located not quite a mile west of our little neighborhood. It's where all the bums lived. Actually, most of them lived down by the Willamette River under the bridges that cross over to downtown

Portland. Burnside is where you see them with their wine bottles or lying in the gutters or on the sidewalks or waiting outside in line at the entrance to the Mission. Chinatown was there too, with its humble-looking restaurants and bars that were mostly fronts for the gambling that everyone knew went on in the back.

Gypsies lived on Burnside as well in some of the old deserted storefronts. The womenfolk could be seen standing on the corners of Second and Third in colorful dresses and heavy makeup. There were old men hanging around, many who lived in some of the old fleabag hotels and apartments, and an occasional woman appeared in rags carrying bags or pushing a grocery cart full of belongings. It was a rather colorful and unique section of town, and quite exciting for young guys like us.

"Don't slam the . . ."

Wham!

"What's for dinner?"

I ate. I slept. I went to school. I got beat up. I shot pool with Steve, and then I did it all over again. Life was good.

"I made meat pie," Mom said in her "I know you don't deserve it, but here it is because I'm such a wonderful mother" kind of way.

I forgot about my day. A guy can put up with a lot as long as there's a good meal waiting for him at home.

CHAPTER TWO

The fifth grade went by slowly and painfully, with emphasis on the pain. Not only did I absorb routine beatings from the various bullies, but my English teacher unknowingly tagged me with a nickname that followed me all through school.

"John," Mr. Sorrel said rather firmly, as he always did when speaking to me. You see, since moving into the Buckman neighborhood, I sort of fell in with a couple of the class clowns. Quite often, I could be found trying to outdo Robby Fuller and Mason Brine. Robby was a wisecracking cocky little pipsqueak of a guy whose big mouth and wicked wit seemed to make up for his lack of stature. Mason Brine, the other member of our comedy team, who I competed with for laughs, was a very obese, obnoxiously funny guy who used his comedy to turn people's attention away from himself, usually at someone else's expense. Then there was me. I just liked to make people laugh to feel like I was somebody, like I had a legitimate excuse for taking up space and breathing air. The three of us became the scourge of the fifth and sixth grades. After the sixth grade, they made sure we were never in the same classes together again.

"Uh, yeah," I answered. If I had a tail, it would have been

between my legs. Mr. Sorrel was no one to trifle with. He wasn't just the English teacher. He was also the vice principal.

"Where is your homework assignment?"

"Uh, my homework?" I asked with all the saintly innocence I could muster.

"Yes, your homework," Mr. Sorrel demanded as he slipped around behind my chair and grabbed hold of that tender area between the shoulders and the neck with his large, strong, stevedore-type hands and squeezed. We called it "the claw." You did not want to get the claw from Mr. Sorrel. He may have been an English teacher, but he was no wimp. He was about six foot one, and not skinny and certainly not fat. He was kind of a studly type guy with a quiet assurance and confidence. I don't know what he was doing at an elementary school. He would have been better suited playing quarterback for the Rams, or maybe serving as an agent for the FBI or something.

"If you do not turn in your assignment by the end of today, your name is mud." That did it. My name from that point on was Mud.

"Hey, Mud," Fran Tarkin called, trying out my new name. She was instrumental in advancing it throughout the student body. Fran was a skinny, awkward girl with freckles and sandy-colored hair and a strange, yet outgoing personality. She was one of those quirky kind of nerdy kids who always seemed to stand out from the others. But I liked her.

"Nice name," she said. If I were to see her today, I would be willing to bet money that the first words out of her mouth would be "Hey, Mud."

"Thanks," I muttered as the pain from the claw started to subside. I was starting to get a little tired of Mr. Sorrel and his claw. Actually, I was way past tired. The more I thought about it, the more I figured something should be done. In fact, I was determined to do something about it myself, and I did. By the time the fifth grade was over, Mr. Sorrel no longer laid a hand on me. I started doing my assignments, and he left me alone. I got A's the rest of the year in English.

Ringgg . . . went the bell and I was off to my homeroom for the final forty-five minutes of school. Mr. Woodall was my sixth grade homeroom teacher. He was kind of lean and dressed rather casually. Most of the male teachers wore shirts and ties, but Mr. Woodall was too cool for that. All the girls thought he was cute. Or . . . he thought all the girls thought he was cute. Either way, he had a pretty good opinion of himself. Whether it was warranted or not, I couldn't say, and didn't care. He was just a teacher.

"John," Mr. Woodall said with emphasis after having to break up me and Robby Fuller, with whom I was trading insults. "You have an IQ of ninety-six." Now, why he said that or what he meant, I did not know. Ninety-six is like average, right? Not much of a slam. I actually thought it was a compliment.

"Uh, thanks," I replied.

I didn't pay Mr. Woodall's comment much attention. I started thinking about the next morning's first fitness class. Mr. Lawnboy, our PE teacher, had announced that morning during gym class that he was starting a before school fitness program. It was to get us whipped into shape. He made a special point of inviting me and some of the other fat or wimpy kids personally. At first, I was offended by Mr. Lawnboy's lack of tact.

"You don't want to be a fat weakling all your life, do you?" Mr. Lawnboy asked with gusto, causing his own Twinkie and Moon-Pie constructed midsection to jiggle violently.

"No," I barely managed to say with my throat beginning to tighten and tears welling up in my eyes.

"Good!" Mr. Lawnboy exclaimed in his robust self-absorbed sort of way, not noticing my discomfort. "I'll see you first thing in the morning."

I wasn't sure if I was going to go as the final bell rang and

I headed down the hall. Mr. Lawnboy's speech hadn't exactly inspired me. I turned the corner heading toward the door and freedom from Buckman's hallowed halls when standing in front of me, barring my way, were Joey Aardema and Many Garcia. They were the two main cogs in the wheel of the "The Gang" that included several other low-life types that terrorized the school. In those days, we only had one gang at Buckman Elementary, but one gang was all that was needed to keep us in fear. I gulped as the fear—terror, really—welled up in my chest and stomach. These guys meant real trouble.

Joey Aardema had light olive-colored skin, black hair, fine handsome features, and intelligent fiery mean black eyes. He was on the small side for his age, and slight of build. His father was half Afro American and part Filipino and Irish, and his mother was Mexican with a mixture of Anglo European ancestry. Many Garcia was third-or-fourth-generation-Mexican American, and was very tall with long legs.

The other members of the gang represented our racially diverse neighborhood rather nicely. There were a couple of white kids with mixed European backgrounds, one Asian, one with some kind of Middle-Eastern heritage, and two Afro American blacks along with Joey and Many. They were an equal-opportunity gang without any reservations toward one's creed or color. It was quite a refreshing attitude for the times. Of course, this was not what I was thinking at that moment. Frankly, I didn't really care.

"Where do you think you're going?" Many asked as he swung one of his long legs up, kicking my books from my hand and sending them and my papers in every direction. Many was well-known for his kicking ability. He would often get in fights where he wouldn't use his fists at all, just his feet, and win.

"What do you want from me?" I asked, shivering right down to my toes and wanting to run, but knowing it wouldn't do any good. No, this time I was going to get it, and get it good. Ever since my little big-mouth brother slung some ethnic epithets their way, I'd been a hunted man. Actually, Curt was the hunted. I was just the one who got caught.

"Well, for starters, give us all your money," Joey demanded with his sinister trademark sneer. Joey was scary-looking. Many was tough, with his long legs and kicking attributes, but Joey was the scary one. He was one bad dude.

"I don't have any money," I almost whimpered.

That was all that was needed. Many let me have it right in the gut with the pointy toe of his Beatle boot. I doubled over as the air rushed out of my lungs. I felt a blow to the side of my face, then my arms, and then my back as I was kicked repeatedly. I lay gasping for air on the hallway floor. Kids were standing around watching. Where was a teacher?

It didn't last long, although it seemed like forever. I picked myself up off the floor with tears in my eyes and welts forming on my face and on my arms where I tried to shield myself.

"Go home to Mama, fat boy," someone said.

Joey and Many were gone, but now I had to walk the gauntlet of onlookers. This was worse than the beatings. It was always the same—the looks, the jeers, the total aloneness. That did it. I decided right then and there that I was going to do something about it. Mr. Lawnboy's early morning fitness class was a good place to start.

CHAPTER THREE

I got up early. The sun was still hidden away, and the birds—at least, the ones that were still hanging around through the winter—had yet to start their singing. As I stepped into my pants, I could feel the bruises from the day before. With each stab of pain came an even stronger resolve to put a stop to the bullying, put a stop to the snickers, the jokes, the hurt.

I ate some cereal, checking the ingredients to see if they contained anything of value. Oats, sugar, and chemicals—at least, I assumed they were chemicals since I couldn't pronounce them.

"I'd better get me a box of that "Breakfast of Champions." I said aloud to no one since I was alone in the kitchen.

I thought about the day before as I looked at my reflection in the side of the shiny toaster that adorned our humble kitchen table.

"Better make that two boxes," I mused as I grabbed my towel and stuffed it into my gym bag along with my shorts, T-shirt, and jock. I was ready.

Mr. Lawnboy was there in the gym, as were several other boys from the sixth and seventh grades. Most of them were either skinny or weak—or, like me, fat and weak. I felt a little self-conscious in my gym shorts, and I wasn't really sure if I had the jock on right. I certainly wasn't going to ask anyone what the proper procedure was for putting the darn thing on.

We started with jumping jacks and then other aerobic type stretching exercises, and I was doing okay. Next came the sit-ups, followed by push-ups and rope climb, or in most of our cases, the "rope hang." All in all, we worked out for about thirty minutes—at least those of us who hadn't already nearly died from exhaustion and was now sitting on the bench wheezing.

I felt pretty good. I had done every single exercise and not once had I stopped or lagged behind. I could hardly breathe and my heart was pounding like a jackhammer and there were funny little stars all about my head, but I was still on my feet.

For the next six months, every morning without fail, I was there in the gym for a thirty-minute workout before school. I was beginning to lose a little weight, and I was up to ten perfect pushups. That was when Mr. Lawnboy informed us that the early morning exercise program was being canceled. Just when I was starting to feel like somebody, like there was hope, like I wasn't going to have to spend my whole life as an overweight punching bag, it was all gone.

The rest of the sixth grade went on as usual, with me disrupting class to get a laugh and the bullies disrupting my face for the same.

"Why don't you go out and do something, for goodness' sake. It's summer vacation, and all you do is mope around the house and get underfoot," my mother informed me with her patented pained expression etched into her face.

"There's nothing to do," I said for the umpteenth time.

"Go get a tan," she said again, as if a tan was the answer to all that troubled me.

"Right."

To get a tan, which seemed a rather random, if not weird

suggestion, meant that I would have to move, and for some reason, the summer before seventh grade, moving was not what I wanted to do. I got even heavier.

The summer went by slowly, but go by it did, and once again I found myself at Buckman Elementary. This time, however, I was in the seventh grade. How I managed to convince my teachers that I was worthy of moving up, I don't know. There weren't many changes except that Joey Aardema had graduated to high school, and it was now up to Many Garcia to carry on the reign of terror. Since Many was in the seventh grade, he felt that he had something to prove—or so it seemed since he seldom messed with me other than an occasional kick to the gut in passing. No, Many was after bigger game. He spent most of the year challenging the entire eighth grade to battle, and he did quite well too.

With this newfound liberty, I started to feel almost human, and when Mr. Clare asked me if I wanted to go out for our flag football team, I had just enough confidence to say, "Sure, I'll give it a try." I loved football. Every waking moment that I wasn't being run down by bullies or dodging them, I was playing or watching football. I wasn't very fast, but I did have a knack for it. I could catch just about any ball that came my way, and my throwing arm wasn't too bad either. The problem was that my confidence was so low that nobody knew how good I was. I would often be the last one chosen to play, and then they made a lineman out of me. Sure, I was big and I could block okay, but I could do the other stuff too, but I rarely got the chance. The boys with the confidence and flair got the good positions.

"Okay, John. You line up over there with the lineman," Mr. Clare ordered.

But at least I get to play, I thought. I was a lineman, but I was going to play.

Every day after school, we practiced, and then every Thursday, we got our butts beat. We won one game that year.

I thought I did okay, but our team stunk. Mr. Clare was a nice guy and a good teacher, but not much of a coach. It didn't matter. Football was dropped. No more flag football for Buckman Elementary, and again went my hopes of amounting to something other than an outlet for expressions of angst and testosterone overflow in young American males.

There weren't many milestones or events of significance in the seventh grade after football was dropped except that Steve and I began to grow apart. Our interests were different. As I began to notice girls, I started to think about things like taking a bath more than once a week. I started brushing my teeth after eating to make them clean and white instead of simply brushing after a meal to prepare my mouth for a wad of bubble gum. Steve wasn't ready to join society, but I was. I wanted to be normal. I wanted to fit in. I wanted to be somebody.

The last bell rang long and loud. Seventh grade was behind me. I did it again. I graduated once more, and this time to the eighth grade.

The class cleared out in a hurry, and I was left alone with Mrs. Wood, who was busily shuffling papers and looking relieved and eager to be away herself. I got up slowly, trying to stave off the inevitable—another lonely summer—and shuffled toward the door, wondering what I would do for the next three long months. As I went through the doorway leading to freedom or captivity, depending on one's perspective, I bumped into someone as they rushed through the door, knocking their papers all over the floor.

"Excuse me," I said as I looked straight into the most beautiful green eyes in all of the seventh-going-on-eighth grade.

Bunny smiled that smile that drove every boy crazy and said sweetly, "It's okay. My fault," as she brushed her golden brown–with–heavenly–streaks–of–yellow locks from her eyes. "I wasn't watching where I was going."

I just kind of stammered and grunted something unintelligible and then began helping her pick up her papers.

"Sorry," was all I could think of to say in a voice that was not my own—as I straightened and handed her a wad of papers. Perspiration began to form on the palms of my hands.

Bunny just smiled as Shirley Thompson and Suzy Baker, her two best friends, strolled up. The smile vanished, and so did Bunny. Her friends were not going to catch her in the company of someone like me. It might seem trivial except it happened much too regularly, and again, I'd had enough.

As I walked home, I began taking a personal inventory. In my mind, I listed all the reasons why a girl like Bunny would like a guy like me. That didn't take too awfully long. Next, I listed the reasons why she would not be attracted to me. Now *there* was a list. I stopped right there on the corner of 18th and Pine and sat down on the curb. I carefully extracted a blank piece of paper from my notebook and wrote 1. I was fat. 2. I was weak. 3. I wasn't cool.

I stopped right there. I didn't want to push myself over the edge. That was plenty to work on, especially since I only had three months to make the transition from a dud to a stud. I was, however, determined to do it.

CHAPTER FOUR

That evening, I fixed a couple of tuna and lettuce sandwiches, stuffed them into a plastic bread bag, and then carefully into a brown paper sack along with an apple and . . .

"No," I said to myself firmly. "No cookies." I pushed them aside and put my lunch in the fridge. Then I pumped up my football and crammed it into a backpack I had attached to the carrying rack over the back wheel of my Schwinn 10-speed. It was an old bike, not much to look at, but it worked. I shoved the pump, a set of wrenches, screwdrivers, and patches into the pack as well, leaving just enough room for my lunch. I rolled up a towel and fastened it to the upper frame of the bike. I was ready.

There was this one time when my Uncle Willie took my little brother and sister and my mom and me on a picnic. I guess he felt bad because his brother ran off with another woman. Anyhow, it was nice of him, and we had fun. He took us to Sauvie Island.

Technically, Sauvie Island (pronounced "Sophie's" island by us locals at the time) is an island because it has a narrow slough that oozes off the Columbia River separating a section of land from the main body. The island was used almost exclusively for farming except along the river, where there were sandy beaches. Not many people from Portland were aware of Sauvie Island in the old days. The Portland hills cut right through the heart of Portland, totally isolating a fair-sized chunk of the city. The northwest part of Portland was mostly industrial and businesses, with a few older neighborhoods here and there right up to the top of the hill. One moment, you were in a busy, vital part of Portland, very close to the core area, with tall buildings and bustling crowds. The next, once you crested the hill and coasted down the other side, you were in kind of a rural setting with the river on one side of the road and wooded hills on the other. Sauvie Island was only about five miles from the edge of town, but it just wasn't in an area where most folks would go to have a picnic. That's what made it so great. No one knew about it except for some old timers who could be found with their lines in the water at Social Security Point and the farmers who lived there.

The beaches on the river side were long and sandy and a good hundred yards wide. Log pilings were sticking up, about three feet or so, out of the water, depending on the tide, that went out a good three hundred feet toward the center of the river and were placed every two hundred yards or so the length of the island. They were great for walking out into the river where the current was swift, to cast your line into the deep channels where the big sturgeon were holed up. The pilings were to protect against erosion, I later deduced, but were put to good use for diving, fishing, and the like.

That's where I was going. I had only been there once, but it was perfect. My plan was to get in shape, and if I could have some fun too, so be it.

I lay in bed for quite a while, thinking about the next day, unable to sleep. I worked it all out while I was lying there. I would get up before dawn every day and start off by doing as many pushups as I could. Then I would grab my lunch and stuff it into my pack and ride out to Sauvie Island. Once there, I would do some more push-ups and a set of sit-ups and leg lifts. Then I would run along the beaches until I was too pooped to go any farther. Next, I would swim and have fun until I was starving hungry. At that point, I would eat my lunch and then do more push-ups and sit-ups and throw the football around while my food was settling, then go back to swimming until it was time to go home. Good plan! I would be a stud before I knew it. I couldn't wait for Bunny to see the new me.

The next thing I knew the alarm was ringing. With puffy eyes, I strained at the clock. "Yep, it's time to get going." I quickly pulled on my cut-offs, sweatshirt, and tenny runners and ran to the kitchen. Next, I wolfed down a bowl of cereal and a banana, swallowed a vitamin pill, and headed for the door, conveniently forgetting to do the push-ups.

"Wait a second," I said to myself. "I got to do this right." I went into the bathroom and promptly brushed my teeth. There was nothing I was going to overlook in my quest for studdom. If it meant brushing my teeth three times a day and washing behind my ears, so be it. I was a man possessed.

The air was crisp and the sun was just beginning to show in the east as I got a leg up on my bike and began to pedal in earnest toward Sauvie Island and what I hoped would be a new me.

I was elated. Over the Burnside Bridge, which was home for the bums, I pedaled. We called them "bums" in those days because the term "homeless" hadn't made its way into our vocabulary, and besides, they had a home down by the river. They had built nice little shacks from plywood, cardboard, discarded sheet metal and such, complete with smoke holes in the roofs and little fireplaces. It was rather an exciting lifestyle living under a bridge without any cares, or so we thought until that one day in December. The wind was pushing the cold air from Eastern Oregon down the Columbia River Gorge and freezing everything in its path. I was walking down to the Willamette River with Steve to skip rocks across the ice when we saw several police and rescue workers down under the Burnside Bridge. They were loading up what appeared to be three old men in rags into the emergency units. The men were white and stiff, with eyes frozen open. I gained a new perspective that day.

I sped by a couple of early risers who were finishing off a bottle of cheap wine. I wondered where they got it so early. I didn't think they could legally purchase alcohol until after seven a.m. No matter—they were on their way, and so was I.

I picked my way carefully through Skid Row, trying to avoid the more seedy areas, and dodged an occasional drunk on the sidewalk. Once through Chinatown, it was clear sailing. Through the back streets of Northwest Portland with row houses and small storefronts and other businesses crowded together I rode until, with plenty of huffing and puffing, I topped the hill where the giant ten-story Montgomery Ward store was located. Once around the store at the top of the hill, it was down and around to just about sea level again. The Portland hills are about a thousand feet or so in elevation, with the downtown area just over sea level. To get to where I was going, I either had to go up and over the hill or go along the highway next to the Willamette River. The river cuts through downtown on its way to the Columbia another six miles or so to the north, as the crow flies. The Willamette River jogs to the west as it goes through town, cutting off all other options. Riding a bike on that old, narrow, heavily traveled highway was suicide, so up the hill I went.

I was panting heavily as I coasted down the backside of the hill. I had come about five miles and had only five more to go to get to the Sauvie Island Bridge.

Once down the hill, I was in a whole new world. One minute, I was in a busy, vital part of the city, and the next, I wasn't.

Past a couple of junkyards I rode as a dog sounded out his disapproval. Past the docks with the immense ocean-going ships being loaded with large cranes swinging cargo into holds beneath their decks. Past a palm reader's house with a large hand that said "Fortunes Told" where I noticed empty whiskey and gin bottles sticking out of the trash can at the curb. Past a gas station where the attendant was rolling tires into place for display, and past a sign that said "Leaving Portland." I had never crossed the line leaving Portland by myself before. I had never even been to the sign that said "Leaving Portland" before. It must have some significance, but I couldn't figure out what it might be except it would be a long ride home.

I was making good time. I might be a fat boy, but I was no slouch. I had been going for about an hour without stopping, and there it was just up ahead—the bridge. If you weren't looking for it, you wouldn't see it. It was off to the right, and there were large Douglas fir trees blocking the view. There was a sign, a small sign however, that read simply "Sauvie Island."

I turned to the right and coasted down over the small two-lane bridge to the island. At the end of the bridge, the road continued for about an eighth of a mile and came to a T. Either way would take you to Marshall Beach, which was my destination. Since the road was a circle leading back to the bridge, it didn't matter which way I went, but which way was shorter? I went to the right. About twenty minutes later, I pulled onto Marshall Beach. I had forgotten how large the island was. Leading onto Marshall Beach was a short driveway through about a dozen dilapidated trailers that housed farmhands and a couple of elderly people. The paved driveway ended where the sandy beach began at the only retail establishment on the island.

The Marshall Beach Inn was a hamburger joint that also served cold beer and boasted a jukebox that would get revved up every Friday and Saturday night. The locals would come, drink beer, and have a rowdy good time. Sometimes if Mrs.

Marshall (that's what we called the lady who owned the beach and all its fine facilities) was in one of her jovial moods brought about by an occasional nip from a small bottle she kept tucked away in her purse, which never left its place at her side with a strap over her left shoulder, she would hook up the jukebox to the outdoor speaker and blast the whole beach with Patsy Cline and Hank Williams Sr. for all of the sunbathing public, which often approached fifty people on a warm and sunny summer Saturday. If Mrs. Marshall wasn't looking, we would sometimes sneak into the lounge section of the diner and slip a quarter into the jukebox and play Steppenwolf's "Born to Be Wild" or Jimi Hendrix' "Purple Haze" and really rock the beach. Mrs. Marshall would rip out the plug and savagely curse us over the loudspeaker, to the delight of the crowd as well as our own. I don't think she was all there, and the booze probably didn't help much. Sadly, neither did we.

I rode my bike to the end of the drive, and then proceeded onto the beach, half-pushing and half-carrying it through the sand. I made it! I had pedaled approximately fifteen miles, as near as I could figure. Probably a little more than that, and I had made it all the way without stopping except for traffic lights.

I threw down my bike and tore off my shirt and shoes. I was supposed to start exercising, but I couldn't help myself. The morning air was cool as I ran for the water, however, I was soon swimming and diving off the pilings and having a ball. I was the first one on the beach, but it wasn't long and there were a half dozen other kids doing the same as me.

After what seemed to be hours, I pulled myself from the water to rest and have some lunch. Sitting by my bicycle was a boy about my age or a little older with a lean sort of rangy look with muscles that most eighth graders would not be seeing the likes of for a few years, and not after some considerable hard work. My backpack was open, and I noticed that a brown paper bag was crumpled next to my bike. Sitting on the backpack as if on display was an apple core. I was tired from the ride and from the swim and I was hungry. For some reason, I don't know what it was, I was not scared. I felt this kind of nothingness from deep inside. It was like all the fear was all used up, and there was nothing to replace it except . . .

I looked first at the apple core and the crumpled bag that had formerly held my lunch and then back at the well-defined stranger.

"You eat my lunch?" I asked with no show of emotion.

"As a matter of fact, I did, and it was good, too," drawled the strange boy as he drew himself to his feet. He was taller than me, and I could see that he was older too. "Why? What are you going to do about it?" he asked. He began to laugh.

I hit him. I don't know what came over me. All those years of taking abuse from bullies, running away, being humiliated, being made to feel like I was the lowest form of life were enough, I guess. Something snapped. I hit him again. I didn't feel a thing—no fear, no pain, no nothing. I hit him the third time, and he went down to his knees with his hands over his face with blood coming from his nose and lip. I stood there waiting. I thought for sure he would get up and beat the tar out of me. He was bigger, and if those muscles were any indication, he was stronger, much stronger. I didn't care. I was ready to fight. For once in my sorry life, I was ready to fight and even die. I didn't care.

He didn't get up. I gave him a kick. Not a hard kick like many a bully had done to me when I was down, but not a light one, either. I wanted him to get up and get on with it. I wanted to get in another lick or two before he pulverized me. I could take it. After all, hadn't I been taking beatings on a regular basis since as far back as I could remember? Did he honestly think he could hurt me more than those who had come before? I kicked him again, harder. I was feeling a little crazy now. The nothing where the fear had once resided had filled in with anger—tremendous, uncontrolled anger.

"Come on," I yelled, "get up. Fight, you wimp," I heard myself say. I kicked him again, this time as hard as I could. He started crying and curled up in a ball, still holding his face in his hands.

I paused and looked down at my victim. The anger began to slip away as all the feelings of loneliness and despair and fear and self-loathing and sadness, pure sadness that had been holed up in every fiber of my being, welled up inside me at that very moment. I felt terrible, worse than if I had taken the beating. I grabbed my bike and walked away. I had never felt so bad. How can bullies do what they do and laugh? I wanted to cry. In fact, I did.

CHAPTER FIVE

The ride home was a long one. I was tired and hungry. I didn't make good time, like I did coming, but it did give me a chance to reflect on the day's events.

It was true that I had finally fought back. In fact, I had hammered a bully. I had put him down and had him crying like a baby. At first, I felt bad, but other feelings began to surface, feelings connected to my ego that took precedence over all else, especially since I had never had one before. A great thing had happened. I was finally feeling like a real person, someone with worth, someone who counted, someone who never, ever, was going to be a punching bag for bullies again. I started getting cocky. Thoughts of what I was going to do to the next guy who dared to mess with me kept running through my head.

My thoughts served me well, helping the time and the miles slip away, and then I was home.

The next morning, I arose at the sound of the alarm and was soon flying through the back streets of Northwest Portland. I couldn't wait to get to Sauvie Island and continue my fitness regimen of swimming and having fun. I was even more determined to get myself in shape before school started.

The experience the day before seemed to fuel my desire to push myself even harder. I'd had my first taste of self-respect, and I liked it. It was kind of confusing, dealing with all those conflicting feelings. On the one hand, I felt like a louse, beating and kicking someone when they were down and helpless. Then on the other hand, I felt a sense of power and confidence with just a hint of superiority. I felt terrible and yet exhilarated. I pushed the terrible feelings away and went with the exhilaration.

I packed my lunch as I had the day before, and this time, I was determined to be the one who ate it. An image of the muscular kid I had beaten the tar out of came to my mind, and the newfound confidence began to slip away. I started to get a little nervous. What if he was waiting for me? I stopped myself. "No problem. I whupped him once, and I can do it again."

The ride to the island was uneventful, if you don't count the shouting match between the palm-reading lady and some greasy-looking guy with long, unkempt hair and a tattoo of the Zig-Zag man on his right forearm. The guy was taking several empty bottles of something out to the curb, where the garbage can apparently had permanent residence. The palm-reading lady was a little on the plump side with long black hair and bright red lips, dark eyeliner and blazing black eyes wearing an old sort of silky clingy robe wrapped loosely around her. She was kind of attractive in a scary sort of way. I heard her asking in a very loud voice where her wallet was, and her gentleman friend replied with at least as much gusto, as he dropped the empties off at the can next to the curb, and began to make his way carefully back to the house, that she should check her crystal ball. I could hear the lady say something about not needing to check her ball to know what happened to her billfold. Then I heard the sound of glass being broken. But by then, I was too far away to hear anymore. I toyed with the idea of going back to catch round two, but I kept on.

Marshall Beach was just the way I had left it. The sun was shining low in the eastern sky, and the air was fresh and warming. I locked my bike up under a tree and decided to do some jogging while I waited for the air to warm a little more before going swimming. Originally, my plan called for callisthenics and running before swimming. Of course, the day before did not quite go as planned. I had hopped into the water as soon as I got there and never did get around to the push-ups and stuff.

I stretched out my legs, which were a little stiff from the bike ride, and began jogging at a slow pace along the beach. I ran east along the deserted beaches, huffing and puffing. There were fir trees mixed with a few deciduous types and bushes lining the beaches growing closer and closer to the river until there was nothing left but trees and bushes right down to the water. There are always bushes on this side of the Cascade Range. You can hardly go for a walk in the woods unless there's a trail to follow because of the thick undergrowth. I turned around and ran the half mile back to Marshall beach and then continued huffing and puffing toward Social Security Point on the western tip of the sandy portion of the island. As usual, there were four or five old guys with their lines in the water and their poles propped up on wooden forks made from limbs of a tree. They sat in a wooden bus-stop-type structure, one of many that dotted the beach and kept the rain and sun off as they fished and told stories to one another, often sipping something from a thermos. They looked up and smiled as I struggled to jog by without appearing winded or fatigued. I ran a little farther and then stopped to rest.

Not bad, I thought. I had run a mile and a half or more without stopping. I was gasping for air with my hands on my knees, but I felt good. I dropped right there on the spot for some push-ups. I struggled to do five. Earlier that morning, I was able to pump out seven pretty good ones, but now my arms were kind of rubbery. I sat down and commenced doing sit-ups. I stuck my toes under a large piece of driftwood for some stability, placed my hands behind my neck, and ripped off twenty as I gasped for air and flung my hands toward my toes to try to get some momentum going. Then as I was lying flat on my back, I raised my legs up and then lowered them until my sizable stomach burned. Didn't take long. After a considerable rest, I dragged myself to my feet and did five bends and thrusts. Man, I hate those things.

I walked and stretched and then began to jog back to Marshall Beach. My legs and arms felt like rubber and I was having difficulty making my way, but I continued on past the old guys. Finally, after much huffing and puffing, I found myself lying in the sand at Marshall Beach. After resting for a while, I gathered all my strength and pulled myself to my feet.

There he was. The kid I had beaten to a pulp. Somehow he looked bigger than I remembered. He was walking toward me with a determined scowl on his swollen face. For some reason, at that very moment, I did not take much satisfaction in seeing his marred countenance. His left eye was swollen practically shut and his lower lip was cut and puffy and his nose looked a little crooked. All my cockiness and newfound confidence was gone, replaced by the terror I knew so well. I froze. All I could do was stand there as he closed the gap. Wouldn't do any good to run even if I could. After all the miles on my bike and the jogging, my legs were not very functional.

He was standing right in front of me now, and without any hesitation, he hit me square on the jaw. Down I went. I had been hit hard before, but that one was a record breaker. I don't know if I lost consciousness or not. All I know for sure is that I don't remember what happened after that first punch. The next thing I do remember is seeing this giant marshmallow and thinking, how in the heck am I going to find a stick big enough to roast it properly? As the cobwebs began to clear, I realized that I was lying on my back looking straight up at a very large white puffy cloud.

"Are you all right?"

"Huh?" I Managed. Someone was talking to me.

"Do you want me to go get Mrs. Marshall?" asked the voice.

Marshall? Marshall who? Dillon?

"Why would I want Marshall Dillon?" I asked. Apparently, the cobwebs were still hanging around some.

I glanced to my right and saw where the voice was coming from. There was a boy about my age standing next to me. I shook my head a couple of times and then started to get up. I don't know why, but I hurt all up and down my legs, chest, stomach, back, and head.

"Ow," I whimpered. "What happened?" Normally I would be crying at a time like this, but I hurt too badly for tears to do any good.

"My brother, Tom, beat you up."

"Your brother?" I looked a little closer at the source of the voice as I stood somewhat uneasily. The brother of the assassin was a bit shorter than me, but very skinny, with reddish hair and freckles.

"You don't look like your brother."

"Thanks. He's my step-brother."

I looked in all directions to see if Tom was still around.

"What did you do to tick him off?" asked the skinny step-brother. "He's a jerk, but normally he doesn't pound someone unless he figures they deserve it."

"Yeah, well, I guess he was mad because I beat him up yesterday."

"You?" He scrunched up his nose and furrowed his brow in disbelief. "You beat up Tom?"

I didn't say anything. It was hard to believe that I could

have beat up anybody, let alone some guy with muscles all over his body.

Tom's little brother was looking me up and down with a questioning look on his freckled face. "I knew that someone got the best of Tom yesterday when he came home with a black eye and his nose about broken off, but are you sure it was you?"

"Yeah, I think it was me," I said, not so sure any longer myself.

"Wait. You hit Tom in the nose?" he asked with a look that said he had just discovered the meaning of life.

"I don't know. Maybe," I replied, wondering what he was getting at.

"Yes, you did," said the all knowing little brother. "Tom may be big and strong, but he has one weakness—his nose. You punch him in the nose, and it's all over."

For some reason, knowing this didn't make me feel any better. I guess I wasn't the stud I had briefly thought I was. I had simply gotten lucky. It was nice while it lasted. Reality was sinking back in, and I hated it.

I stood there for a while just looking around, feeling the soreness from the recent encounter. The sun was now high in the sky, and I was hot. What the heck. I wasn't going to let a little assault and battery ruin a fine summer day. I gingerly made my way down to the water and eased in. It was cold, but felt good. Maybe it would help keep some of the swelling down. Goodness knows there were plenty of sore areas that might have swollen up on me.

Tom's little redheaded step-brother had followed me and was swimming around in three feet of water.

"What's your name?" I asked as I sized him up.

"Greg. What's yours?"

"John," I answered, beginning to feel better.

"Wanna go dive off the pilings?"

"Okay."

I practically forgot all about the beating I had received as Greg and I began to get to know each other. He was in the seventh going on the eighth grade, just like me. He attended a small school on the island that had kindergarten through high school all in the same building. There were only fifty-three students who attended Sauvie Island Elementary and High School. Most of the students lived on the island. The school was too small for a football team, so Tom and two other boys were allowed to play for Scappoose High just down the road, and of course Tom was the star running back.

We swam and talked and had a great time. Greg and I had a lot in common. Neither one of us had a dad. Well, Greg had a stepdad he called Bob, but Bob didn't pay much attention to Greg. Tom got most of the attention since he was Bob's real son.

Bob was a farmer on the island, and Greg and his mom had moved in with him and Tom after tying the knot two years earlier. Greg's real dad split when the going got a little rough. Apparently, there was this cocktail waitress he had been on friendly terms with who had a husband over in Viet Nam. The husband came home one day, and Greg's dad left.

The next day found us together swimming and throwing the football around. It turned out that Greg, although thin, didn't have much in the confidence and self-esteem department either. They probably had a shortage of fat or weird kids to pick on at Sauvie Island Elementary and High School because, Greg, who seemed pretty regular, still got his share of abuse. So we did push-ups together and we ran together, swam together, and threw the football together in the name of fitness and with the hope of becoming the inflictors instead of the inflicted. We also explored the island together. Greg's big brother, Tom, was around, but except for an occasional slap or kick, he left us alone.

Sauvie Island, as I discovered that summer, was comprised of about 24,000 acres of farmland interspersed with marshy areas, tall fir and deciduous trees, small lakes and ponds with sandy beaches on the Columbia River side, and brush and trees on the slough side. Greg's step-dad grew sweet corn mostly, as did many of the farmers, on about five hundred acres of land that he leased, and apples on about one hundred and fifty acres that he owned. He was a workaholic, which was good for the bottom line but was a bit hard on his relationship with Greg's mother.

As Greg and I first began the running part of our exercise regimen, we had trouble covering much ground. After two months of diligent effort, however, we were cruising around the island with a lot less effort, especially when we had some place to go. Every day was an adventure with something new to see. The ponds we discovered were full of fish, and we spent many an hour catching bluegill, crappie, tiger perch, catfish, bass, pumpkin seed, carp, suckers, chubs, and several unnamed varieties. In the river we added sturgeon and shad to the list. There were salmon and steelhead out there too, but we had to go to Social Security Point to get them, and we didn't like the idea of having to share our fishing spot with a bunch of old guys. Some of the fish that went unnamed may have been trout, but neither of us had done much trout fishing. I was a city boy used to fishing down by the sewer pipes on the Willamette for carp and suckers. Greg hadn't done much fishing until I came around, so our knowledge was limited.

The summer went by quickly, and soon it was time for me and Greg to face the inevitable. We'd had a lot of fun, and although we couldn't see much difference in our appearances, we were in much better condition than when we started. Three months of riding a bike thirty miles a day would get a guy in good shape, especially with all the running and swimming and push-ups and stuff except for one thing. I did not ride my bike every day like I had originally planned. I slept over two or three nights a week at Greg's, and his mother often gave me a ride home on the other nights. We said our goodbyes and committed ourselves to spending all of next summer together as well.

"I'll give you a call after school tomorrow," I said as I rode away. The summer was over, but not our friendship.

CHAPTER SIX

I got dressed slowly. I wasn't sure how I was going to like the eighth grade. Sure, finally I was one of the big guys. No more upperclassmen swaggering around, but for some reason, I was feeling a bit apprehensive. I had worked hard all summer to build muscles, and for all my effort, I couldn't see that I had much to show for it. I was still fat. Maybe not as fat as I had been, but nevertheless, there was still plenty around the old midsection. I tucked my shirt into my new pair of Levis. I had begged and pleaded with my mom to get me Levis. She would usually buy us those goofy imitation denim rejects that say "I'm a dumb weirdo. Come beat me up." I looked at my reflection in the mirror. Yes, it was true that I was still fat, but I was somehow different. My hair was yellow from the sun, and my face and arms had a brown color that was not unattractive. I flexed my muscles. Yup, I think I saw some movement. *There just might be some hope,* I thought as I headed toward the door.

"Look out, Bunny. Here I come."

The first day of school as an elite member of the Buckman Elementary ruling class went well right up to the final bell when . . .

"Hi, Bunny." I did it. I said hi.

"Hi," she said back with a hint of a smile. Bunny had a way of smiling with just a trace of a gleam in her eye that drove all of us boys crazy. When Bunny smiled and gleamed, we all acted a little goofy.

Okay, I told myself. *No guts, no glory.*

"Bunny, can I walk you home?"

I was expecting Bunny to act surprised, maybe put off a little or just disinterested, but the look in those pretty green eyes more than just surprised me. I saw fear.

Why would Bunny be afraid of me?

She wasn't. The next thing I knew, I was intensely aware that the hall floor had just recently been waxed and buffed. Old Joe the janitor was not one to half step, especially the first day of school.

"What do you think you're doing, talking with my girl?" asked a strange voice that was obviously attached to the hands that were pressing my nose into the nice shiny floor.

I didn't know who he was, but I did know that he was heavy and strong. I couldn't move a muscle. I tried to mumble some kind of explanation for my brash behavior, but that only seemed to make him madder, since he then began to slap at the back of my head several times before finally releasing his hold. The voice then stood up and allowed me to do the same. As I gathered myself together and stood, I sucked in a breath of air and held it. The square-cut jaw, large brown eyes, dimpled cheeks and chin, wavy brown hair, six foot-one inch muscular frame was that of Rodney Skylark.

Rodney Skylark was the son of Coach Buddy Skylark, the varsity football coach at Washington High School. Rodney had played Pee Wee football since he was five and was now the starting quarterback for the Washington varsity team as a freshman. I didn't know Rodney personally, since he'd spent his grade-school years at Laurelhurst Elementary over in the uppity Laurelhurst neighborhood. I did, like everyone else, know his reputation. He was the fastest, strongest, and most athletic kid who had ever lived in Portland. He was already being projected as a sure-fire pro. The only thing people couldn't agree on was whether he would be a pro football, basketball, or baseball player. He excelled in all sports, so I guess it was an honor to get roughed up by such a celebrity. One day, I could look back and tell my grandchildren that the great Rodney Skylark had pushed me down and slapped me around and humiliated me in front of the prettiest girl in all the world and I did nothing about it. I did not like the sound of that.

"You go near Bunny again, and you'll be sucking your meals through a straw," Rodney warned.

"It's Mr. Sorrel!" I shouted, pointing with my left hand.

Rodney turned his head to look. I reared back and then brought my right fist forward with all the strength I could muster. It had worked once—it might work twice. I hit him square in the nose as he was turning back to look at me. Splat. His nose flattened, and blood shot all over his sanitary white T-shirt. I don't know exactly what happened next except that I did not lie down. I fought with all the power within me for a split second or so. It wasn't near enough. I don't remember getting beat this bad, this quick ever before. Unlike Greg's big brother, Tom, Rodney was supercharged from the blow to his nose. It was like I unloosed a caged animal.

I came to my senses in the nurse's office, getting a whiff of smelling salts from Mrs. Whitmore, our school nurse. I hurt all over, and as my head cleared up, I was beginning to remember what had happened. I had stood up to the strongest, fastest, and most athletic kid who ever lived in Portland—and lived. Now I could tell my grandkids about the time I almost whupped the famous Rodney Skylark, and if he was a year or two or maybe three younger and five or six inches shorter with seventy or maybe eighty percent fewer muscles, I would have.

Something else was beginning to sink in. I didn't hurt any more after a beating when I fought back than when I didn't.

"You alright?" Mrs. Whitmore asked. "How many fingers?"

"Two."

"He's okay—just got his bell rung a little bit. I'll give him a ride home." Mr. Sorrel was addressing Mrs. Whitmore.

Now I was in for it. Mr. Sorrel was going to give me a ride home. The very least would be a lecture and a full report to my mother.

Mr. Sorrel didn't say a word about the fight. He just made small talk like we were a couple of the guys going home from work or something.

"See you in school tomorrow," he said as I climbed from his shiny new GTX with a 440 magnum and a four speed. Mr. Sorrel was cool.

"Right. Thanks for the ride."

I walked through the door of our dilapidated flat. It might have been a dump, but my mom did keep it clean and nice. I stopped at the mirror in the hall and stared. My face looked like a raw sausage patty with a nose and lips. I checked, and to my surprise, found all my teeth intact. "Good. I still have a future in modeling." I took a step back to take in the rest of me. "Modeling tanks, maybe," I decided.

My mom didn't fuss much about the new face I was sporting since my appearance seemed to change fairly regularly. I ate my dinner and went to bed. The next day found me walking through the side door of Buckman Elementary.

"Hey, John. I heard you broke Rod Skylark's nose." Mike Stevens, the toughest kid at Buckman, stood directly in front of me, blocking my way. Mike's stern look melted and he smiled. "Nice job. I was hoping to do that myself one of these days."

Mike was a good guy and I had always got along with him —or at least, he tolerated me. Now there was a look of respect in his eyes that had never been there before.

"If your face is any indication, Rod's broken nose was costly," Mike lamented as he looked me over.

"Yeah, but it was worth it," I said bravely. I was a new man.

All that day, all anyone wanted to talk about was how I hammered old Rod Skylark senseless. It was all over school. I had been elevated from zero to hero.

After my last class, I saw Bunny again at her locker. I wasn't certain what I should do. Rodney Skylark was probably coming to get her. I didn't want to see him again.

I walked by and quickly said, "Hi, Bunny."

Bunny glanced my way, then nervously looked up and down the hall before she said, "Hi."

I thought about stopping for a second, but I kept seeing the face of Rodney Skylark in my mind's eye. Instead, I continued on my way down the hall, picking up my pace as I went. I might have found some courage the day before, but I wasn't stupid.

Something about the nervous way Bunny acted when she saw me started my mind chugging away. Why, I kept asking myself, was she so afraid when Rodney showed up? Why was she afraid again when I said hi? The first thing that came to my mind was that she was afraid for me. Of course, this is what I wanted to believe, but it just didn't ring true. If she was concerned for my welfare, she would have acted . . . well, concerned. It was not, however, concern that I detected in her eyes, but fear. Afraid of what, then, if not for my safety?

A cold chill ran through my veins as it finally sank in. Bunny was afraid of Rodney. What he was doing to make her afraid, I didn't know. What I *did* know was that I wanted to get that guy like I have never wanted anything before. I stepped out of the side door of Buckman Elementary into the bright sunshine and right into the path of Rodney Skylark. Gulp. *Now was my chance.*

Rodney just stood there with tape across his broken nose, not saying a word. His brown eyes were boring right through me. Now I knew how those soldiers in combat feel when they lose their nerve. I hadn't developed a lot of nerve up to that point, and what I had was gone. I was scared. *Petrified* was more like it. I knew that if Rodney wanted to, he could literally rip my head off, and there was nothing I could do about it.

"Out of my way, puke," Rodney demanded as he gave me a powerful shove that knocked me backwards and off my feet. Of course, he kicked me as he walked past.

"You want any more?" he asked, laughing.

"No," I said very meekly, my voice quavering.

I got up and started walking home. I wasn't hurt, but I wasn't the same guy who broke the nose of the strongest, fastest, and meanest kid in town. I was the guy bullies use for a punching bag—again.

For the next several weeks, I just moped around the house, thinking about how Bunny was probably being abused and mistreated by Rodney, and there was nothing I could or would do about it because of my cowardice. When I went to school, I started sneaking into class early to avoid the kids in the hall and in the playground like I used to when I was an underclassman. After school, I would get away quickly before Rod showed up or before anyone else might get an idea to have some fun at my expense. There really wasn't anyone now that Many Garcia, the last member of "The Gang," had moved away who was giving me trouble except Rodney. It's just that I was afraid of everyone. I had lost all of my hard-earned self-confidence and self-respect. I no longer sought

Bunny out to say hi or to catch a glimpse of her smile. I think I was even worse than before. I had no friends except . . .

"Hi, Greg. It's me, John." I never had called him the first day of school like I said I would, and for some reason, he hadn't called me either.

"Hey, how's it goin'?" Greg seemed a little surprised. "I didn't think you were going to call."

"Oh, yeah. I was going to earlier, but our phone was out of order," I lied.

"Right." Greg didn't believe me. "So, what's going on?"

I hesitated for a moment, and then I told him everything. I told him how I went to school on the first day and that I asked Bunny if I could walk her home. I told him how Rodney took exception to my interest in Bunny. How I plowed Rodney Skylark in the nose and how he beat me to a pulp and how he harassed me whenever he saw me. Then, not without some difficulty, I told him how I was now afraid of my own shadow and that I'd been moping around for weeks not wanting to call 'cause I felt like such a loser.

"Yeah, I thought something was up when I called two days after school started and your mom said you didn't want to talk to anyone."

"That was you?"

"Yeah."

"How's everything at your school?"

"Better. Tom has been sticking up for me and showing me how to stand up for myself and stuff. I don't know what's come over him, but now if anyone gives me any grief, I just tell Tom, and he takes care of it."

"Yeah? Huh. Sounds good," I lamented, thinking how it would be if my older brother Scott was in school with me. Boy, things would have been different.

"Hey, why don't you ride out here Friday after school and spend the weekend?"

"Yeah, that's a good idea. We could do some fishing or something."

We made plans for the weekend. Greg said he could get some of the guys from school and we could play some tackle football on Marshall Beach. My spirits lifted. I was going to have some fun.

CHAPTER SEVEN

The next two days went by slowly, but Friday afternoon finally arrived and I was off for Sauvie Island as soon as the bell rang. I had packed my bag the night before and I rode my bike to school so I wouldn't have to waste time going home first. My mom was a little reluctant as far as letting me go to the island since the weather hadn't been good lately, but she was probably tired of me moping around the house, so she relented.

The weather was a little nasty, but the heavy rain had let up, and there was just a light drizzle coming down. A light drizzle to an Oregonian is like a day filled with sunshine. Listen to the area weather report and you'd think you would get the same report most every day—rain. It just isn't so. We have heavy rain, light rain, moderate rain, showers, light showers, heavy showers, moderate showers, drizzle, heavy drizzle, light drizzle, moderate drizzle, misty conditions, heavy mist, light mist, moderate mist, thunder showers, rain mixed with snow, sleet and hail, wind-driven rain, and we even on occasion have sun mixed with rain, but not too often. Now, in the summertime from July 5th, after the big fireworks displays and picnics, through August just before Labor Day, it is pretty dry and sunny. But like I said, there was a light drizzle coming down as I jumped on my bike and headed for the island.

I rode hard, wanting to put as much distance between Buckman Elementary and myself as I could and as quickly as I could. I was still having problems with my nerve. How could I have enough guts to punch Rodney Skylark in the nose and then the next minute be afraid of my own shadow? What was wrong with me?

I turned my thoughts off as I sped past the large palm and caught a glimpse of the palm-reader's boyfriend sitting on the porch with a contented look sipping something from a bottle. I guess they must have made up.

I made good time with the constant drizzle helping to push me on. I pulled up to Greg's house completely drenched, with a black streak of mud and dirt up the back of my pants and coat. I had some fenders at home, but I hadn't got around to putting them on. It's like when it's raining and I need to use my bike, I don't have time to put them on, and when it's sunny, I don't need them.

I pulled into Greg's garage and pounded on the door to the kitchen.

"Hey, Greg, I'm here," I shouted, "and I'm wet."

Greg said hi and led me to the laundry room, where I changed into my dry clothes, including socks, underwear, and an old pair of tennis shoes that were all tied up in a plastic bag that I had tucked into my knapsack. When you live in Oregon, you have to be prepared. Greg showed me how to work the washer, and I threw everything in there, including my tenny runners, with a generous amount of soap.

I made my usual salutations to Greg's parents, and then Greg and I made for the barn and started to make plans for the rest of the day.

"What do you want to do?"

"I don't know. What do you want to do?"

After some extensive give and take, we collectively decided

to eat some dinner, watch a little TV, and then call it a day. Good plan.

The next morning, we were up and out of the house as soon as the sun had climbed over the horizon. Greg grabbed some bananas and muffins for a little sustenance, and we were off to meet the guys for our game.

Everything was arranged. We were to meet at Harry's house by 8:00 am. Harry was sixteen and had access to his dad's pickup truck, which would hold ten of us easy. Then we would drive the mile and a half to Marshall Beach and have our game, rain or shine. Fortunately for us, the sun was peeking around some big fluffy white clouds, and those big dark ominous types were, at least for the present, not to be seen.

We pulled into Harry's around seven thirty and waited as his mother proceeded to fix his breakfast while Harry could be heard protesting. We threw the football as we waited, and some of the others joined us.

"Hey, George," Greg hollered as a husky kid with glasses and short brown hair and lots of zits rode up on his bike. There was another guy named Mike who pulled in behind. Mike had red hair and freckles and didn't say much. Before long, there were about ten of us waiting and snickering as we listened to Harry's mom nag her son.

"Now, Harry, make sure you get back in time to watch your little sister so I can go to the store, and brush your hair. You look like a porcupine."

"All right," Harry replied mournfully.

"Now, come here and give me a kiss before you go."

We loved that last part, and the guys let Harry know that we heard every bit.

"You better knock it off or you'll all be walking." Harry was serious, so the guys switched their focus to Mike and his dad's cleats that he was wearing. They were at least three sizes too big.

"What are you doing with those things on? You got an audition with the circus later?" asked one of the guys as we all laughed our collective butts off.

The guys and I hopped into the truck, and away we went. It was a little crowded, but we were soon turning onto Marshall Beach.

We chose up sides, and Greg and I ended up on opposite teams. As usual I was relegated to the line.

"Okay, fat boys on the line, and you know who you are," announced our captain, a tall, confident kid, as he looked right at me.

We kicked the ball off to the other team and raced down the sandy beach, where a small kid scooped up the ball and slipped past three defenders who had misjudged his quickness. I came running down the field in back of the initial point of attack, since excessive speed was not one of my shortcomings, and as the slippery little guy came bounding around the three overachievers, I was right there. I slammed full into him, sending him backwards and causing the ball to pop loose. A kid named Billy jumped on it. It was our ball.

We were pumped, and our captain called for a pass play. We took our places. I hunkered down next to center, another fat kid, and across from a tall, slender guy with glasses who was glaring at me. There's something about the game of football that brings out the animal in a person. It was obvious that this guy I was lined up on was thinking he was going to take my head off. Normally in a situation where I might be confronted by someone wanting to do me bodily harm, I would be scared to death and would do all that was in my power to avoid a confrontation.

In football, however, it's different. There's some kind of transformation that comes over you when you're on the field lined up against a bunch of guys who're going to do their very best to take you out and send you home in a body bag. It's different, and I can't explain it. All I know is that when I play football, all I can think about is getting the other guy worse than he gets me, and loving every minute of it with all of its pain and blood and agony.

"27, 32, 3." The ball was snapped to our captain, the quarterback. I lunged forward with all my might and all my strength and all my pent-up emotion, not to mention my considerable bulk. I drove forward with hands clenched next to my chest with elbows extended, driving my legs as one would jackhammers. I caught the tall, lanky kid just as he was starting to come up out of his stance. I stood him up and then knocked him back. Down he went. The pass fell incomplete, but I felt exhilarated. The tall kid got up and was mad as a hornet. I just smiled and went back to the huddle.

Our captain called another pass play, and again I lined up opposite of the tall, lanky kid, who now had a serious scowl and a look of complete determination.

"21, 4, 18." The ball was snapped, and again I drove forward, elbows extended, and again I drove the tall kid back, and down he went. The pass fell incomplete again.

Our captain was not the best passing quarterback, but he was observant.

"Can you take Robert out again?" The tall lanky kid had a name.

"Yeah, I think so."

"Okay, I'm running right behind you. On three."

We lined up again. This time, Robert, the tall kid, had a different look on his face, but I didn't have time to analyze it.

"Three."

And again I drove forward, and again I pushed him back, and again he went down. Our captain slipped through and picked up the yardage for the first down.

This time, however, Robert didn't go back to his huddle. He came after me. I saw him out of the corner of my eye and was able to get out of his way somewhat. As he charged forward to tackle me, I gave him a stiff arm to the head, which pushed him to the ground. He jumped up and came at me again. He approached me with more restraint and a better focused sense of purpose. Robert closed in on me with his fists up, ready to do battle. I knew that I was stronger and bigger. I had just proved it by flattening him three times in a row, but I still froze. He swung awkwardly, hitting me a glancing blow to my cheekbone. I backed up. I was scared and looking for a way out.

"Hold it," snapped an authoritative voice.

I looked up, and there was Tom, pushing his way through the on-looking boys circled around us.

"I thought you guys were playing football." Tom just stood there looking stern, and that was enough.

"That's right, and it's still our ball first and ten," exclaimed our captain, who had grabbed the ball and placed it on the appropriate yard line. "Let's go. Huddle up."

Robert dropped his hands, but the look of anger and determination was still in his eye. I had a feeling the game just wasn't going to be as much fun.

We played the rest of the game without incident. Tom stayed to watch, which seemed to keep the hotter heads from boiling over and I didn't play with the same intensity after that. I was afraid that if I flattened Robert again, he would come after me. Silly, I know, but there's something about confronting someone who wants to take you apart outside the confines of football that's very intimidating—at least, it was to me.

Our team won by three touchdowns. They couldn't stop our running game. Even though I took it easy on Robert, I was still able to push him around enough to clear some holes for our running game without causing him to boil over.

We got cleaned up at Greg's and had some lunch out on the porch. Greg went inside to get another soda as Tom sat down next to me on the porch railing.

"What was all that about with Robert?"

"Oh, he just got a little mad 'cause I pan-caked him," I answered

"No, not that. Why did you let him push you around? You looked like you were scared."

I had hoped that it all had happened so fast that no one had noticed how afraid I was. Tom saw.

"Afraid of Robert?" I tried to sound confident.

"Yeah, Robert." Tom spoke quietly. "You know, you're bigger and stronger than he is. He can't hurt you. So why are you afraid of him?"

"Well, uh," I stammered, trying to think of the right thing to say and then finally settling for, "I don't know."

"You're not afraid of getting hurt, are you? You wouldn't play football if you were afraid of getting hurt. So, what is it?"

I didn't answer. I kept my eyes on the old wooden planks on the floor of the porch.

"Greg says that you get beat up all the time at school, that you're afraid to stand up for yourself."

I felt tears well up in my eyes. I felt so helpless and ashamed, so alone.

"You don't have to let the fear tell you what to do. That's what you're doing—you're letting the fear take control. You're letting the fear tell you that you're weak, and that even a wimp like Robert can whip you. It's not true. You're not weak. I know. I'll never forget the beating you gave me that day on the beach." Tom spoke solemnly. He seemed to care how I felt.

"What do I do?" I asked desperately in a husky voice, tears streaming down my cheeks.

"You start right now by telling yourself that no matter how you may feel, how afraid you may be, you are the one in charge and not the fear. Every time you see yourself in the mirror, you say, I'm in charge, and I'll do what I need to do no matter what. Nothing will get in my way. Fear is not in charge. I am."

Greg was standing at the door and had heard much of

what was said. "That's right—that's what I do, and it works. I'm not afraid like I used to be. I tell myself that I'm in charge, not my fear or any other emotions."

The three of us talked for some time about fear and life and how crazy all of it sometimes seems. Greg and Tom had been through a lot for their young years, growing up in broken homes until their parents married one another. Fear and insecurity were not unfamiliar to them. Tom had a counselor at school who had taken an interest and was helping him overcome some of his problems. Tom in turn was helping Greg, and now they were both trying to help me.

To learn that Tom was afraid and that he'd had similar problems was hard to believe at first. Tom admitted that he didn't always deal with his fear as he should. Like the day he ate my lunch. He said that he would sometimes pick on smaller or weaker kids to make himself feel superior, but after his encounter with me and some counseling, Tom had rethought his position on what it meant to have courage. Beating someone up was not a courageous thing to do. Courage is standing your ground when you're right and doing what's right in the face of ridicule, or worse.

"The first thing you need to do, besides the positive reinforcement stuff in the mirror," Tom said in a knowing way, "is to do things that will give you confidence. There's nothing like being strong and fast and in good physical condition to make a guy feel like somebody. I wasn't always the physical specimen you see before you." Tom stood straighter, flexing his muscles beneath his snug T-shirt. "As you are now, I once was. And," Tom was speaking intently now, "as I am now, you can become."

"Yeah," I agreed, "very inspirational." *Laying it on a little heavy*, I thought. "I've been working at getting in shape, but not with much success." Actually, I hadn't done a whole lot of anything resembling exercise since summer. Most of the meager muscle that had begun to show had gone back to jelly.

"Well, it's time to step it up. If you want to feel good about yourself, you need to give yourself some reasons, and right now, you look like you could use a couple," Tom was now looking me over with a pained expression on his face. "It's going to take a lot of hard work, but you can do it."

"Okay, what do I do?" I was game. Tom was the sturdiest-looking dude this side of Rodney Skylark, and I wanted to be sturdy too. I could hardly wait for Bunny to see the new me I was going to create.

"It's late. I'll set you up with a fitness regimen tomorrow, and we'll get a workout in too." Tom headed inside. "See ya in the mornin'."

Greg and I talked a little more and then headed to bed ourselves. I couldn't sleep right away. Thoughts of bulging biceps and triceps and all the other "ceps" kept running through my mind. I was going to do it! I was going to get myself in shape and look good and feel good, and nobody had better mess with me if they didn't want some serious trouble. No longer would I let fear rule me as it once had. No longer would I be a slave to my emotions. I would be master of myself and anybody else, for that matter, who got in my way —was the last thought that went through my mind as I drifted into unconsciousness.

CHAPTER EIGHT

The next morning, we were up and ready. Greg and I came downstairs together, and there was Tom at the kitchen table, jotting something down in a notebook.

"Hey," he said in greeting. "The first thing we need to do is discuss your lifestyle and make changes where they're needed." He wasn't messing around. No time for pleasantries.

"What about some breakfast first?" Greg asked, clutching his growling stomach.

"No breakfast, lunch, dinner, or snacks until we get this daily regimen worked out."

I didn't know why Tom was being so strongly supportive. I almost wished he would back off a little except I needed it and I knew it. I guessed I could endure a little of his pushy tyranny.

"Okay. What do you want to know?"

For the next twenty minutes, Tom asked me about my eating habits, sleeping habits, and all the physical aspects of my dull life. I answered as honestly and as openly as I could without revealing any truly deep dark secrets.

"That's all I need for now." Tom got up from the table. "Don't eat a thing until I get this done." He went to his room.

For the next two long hungry hours, Greg and I amused ourselves playing ping pong. We played bravely on, slamming the ping-pong ball back and forth while our stomachs called out for sustenance—begged, even. We were beginning to wonder if all this was worth it when Tom finally appeared.

"Here it is." Tom held up his notebook and looked directly at me. "If you follow this plan, you will be the new stud-muffin extraordinaire of Buckman Elementary. The women will swoon and the men will cower."

"Sounds good to me." I was ready.

For the next hour or so, Tom, Greg, and I went over my new plan. It went something like this—Monday morning, up at six. Put on sweats or suitable exercise clothing and stretch for a good five-ten minutes. Jog at a slow pace for six minutes. Do fifty sit-ups and then as many push-ups as possible. Jog for ten more minutes at a quicker pace. Do as many leg lifts as possible. Do twenty bends and thrusts, doing a push-up when in the extended prone position. Shake it off and stretch for another three minutes. Do three sets of curls, using moderate weight. The first two sets should be easy, but the last should be very difficult. Shake it off and do three sets of kickbacks, then three sets of flies and then three sets of lat stretchers. Then do another fifty sit-ups, push-ups until muscles fail, and jog for another ten minutes as a fast as possible. Walk it off, stretch, and hit the shower.

Then go to school, where I'd do three sets of pull-ups in the gym. After school, go for a swim at the Buckman pool for an hour, doing laps the whole time. After the swim, walk home at a brisk pace. Once home, stretch, and then it's free time for homework, chores, etc. No sitting around unless doing homework. Must be actively involved in some kind of physical activity during all waking hours. In bed at eight.

Tuesday, up at six. Stretch for five-ten minutes. Do jumping jacks for three minutes. Skip rope for five minutes. Do three sets of lunges, strapping on weights as they become easier. Do twenty bends and thrusts without pushups. Do fifty sit-ups. Stretch for three minutes. Bench-press three sets with moderate weights. Do three sets of incline and decline dumbbell presses. Do another set of sit-ups. Stretch for three to five minutes. Jump rope for ten minutes. Do three sets of leg-lift crunches. Work out on punching bag (old duffel bag filled with rags hanging from the ceiling in the basement) for ten minutes. Stretch, walk it off, shower, eat, and run to school, where I do three sets of chin-ups. After school, more laps at the pool and then run home.

The next week, it switches. The Monday, Wednesday, and Friday workout becomes the Tuesday and Thursday workout, and the Tuesday and Thursday workout becomes the Monday, Wednesday, and Friday workout. Saturday becomes the marathon exercise day, starting with a bike ride to the island at first light. Once at Greg's house, Tom will give me and Greg a thorough PT (physical training) test. He'll time us in a one-mile. He'll have us do as many push-ups as we can without stopping, check to see how many sit-ups and pull-ups we can do, how many bends and thrusts in sixty seconds, and then we'll max out on the bench press.

After a morning of testing, we'll eat a big lunch and then play football or practice our fundamentals through the entire afternoon. Sunday will normally be our day of rest. We'll start off with a weigh-in and take stock of our progress. Next, we'll make plans and set goals for Monday through Saturday, adjusting the regimen as we go for optimum growth. Then we'll just goof around the rest of the day.

"I don't know if I can do all this stuff." I was almost whining.

"Just do your best, and after a while, it will become easy. Of course, before that happens, I'll be increasing the degree of difficulty and adding a few more exercises." Tom was beginning to sound a little sadistic.

Next, Tom went over what we could eat. By this time, I realized that Greg was getting the same makeover as I was.

"Why are you doing all this?" I asked.

"I need it too," Greg explained simply.

I had forgotten that Greg, even though he was thin, had his share of challenges.

Tom then proceeded to tell us what we could and could not eat and when we could and could not eat it. Greg's diet was a little different than mine, since he needed to gain weight where I needed to lose it. Essentially, Tom wanted me to eat lots of fresh fruit and vegetables, lean meats, low-fat milk, whole grains, drink lots of water and cut out margarine, mayonnaise, etc., using good extra virgin olive oil instead. No fried foods, and sweets and absolutely no unauthorized snacks. He also suggested taking daily vitamin supplements.

"Whoa, there. Who died and made you surgeon general?" I was getting a bit concerned. "No sweets or snacks?"

"No! None!" Tom was adamant. "Not if you're serious about becoming more than just a blob wheezing your way through life, afraid of your own shadow and never experiencing the joy of being your own man and setting your sights on something and getting it . . ." Tom paused for effect. "Like Bunny."

That did it! "Okay, let's get to it."

We started off with a healthy breakfast. I had two soft-boiled eggs, no butter, two pieces of toast with just a smidge of peanut butter and honey, an apple and a large bowl of nine-grain mush with a dollop of honey. Greg's diet was similar except without limits on the high-calorie items.

Next was the evaluation of our physical condition. I bench pressed eighty pounds and Greg managed seventy-five. Tom ripped off two hundred and twenty-five pounds five times for our benefit.

"Just two years ago, I struggled with ninety pounds just like you guys. The coach gave me a workout program real similar to yours, and put me on a weight-gain diet like yours, Greg. The rest is history." Tom didn't have much use for humility. "I wanted to be strong and confident. I was tired of getting picked on. Nobody picks on me anymore."

Tom continued to test us and to jot down the results. It was obvious that Greg and I had our work cut out for us.

We played football after our workout and testing, and then, we weighed in. There was an old floor scale for cattle in the barn that we used to weigh ourselves. We also stood against the wall and marked off our heights and measured them with a tape measure that Greg pilfered from his mom's sewing box. I was five feet six inches and one hundred and ninety-three pounds. Greg tipped the scales at one hundred and ten pounds standing five feet three inches. Tom weighed one hundred and seventy-five pounds and stood five feet eleven inches. Of course Tom wrote it all down in his notebook.

When I got on my bike and headed for home, I felt for the first time in my life like things were going to be different. I had hope.

CHAPTER NINE

At first, the early morning fitness routine was a little hard to get used to. After a couple of months of struggling with the concept of early to bed and early to rise with physical endurance in the form of pain and agony in between, I began to see results. I began to feel good. Last summer, I felt good after all the bike riding, running, and swimming. I was beginning to feel that way again. Where smooth, rounded lines once were, the hint of muscles began to show. Where a large off-road all-terrain spare tire had once adorned my waistline was now more of a steel-belted radial. I was starting to enjoy the workouts too, or at least tolerate them with a little enthusiasm. I missed a few days at first, but did better as I went. After a while, my regimen became habit, and a missed workout left a hole that needed to be filled.

School was better too. I was no longer suffering from depression or paralyzed by fear whenever a possible antagonist, real or imagined, would come into view. Rodney Skylark was my only real concern, and I stayed away from him.

"Okay, John. Get on the scale." Tom was businesslike as usual. He was holding his clipboard and jotting down information in the proper columns as Greg and I weighed in. It was the eleventh week of our new program. Greg weighed one hundred and fourteen pounds, up four pounds. He was ecstatic. He had been working very hard and was eating like a horse, trying to put on weight. On the other hand, I had been working hard too—or at least I thought I was. I had started to establish some good habits and was gaining some strength, but I was still eating more than I should. The old platform scale that had weighed many steers, heifers, cows, and bulls creaked from the sudden stress of my full weight coming down on it.

"One ninety-three." Tom noted without expression. "How can you go eleven weeks working out every day and not lose any weight?" he wanted to know.

"I don't know." I was dejected. I had worked so hard, and for what? Nothing, that's what. I hung my head and climbed off the scale. I was ready to call the whole thing off and join the nearest monastery.

"Wait a minute. Stand up straight," Tom demanded as he gave me an intense once-over. "Stand against the wall."

I stood next to the wall in the barn where the marks were still visible from our previous measuring some eleven weeks prior. Tom placed a stick on top of my head.

"Just as I suspected—you've grown. You are now five feet six and a half inches." Tom did some scribbling and scratched his head a couple of times and then scribbled some more and then wrinkled up his face and then scribbled some more. "There," he said with a satisfied look. "The one-half inch you have grown is the equivalent of losing a pound and a quarter."

"Great. Now all I have to do is grow another foot and a half." Tom's calculations were not helping.

"No, you're not looking at this the right way. If you continue to grow and reach the height of… say, five feet ten inches and keep working out, you'll be just right. Muscle weighs more than fat, and by turning your extra inches all into muscle and by growing, you'll be in great shape." Tom was speaking excitedly now. "It might take you a couple of years to grow the necessary inches, but by the time you do, and as long as you keep working out, you will be one chiseled dude."

Tom was making sense. I quickly ran the figures through my mind. If I grew to six feet, which was very likely since my older brother Scott did, I would be six feet tall and weigh one hundred and ninety-three pounds, all of which would be muscle. It did make sense. Jack Snow, my favorite wide receiver for the Los Angeles Rams, weighed one ninety. All I had to do was keep working out and running, and in a couple of years, I would be six feet tall and lean. Whoa there—put the monastery on hold!

"You're right! I'm on my way!" Visions of a washboard stomach and veins popping out all over my greased-down body were going through my mind. I could do it. *I will do it. All I have to do is keep working hard like I am, and nature will run its course.*

Since it was Sunday, our day of rest from heavy workouts, Greg and I just wandered around the island making plans for the future. We walked over to Marshall Beach to see what was going on. Usually on Sunday afternoons during the off-season, Mrs. Marshall would open up the Island's burger slash beer joint to the locals and they would all get falling-down drunk and carry on like a bunch of loonies. Sometimes they would fight.

One time, Old Roy, a regular at the beach, accused Bob the mailman of messing around with his wife, Gloria, who was fifteen years younger than himself. Well, Bob denied it, but Old Roy kept going on and on about Bob and Gloria fooling around behind his back, so finally Bob had enough. He walked over to Gloria, a wild redhead who stood about five feet ten inches with a Dolly Parton wig giving her another eight inches on top of that. She had a full set of curves like Dolly too, which attracted the attention of most of the men folk, especially when she was swishing around, which was most of the time. Bob stopped right smack-dab in front of Gloria with everybody in the place, including Roy, watching. He slipped his arms around the big redhead and said with enthusiasm, "If I'm going to get accused of something, then by George, I'm going to be guilty!" With that, he pulled her tight and planted a great big one right on her large bright-red lips. That's all it took. The whole establishment was in an uproar. Roy tried to choke Bob to death with Gloria slamming her purse over Roy's head. Everyone else sort of chose up sides and commenced to brawling. It was a wonderful thing!

After the riot, we got the whole story from Jody, Mrs. Marshall's part-time cook. He would have been her full-time cook except he had to report back to jail every Sunday evening. They let him out on a work release program from Friday morning through Sunday, the Pub's busy time. Anyhow, according to Jody, Gloria left Roy and drove away with Bob the very next day when he came by in his mailman's jeep delivering the mail. There was seldom a dull moment on the island, and Greg and I were hoping for some similar action as we strolled in sight of the diner.

Greg was still pumped from the four pounds he had gained, and I was feeling good about the progress I was making as well. The day before, Tom had checked us for strength. Both of us were getting stronger—not a lot, but stronger. Becoming a stud doesn't happen overnight.

"Next year is football, you know," Greg informed me, "and all this exercise will give us an advantage over the rest of the guys. In fact, I wouldn't be surprised if we could make varsity if we picked up the pace a little bit and practiced more."

"Yeah." Can't argue with that kind of logic, I mentally agreed. "When you're good, you're good, and when you happen to be Greg and John, you're even better."

"That's right!" Greg returned agreeably.

"You know, when we make varsity, we're going to have to get ourselves a car to haul all our women around in," I surmised.

"Wouldn't be right to make them all walk."

"No, it sure wouldn't. What kind of car you gonna get?"

Greg sat rather stoically for a moment or two. "I want a 65 GTO with a 389, tri-power and a 4-speed with Positraction. How 'bout you?"

"67 GTX," I said matter-of-factly, "with a 440 magnum, 4-speed."

"Yeah, those are cool," Greg agreed.

We sat on a picnic table near the Pub and watched the locals come and go, talking about girls, football, and cars. Bob and Gloria rolled up in Bob's mailman jeep, which he liked to drive when he was off duty to impress the civilian population. Roy came along a little later with his new girlfriend, Sonny. Sonny was from Scappoose, just west of the Sauvie Island turnoff. She worked at the Blue Bird Lounge as a cocktail waitress. Sonny was shorter than Gloria, but was sporting that same sort of "makeup is everything" look, that seemed to be all the rage with your overachieving man-eater types. Everyone seemed to be okay with the new arrangement, and to our dismay nothing of interest happened all that afternoon not counting the cat that caught fire.

Someone had spilled some hard liquor on it, and someone else soon after threw a burning match to the floor where the cat just happened to be. The diner only serves beer and wine, but there is always a bottle of hard stuff to be found amongst the patrons. The flaming cat was quickly dealt with by a fast thinker who sloshed a pitcher of beer on it before any real harm was done.

Greg's mom offered to give me a ride home. I refused. I wanted the exercise. From that weekend on, there was hardly a single waking moment of the day that I was not aware of the calories that I was or was not burning. Each morning, I arose to my exercise regimen, and every evening, I finished the day with more of the same. Each day, I grew closer to my goal. I began to be obsessed in a good way—or at least, I think it was a good way.

It was paying off, too. Not that the girls had actually noticed me yet or that Bunny had left Rodney Skylark for me or that my mere physical presence sent chills through the dominating portion of the male populous of the eighth grade or anything like that. No, it was a more of a quiet kind of confidence and self-respect that started growing within. When I looked into the mirror to heap on positive affirmations, which I had become accustomed to doing, I started looking deeper and deeper into my own eyes. I began to like what I was seeing.

There's something about pushing oneself beyond one's physical capabilities repeatedly until it becomes doable and then reaching out and beyond again and succeeding and growing and doing it again and again that changes more than one's muscle. It builds something inside as well. I felt good.

The days rolled into weeks and the weeks into months and the exercise went on. By school's end in the first week of June, I weighed in at one hundred and ninety-two pounds. After seven months of working out and running and bike riding and playing football with the guys on the island, I had lost only one pound. I grew two full inches, however. I was now five foot eight. Greg had grown too. He was now five foot six inches and one hundred and seventeen pounds. We were making strides.

CHAPTER TEN

It was the first day of summer vacation, and Greg and I had a very serious summer planned. We were going to pick berries in the morning for school money and then work out, run and work on our football skills, and finish up with a swim each day. When berry season ends in July, we would pick beans, and by the time beans had run their course, we would buck hay for Greg's step-uncle, Whit. Uncle Whit had three hundred acres of hay just south of Portland a few miles. Plus, Greg's dad always needed help stacking hay or something on the farm.

This plan of ours would ensure us a summer of muscle-building hard work and exercise, including plenty of time to work on our fundamentals to get us ready for our first year of high school football. We would also earn a little cash for new duds to slip our svelte, hard-as-nails, bodies into for school. We were men with a plan. We could not be stopped.

To make our summer plan work meant that I would have to stay over at Greg's place at least Monday through Friday to be able to get up and be off berry picking by six am. It took a little convincing, but my mom gave her permission, and Greg's folks were okay with it.

I made my way carefully through town on my bicycle, which was loaded down with all the stuff I would need throughout the first week of summer. I packed extra clothes and the like, but it wasn't the clothing that made the bike sway the way it was. It was the fifty pounds of weights I had placed at the bottom of my pack and strapped to the back of my bike that was making the ride interesting, as they would slip from one side to the other. I was bringing two twenty-five-pound cast-iron plates that I had found at a garage sale to add to our collection in Greg's barn. Now we would be able to put three hundred pounds on the bar for serious bench work. Of course, neither Greg nor I were anywhere near the three-hundred-pound mark, but to be a studly member of the Washington High varsity football team, a three-hundred-pound bench press was a must.

School had let out for the last time at Buckman Elementary for me and the other former eighth graders. We had a little ceremony where Mrs. Walters, our principal, gave a speech about life and our commitment to learning and zzzzzz. I awoke to loud cheers, and the next thing I know, I was running home as fast as I could to grab my bike already loaded the night before. Then I headed for Greg's for a summer of serious hard work and total commitment to self-improvement in the form of football fundamentals and conditioning. Swimming and camping and fishing were also figured into our plans. We were going to work hard, but we planned to play hard too.

The sun was shining bright and warm, and pedaling over the hill took a little more effort than normal with the extra weight. Sweat was pouring from my pores as I grunted and peddled up over the crest of the hill over a thousand feet above Portland's downtown. It wasn't long before I was coasting down the other side right past the large palm. The palm-reading lady was sitting on her porch with a man I hadn't seen before. They were looking rather chummy. I guess the dark-haired greasy guy with the Zig-Zag man tattoo was out of the picture. I felt kind of sad for him, and a little disappointed. He kept things interesting.

The corn was well on its way of being "knee-high by the fourth of July," I noticed as I turned left at the Y in the road after rolling down off the bridge leading to the island. I had never taken the left fork before. The right turn on the island was supposed to be shorter, but since it was one big loop, I thought I would do a little investigating. Greg and I had explored all of the beach area and most of the farms and marshy wooded area on the right side of the island, but the left side was still a mystery.

I peddled past cornfields and peach trees and an assortment of other crops that I could not identify. There were small farmhouses that were probably built sometime after some of the first dams on the Colombia went in. From what I learned in school, the dams changed some of the landscape, exposing some land masses that were quickly gobbled up for farms and such. There were newer homes too here and there, with large barns and horses and cows and all the regular farm animals you'd expect to see.

I rode on, and soon up ahead I could see the school. I knew it was over on this side of the island, but I had yet to see it. It was an old wooden building with what appeared to be a fresh coat of white paint and a new charcoal-black shingled roof. It looked to be big enough for the fifty or so students who attended there, but not much bigger. I peddled over the front lawn and around back to investigate.

Behind the school building was a large grass field that needed mowing, complete with a red cinder track and a baseball diamond with a rickety old backstop. There was a play area for the younger kids with monkey bars, teeter-totters, and a slide. Directly behind the school building was a basketball court with two baskets sporting metal mesh nets.

I stopped my bike at the monkey bars when I noticed a

girl dribbling a basketball. She shot the ball into the air and over the basket. It went rolling right up to where I was straddling my loaded-down bike. I just stood there for a moment, not sure what I should do. However, the girl seemed to know exactly what I should do. She stood there with her hands on her hips, waiting for me to do the gentlemanly thing. So I did. I got off my bike, carefully laying it on its side, grabbed the ball, and threw it to her. She smiled a big, friendly smile and started dribbling, and again—shooting the same high arcing shot which sent the ball over the hoop and right back to where I stood. This time, I knew what was expected, and without hesitating I scooped up the ball and tossed it to her.

"Thanks," she said, smiling that same big friendly smile. She caught the ball and continued her dribbling and shooting routine with about the same results.

I shagged a couple more balls for her, trying to be cool while I scoped her out. She looked to be maybe a year younger than myself, a little on the skinny side with strawberry-blonde hair, blue eyes, and a few freckles. She was kind of cute in an outdoorsy sort of way. "You live around here?" I finally asked. Girls always made me nervous, especially cute ones.

"Yes, I do," she said, smiling that big smile again. Something about that smile stirred up butterflies in my stomach. "Over there." She pointed to a large old farmhouse with several barns and fields full of young cornstalks on the other side of the schoolyard.

We exchanged information—name, rank, and serial number, or to be more precise, name, school, and age. She was easy to talk to, with a comfortable, easygoing personality. Her name was Sally, and she would be in the eighth grade that fall. I enjoyed talking to Sally, but I had to get going. Greg was waiting, and we had to get started—big, cute, stomach-churning smiles or no. There were only three months before practice started for the freshman football team and we had to be ready. I couldn't let some girl distract me from my mission.

"Well, I got to go, Sally. Greg and I have a lot of work to do to get ready for football." Sally knew Greg and Tom from school. Everybody knows everybody on the island.

"Some of my friends and I hang out at Marshall Beach quite a bit," Sally said, smiling again. "Maybe I'll see you there?" It was more of a question than a statement.

"Yeah, maybe," I replied. I was beginning to wonder what the guys would think about me fraternizing with an eighth grader. "I'll see ya," I called out as I began pumping the pedals and moving on down Sauvie Island Road to Greg's. I looked back and saw her walking to her house behind the school with the ball tucked under her arm. For some reason, I had the feeling I might have blown it.

"Blown what?" I asked myself aloud. "After all, she's just an eighth grader. I don't need no girlfriend. I'm looking for a real woman, a freshman, like Bunny."

Of course Rodney Skylark might have something to say about that. A cold chill ran through my veins as visions of Rodney came to the forefront of my mind. I set my jaw tight and my resolve even tighter. Three months of summer, and I was going to make the most of it.

Greg was in the front yard doing pull-ups from the limb of the old cherry tree as I rolled up to his house on my loaded-down 10-speed.

"Eleven," Greg grunted as he dropped from the limb. "That's a new record. How many can you do?" Greg asked, bypassing any salutations and the like that might generally be customary between friends who hadn't seen each other in a week.

"Last count was five," I said, not without some pride. Greg could do eleven, but he was a lot lighter.

"Go ahead. Let's see what you've got," Greg demanded.

"Okay," I said.

With a sense of purpose, I laid my bike on the lawn and started swaying my arms around and shaking them out to get loosened up. There were actually some muscles in the limbs that I was swinging. I could feel my biceps twitch as I flexed. For the past seven months or so, I had stayed true to my quest for physical fitness. I had not strayed. I had not made great gains, but Tom assured me, repeatedly, that they would come.

I stood on a small wooden box and grabbed the smooth lower branch of the large old cherry tree in one hand and then the other. I allowed myself to hang, kicking the box to one side, arms fully extended. I pulled myself up, pushing my chin over the limb. The first one felt good. I quickly lowered myself, trying to gain some momentum. Once at the bottom, without pausing, back up I went, and again my chin went over the limb. Then three. Then four. My chin went up and over the branch without too much effort, although I was breathing hard and grunting heavily on the upward swings. I had established the needed rhythm to go for a personal best—I could feel it.

The fifth upward swing was not, as the first four, but with some effort, I got it. I could feel my strength beginning to wane. I just had to do one more. I dropped to the fully extended position and jerked up with all the strength I could muster. I literally bounced up, struggled a moment to get my chin over the limb for number six and a new personal best, and then dropped and bounced again. I got three-fourths of the way up and then reached down inside to some inner reservoir and pulled until my chin was just over the limb. I dropped to the ground in a heap, panting, coughing, and wheezing.

I had done it—seven pull-ups and every one a keeper, no cheaters or wimpies. I was elated.

Greg was too. "Way to go, John baby. That's the way." He continued to barrage me with similar "atta boys" while I struggled to regain my composure.

Finally, I was able to rise to my feet and catch my breath somewhat as I beckoned Greg over to my bicycle. "Here," I said haltingly between pants as I reached into my pack on the back of my bike. I pulled out one, then two twenty-five-pound plates. "Now we've got three hundred pounds!"

"Let's go!" Greg hollered as he grabbed one of the plates and began running for the barn with me and the other plate following right behind.

We previously had moved the weights out behind the barn into the full sun so as to work up a full sweat and catch a few rays as we worked out. Nothing worse than a hard body cut to the bone without some color. We excitedly placed the plates on the rack that held the extras. It would be a while before we actually needed them, but it gave us a good feeling knowing that we would be able to load up three hundred pounds on the bench when the time came.

We looked on our weight collection with much satisfaction. I had brought my one hundred and ten-pound set from home a few pieces at a time. It included two adjustable dumbbells as well as a five-foot 5 foot bar. Getting the bar to Greg's on my bike was the tricky part, but I managed. The rest of the weights came a few at a time. Tom had a six-foot bar and another hundred and fifty pounds, as well as a curl bar and a few solid weight dumbbells. We constructed the bench with some lumber left over from a shed Tom's dad had built. He welded a bunch of pipe together for a very stout support for the barbell, complete with a safety bar on either side of the bench so we wouldn't get crushed from the massive weights we were lifting.

We loaded up the bar with two twenty-five-pound plates plus two five-pounders for a total of eighty-five pounds including the bar. I assumed the position of spotter. Greg ripped off four reps on his own, and I helped him through three more to give him a good workout.

"Arrghh!" The beast in Greg was stirring.

"My turn!" I said enthusiastically. The bench press was my specialty. I had trouble keeping up with Greg when it came to pull-ups and Greg could run faster and farther than I could, but I was stronger on the bench.

"Here." I handed Greg a ten-pound plate to replace the five-pounder as I grabbed another.

"What's this? You think you're King Kong or something?" Greg did not like the fact that I could bench more than him. He was very competitive, but so was I.

"That's right," I said, swaggering around the bench, shaking my arms in preparation. After making a show of loosening up, I laid down on the bench and grabbed the bar, which now weighed ninety-five pounds. I pushed it up into position, let it down to my chest, and then pushed it up again, shaking a little.

"I don't think King Kong ever struggled with ninety-five pounds," Greg exclaimed gleefully as he noticed my shaky ascent.

But that was the first rep, and sometimes it takes two or three before they come smoothly.

"Two," I grunted as my arms extended over my chest. "Three." Grunt. "Four." I exhaled forcefully as the bar went up. Then with much effort but signaling Greg to back off, I managed the fifth. Greg helped me place the bar on the rack slightly behind my head.

"Wow," was all he had to say.

I was making some serious gains. Tom had said they would come. The best I could ever get before was two reps with ninety-five pounds. I was on my way.

We continued our workout doing curls, kickbacks on the curl bar, flies while standing and lying on the bench with dumbbells, and overhead presses, standing and in the incline and decline position again with the dumbbells. We also did some chest pulls, standing and bent, and pullovers on the bench with the curl bar. Then we did an assortment of exercises that we had no official names for, but hurt just the same.

After the weights, we went back into the barn and looped a rope through a large pulley that was hanging from a rafter. We hooked one end of the rope through the handles of a metal laundry tub full of rocks, and we tied the other end to an O ring Tom's dad had welded to an old set of stingray handle bars from a bicycle that had been hanging around. We then commenced doing lat pulls and triceps extensions.

After considerable grunting and much sweating, we were pumped. Blood had swollen our muscles to their maximum limits. We were into the strutting-around flexing part of our workout when Tom showed up.

"Very impressive. Did you do your stomach?" Tom, always the party pooper, wanted to know.

"Uh, no. We were just getting to that part." Greg wasn't completely lying. The "no" part was true. Greg and I would often get to strutting around, doing all the glamour lifts, and forget about doing our stomach stuff. We hated doing crunches and leg lifts and sit-ups. They just hurt and weren't much fun at all.

"That's right," I chimed in.

Tom looked at me and then at Greg with the same disdainful look that we had seen many an afternoon.

"Okay, one more time." Tom had given us this same speech several times before, and here it came again. "If you want to become strong and make steady gains, you must not neglect any one part of your body. It's all connected. If you don't work your stomach, you won't be nearly as strong as you could be. Not working one area of the body will actually hold back the other areas. Don't neglect your stomach. It's what keeps your legs connected to your chest and arms. If you have a weak midsection, it's like having a body that's divided, and a divided body is not going to be as strong as one that is securely connected."

"Words of wisdom, I'm sure," I said rather sullenly. "Okay, Greg, hold my feet."

Greg held on to my feet as I did my sit-ups and then we switched. Next were the much-hated crunches, followed by the equally unpopular leg lifts. We gave a good effort. We knew Tom was right. Besides, you can't get that washboard look without some work, and a washboard stomach is mandatory for attracting babes on the beach.

After another set each of stomach exercises, we put on our cut-offs, Converse low-tops, and T-shirts for our run over to Marshall Beach for a swim. It was now seven thirty. We had two more hours of daylight, and the air was warm. The Columbia River would be a bit cool yet, since it was still early June and the snow was still melting and flowing from the nearby mountains of the Cascades, but tolerable.

We used to ride over to Marshall Beach on our bikes, but we would no longer allow ourselves the luxury. It was nearly two miles one way, so a good run was mandatory if a swim was in the works.

As we jogged along, I began thinking of that cute girl with the freckles and strawberry-blonde hair, and that same butterfly feeling in the pit of my gut resurfaced.

"Greg?" I huffed. "Do you know Sally Rayfield?"

"Yeah, I know her. Why?" Greg replied with a disturbed tone.

"Oh, no reason. I met her at the school on the way over." I tried to sound indifferent as if I was just trying to pass the time with conversation.

Greg looked at me intently, not buying it, as we huffed and puffed down the narrow paved road that leads to Marshall Beach.

"So . . . what?" Greg wanted to know.

"So . . . what *what*?" I asked back.

"So, why are you interested in Sally Rayfield?"

"Oh, I don't know. Just curious."

"You like her?" Greg wasn't really asking.

"Like her?" I sputtered. "She's just a kid."

"Right." Greg grunted. We continued huffing and puffing toward Marshall Beach without talking for a spell.

So, what if I did like her? What's it to Greg?

"Well, what if I do like her?" I blurted between breaths.

Greg was taken by surprise. It was obvious from the blank look on his face that he hadn't given it another thought. "Huh?"

"Nothing," I said quickly.

"Oh, you're still thinking about Sally Rayfield. I thought you were holding out for Bunny."

"That's right. I am," I said with conviction as a vision of green eyes, shimmering light-brown hair with blonde streaks, and clear, smooth skin flashed before my eyes. Sally Rayfield was forgotten—at least for the present.

Marshall Beach came in sight. Greg started running faster, and I fought to keep up. The closer we got, the more we increased our pace until we were both going full tilt. Of course, Greg was now pulling away from me.

I ran as hard as I could, keeping Greg in sight. He rounded the corner and I followed, but by the time I caught up to him, he had already ripped off his shirt and was plowing into the river. After a few more huffs and puffs, I found myself swimming beside him.

We swam vigorously. Everything we did, we did vigorously. Every movement during the course of a day was part of our workout. Going to the water fountain at school was used to build muscle. We would bend over to get a drink, not using our hands and arms to prop ourselves up, but we would flex and squeeze our stomach muscles and then straighten up, flexing all the way. Sitting at our desks, we would place our arms under the desks and pull upwards, working our biceps, shoulders, and pecs. We would never walk if we could run. We would never sit and be idle. We were all about fitness. Every waking hour of every day except Sunday, we worked our bodies. One day a week, we rested from our runs and workouts and muscle flexing. Proper rest is equally, if not more, important as the exercise. We were serious, and it was beginning to pay off, as my record-breaking pull-ups and bench press had demonstrated.

Twilight in June is long and bright in the more northern latitudes, and although Oregon is not Alaska, the light in the sky still doesn't completely go away until sometime after ten p.m. It must have been getting close to that time, as we were losing sight of much of Marshall Beach from the water. We got out, put our shirts on, and began to jog back to Greg's. Jogging home is always harder and seems longer than jogging to the beach, but we made it. We did our customary push-ups at the end of our run without much enthusiasm, having spent much of our energy, and headed to the kitchen to get some supplies for the night. After stocking up on leftovers from dinner and some cookies and milk, we headed out to the tent staked out beyond the barn.

The barn was situated to one side and slightly in back of the house and right next to the orchard of apple trees. The orchard was shaped like an L, making a turn about sixty feet behind the barn and going clear over to the rows of sweet corn on the other side of the house. We made camp on the far side of the apple trees directly behind the barn. There was a small creek that ran right through our camp and dumped into a fair-sized pond. At night, we would build a large fire and throw our baited and weighted lines into the water at the mouth of the creek. The catfish hung out there, and we would catch a mess of them. There were bass, crappie, and blue gill in the pond as well. Tom and Huck never had it so good.

Some nights, if we had any energy left after picking berries or bucking hay, pumping iron, running, swimming, and football, we would sneak out and run all over the island, exploring and spying on the neighbors. Generally, we would have to do our night maneuvers on Saturday evenings or we would be too tired the next day to work or anything else. By the end of summer, our Saturday night excursions took us clear to the other side of the island where the Columbia makes its split, forming the island. There we discovered the houseboats. Of course we knew they were there because we could see them from the road when we passed over the bridge, but we had never taken a close look until one clear and moonlit Saturday night.

We snuck into the houseboat parking lot just off the main road. The house boats lined the slough with garages directly behind them facing us as we entered the parking area. There were three bright floodlights on poles along the row of garages. We kept to the dark recesses of tall Douglas fir trees along the perimeter. We couldn't see much from where we were positioned. The garages blocked much of our view of the houseboats. We would have to cross under the lights to get to the paths alongside of the garages that led to the twenty or so floating homes. There were another twenty or more on the mainland side separated from the island by about two hundred feet of water where the Columbia flows into the slough. The slough was wide at the mouth, but narrowed considerably as it flowed west. The houseboats lined the wider portion of the waterway.

We could hear music blaring, with loud voices and laughter intermingled. Someone was having a party, and we just had to see what was going on.

After studying the situation we deduced that there was no way of gaining a good spying advantage from the bank. There were thick brambles and trees on either end of the string of houseboats that were impenetrable.

"We've got to go by water," Greg announced grimly. "There's no other way."

"Right," I agreed.

We retraced our steps to the main road and lightly jogged

west toward the bridge. Our tennis-shoe clad feet were quiet on the pavement. The air was mild and the moon was bright, giving us some relief from the darkness. Once we made the bridge, we took the path that led down to the slough and under the bridge. There, we immediately took off our shoes and shirts, and with nothing but our cut-off Levi's and a load of bravado, we entered the water.

The slow-moving slough was a little cool at first, but became quite comfortable once we got used to it. Slowly and quietly we breast-stroked toward the houseboats lining the bank. They weren't more than two hundred yards away. We kept to the island side so as not to be detected in the moonlight, which seemed quite bright on the water. There were large limbs from fir trees lining the bank of the slough that extended out a good fifteen feet or more shielding the light from the moon. We swam in the dark under the limbs hanging about eight feet above our heads, but could see the lights from the houseboats ahead and the moonlight shimmering on the water in the center of the slough. As we drew closer, we could hear laughter and music, and saw people on the deck of one of the large and more spacious floating structures.

Where the large old-growth Douglas fir trees stopped, the row of houseboats on both sides of the slough began. We slithered up to the first house which sat upon several huge logs. It was one of the smaller and older homes with what appeared to be one main room with a kitchen, living area, and what we figured was a bedroom and a bathroom. It had a small deck in front with a sliding patio-type door decorated with fishnets, colorful Japanese glass buoys, dried-out starfish, and an assortment of shells and driftwood. Some of the driftwood was rather large, placed in a decorative manner here and there. A couple of fishing poles were leaning against the house with a white bucket and what appeared to be a large beat-up metal tackle box. There was a soft light coming from the interior, and the movement of light from what we presumed was a television in the corner out of our sight. We couldn't see anyone, so we moved around the deck and swam up to the next one.

Again, we didn't see anyone—just the usual lawn chairs and assorted marine-type decorations. The first five or six boats were of comparable size and style, followed by larger boats with much larger decks for entertaining. Across the slough, the houseboats were similar. The smaller ones were in the narrow part and they became larger as the waterway widened. The small boats all had patio-type sliding glass doors leading to small decks. We could see television lights flickering in some, and could hear the sound of Johnny Carson coaxing laughs from an audience and a newsman going off about a demonstration in Berkeley. All the while, the sounds of the party became louder as we swam closer. None of this would have been all that exciting to the average citizen, but Greg and I were thrilled. Our blood was pumping as if we were Navy Seals on a special assignment deep in enemy waters. The houseboats held the secret, and it was our job to find out what it was. We slithered on.

Sure enough, the last of the little houseboats held a secret all right, but not one of any political importance—if you don't count the local branch of the federal post office or the crowd over at the Marshall Beach beer and burger bar. As we silently crept through the water to get in front of the last little houseboat, we could see into the semi-lit interior. There to our surprise were two familiar faces—Bob the mailman and Sonny, the new girlfriend of Roy. They were lounging on the couch under a blanket. I guess Bob had a thing for Roy's girlfriends. First it was Gloria, and now Sonny. They were talking, and every once in a while, Bob would give her a kiss.

We had seen enough. As interesting and exciting as Bob the mailman's love life was, "gag," we had to move on. After all, a Navy Seal cannot limit himself to witnessing acts of indiscretions. Besides, Bob taking up with another of Roy's girlfriends was not the news it once was.

We focused now on the party sounds coming from the largest of the houseboats near the end of the line where the slough was rather wide. We slid by a couple of the larger floating homes on logs without any trouble, but there directly in front of us on the deck of the next one were a man and a woman standing at the rail facing the slough. They were talking. They each had a large drink of something they periodically took sips from. There was no way of getting by them unnoticed. I signaled Greg to retrace our strokes. We pulled back around to the side of the neighboring floating house out of sight.

"Now what?" Greg whispered tersely as we treaded water.

I looked all around. "We've got to go back and swim to the other side and then make our way along the houseboats, staying in the shadows." I pointed to the line of houses on the other side of the slough. "And then we'll swim back over to this side once we get down to the end. They won't be able to see us."

Greg scrunched up his freckled face as he peered intently at the row of houseboats on the opposite side of the slough.

"Right. Let's go." He was game.

We quietly retraced our strokes. Back under the limbs of the trees, we crossed over to the other side. There was only about fifty feet of water separating the two banks at this point. We would be hidden completely from view except for about fifteen feet in the very center of the slough. We could have gone down the slough another fifty feet or so, and crossed, with no danger of detection, but it wouldn't have been nearly as exciting. Besides, what's a little danger to a Navy Seal?

We breast-stroked as quietly as we could to the other side. Once there, we studied our surroundings and made sure that we had not been seen. We could just barely see two silhouettes across the slough on the deck of the houseboat where our forward progress had been halted. From their body language, we deduced that they weren't aware of anyone else in the vicinity. They were too busy with each other to notice silent invaders such as ourselves.

We crept along through the cool water, staying close to the houseboats under the protection of the shadows. We glanced into each one as we passed without detecting anything of interest. This side of the slough was rather boring.

We continued on past the couple on the other side who had caused us to alter our plan. We could hear the sounds of music and laughter coming from a very large houseboat on the island side getting louder as we made our way toward the Columbia. There were a dozen or so people on the large deck of the houseboat dancing and carrying on like people do when they've had enough drink to take away the usual inhibitions, but not so much that they were falling all over themselves. The houseboat had large French-type doors that exposed the entire back portion of the boat when opened, which they were. We could see another couple of dozen people in the interior of the boat, and there was a band visible in the back recesses next to what appeared to be a bar. The lights were turned down somewhat for atmosphere, which made our spying a little more challenging than we had hoped. We were definitely going to have to swim over to the other side to get a closer look.

We continued on. After a few minutes of uninterrupted slithering in the dark shadows, we reached the end. Two hundred feet of water separated us from the other side. The Columbia River was to our right, and the houseboats along both banks of the slough to our left. The moon shone brightly on the water, but from this angle it didn't appear that we would be seen by anyone on the party boat. There were another three or four houseboats and a fairly large cabin cruiser at the end obstructing the view. We swam for the other side.

The water was still cool, but comfortable, and there was no discernible current. However, we could see, from the light of the moon, out over much of the mighty Colombia River to our right as we swam to the north bank of the slough. It had the appearance of great movement toward its final destination. The Pacific Ocean was about eighty miles to the west. I felt rather small at that moment. If Greg and I had gone a little farther out, we would have been caught up in the current and possibly washed out to sea and deposited on some beach somewhere for the gulls to peck and scratch at. Of course, the crabs would get their share as well. That is, if a great white shark didn't chew up our limp and bloated bodies first. I shuddered and decided I would direct my thoughts back to the task at hand. I swam toward the houseboats on the opposite bank of the slough.

As I swam, with the dangerous currents heading out to sea not more than a dozen feet to my right, I realized that Greg and I, over the course of the summer, had become quite good swimmers. Our bodies had become stronger from working hard and as Mother Nature had run its course. It had been a very good three months. We hadn't earned quite as much money as we had planned. The berry picking was so monotonous that we found ourselves running off early to swim or fish in one of the many ponds on more than one occasion. But every day, we worked hard at our goal of becoming physical specimens. We never missed a workout, and there was never a day that went by that we did not run, swim, and throw the football around.

After a hard day of bucking hay for Greg's uncle or picking berries or beans in the hot sun or helping Greg's dad with chores, which happened more and more frequently, or after a hard workout with the weights, we would grab the ball and head for Marshall Beach to give the girls who were there sunbathing a treat.

Greg and I had become quite tanned, and my hair was

bleached blond from the sun. We were a couple of Greek gods. I still had more than a little gut with side handles and Greg was still kind of skinny with lots of freckles, but that didn't muddle our self-perception any. To our way of thinking, we were hot commodities—at least in the world of early pubescent adolescence. And we would not deny the young women of the world a chance to see what we had to offer.

One extremely warm and sunny day in August after a hard day of bucking hay for Greg's uncle, we were throwing the football, running routes, flexing, and generally just looking good for the masses at Marshall Beach when the ball flew over my head, bounced, and rolled into the outstretched arms of a familiar face. At first, I didn't recognize the strawberry-blonde hair and blue eyes. My heart skipped a beat, though, when I realized who it was.

"Hi," Sally Rayfield said with a smile as she handed me the ball. It was that same smile that had haunted me from the day that we met in back of Sauvie Island Elementary and High School almost two months earlier. She had a nice tan going and looked good in her modest one-piece bathing suit. She was still a little on the thin side, but that smile made up for anything she might have lacked.

"Hi," I said back nervously as I took the ball.

"Haven't seen you around. Whatcha been up to?" Sally asked ever so sweetly as if she were a spider trying to lure her prey into her web.

I stammered something unintelligible just as Greg came to a running stop in the sand beside me.

"What's up?" Greg demanded, obviously not under the same spell in which I was totally entrapped. I don't know what it was about Sally, but she did seem to exercise some sort of power over me. While it was true that pretty girls made me nervous, it was also true that even Bunny, the goddess of my dreams, the babe of babes, the most beautiful woman in all the world, didn't cause the sort of discomfort that I was now experiencing. It was also true, and perhaps even stranger, that although she was cute with an admittedly great smile, I didn't consider Sally Rayfield to be pretty—well, at least not Bunny kind of pretty. She had a nice look, but . . .

"Are we going to play ball or what?" Greg demanded with a bit of a disgusted look on his freckled face. He took the ball from my hands and ordered, "Go long."

So I did. I sped off in the deep sand, not turning to look back until I was at what I figured to be the limit of Greg's throwing range. I wanted to put as much space between that Sally Rayfield and myself as possible. I looked back as I began drifting to the right. Greg threw a beauty, leading me perfectly. The ball dropped softly into my outstretched hands and then continued its course to the ground as I stumbled and bumbled into a heap on the sand. Yep, she was bad news.

Greg and I managed to steer our football maneuvers down the beach on the very next route, away from Sally and her snickering friends.

I was thinking of Sally now as Greg and I closed in on the other side of the slough. I had thought of her often after that meeting on the beach, but had managed to stay away from her. I just couldn't for the life of me sort out my feelings. On the other hand, it was very clear in my mind how I felt about Bunny. Bunny was everything to me. She was what kept me going, the reason I would go for that extra rep on the bench or that extra sit-up.

We could hear the music and sounds of voices intermingled with laughter coming from the party boat, our final destination. A good Navy Seal always has a plan, or at the very least, a good reason for placing himself in danger. Unlike our Navy Seal brethren, however, we had no real plan or reason to be there. We just wanted to sneak a peek. We had made our way past the three large houseboats and then around the cabin cruiser parked next to the party boat. Here we had to be careful. There were several people on the deck not more than twenty-five feet away. The light of the moon was blocked by the large cruiser as we slipped around the nose and slid along its side, keeping to the darkness.

Our eyes were wide open and our blood was pumping enthusiastically as the excitement of the moment registered.

I caught Greg's eye as we treaded water in the darkness provided by the cruiser and motioned with a jerk of my head toward the side of the houseboat. We made our way silently, and once we passed the last portion of the deck, we swam the twenty-odd feet over to the floating house. It was dark between the large cabin cruiser and the houseboat, and we were relatively safe from view. We clung to the huge logs that kept the structure afloat as we gathered ourselves.

"We need to get around to the front to see inside," Greg said.

"Right," I agreed. "Let's go."

Greg started out and I was right behind him as we worked our way along the side of the deck toward the front. We couldn't see anything from where we were swimming. The deck was a good three feet above our heads, and we could hear people talking directly above. Our goal was the ladder positioned off to the far side of the deck directly in front of the large French doors that had been flung open for the party. By climbing up the ladder, we would be able to see all that there was to see.

From the voices we heard, we determined that there were about eight people on the deck. As we swam for the ladder, I could see a forearm and hand sticking out over the rail. The hand held a cigarette, which was flicked in our general direction. The ash landed in the water next to me. There were two other people standing at the rail that we could see quite clearly. All they had to do was look down and we would be caught. We crept on.

We made the ladder without being spotted. Holding on to the bottom rung, we listened. The band at that moment was between songs. We could hear voices mingled with laughter. Someone was saying something about some property that he had invested a lot of money in, and another guy was trying to impress some girl with a lot of big talk. There was another voice that sounded oddly familiar. A cold shiver went through me. I knew that voice. Or was the water chilling me? I listened intently. Greg nudged me and motioned up the ladder. We both reached up for the next rung and began to make our simultaneous ascent. We moved very slowly, and I heard that voice again. It had a familiar arrogant flavor that caused my stomach to tighten, but I couldn't make out the words nor put a face to it.

We had managed to pull ourselves up to the top rung. It was a tight fit, but neither one of us wanted to wait for a turn. As we gathered ourselves to sneak our peak over the floor of the deck, I heard another voice. It was clear and feminine and sent butterflies loose all through my guts. At the sound of that familiar angelic voice, I forgot all else, and popped my head up over the top rung into full view of anyone looking in my general direction. It just so happened that there *was* someone looking in my general direction, and at the sight of my wet head and naked upper torso popping up out of the deep like a scene in a cheap horror flick, she screamed.

After that, it was pure chaos. Everyone on the deck was yelling, and I heard someone say something about getting his gun and someone else saying something about calling the police. Then the outside lights turned on and the whole area was lit up like noonday. Greg pulled me back down the ladder, and off we swam as fast as we could in the direction of the bridge where we had left our shirts and shoes. Behind us, we could hear shouting as the partiers watched our hasty retreat in the bright light. A few more hardy strokes toward the bridge and we would be in the shadows. Although the moon was still shining brightly, it would be difficult for anyone standing in the light of the houseboat to see us. We swam as hard as we could, neither one of us saying a word.

Thoughts and visions of the owner of that sweet, familiar voice raced through my head as I swam for my life, but they were quickly pushed aside by the recollection of the other voice, the voice of Rodney Skylark.

I abandoned the thoughts of Rodney and Bunny as we swam past the houseboats, many of them coming alive from all the racket from the party boat. Even Bob the mailman had managed to pull himself from his comfortable perch on the couch and his borrowed companion to see what all the excitement was about. He stood on the deck of his houseboat, quietly watching us swim by as he took a swig from a stubby brown bottle.

We reached the bridge in short order and pulled ourselves from the water. We grabbed our shoes and shirts and were about to put them on when I heard something.

"Listen," I demanded.

Greg stopped dead in his tracks and cocked an ear. We could hear voices and shoes slapping on pavement coming our way.

"Come on," I said as I grabbed my gear and waded back into the water.

Greg followed, and we quickly made for the other side. The slough was only about thirty feet wide at the bridge. We were just about to the other side when we heard voices up on the road from the opposite bank from where we had just come.

"Come on. They might be down there," an authoritative voice called out to his companions.

We could hear the shuffling sounds of the posse climbing down the uneven trail that lead to the slough under the bridge. The beams of a couple of flashlights darted about.

"Over here," Greg whispered, motioning to a large tree just to the side of the bridge up on the bank. We quickly pulled ourselves out of the water and slid behind the Douglas fir.

The posse was now at the water's edge on the other side of the slough, shining their lights in earnest.

"Where the heck could they have gone?" rang out a questioning voice.

There was a lot of excited chatter and cursing, and then we heard the authoritative one who had obviously taken charge. "Let's look on the other side."

Our hearts sank, but our minds began to race. They were coming. We could try to climb the rocky trail to the top of the bank barefoot and run like crazy before they had a chance to climb the bank and cross the bridge. Our bare feet wouldn't take those sharp rocks, and if we took the time to put our shoes on, our pursuers would have us for sure. There was only one thing for us to do. We looked at each other and then at the top of the rocky bank and then toward the water. We didn't hesitate. We could see the last of the posse climbing up the bank on the other side as we entered the slough. We stayed directly under the bridge as we swam for the other side, which turned out to be a good thing. The men were shining their lights down on the water as they raced across the bridge. We reached the bank and pulled ourselves out of the water and immediately climbed the not-nearly so rocky trail that lead back up to the road in our bare feet as we heard the voices of the posse climbing down the opposite bank.

Once to the road, we ran to the other side and into the woods. There we caught our breath as we put our sneakers on. My socks and T-shirt had been abandoned, as had Greg's. We listened for a moment. The voices had split up. It sounded as though some were on the other side of the bridge and yet another group had crossed back over but were now moving off down the road. We couldn't see a thing amongst the trees, so we carefully and quietly crept back out of our wooded haven and made our way around it, going in the same direction as the posse. We only had to go maybe a hundred feet or so, and then the trees ended and a large field of hay and our escape were waiting. We made the hayfield without incident. Once there, we threw caution to the wind and began running just as fast as we could. We were not seen.

CHAPTER ELEVEN

I stood in front of the hall mirror in our turn-of-the-century apartment, admiring my reflection. My hair was bleached blond from the sun like the surfers of Southern California, and my skin was a golden brown. I could feel muscles beneath my new clothes. There was still a fairly sizable bulge around my midsection, but I felt good. I was sporting new Levi's 501 jeans that I had sent through the wash with bleach at least six times so they wouldn't look new and a Los Angeles Rams jersey with the number 47. I didn't know who #47 was, but I didn't care—the Rams were my team. Topping off the ensemble were my brand-spanking-new bright-white Converse low-top tennis shoes. The days of my mother choosing my clothes were history. I was cool, and there was just no denying it.

The summer had been a good one. Even though our goal of becoming total studs was not completely realized, we had made considerable progress. Just the day before, Greg and I had taken our last test of our physical prowess for the summer. I was now able to bench-press one hundred and ten pounds six times, and I pushed one hundred and forty pounds one time. I also pumped out thirty-three good push-ups and eight pull-ups. I felt like King Kong.

Greg's mom took us shopping a few days before summer was over to get our new school threads. I had managed to save one hundred and eighteen dollars from picking berries and beans and bucking hay. It was a good feeling, being self-reliant. Money in the pocket honestly earned through hard work in the hot sun makes a man feel . . . well . . . manly. I smoothed a wrinkle in my jersey, ran a hand through my blond mane, gave myself an appreciative wink, and headed for the door. *Look out, Washington High. Here I come.*

I decided to walk. It wouldn't look right riding my bike to school.

It was a clear and mild morning in September, and the leaves on the trees had not yet begun to turn color. Autumn in Western Oregon comes rather late sometimes, due I guess, to the consistently mild seasons. I walked along with a bounce in my step that was not there the previous September. I felt glad to be alive.

Once at school, I began to renew acquaintances. There were a lot of new faces. Washington High School drew from a much larger area than Buckman Elementary. Some of the new faces were girls—cute girls. High school had promise.

Math was my first class. Next was shop, then science, followed by health taught by the PE teacher and coach of the freshman football team. Mr. Bumwack was pretty cool and asked for a show of hands of those who would be staying after school to try out for the freshman football team. He seemed really pleased to see eight out of the twelve or so boys raise our hands. He looked us over very thoroughly, giving each of us an approving nod.

"Those of you trying out for football, call me Coach. For the rest of you, I'm Mr. Bumwack." Coach was setting up the football players as elite citizens, and the eight of us had absolutely no problem with this particular class distinction. Football Rules.

After health was lunch, followed by PE, and then last period was study hall in the library.

My classes went by fairly quickly. Most of the time was spent getting organized and introducing ourselves to each other and stuff like that. I finally found myself in study hall for the last period. I was just getting settled into a chair at one of the tables when I heard an angelic voice behind me.

"Mind if I sit here?"

I turned in my seat, and there stood Bunny. Her hair was a bit lighter than I remembered with golden streaks throughout. Her green eyes were shining bright, and her clear skin was tanned. She was smiling sweetly, waiting for my reply.

"Sure, Bunny," I half stammered. I pushed my books to one side, trying to make room for her. It was a small round table, big enough for maybe four. Bunny sat down next to me.

"Thank you," she said looking at me with a surprised look on her pretty face. "John, I didn't know it was you. Where did you get that blond hair?"

"I . . . uh, the sun," I stammered. Just once I wish I could manage some sort of intelligent dialogue with Bunny without coming off like some sort of dip.

"Looks good."

Looks good? Bunny said my hair looks good. Now we're getting someplace. Okay, what do I say next? Something suave . . .

"Your hair looks good too." I think I did it again. That must have sounded dorky. It sounded dorky to me. Of *course* it sounded dorky. I'm a dork, aren't I?

"Oh, thank you," Bunny replied kindly.

She's handling it well—I have to give her that. Not only is she showing great patience but she has a sharp mind too. Say something else, quick, something cool.

"You're welcome." *Yep, cool runs all through my veins. This is going to be a long study hall.*

We didn't say much after that. I made like I had lots of work to do and went to shuffling papers and looking studious. Bunny opened up her journal and began writing. If only it was me she was writing so intently about.

I actually did manage to get a little work done, if you count connecting the dots and working a crossword puzzle in a *Highlights* magazine that had been left on our table. I was searching for the next dot to form *some* sort of animal when I felt a change in the atmosphere. I imagine it was something like the feeling in the air just before a large funnel cloud touches down. Since we've never had a tornado around these parts, at least in my lifetime, I wasn't sure what that would feel like. Just the same, I looked up to see a nervous smile appear on Bunny's most kissable lips—even in the face of a dangerous twister, I still had time to appreciate some of the finer things in life. My thought process changed, however, as the heaviness in the air and Bunny's tense countenance finally registered somewhere deep in my gut, which began sinking as soon as Bunny's kissable lips left my mind. I turned to see what had Bunny smiling so nervously.

"Hi, Rod." Bunny greeted the presence behind me with what I felt was forced enthusiasm.

There he stood, tall and threatening. Rodney Skylark was glaring down at me. The fear jumped up into my throat as it had hundreds of times before. My heart began beating wildly as my palms got clammy and the rest of me began quivering. All these months of running and working out, becoming stronger and faster, and the fear was still the same, massive and uncontrollable.

I didn't say a word. I just waited for my punishment like a convicted con on death row. It was inevitable. There was nothing I could do but take it.

"Whatcha doin' sittin' next to this puke?" Rodney demanded. He had an air of superiority that I'm sure was of world-class proportions. I believe it was Rodney's own sense of his self-worth, however, that saved my bacon.

"Come on." Rodney stood there with his patented look of vast superiority as he waited for Bunny to gather her things. I guess I wasn't worthy of a beating at this time.

As Bunny took her place at his side, he looked down at me with a scowl and warned, "Next time, find a seat somewhere a little safer if you want to keep your face intact." They walked off.

I didn't say a word. The old ways were back—again.

I shuffled my papers on the table, trying to regain my composure. The other kids were filing out of the library. After they all had left, I stood, tucked my books and notebook under my arm, and headed slowly toward the door.

It was time for football. I didn't feel like playing football. I felt like curling up somewhere with a couple dozen Ding Dongs and eating myself into a sugar-induced coma and never waking up.

"Hey, John!" It was Fred Homestead, a new kid I met in first period. "Let's go!" He couldn't contain his enthusiasm. "Are you ready for some football? Blood and gore and guts with veins in my teeth." He was quoting Arlo Guthrie. "I am going to hurt somebody." Greg now using some of his own material.

Fred continued on with his violent machismo ramblings while I passively fell in beside him on our way to the gym.

Fred had attended Laurelhurst Elementary in the Laurelhurst neighborhood, same as Rodney Skylark. Like me, Fred was a year younger than Rodney, so he hadn't been in any of his classes. I'd met Fred in math class that very morning, where we hit it off immediately, having a lot in common. Fred was about my height, which was now about five feet eight and a half inches, and a little bit heavier than my now low of one hundred and ninety-one.

He also wanted to play football in the worst way. We'd spent the entire math class talking about how we were going to kick some serious butt out on the gridiron. Fred had been running and lifting weights in his garage all summer in preparation for freshman football. We talked about our physical condition and the gains we'd made over the summer. We also talked about our goals, which included playing college ball, dating all the cheerleaders and their friends, and maybe their sisters and their sisters' friends, and of course playing in the NFL. If any of the words Fred uttered were true, he was probably a bit stronger than me, but after all the running I'd done over the summer, I'd be surprised if he could beat me in a footrace or match my endurance.

"I'm gonna rip their hearts out and have them for lunch," Fred said with fire and a scowl on his round, cherubic face, with long strands of blond hair hanging in front of his blue eyes, that gleamed brightly. Fred's countenance exuded innocence and mirth. He was a good-natured guy and easy to talk to and very likable in a Gomer sort of way. Right now, however, all he wanted to do was tear somebody's head off.

"Save some for me," I managed, gathering myself somewhat, although far less enthusiastic than Fred. He didn't seem to notice.

We strolled into the gym as Fred's rhetoric began to take the shape of rhymes.

"Roses are red, violets are green, I'm gonna rip out their guts and stomp on their spleen." He was definitely on a roll.

Once in the gym, Coach Bumwack lined us up and took roll. We had already signed up for football and turned in our permission slips, along with notes from our doctors saying we were healthy enough to receive massive amounts of physical abuse.

"There are sixty-three of you trying out for the freshman football team," Coach Bumwack barked in his raspy, but powerful voice. "There are only fifty spots available," he continued, his craggy old face getting stern and serious with both brows knitted. "Some of you will not make the team. In fact, I don't care how good you are—if you don't give me one hundred and ten percent, you won't make this team." Coach Bumwack paused, letting this sink in.

"Okay," he barked, "dress-down and meet me on the field. You've got three minutes. Go."

We were gone. All sixty-three of us raced for the stairs leading down to the boys' locker room. Rodney Skylark had left my mind and was replaced with a larger fear. I was scared to death of being one of the ones who didn't make the team.

I ran as hard as I could. Everybody was pushing and shoving all the way as we crammed through the narrow stairway. No one wanted to be the last to take the field. I was about to push past a small guy with glasses who was just trying to go with the flow when I stepped on someone's foot. I felt my right ankle buckle as I was being pushed from the rear. A moment later, I found myself at the bottom of the stairs as the last of the freshman football team completed its journey over my bruised and battered carcass.

I didn't think I was hurt as I tried to leap to my feet, but the moment I put my weight down on that ankle, I knew that my chances of making the team had just decreased dramatically.

I hobbled into the locker room and started dressing down as quickly as I could. Some of the boys were already heading out to the practice field. I was feeling panicky. A large lump was swelling up in my throat. I had to fight back the tears. The pain from my sore ankle was no big deal, but the frustration and fear of losing the only thing, the only light in my bleak tunnel, the only thought of virtually every waking hour—when I wasn't thinking about girls—was slipping away. I tied the last shoelace and jumped to my feet and began to hobble as quickly as I could through the door leading to the practice field.

Coach Bumwack had the boys lined up ten across and six deep and spread out at arms' length for loosening-up exercises when I came hobbling up.

"Glad to see you could make it," the coach barked as I slunk around to the back to take my place.

After a half hour of stretching and warm-up exercises, we were divided into groups of ten and began to run some passing drills. The coach and his three assistants watched us intently, jotting down notes on their clipboards and blowing their whistles whenever the mood struck them. I wasn't doing too well. I got through the exercises without any problem, but this running stuff was not working. My ankle was sore and getting quite swollen.

Tweet!! Coach Duemage, the pudgy assistant coach and biology teacher assigned to our group, blew his whistle. "What is wrong with you?" he asked as I limped through a pass pattern and dropped the ball that was thrown a little too far for me to reach in my present condition. "You got a broken leg, or you just doggin' it?"

Tweeeeet!!! "Next," said the little pudgy coach without any compassion. It was his chance to feel like a man, at least in his mind, and he was enjoying himself.

That was pretty much how the first and last day of practice went. Coach Bumwack and his assistants got together and compared notes as we ran laps around the field. I, of course, was well behind the pack—trying not to limp. After a few laps, we were called over to where the coaches were and lined up. Ten names were called off. We were asked to stay, and the others were dismissed and told to be on the field ready to go at three fifteen the next day. Those of us who remained stood with our heads bowed. We knew what was coming.

Coach Bumwack stood before us, looking studiously at his clipboard. I think he was trying to find just the right words.

"I'm sorry, boys, but I have to get the squad down to fifty. I wish I could take you all, but I can't. Thanks for coming out." He stood there for a moment without expression, looking us over, and then turned and walked away.

I knew it was coming, but I was still not prepared for it. I was stunned. I just stood there.

The other boys began to make their way back to the locker room, where sounds of gleeful shouting and merriment could be heard. Each time the door leading from the boys' locker room opened, the field was bathed in the sounds of adolescent bliss. They had all survived the first cut. Using the math that I somehow managed to learn through my first nine years of school, I deduced that there would be three more cut to make an even 50. But for now, the remaining fifty-three boys were victorious, and I was a loser.

What else is new? I've always been a loser. Why should it be different now? With my head bowed, my eyes filled with water. There was a giant hole in my chest where once my heart resided.

Somehow, I managed to find my locker and began to dress down for a shower. Fred was there tying his shoes as I walked up. He didn't say anything. I averted my eyes from his.

Finally, Fred found his voice. "What happened? I saw you limping around out there" He had finished tying his shoes and was just sitting there on the bench, waiting.

I didn't look up. "I got cut," I almost whispered with my throat swollen tight and the tears about to burst loose.

Fred sat there for a moment, thinking. "But what happened?"

I didn't reply. I couldn't. I knew if I tried, the tears would come. I just sat there on the bench with my head bowed, making like I was trying to untie my shoe.

Fred must have sensed that I needed some space. "I'll talk to you later. I got to get home for dinner."

Fred left, and I took a long shower. That was a mistake. As

I was toweling off, the varsity football team entered the locker room.

They came storming in with their pads and helmets, looking like warriors returning from battle. They were cocky, loud, and they were big and they were bad. The Washington varsity football team had gone to state the last four years straight, and now with Rodney Skylark as their starting quarterback, they were expected not only to go to state the next three years, but to win the whole darn thing.

To say that I felt intimidated would be a bit of an understatement. I was petrified. Here I was, a freshman boy among men. I was a loser who couldn't even make the first cut of the freshman football team and there I stood, totally naked before them. I hoped they wouldn't take notice of me, but of course they did.

"Hey, what have we here?" asked the first of the warriors in passing.

"Looks like the Pillsbury Dough Boy," suggested another of the monoliths.

"Well, ain't he cute."

"Must be a reject from the freshman team," exclaimed yet another, hitting it right on the head.

I grabbed my underwear and was trying to get a leg in as quickly as I could. I wanted to get out of there fast. I had forgotten about my injury, and as I lifted my left foot, pain shot through my bad ankle that was supporting my entire weight. I toppled over, bumping into a very large and dirty football player who had taken up residence in the locker next to mine.

"Hey," he grumbled, giving me a shove with his elbow.

Backwards and over the bench I went, hitting my head on the hard locker-room floor. I lay there naked and dazed for a moment or two as the entire varsity football team roared with laughter.

Someone threw my clothes into a corner. I got dressed the

best I could with my ankle making it very difficult to get my left leg into my pants without sitting down.

I hobbled out of there without tying my shoes as various members of the team continued to skewer me with creative verbal harpoons. My life was over.

CHAPTER TWELVE

The walk home from school was long. My swollen ankle didn't make the trip any easier, but I could live with it. The pain in my heart, however, was another matter.

I was thankful for the rain that poured from the sky, camouflaging my tears. I could no longer hold them back. They came in torrents. I didn't want to live. I had nothing left to live for. All those years of disappointment were taking their toll. Why did I have to be a fat kid whose dad ran out on him? *Not only am I not worthy to be a son, but I'm not good enough to play football like almost every other boy with the exception of a few wimpy rejects, which apparently includes me.*

I stopped at the corner of Ash and Stark Street four blocks down from my house and leaned against the telephone pole for support. I let the convulsive sobs run their course in the heavy rain.

A car pulled over to the curb and stopped. It was Mr. Johnson's '58 Chevy Impala. Mr. Johnson was the janitor at Washington High. He also filled in at Buckman if someone was sick or if they needed extra help. He was a likable old guy who always had time for us kids with a friendly word or two. He rolled down the window on the passenger side of his car.

I pulled myself away from the telephone pole and quickly wiped my eyes as I tried desperately to stop the flow of tears.

"Get in. I'll take you home." Mr. Johnson sounded a bit gruff, like he always did, but in a likable sort of way. He was over six feet tall and broad shouldered. He claimed to have played some professional football before he hurt his leg in an accident. "Don't you know it's raining cats and dogs? Don't you have any sense at all?" Mr. Johnson knew I had been crying, but he wasn't about to let on that he knew.

"That's okay," I heard myself say. "I like walking in the rain."

Mr. Johnson looked at me sternly with his normally kindly dark eyes and repeated, "Get in," and added, "Where do you live?"

So I did as instructed and I told him where I lived. I didn't want Mr. Johnson to know that I that I didn't make the football team, but I had the feeling that he'd already figured it out. I was right.

"So, you got cut," Mr. Johnson declared, not mincing words as I settled into my seat on the passenger side of his Chevy.

He pulled out into the street and headed toward my house just a few blocks to the north. I didn't say a word, what with my heart pushing up into my throat. I didn't know what to say even if I could speak. What was there to say? I got cut on the first day of practice. I was a big loser. End of discussion.

Mr. Johnson looked at me intently as he pulled over to the curb next to our run-down fourplex.

"So, what are you going to do about it?" he asked.

What was I going to do about it? I couldn't believe such a question. What was his problem? I didn't make the team. What was there to do about it other than maybe crawl under a rock and die? I could feel anger begin to creep in and push aside my feelings of self-loathing, self-pity, and shame.

"What *can* I do?" I shouted, tears of anger now welling up in my eyes—replacing the tears of self-pity. I leaped out of the car, slammed the door, and hobbled up the stairs as quickly as I could. I didn't look back as I limped through the old scarred and battered Victorian door that led into my home and sanctuary. There it was safe. There were no football coaches who could cut me or thugs who could thump me. Besides, my mom kept the refrigerator stocked, and sometimes that's all a guy needs to forget his troubles. In fact, the fridge was often the first place I went when things weren't going quite right, or even if they were. I made my salutations to Mom and family by asking what was for dinner while I took a long, hard look in the fridge. There was a chocolate cream pie in there. Things were looking better all ready.

Once the euphoria of a good home-cooked meal topped off by one of my favorite desserts had worn off, I was left thinking of my wasted life. I was fourteen years old and I hadn't amounted to anything. Too fat and slow to play football. Sure, the sprained ankle didn't help, but it was in the stars. I was destined to be a loser. Maybe there was some of that chocolate cream pie left.

Getting out of bed the next day was not an easy task. I had no energy. If it wasn't for the smell of bacon frying in Mom's big black cast-iron skillet, I might never have made it. I had no reason to get out of bed aside from the occasional meal and/or snack. School, without football, certainly held no drawing power any longer. No football meant I would probably never have a chance with Bunny.

"Bunny!" I said aloud from the prone position in my bed from which I had no plans of moving from unless, of course, my mom would not cooperate by bringing me my meals. "Bunny," I said again, this time rather dejectedly. Bunny would have nothing to do with a fat slob who couldn't even make the freshman football team. I lay there thinking about

Bunny and football when the smell of toast began to blend in with the bacon. Time to get up.

I managed to get dressed after breakfast and shuffled off to school. The closer I got, the more dejected I became. Everyone would know that I didn't make the team. That I was still a loser even after all the work I had done.

I turned up the limping action as I went through the Stark Street entrance to Washington High. I wanted everyone to know that there was a very good reason for me not making the team. It didn't appear that anyone had taken notice of my obvious condition except for Mr. Johnson, who was coming out of the boiler room as I limped by.

"Hey, Gimp," Mr. Johnson greeted me in a challenging manner as he stepped in front of me, blocking my way. "You going to ask the coach for another shot?"

I looked up into his expectant face. Mr. Johnson was a kindly old guy who would joke and horse around with us kids and usually had an encouraging word or two in passing, but he was acting a bit out of character at the moment. I guess he wasn't ready to let me quit on life, even though I already had.

"The coach don't want me," I stated flatly.

Mr. Johnson's eyes became hot and burning as they looked deep into my own. "That's because you have not given him a reason to want you," he said emphatically. He side-stepped to halt my attempt to go around. "You need to talk to him. Tell him that you hurt your ankle and weren't able to give a good showing, and that you'd like another chance to make the team. Tell him you'll do anything he says to get yourself ready. Then no matter what he might say, you start working your butt off. If you whip yourself into a football animal, there's no way he'll keep you off the team."

I just stood there, waiting for the speech to conclude so I could go about my business.

"Let me tell you a story," Mr. Johnson continued, his tone softening some.

Great. Now he wants to tell me a story.

"I wanted to play football as far back as I can remember, but it was just me and my mother and my three younger sisters. My dad died in a logging accident. A tree fell on him when I was twelve. I had to sell papers to help out, and when I got to high school, I took a job in the evenings pumping gas. There was no time for football—we had to eat. The summer after I graduated from high school, my mama finally got her schooling done and got a job as a nurse so I didn't have to support the family any longer. I still wanted to play football, so I went and talked to the coach at Portland State and asked him what I needed to do to make his football team.

"You know what he told me?" Mr. Johnson asked as his shaggy graying eyebrows rose up slightly. "He told me that if I was willing to work as hard as I could, I might have a chance. It was up to you, he said."

Mr. Johnson looked me straight in the eye. "It's up to you." With that, the large man moved away.

I stood there in the hall for a moment as those words began to sink in. *It's up to me.*

I went to all my classes that day in a bit of a cloud. Mr. Johnson's story kept running through my mind, along with the words *It's up to me.*

After school, I hopped onto a bus going downtown. It cost me a quarter each way, but I needed to do some research at the main library.

The year before, I'd had to do a report on Prohibition for social studies, and my teacher directed me to the downtown library where I could access info off old newspapers recorded on microfilm . . . or was it microfiche? I never did figure out the difference. Maybe there was something on Mr. Johnson in the sports page of an old *Oregonian* newspaper.

I got off the smelly old diesel bus and limped two blocks south to the main library. It was a very large building occupying an entire block with four floors up and one down. I climbed the stairs, taking one at a time, at the front entrance and then went to the basement where the microfilm was kept. After searching the catalog, I found the year I was looking for. I got the number and went to the desk. The librarian lady soon had me hooked up at the viewer machine thing-a-ma-bob and I was on my way searching *Oregonian* newspapers starting in September of 1938. Mr. Johnson was about fifty in my estimation, so he must have played college ball about thirty years prior. I looked through all the sports pages in 1938 and found nothing. However, in the Sunday, October 3rd, 1937 *Oregonian*, I found an article about the Portland State Vikings with a picture of Julius Johnson scoring the winning touchdown after intercepting a pass against Oregon State.

Bingo! According to this article, Julius Johnson—or JJ, as the reporter called him—was a stud senior linebacker for the Vikings. He had walked on at Portland State having no prior playing experience. I found several other articles on the Vikings with Julius Johnson mentioned and one at the end of the season with him featured, focusing mainly on his future in the pros.

The library was getting ready to close when I found an article about Julius Johnson playing for the Cleveland Browns in 1941. According to the article—he was doing quite well as a starting linebacker before being drafted into the Army.

It was true. Mr. Johnson had played college and pro football.

On the bus ride home, I thought about how Mr. Johnson had made the team at Portland State without even playing high school football. He had made up his mind that he was going to play, and by the time he was a junior, he was a starter and had earned a full scholarship for his remaining two years. Remarkable.

"It's up to you," I said aloud, getting strange looks from the other passengers.

"It's up to me," I said very softly so as to not attract any more attention. It's up to me.

The rest of the evening, I stood in front of the mirror in the bathroom, practicing my speech for Coach Bumwack. I was going to tell him about my ankle and ask for another chance.

"Look here, Coach," I said with confidence to my reflection. "If you want to win football games, you might want to give me another shot." *Mmm, I like that,* I thought.

The next morning went by very slowly. Each minute was accounted for. I was going to approach Coach Bumwack right after health class. I don't know why I felt so anxious and nervous, but I did. My gut was in a knot all morning. I couldn't even eat my breakfast, and my mom had fixed French toast with those little brown n' serve sausage links she occasionally got when they were on sale.

The walk to school seemed to take forever, as did my first three classes. However, time did pass as the knots in my gut continued to tighten and twist. I had the speech memorized. I had been running it over my mind all that morning. "Coach Bumwack," I would say, "I would like another chance to make the football team. You see, I sprained my ankle just prior to tryouts and didn't give a very good showing of myself. I can do much better once my ankle has healed, and I'm willing to work hard and do whatever it takes to make the team." That should do it.

Health class was winding down. My fellow students were passing the photos of advanced athlete's foot and foot funguses to the front when the bell rang and everyone made a mad dash for the door. I stayed in my chair with a stack of 8 X 10 glossy photos of rotting feet, waiting for my chance to talk to the coach.

"And remember, clean feet are happy feet," Coach Bumwack said, ushering the last of the students out of the classroom. He turned to look at me sitting at my desk.

"What are you doing with those pictures? You weren't really going to take them home, were you?" Coach Bumwack asked with a disgusted look.

I had forgotten about the photos, and in my nervousness, I had tucked them in with my books.

"That's kind of sick, don't you think?" asked the coach as he reached for the photos.

I turned red as a beet. I did not want his foot pictures. I handed the glossy photos of nasty-looking feet back to the coach.

"Coach Bumwack, I . . . uh . . . uh . . ." I stammered as I tried to remember how my speech went.

"Whoa there," interrupted the self-absorbed head of the freshman football team with a glare. "That's Mr. Bumwack unless you're a member of the football team."

"Right, sorry, uh, Mr. Bumwack." I searched my brain for the words to say, but they were gone. Nothing left but mental goulash.

"Is there something I can do for you?" He asked sternly. "It's time for my lunch, and I got to get to it."

"I . . . uh . . ." I repeated—having trouble putting together more than one syllable.

"What?" barked the impatient coach.

"I wanna play football," I almost whimpered. This was not going as I had hoped.

The coach looked down at me where I sat in the front row of desks. He had a very distasteful look on his puffy, heavy-lined face.

"You had your chance, son," the coach said quietly without feeling. "Better find something you're more suited for." With that, Mr. Bumwack straightened himself, turned, and headed toward the cafeteria, where thick-crust pizza and French fries covered in special sauce were waiting for him.

I sat there in the empty health class staring at the

statement on the blackboard. The words *Clean Feet Are Happy Feet* kept rotating through my brain, pushing out all else. I felt like a zombie. I was totally numb. I could walk over hot coals barefoot and not have winced. Once again, I was a miserable wretch.

Time for lunch.

Even in the darkest of emotional abysses, I had time for a meal. In fact, it was food and sometimes only food that kept me connected to the world of the living. With a plate of spaghetti and some garlic bread in front of me I felt alive and nurtured. Without it, I felt alone and lost.

I got through the remainder of the day. How, I don't know. I don't remember anything up until the moment I was heading toward the northeast corner door to go home when Mr. Johnson stopped me.

"Well?" he asked expectantly.

I looked up into his hopeful and kindly dark eyes.

"Coach Bumwack said I had my chance and that's that," I reported blankly. I pushed on past Mr. Johnson, who stood there not knowing what to say. Even Mr. Johnson, with all his wisdom and life experience, was at a loss for words or a course of action, and so was I. Other than my plan of a slow Twinkie-induced death, I was out of options.

I was headed toward the little mom-and-pop convenience store that was called, coincidentally, Mom & Pops, to load up on said Twinkies when Mr. Johnson pulled alongside me in his classic Chevy.

Here we go again. Sorry, Mr. Johnson, I thought to myself. No tears today. I don't have any left.

Mr. Johnson reached for the door handle on the passenger side and flung the door open with his large strong right hand. He looked at me sternly. "Get in."

I was about to tell Mr. Johnson no thanks and continue on toward the store, but there was something in his eyes. I got in.

I sat there on the passenger side of his '58 Chevy Impala, waiting.

Mr. Johnson looked at me intently for a moment or two. "Do you want to play football?"

"Coach Bumwack . . ." I began.

"Do you want to play football?" Mr. Johnson asked again, interrupting my story of rejection.

I looked down at my feet. *Clean feet are happy feet* started going through my brain.

"Do you want to play football?" Mr. Johnson asked softly for the third time.

I kept looking at my feet, but I did manage a shaky "Yes."

"Can you spare a few minutes?"

"I guess so," I mumbled.

Mr. Johnson gave the gas pedal a push, and the three deuces sitting on top of the motor started sucking air and blowing the fuel and air mixture through the stock manifold to the hungry cylinders. The tires broke free for a moment or two as Mr. Johnson guided the beast into traffic. About a minute later, we pulled into the back parking lot of Washington High School where the teachers and staff parked their rigs.

"We aren't going to talk with Coach Bumwack, are we?" The knot in my gut was coming back.

"No. There is, however, someone else that might be able to help." Mr. Johnson's eyes began to twinkle again as he smiled slightly. "Come on."

I followed Mr. Johnson through the back door that led past the boiler room to the back side of the gym, where the athletic department was situated. The athletic department was probably once a classroom. It had since been divided by partitions, filing cabinets, and wall lockers to form individual office space for each of the coaches. Each little cubicle had a double wall locker, filing cabinet, and desk. The head football coach, Buddy Skylark, had what appeared to be two cubicles together with some additional chairs for guests.

We made our way through the maze of cubicles to the back, where we found the junior varsity coaches' cubicle. There were two double wall lockers with their back sides out, forming a doorway with a piece of burgundy cloth with a big gold W hanging between them as a door. To one side at eye level, there was a small name plaque that said *Coach Wurthlin, Junior Varsity Football.*

Mr. Johnson knocked on a wall locker.

"Yo," came the response from within. "Enter."

Mr. Johnson pulled back the curtain and ushered me in, following right behind. The two men exchanged hearty handshakes.

"This here is the young man I was telling you about," Mr. Johnson said by way of introduction.

Coach Wurthlin gave me a quick once-over and then looked me right in the eye.

"Do you want to play football?" he asked, getting right to the point without show of emotion on his youthful face. I didn't know much about him except that he had only been teaching for a couple of years and had served in Vietnam. He taught social studies, and I gathered he was well liked.

"Yes, I do," I told him.

Coach Wurthlin studied my face for a moment. He wasn't a big man—average height and weight, I figured. But there was a presence about him that seemed to take up additional space. "Are you willing to do what it takes?" he asked, his brow beginning to furrow.

"Yes, I am," I replied, and this time with feeling. I wanted to play football more than anything I could think of. My first two days of high school had been an emotional nightmare.

"Mr. Johnson tells me that you didn't get a fair tryout. I can't let you try out for the junior varsity unless you're either on the freshman team or are at least a sophomore." Coach

Wurthlin paused for a moment, gathering his thoughts. He ran a hand over his dark-brown curly mop of hair. He was a handsome man with a stern but pleasant way about him. He was a leader. Some men take it upon themselves to be leaders. They take charge, bark, and manage to get some to follow. Then there are men people are just inclined to follow. Not because of anything they might say or do. They're just natural-born leaders. Coach Wurthlin was a leader.

"Here's what I can do. I can let you work out in the weight room with the JV team, and I'll get you a partner to team up with." Mr. Wurthlin paused for a moment to look for a reaction. He must have seen what he wanted in my face because he continued. "I will expect you to lift every day with your partner and follow the workout program, which includes running and doing drills, and report to me here in my office every Tuesday during your lunch period. If you show what I consider to be a strong work ethic, motivation, and commitment, you'll have a fair shot to make the JV squad next year. It's up to you."

There were those words again. I looked into the strong and clear brown eyes of Coach Wurthlin as I fought to keep the tears from welling up in my eyes.

"Okay," I barely managed with my throat tightening.

Coach Wurthlin smiled a big, warm smile and gave me a strong pat on the back.

"Good," he said with gusto. "Come on down to the practice field after school tomorrow and I'll introduce you to your partner."

I turned and left the cubicle without saying a word. I couldn't speak. I knew if I tried, I would start blubbering like a little girl again. I didn't want to go home with Mr. Johnson in such a vulnerable condition, so I went down a short hallway leading into the depths of the school. I turned the corner and headed toward the exit on the other side of the building. Mr.

Johnson would say goodbye and give me just enough time to get away, I was hoping.

Whether I gave Mr. Johnson the slip or he just let me go, I don't know. I did manage, however, to walk home without him trying to give me a ride. All the pent-up pain and self-pity had come to the surface again, and I had to get it under control before I could face anyone. I didn't know why I felt the way I did. After all, I was getting a second chance.

CHAPTER THIRTEEN

The phone rang as I was wolfing down the last hunk of meatloaf, my eyes roaming the table for more.

"John, it's for you," called my little sister from the phone in the dining room.

I left the kitchen feeling like there was a void in my person that meat loaf hadn't filled. "Hello," I said into the telephone.

"Hey, John," greeted a familiar voice.

"Hey, Greg." I was actually glad he called. He had tried to get a hold of me after the first day of school, but I told Curt to tell him I couldn't come to the phone.

"How's school?" Greg wanted to know. "What position do they have you playing?"

Greg paused for a moment to let me reply, but I didn't answer right away. I was trying to think of how to tell him I didn't make the team. I thought for a moment of telling him that.

I was on the JV team. After all, I would be doing drills with one of the guys and I was lifting weights with the team, so I was practically a member. I would only be telling half a lie. But even half a lie was more than I could ever hope of sliding past Greg. He would know right off by the sound of my voice that I was lying. Besides, lying is for cowards. If I was ever going to be man enough to make the JV team, I had better be man enough to face reality.

"I didn't make the team," I replied solemnly.

"Huh? What?" Greg asked intelligently.

"That's right. I got cut the first day."

"How? Why? What?"

"I sprained my ankle just before practice, and that was that," I explained, trying to make light of it. "But," I said before Greg could jump in with more of his one-syllable inquiries, "I'll be working out with the JV team in the weight room and practicing and running drills with one of the guys on the team. Coach Wurthlin, the JV coach, says if I work hard, I can play on the JV team next year."

Greg and I shot the bull for some time. Of course he had to know all the sordid details of my failure. By the time we got through talking about my involvement with the junior varsity, it had taken on quite a luster. Not many kids skip the freshman team and go straight to the JV team. It was all a matter of perspective, and by the time Greg and I were through discussing it, I was NFL bound.

Greg, on the other hand, was doomed to a year of slugging it out on the Scappoose High School freshman team. The coach needed wide receivers, and Greg had the speed and decent hands. He also informed me that he would play at one of the defensive back spots. So far it was looking like he would start on offense and play a backup role on defense, and the coach was trying him out at running back punts and kickoffs. There was a chance, though, that Greg could play some on the JV team too because of a lack of numbers. Small schools do have their advantages.

I went to sleep that night with a light heart. The burden of being a loser had once again been lifted.

Fred was sitting at Mrs. Roberts' desk as I walked into my first-period math class the next morning.

"And now, class," Fred said in a high nasal voice, trying to sound like Mrs. Roberts. "Open your books to page 131, subtract thirty-one, add four, divide by two to the third power, multiply by negative two, add eighty-three, and then do all the problems on that page that have double digits for an answer."

"Hello, Fred," greeted Mrs. Roberts, who had slipped in behind him about halfway through his dialogue. He should have known something was up when the laughter died suddenly in the middle of his act, but Fred, ever the showman, had pushed on.

After Fred was unceremoniously directed to his seat next to mine, Mrs. Roberts soon had us all focused on math, which does not mix well with mirth. There's nothing like a shot of algebra to take the fun out of life.

During the lulls in the math lecture, I was able to inform Fred of my good fortune. He was thrilled for me. Fred was a good friend.

The day dragged on, but eventually the last bell rang as I was sitting in the library for study hall, intently studying the contours of one Bunny Carlson through a slit between stacks of books piled in front of me. Bunny gathered her things and headed toward the door. Rodney Skylark met her there, and together they went their way.

What did she see in that chump? Of all the guys in the world, why would someone of Bunny's obvious caliber want anything to do with a mean, arrogant jerk like Rodney Skylark, especially with a man like me around?

I came out from behind my protective book barrier and remembered that it was time for football.

After putting on my workout attire, I quickly made my way to the junior varsity portion of the field. The freshman team, other than for tryouts, usually practices on the Buckman field three blocks away. The varsity and the JV teams share the field adjacent to Washington High School. It wasn't a large area but the two teams managed.

I was the first on the field, but it wasn't long before Coach Wurthlin and Mr. Johnson showed up, with a few of the players beginning to trickle out of the locker room wearing their practice gear including full pads. Apparently, Mr. Johnson was an assistant coach.

"Hello, John," Coach Wurthlin greeted me with a pleased look. "Tell me, what position do you see yourself playing?"

He looked at me intently as I struggled to get the words out. I knew exactly what position I wanted to play on both offense and defense. The problem was, I was built like a lineman, and that's what I always played. It never seemed to matter that I could run good routes, albeit a tad bit slowly, and I could catch anything I could get a hand on. I was always relegated to the line whenever a group of us kids would get together for some playground football. I swallowed hard.

"I want to be a wide receiver and a linebacker." There. I said it. My knees were shaking and my palms were sweating. I would play any position just to be on the team, but I had to try.

"Wide receiver, hey?" Coach Wurthlin replied thoughtfully as he looked me over. "Well, John, to be perfectly honest with you, you're not built like a wide receiver—not that you can't turn yourself into one, or at least a tight end—but we always have a need for good lineman."

Coach Wurthlin hadn't laughed or even smiled at the thought of me as a wide receiver. In fact, he had made reference to the possibility of turning myself into one, probably through much hard work and perhaps involving a growth spurt. I didn't have much control over my height, but I could handle the hard work part.

"However," the coach continued after pausing for a moment, "if you really want to be a receiver, there will always be an opportunity to switch from one position to another if you work really hard and are able to show me that you can do it. I always play the best player at each position, and I don't care if a lineman might be a little bit on the small side or if a receiver is big as long as they can get the job done. Of course, I'm the one to make that decision, and I have to do what's best for the team."

That was all I wanted—a chance.

"If you're serious about becoming a receiver, come see me after practice and we'll talk. For now, go fall in with the lineman," Coach Wurthlin said with an enthusiastic smile on his youthful, but rugged face.

"You mean I get to practice with the team?" I asked incredulously.

"You won't be practicing *with* the team," Coach Wurthlin explained, trying not to burst my bubble. "You will be assisting Coach Saunders. I expect you to pay very close attention to everything that's going on. Coach Saunders will give you a drill program as well as a workout program, and you'll be working directly with him so you won't need to check in with me every Tuesday like we had discussed. However, my door is always open."

"Okay, Coach!" I was pumped. I began running over to where the small group of large lineman were stretching when I stopped in my tracks and jogged back to where the coach was standing, now looking intently at a clipboard.

"Coach Wurthlin?" I asked sheepishly as he looked up from his board and directly into my eyes. I had the feeling he could see into my very soul.

"Coach, can I still come by after practice and talk to you about becoming a wide receiver?" I asked needing reassurance.

"Sure. I'm in my office by five, every night until six."

That was all I needed to hear.

Coach Saunders was a volunteer. His son, David Saunders, had played four years of football at Washington

High before being offered a scholarship to Montana State. Coach had helped out when his son was here and just stuck around. He had been an offensive lineman himself playing four years at Oregon State. He was a big man. He had to be six foot five or so and over three hundred pounds. He kept a whistle around his huge neck—if you could call it a neck. He didn't really have one. His head just seemed to sit on top of his very large shoulders. He was a nice guy, and put me to work keeping track of the time for each drill. I also got to hold the clipboard and inform him of what was next on the practice agenda after each drill was completed.

"Okay, that's good. Now give me three laps and head for the showers," Coach Saunders barked, dismissing the team for the day. "Laughton," he added before the tired linemen shuffled off on their run around the school's practice field, "You and Smith come see me before you go inside. You two will be working together. And Smith, you watch these guys and make sure they do all three laps, and I want to know who comes in last." There was just a hint of something twisted in his smile when he said that last part.

The linemen trudged around the track, giving me a dirty look each time they passed. They stayed in a tight group for the entire three laps until the last final hundred yards, when it became an all-out footrace. A kid named Henry Morton, #82, came in first, and the rest of them were close behind except for a single lumbering giant who came in several yards behind the pack. Gary Laughton, #78.

Gary, from what I had deduced from watching all of them intently during their drills, was the least gifted. Or maybe I should say, he just wasn't quite up to speed yet. Anyhow, it was obvious that he needed the most work. That's probably why he was being assigned to work with me. Of course, this was all speculation, but it looked pretty obvious and I had to admit, it made sense.

I was waiting at the end of the field with clipboard in hand as Gary Laughton wheezed by and came to a stop. He bent over and rested his hands on his knees, trying to get his breath. The other linemen were already making their way to the locker room, not needing to take time to recuperate as Laughton did.

I looked over the large JV lineman as he began to get his breath back. By this time, he had succumbed to the pull of gravity and was lying on his back. He was big, by far the biggest kid on the team. He was not in real good shape, though. He was about six foot three or four and close to three hundred pounds.

After another moment or two, Gary started to take notice of his surroundings. He looked up and saw me standing by attentively. He smiled sheepishly as he made the attempt to regain his feet. No small task, but he managed. As he drew himself to his full height, it was clear that Gary had what it takes to fill up a spot on the offensive line. He was huge, but it was also obvious that most of his bulk was soft. He needed work, but so did I. I was excited by the prospect. I couldn't wait to get started.

"Well, I guess it's you and me," I exclaimed trying to bridle my enthusiasm.

"Yeah, right," Gary responded.

It was obvious that Gary did not exactly share my passion.

I took a long, hard look at the large, soft offensive lineman.

"Gary, don't you want to play football?"

The question took Gary by surprise. Actually, I was a bit surprised at the question myself. Just the same, I looked deep into his eyes and waited for a response.

Gary's countenance hardened. You could tell that he didn't like the fact that a young punk a full year younger, a hundred pounds lighter, and a good six inches shorter who couldn't even make the freshman team was questioning his desire and manhood.

For a moment there, I thought he might squash me like a

bug. I had definitely stirred something in the large breast of the mammoth sophomore lineman. Just as quickly, though, Gary's face softened and just a hint of smile began to show itself. It was his eyes mostly. Where one instant they were dark as night, the next they were shining brightly.

"Yeah, I want to play football," Gary said with conviction. "How about you?"

It was Gary who was now looking for a response.

"More than anything," I answered.

That first afternoon, Gary and I spent getting to know each other and making plans for our workouts together.

Gary was a lot like me except a year older. He lived with his grandmother and twelve-year-old sister. His mom died when he was five, and his dad just went away. He, like me, had always been on the chubby side. The only real difference was that Gary was always a lot bigger than the bullies and didn't get picked on all that much. Other than that, we basically had the same goals. We both wanted to be somebody. Gary figured that through football, he could mold himself into something other than a large fat kid. We both had a long way to go.

Coach Saunders had a simple plan for the two of us. During practice, I was to assist the coach and learn. Upon conclusion of practice, we were both to run a few drills designed to make us better, stronger, and more agile linemen. After that, it was the showers for Gary and laps for me. Also, every morning at six thirty, I was to be dressed down and on the weights with Gary until seven forty-five, giving me fifteen minutes to shower and change before school starts at eight.

I went home that evening without talking to Coach Wurthlin about being a wide receiver. I had plenty of time to for that later. I knew what I had to do. I had to lose weight and get fast.

The next morning, I was in the weight room bright and early. In fact, I was a good fifteen minutes early. I had to bang on the door. Fortunately, Mr. Johnson was in the area to let me in.

I warmed up and stretched while I waited for Gary. Other members of the JV team began to stumble in. The weight room was decent in size with two Olympic benches, two slant board stations, two squat stations, two curl stations, a full rack of dumbbells from two to one hundred pounds, two full universal gyms, four adjustable sit-up stations, an assortment of oddball fly and lat pull stations, and mirrors along the walls. It had pretty much all that a guy needed to mold himself into a bone-crushing machine.

The coaches of the three football teams divided the workout times. The freshman worked out after practice, the JV team was in the morning, and the varsity got a full period just before lunch. Coach Skylark would make the team work out through much of their lunch period as well.

Once Gary was there, he quickly outlined our workout routine. Chest and arms one day, lats and shoulders the next, and legs on the third day. Then we'd repeat the sequence with Saturday as leg day. Since the school was closed on Saturday, we were expected to do our leg work-out on our own.

The coach had Gary on a fairly light workout regimen with lots of reps. I think he wanted to firm him up some first. I found Gary's workout to be almost too easy. Greg and I were lifting heavier. I kept up with Gary without any problem, and that seemed to irritate him.

I set the forty pound Olympic bar with two twenty-five-pounders back on the supports after benching ten reps.

Gary scowled at me as I got to my feet.

"Slip a twenty-five on each side," he demanded.

It was obvious that Gary intended to put me in my place.

I did as I was told. I was actually hoping that Gary would show me up. There was now a total of one hundred and forty-five pounds sitting on the supports as Gary slid into position.

"You want a spot?" I asked.

Gary just glared at me as he pushed the bar up and then lowered it to his chest. The bar went up three inches as the soft behemoth grunted, and then settled back down on his chest. He couldn't lift it.

Without saying a word, I reached down and helped Gary push the bar up and slide it back into place on the supports.

Gary just laid there for a moment, then sat up and looked me right in the eye. He was embarrassed and dejected, and I thought he might cry.

"Gary," I said firmly, "all this means is that we have got to work even harder."

The sadness in Gary's eyes vanished. A look of determination took its place.

"You're right," Gary said softly through tight lips and a set jaw.

The big, soft lineman stood up and took off one of the twenty-five-pounders as I did the same. Gary then ripped off six reps on his own and three more with me helping. We didn't speak during the rest of the workout except to direct one another to the next station and how much weight to put on.

Practice was uneventful that day, except I noticed that Gary was still quite grim. He worked hard. He was again the last one around the track at the end of practice.

Coach Saunders hadn't asked me who had come in last the day before, and I hadn't volunteered the information. I had no intention of doing so today either.

I waited for Gary to catch his breath as he was again lying on his back.

The coach had informed me that Gary and I were to run the tires and work on coming hard out of a three-point stance. That's just what we did. The tires were killing Gary, but he insisted on doing several more sets than we were instructed to do. Then we worked on driving out of the three-point stance and running hard down the field for several yards. Afterwards, we hit the blocking sleds. Again, Gary insisted on doing more than required. After about forty-five minutes, the two of us were bent over, hands on our knees, gasping for air. My legs felt like rubber. Gary hit the showers, and I lumbered around the track three times on wobbly legs.

Gary and I worked hard together. We pushed one another. Every day, we tried to do more than the day before. The games came and went and Gary didn't play in any of them, but he didn't get discouraged. We seemed to feed off one another's desire to make something of ourselves. We never really talked about it. We just gritted our teeth and worked hard and then harder. We were making progress. By the end of the season, Gary was no longer the last one around the track, and we were both getting stronger. Gary especially was making great strides in his strength. He quickly passed me by, which made me work all that much harder.

The season was over. All of the players, including myself, met with Coach Wurthlin to discuss goals and conditioning in preparation for next season. Gary and I were the last to speak with him, and he had the two of us come in together.

"The two of you have made great strides," the coach began. "I've seen how hard you've been working, and it's paying off. You keep up the hard work over the rest of the school year and this summer, and I can see you playing and perhaps even starting next year." He was looking intently at Gary.

"And Smith," he added, "I really appreciate your hard work and determination. You keep it up, and there will be a spot on this team for you as well."

That was all I needed to hear. I couldn't wait to get out of the coach's office so I could pump some more iron and run some more wind sprints.

The coach handed each of us several typed-up papers diagramming our workouts and drills, complete with a log to record our progress.

"I want to see both of you with your logs every first

Monday of each month right after school here in my office."
The coach was looking very intently at the two of us as he
spoke. "I think that the two of you have great potential." He
paused, letting that sink in. "However, one's potential is only
achieved by working as hard as you can. It's up to you."

"It's up to me," I said to myself.

CHAPTER FOURTEEN

I pulled myself off the ground, trying to get my wind back after advancing the ball six yards on a run off tackle. The whole defense was keying on me. They knew I was getting the ball. Everything we had tried had failed—that is, until the coach switched me from wide receiver to running back and started calling my number. Joey, our fourth-string quarterback, had been rendered totally ineffective. Not that he had the skills to get the ball to his receivers, which he did not. Joey was really a second-string senior linebacker and hadn't played quarterback since junior high. But somebody had to be the quarterback after losing the other three in the first half.

Northeast Portland's Jefferson High School was loaded with talent. They were big and they were fast. At least four of the guys on their vaunted defense were destined to play Division I ball after graduating. Jefferson liked to run the football, eating up the clock while their defense made sure they would get ample opportunities to work the ball into the end zone. The philosophy was working. The score was 20 to 7 with three minutes to go in the third quarter.

We needed two more yards to keep this drive alive. It was fourth down and two on Jefferson's thirty-two-yard line. There would be no punting. The coach called time and gathered us together. He looked over us sternly, his eyes resting on me.

"The only chance we have is to give Smith the ball and block our butts off. It's up to you, John," the coach said quietly.

That was all I needed to hear.

"Hut one. Hut two. Hut three," Joey barked, the ball hit him in the hands and he simply turned and fed it to me as I came forward to meet him.

"It's up to me." I lowered my head and hit the crease created by our undersized offensive line. There wasn't much room, and I could feel hands grabbing. I kept my legs churning, breaking through several sets of arms, the whole time chanting, "It's up to me."

I heard the crowd roar as I broke into the backfield. Looking up, I could see our Washington High cheerleaders jumping up and down in the back of the end zone. There was something peculiar about those cheerleaders . . .

"John!" A shrill voice rang out. "Are you with us?" Mrs. Roberts' face came into view as I lifted my head from my desk.

Disappointment oozed through my body as I realized it was all a dream. I should have known something was up when all the cheerleaders looked like Mrs. Owens—our esteemed head cook at Washington High School. The somewhat portly Mrs. Owens calls herself the student-body energizer. The word is she has it in for the teachers and uses as much white sugar as is humanly possible in all of her cooking. There is just no end to the amount of torment that a hyped-up student body can inflict on the faculty after one of her meals. Why it seems like, just yesterday when we were treated to a nice hot lunch consisting of a generous slice of honey-baked ham smothered in Mrs. Owens' blue ribbon (Mrs. Owens had actually won several blue ribbons for her cooking and displayed them prominently in the cafeteria) raisin and pineapple sauce, candied yams with a sweet brown sugar and butter sauce and little colored marshmallows, fruit salad—mostly whipped cream and maraschino cherries—a big chocolate brownie with another award-winning (fudge) sauce, and milk with your choice of syrups.

I let my head clear as I rubbed the sleep from my eyes sadly realizing that it wasn't up to me. That is, the team's success wasn't up to me. Not at this point, anyway, but it was totally up to me as far as my own goals and progress were concerned. Again I gritted my teeth and promised myself to work even harder.

At that moment, working harder was all about algebra, a necessary evil if I wanted to play football. I had to keep my grades up. Also, if I wanted to play ball at the next level, I'd better learn what they're teaching. A guy could slide through high school with a C average, but that wouldn't prepare him for college. So I reluctantly turned my attention back to Mrs. Roberts and math.

The weeks went by, and Gary and I, joined by Fred, worked out just as the coach had outlined. Every morning before school, we hit the weights. Every afternoon when school let out, we hit the practice field for blocking drills, tires, wind sprints, and running the bleachers. We worked on coming hard out of a three-point stance and using proper blocking techniques on one another. At the end of each practice, I ran passing routes with Fred covering me as Gary passed me the ball. Gary had a pretty good arm, and Fred was getting so he could stay with me on the short routes—sort of.

The three of us kept track of everything we did in our logs and reported to the coach every first Monday, as instructed. Coach Wurthlin interviewed us individually. He asked us how our workouts were progressing and wanted to see our report cards, making notations and placing the information in a file that he kept on each of his players. He also weighed us and checked our height. He asked us about our eating habits and made a few suggestions. "Eat lots of fresh fruit and vegetables, go easy on junk food and sweets, and take your vitamins," the coach suggested as he handed us a booklet called *The Proper Diet of the American Athlete.*

Fred and Gary hustled out of the coach's makeshift office with their new diet booklets. It was way past dinnertime, and I knew that no door would hit them in the behind. I also felt pretty confident that dinner would be long gone before their diet book would ever be opened.

As I strolled home, I skimmed through the booklet, taking mental notes. For the most part, I had been following the guidelines laid down in the book—with just one little exception. I was still eating too much. "Not too much fruit or vegetables, though," I told myself in a reassuring manner. Just too many starches, fatty junk foods, and sweets. The coach weighed me in at one hundred and ninety-four. Not only had I not lost weight after all these months of hard work, but I had gained. I was feeling discouraged.

As I climbed up the stairs to our flat, I noticed a car parked in front that I hadn't seen before. "Maybe Sandy finally hired on full time with the police department and got himself some wheels," I mused. Sandy was a man in his thirties who lived in the flat next door. He worked part time for the Portland Police Department as an auxiliary officer. Whenever there was a convention or special event, Sandy would be put to work directing traffic or hanging out somewhere complete with uniform, badge, nightstick, and gun. He would generally stop by our place to strut around in full regalia before heading off to do his duty.

I opened the door and heard familiar voices coming from within.

"Hey, John," Greg greeted me with enthusiasm.

"Hey," I replied, trying to mask the joy I felt at seeing his freckled face. I didn't want Greg to get the wrong idea, like I was glad to see him or something.

Greg was with his mom on some errand and had stopped by.

We left our moms with coffee and went downstairs to my basement hideaway. The basement was very large, with laundry hookups and storage rooms for all four tenants. I had laid claim to the largest storage room and converted it over to my weight room.

I turned the tumblers to the combination lock and opened the door. I had soundproofed the walls and ceiling with old carpet that had been rolled up in a corner of the basement. When the door was closed, I could play my stereo as loud as I wanted without bothering anyone. All over the carpeted walls were rock-and-roll band flyers that I collected off telephone poles and the outer walls of some of the hip places in town. My stereo and my album collection were against one wall, and the speakers were hung in the corners. There was an old beat-up easy chair with a blanket over it against the opposite wall, a floor lamp on the right, and an end table to the left. In the middle of the room was a makeshift bench with various dumbbells, curl bar and barbells scattered around, and a pile of plates in the corner ranging from five to twenty-five pounds each.

My brother Scott had come home to stay for a couple of months before joining the Marine Corps. Once he was sixteen, he had more or less moved out on his own. He came home to get mom to give her consent to join the Marines when he turned seventeen, and then he was off to San Diego. The stereo and weights were his. I had just recently discovered them in another storage room when I was cleaning it out. Scott still had a year before he would be collecting them, so I wrote and asked if I might use them. There was also a large mirror up against one wall. I had found it in one of the flats when I was helping Mrs. Goldberg, the owner, get it ready to rent.

Greg hadn't been down to my little sanctuary since the

remodel and was quite impressed. In fact, Greg and I hadn't gotten together since just before school had started six months prior.

"Cool room," Greg enthused. "How many pounds you got?"

"Three hundred and twenty-five in plates," I answered matter-of-factly.

"Wow. Let's pump some iron." Greg was ready.

I put on some rockin' tunes, and we started throwing weights around. First thing I noticed was that Greg was stronger. So was I. I had made some pretty serious gains since summer.

"Hey, let me see you bench," Greg demanded in a challenging fashion.

"Okay," I replied casually, trying not to let Greg know that I was chomping at the bit to do just that.

I hefted the twenty pound bar and placed it in the makeshift holders at the head of the bench. I grabbed a twenty-five-pound plate and motioned to Greg to grab the other. Then as coolly and as nonchalantly as I could manage, I reached for another twenty-five-pounder.

"One more," I simply directed Greg.

Greg raised an eyebrow ever so slightly and then grabbed the other twenty-five-pounder as if it were no big deal.

This was not the response I was looking for. There was now one hundred pounds, plus the bar and collar locks making it one twenty-five even. Normally I'd start out with the bar plus two twenty-fives, do as many reps as I could, then add ten more pounds and so on until I'd get to one twenty-five. I'd manage one or two and once three reps and then I'd gradually take weights off until I was back to where I started and totally spent. I had never even thought of putting more weight on.

"And a ten," I said as if I did this every day. I grabbed a ten-pound plate and placed it on the end of the bar, fitting the collar lock snugly in place.

This time with the impressed look I was hoping for, Greg placed the last plate on the bar and fastened his collar lock.

I shook my arms loose. I felt good. I hadn't done any bench work since Friday. We work the bench every Tuesday and Friday. Our schedule had changed somewhat with more emphasis on legs and overall conditioning. Of course, I did push-ups and sit-ups every morning and evening, along with at least two sets of pull-ups every day as I passed by the support pipe gizmo thing that's attached to the telephone pole on the way to and from school, in addition to my workouts.

However, that morning I was in a bit of a rush to get to school and neglected to do my push-ups, or my early morning workout. You see, the cheerleaders, including Bunny, started their first spring early morning outdoor practice. It's a Washington High School tradition for us guys to stand on the sidelines and ogle, and cheer them on.

After loosening up and taking several deep breaths, I took my place under the loaded barbell weighing one hundred and forty-five pounds. I placed my hands on the bar and pushed up and slightly out. I let the bar down fairly quickly and pushed it back up with all my might as it touched my chest. It went up. Before thinking about what I had just accomplished, I let it drop again, almost bouncing it off my chest and it went up, my arms fully extended. I lowered one hundred and forty five pounds the third time, and again it went up. Once my arms were fully extended, I dropped it again, bouncing it off my chest and pushing with all my might as the bar slowly went up to about three-quarters of the way.

Greg placed his hands down by the bar as if to help, but he didn't touch it. There's a natural phenomenon that takes place when a spotter places his hands near or on the bar, but doesn't help. Somehow, the person benching gains strength from the spotter. Whether it's a psychological thing or whether there's a melding of energies, I don't know. The fact is that often when the person benching is stuck and can't move the bar any further, the spotter can give him strength by placing his hands on or near the bar. Slowly, the bar came up the rest of the way. A personal best by far—one hundred and forty-five pounds four times.

"Wow," was all Greg could say.

I sat up, not saying anything, and looked at Greg. I forgot to play it cool and was in total shock. I didn't have a clue that I had gained that kind of strength. The coach said that the gains would come. Greg's brother, Tom, also said they would come, but somehow, I guess I didn't really believe them. I had hoped. I had hoped with all my being, but I don't think I really believed. I did now.

One hundred and forty-five pounds four times wasn't going to break any records other than mine and Greg's, but it wasn't bad. There were guys on the freshman team who were still struggling with less. However, most the guys on the JV team were benching more. I still had a ways to go, but I was definitely heading in the right direction.

Of course Greg had to try to keep up, and slid under the bar with one hundred and forty-five pounds. Much to my surprise, he ripped off two reps.

"Wow. Not bad," I admitted, "especially for a guy who only weighs a hundred and seventeen pounds."

"Make that one thirty," Greg declared as he removed himself from the bench.

It was true. Hard work and determination pays off. I knew now that if I kept working hard, I would continue to make gains.

"It won't be long until we're the very studs we have dreamed we would be." Greg was speaking as if he had read my soul.

Just then, Greg's mother appeared at the door of my weight room and dragged Greg away.

I sat there in my little sanctuary going over in my mind where I'd been and where I still wanted to be. Building a chunk of granite from a bowl of jelly takes time and a lot of hard work, but it can be done. In fact, I was witnessing firsthand the transformation actually taking place. I had come quite a ways. I was no longer a bowl of jelly. I was much stronger than when I first started in Mr. Lawnboy's early morning exercise program for fatties and wimps. I was much faster, too. I felt good. I might have been a pound or two heavier than when I started, but I was a little taller and my waistline was smaller.

Also, when was the last time someone picked on me? Not counting the harassment from the guys on the Varsity team and the occasional glare from Rodney Skylark, no one had bothered me at all. I'm sure the fact that Joey Aardema was in lock-up for armed robbery and the rest of his gang doesn't bother coming to school any longer helped. I still had a long ways to go, though. Bunny still didn't think of me as being any competition for Rodney, and neither did Rodney. As far as football goes, I didn't even have a place on the bench secured for sure yet. But I would, because it was up to me.

CHAPTER FIFTEEN

Spring came and went. My first year in high school came to a close, and still no Bunny. I was starting to wonder if Bunny was a realistic goal.

I pushed all negative thoughts from my mind as I pedaled my new 10-speed that I had purchased with lawn-mowing money over the bridge that leads to Sauvie Island. Greg and I had been making plans all spring. I hung a left, taking the somewhat longer route. Sally Rayfield lived on this side of the island. I was hoping to get a look at her. It had been almost a year. For the most part, Bunny had been the object of my obsessions, but once in a while, the image of Sally's big smile would edge its way into my thoughts.

The sun was shining bright and the sweat oozed from my pores as I pedaled my bike—dragging a makeshift trailer behind it loaded down with clothes, additional weights, a curl-bar, and a couple of footballs. Greg and I were ready for a serious summer.

We were going to help Greg's step-dad, Bob, do chores from six to noon every day for ten dollars a day. We would feed and water the animals, clean out their pens and stalls, stack hay, move irrigation pipe, dig post holes, and on and on and on. There was no end to the work around there. Greg's step-dad was letting us work just half a day except when it was time to get the hay out of his brother's field just south of Portland. Then we would put in some pretty long days, for about a week, bucking the hay bales. After work, we hit the weights. Once we had our workouts out of the way, we would practice our passing routes, taking turns throwing and catching. Tom said if he was around, he would work with us. After football practice, we would run over to Marshall Beach and swim until almost dark, then run home, get some sleep, and do it all over again.

Greg and I originally wanted to spend every waking hour working out, swimming, and running the island, but his dad convinced us that we needed money for wheels. After all, we would be turning sixteen the next school year. Ten dollars a day for three months is roughly nine hundred dollars. Five hundred bucks could get a nice little Chevy of some kind. Besides, farm work is hard, and good for muscle development.

I cruised by the school where I had first met Sally. There wasn't a soul around. No Sally—just a funny empty feeling in the bottom of my gut. I kept pedaling until I reached Greg's place. Sally was all but forgotten.

"Hey, John," Greg exclaimed as I pulled into his drive and parked my bike in the shade of the large maple in his front yard.

"Hey," I returned with equal enthusiasm. "I got some more weights."

We pushed my bike over to the barn, unloaded the weights, and put them away in the weight room. We were quite well stocked, having duplicate dumbbells, curl bars, straight bars, and all the plates necessary to keep them loaded at the same time. No more unloading one dumbbell or barbell to load another.

Greg and I jumped right in and got a good thorough workout. Once our muscles were sufficiently pumped full of blood we grabbed a football and headed to Marshall Beach at a fast jog in our cut-offs and tennis shoes.

The sun was still fairly high in the sky as we sprinted through the small trailer park, past Mrs. Marshall's combination hamburger stand and beer joint, and onto the beach. The speaker that sits on top of the light pole at the edge of the beach was blaring out a Patsy Cline standard. Mrs. Marshall must be in a good mood. There were maybe twenty-five to thirty sunbathers on towels and blankets, and another twenty or so in the water. It was a busy day at Marshall Beach.

We wasted no time. We kicked off our shoes and threw ourselves into the water. It was cold, but felt good as it washed the sweat and the heat away.

Greg and I raced from one log piling to another several times until we were totally exhausted. I was a pretty strong swimmer and had no problem staying ahead of Greg, but he wouldn't quit. Finally, after several laps, I gave up.

"Okay, you win," I managed, breathing heavily as I stopped at the far piling at the east end of Marshall Beach with Greg right behind me.

"What's the matter? Can't you take it?" Greg struggled to ask between breaths.

"No," I replied without shame.

I pulled myself from the water. Right before my eyes was a familiar face with that big smile I had seen in my thoughts hundreds of times since last summer. I usually pushed the memories of Sally and the butterflies that always seemed to accompany her or even the thought of her out of my mind and focused on Bunny, but I never really could completely.

"Hi, Sally," I said, trying to sound natural as my stomach began twisting in knots.

Sally's smile grew even larger as she pulled herself up off the blanket she was laying on. She was wearing the same modest one-piece swimsuit, but there was something different about it. It seemed to be a little snugger than I remembered. Either that swimsuit had shrunk, or Sally was starting to fill it out. My stomach twisted even tighter.

"Hi," she replied, smiling brightly.

Sally must have gotten an early start on her tan because she had a nice golden glow about her, and her hair seemed to be more blonde than red, and boy, was I feeling weird.

"Hey, Sally," Greg greeted flatly as he dragged himself from the water. "Time to practice our routes."

"Right," I said almost too enthusiastically, thankful for an excuse to get away from Sally. "See ya, Sally. Got to work on our passing routes," I managed to mumble, my voice not sounding like my own.

Greg and I quickly ran over to where we left our shoes and grabbed the football. We ran our routes in the deep sand, hoping to build speed and power. Every now and then, I would sneak a peek in Sally's direction. There she was, lounging around in the sun, watching us the whole time. That made me all the more nervous.

Eventually a couple of Sally's girlfriends arrived, and Greg and I had pass-routed our way down the beach, where I felt a lot more comfortable.

The sun was starting to set, so we took one last dip, then jogged back to Greg's house. We were beat. It had been a good first day. However, the next day, summer really started. We set the alarm for five thirty. Greg's dad gave us an outline of our chores for the day, and it looked like it was going to be a very full six hours.

We were up and at 'em after a quick breakfast. First, we fed the animals and mucked out their stalls. Then we stacked about a hundred bales of hay from the truck and trailer into the barn. Greg's stepdad, Bob, buys hay whenever he finds a deal and then sells it in the winter for a little extra cash. Next we moved a whole bunch of irrigation pipe. Neither Greg nor

I had a watch, and by the time Bob got around to relieving us, it was two o'clock.

"Keep track of the extra hours you work," he told us as he dropped us off at the house.

Man, were we beat. Farm work is hard.

Greg's mom got us a snack, and then we dragged ourselves into the barn for a workout. We did the best we could with our tired muscles. We kind of just went through the motions, but we did manage to stick to our complete workout schedule and then jogged over to the beach for a swim.

The days went by and the work got harder as Bob demanded more and more from us. Rarely did we get off at noon. There was always more work than we could get done, but we always got our complete workout, practice and swim time in. There just wasn't any time left for goofing around.

School started September 7th, and football practice started the 24th of August. It couldn't come too soon for me and Greg. Two-a-days in the hot sun would be a welcome relief.

After almost three months of hard work being pushed by Bob, Greg's sadistic stepdad, along with pushing ourselves to do our workout regimen, our muscles were spent. It took every ounce of strength I had left to lift the last hay bale up to Greg, who was standing midway up the stack. It was up to Greg to get it up to Bob another four bales up at the top. Greg didn't have anything left.

"Here, wait. I'll help you," I said as I climbed up to where Greg was stationed.

The two of us managed to get the last hundred-pound bale of alfalfa hay up to the top of the stack—barely. We practically collapsed right where we stood.

"There. That should do it for today," Greg's stepdad said with satisfaction. "Got another truck coming tomorrow."

"Ugh," was Greg's reply.

"Good," I managed without emotion.

Bob looked us over and chuckled. "How 'bout if I give you guys the rest of the summer off?"

"Really?" Greg asked, not believing his ears.

There were three days left before practice started. Greg and I thought we had died and gone to heaven.

Greg's stepdad nimbly jumped down to our level and then to the floor of the barn. He slapped at the hay clinging to his shirt and pants and stretched out his lanky frame.

"You know," he started slowly, "I'm proud of you boys. You've worked hard. You've given me all that I could ask of a hired hand. Come see me after dinner, and we'll settle up."

He smiled, turned, and headed for the house. Greg and I still sat there on the hay bales, not sure we could move, but we felt good—really good.

"Well, what do you want to do with these three days?" I asked.

"I don't know. What do you want to do?"

"Let's float the river!" I almost shouted.

"Yeah!" Greg returned excitedly. "We can use Tom's canoe."

We made our plans, got permission—which wasn't easy— and asked Tom if we could use his canoe and if he would drop us off on the Willamette River just below Salem. Salem was about sixty miles south of Sauvie Island. The Willamette River begins its life somewhere east of Eugene. It flows northward, once through Eugene, then through Salem and then through Portland on its way to the Columbia just east of Sauvie Island. We figured we could float twenty miles a day pretty easy with plenty of time to swim and fish.

Greg and Tom and their dad Bob had made this trip several times, and Greg knew all the good fishing holes and places to camp along the way. It was now three thirty p.m. on Thursday, and we had until Monday morning when we would report for football practice. If we hadn't been working so hard for so long, we might have used those three days for practice, but we needed some time off. We were totally exhausted and didn't even want to think about football.

We loaded our gear into the pickup, tied the canoe in place, and ran and got Tom off the telephone, which was not an easy task. With him being the biggest football senior stud on campus, the girls wouldn't leave him alone—at least, that was his story. Anyway, he was on the phone a lot.

It was about seven p.m. when Tom helped us unload our gear at the little boat ramp on the Willamette south of Salem. The river was not real wide there. A small island cut through the middle of the gently flowing waterway. The island was where we would stay the night and be on the river at first light.

Tom pushed us off and waved as we paddled over to a small beach head. We pulled the canoe out of the water and started right in setting up camp. We only had a good hour or so before dark.

The island was covered in trees and underbrush, except where we had landed. There was a little sandy section that extended up into the island about twenty feet and was about twenty feet wide. It was a perfect place to camp. We gathered up large rocks from the bottom of the river for our campfire and placed them in a circle in the middle of the clearing. Next we gathered up all the twigs and driftwood we could find in our immediate surroundings, which was significant, and piled it up a few feet from the fire pit. We placed some twigs in the pit with a few larger pieces on top. I gave the little pile a generous squirt of lighter fluid, and laid several large chunks of drift-wood on top. Greg took out the matches, and soon we had a nice bright fire. We laid out our sleeping bags and fired up our lantern.

I lay back on my sleeping bag and looked at the sky. There wasn't a cloud to be seen, and the stars were just beginning to show as twilight was waning.

"Man, this is the life." I sighed as I got comfortable.

There was a slight breeze, and the air was still warm. The

nighttime sounds were beginning to echo across the river. A large blue heron flew over us, looking for its roost, as an owl hooted somewhere in the woods over on the far bank.

"Yeah, you know it," Greg agreed as he lay back on his bag.

"What are you going to do with your money?"

Greg's dad had given us each eleven hundred dollars, which included the extra hours. He said that he would take care of the taxes. That was more money than I had ever seen.

"Well, I guess I'll buy some school clothes and save the rest for a car," Greg answered without thinking, since we had discussed this subject almost every day since summer started.

"Yeah, me too," I added as I felt the rigors of the day begin to take their toll.

The two of us slept like babies on the soft sand, dreaming of fast cars, football, and pretty girls—not necessarily in that order.

Then seemingly in the blink of an eye the night had passed, and the eastern sky began to show forth it's early morning light. We dragged ourselves out of our bags. The air was a little cool as I stirred the fire and threw on some more wood. It wasn't long and we had bacon sizzling in a large black cast-iron pan.

After bacon, eggs, and a couple of bagels, we put out the fire, loaded up our gear, and we were off.

Greg guided the canoe expertly as we paddled. We mostly drifted along with the easy current toward the mighty Columbia. I cast my baited hook toward the bank, letting it settle, and then retrieved it and flicked it again as we drifted.

The banks of the river were densely populated with tall Douglas fir trees and brambles until we reached Salem, the capital. Salem isn't much of a town to look at, and from the river, it was even less impressive. We were through it quickly.

We cruised by farms and forests, sandy beaches and through a couple of small towns. Several times during the course of the day, we cooled ourselves in the river. That evening, we camped on the bank at the edge of a cornfield. We actually caught several fish. We released all but Greg's nice fat bass, which we had for dinner, frying the filets in bacon grease. Again, we settled down under the stars.

The next day, we had to pull our rig from the water when we got to the falls at Oregon City. There was a nice well-worn path that served us well, and we put in at the base and continued down river past more forests and farms and several large mansions and fancy homes lining the river in the Lake Oswego area. Lake Oswego is a bedroom community of Portland where most of the Portland Trail Blazers and other millionaire-types live.

Late in the afternoon, we pulled into a slough that drained into the river downstream a couple of miles from the Lake Oswego mansions. The water was black and didn't seem to move hardly at all. We paddled up the slough for a quarter mile or so and found a grassy section of the bank free of trees. The slough appeared to continue on for a ways, but became much narrower, with many trees extending their branches over the water making it hard to go any farther. Here we tied up the canoe to a large log that was half in and half out of the water, grabbed our gear, and set up camp. We pulled up most of the tall green grass to use as bedding and then dug a fire pit in the dirt. There was plenty of wood, and soon we had a fire. It was nice and cozy in the slough surrounded by large trees and dense undergrowth. There was a small slit high up in the canopy where the sky was exposed to our view. The sun was beginning to set. We baited our hooks and cast them a few feet out into the slough. Life was good, and practice was still a full day and night away.

"You think junior varsity two-a-days will be worse than working for your dad?" I wondered aloud. "I would think that after the last couple of months, we can handle anything."

"You're probably right," Greg agreed. "Except my muscles

still seem kind of stiff. I'm sure glad we got a couple of days off to recuperate before football."

"Yeah, but I bet by the time practice starts the day after tomorrow, we will be chomping at the bit to get after it." I was starting to get my enthusiasm back just as I got a pull on my line. A few moments later, I was pulling in the biggest and ugliest catfish I had ever seen. It had to be ten pounds.

"Wow. What a beauty," Greg said as he netted it.

'Let's eat."

We cleaned the big fish, fried the fillets in bacon grease, served them with ketchup and the last of our bagels. We sat around the fire with darkness setting in and a cool breeze finding its way down the slough. Life was good.

The next morning, we fried up the last of our eggs, wolfed them down with a can of chili, and then broke camp. Soon the two of us were back in the bright sunshine heading for Sauvie Island about twenty miles downriver. It was a beautiful sunny day, and there were all kinds of boats on the river. We had to stay close to the bank to stay out of their way.

We paddled our canoe more vigorously. The river had become much wider and slower as it got closer to Portland. We passed through the town of Milwaukee and past the golf course that lines the river there. We continued on past Oaks Amusement Park, where they set off the fireworks every 4th of July. Soon we were in downtown Portland. We floated under bridge after bridge with tall buildings lining the way.

Portland boasts quite an assortment of bridges varying in age going back as far as the early 1900s. There were a couple of drawbridges, a couple of expansion bridges, a swing bridge, and couple of bridges where the center section lifts up to let the ships pass under. When the Navy fleet comes in and docks between the bridges on the west side for the Rose Festival every June, it's quite a sight to see. It also causes terrific traffic problems, with several of the bridges raised or swung open all at the same time.

Today there was only a small Navy ship without guns docked between the Burnside and Morrison Bridges. Not very exciting, but the fire department's fire boat was out in the middle of the river, clearing out its water cannons. It was a very impressive display, with six water cannons shooting water in all directions high into the air. At least, that's what we thought up until the moment that our curiosity pulled us just a little too close to the falling streams of water and darn near capsized our canoe. We managed to back-paddle and bail out the water before we became a statistic.

The sun grew hotter as the day progressed, and again we were inclined to stop for a swim every now and then. It was a day that we never wanted to end, but time doesn't stand still. Soon we found ourselves at the mouth of the Willamette where it flows into the Columbia. The current picked up considerably, and we paddled like crazy to maintain control as we kept close to the bank. A few short miles downriver, we turned into the slough where we'd had our houseboat adventure the year before. Several of the houseboats had people lounging around on their decks, some swimming and some sunbathing.

"I hope no one recognizes us," Greg whispered as we paddled by nonchalantly.

"Yeah," I returned out of the side of my mouth as I turned to look at the people jumping from the very same deck where we were discovered. "It was pretty dark that night."

As we approached the smaller houseboats, we noticed that Bob the mailman was lying in a lounge chair next to a woman we didn't recognize. What happened to Sonny?

We paddled our canoe under the bridge that leads to the island and continued on for about another half mile. Here the trees were almost touching each other from one side of the bank to the other. A little farther ahead, the slough opened up into a clearing on the island side where the bank became a rocky beach. Tom was waiting with his pickup truck.

CHAPTER SIXTEEN

"One," I grunted as the sweat dropped like rain. "Two," I counted as my feet shot back in the push-up position. "Three," I hollered, my arms bending as my chest touched the ground.

"Ten more," roared an authoritative voice.

With that, it was as if the air had been let out of fifty hot-air balloons at the same time. The junior varsity football team collapsed, facedown, unable—at least for that moment—to push themselves up, bring in their feet, and stand up straight, then repeat that series of motions ten more times in the heat of the late-afternoon sun.

"Four," I managed to utter as I pushed myself up. "Five," I breathed out as I brought in my feet. "Six," I almost whimpered as I stood as tall as I could in the blazing heat.

I was the only one standing.

"Get up," roared the voice of Satan, the same voice that had plagued us all that afternoon, as I was preparing to begin my next bend and thrust. "Four laps and then the showers." Coach Saunders, the assistant JV coach, was still roaring. "And I'd better not see anyone dogging it."

I started shuffling in the general direction of the track with the rest of the team coming to their feet and joining me. The first so-called two-hour practice in the morning actually lasted three and a half hours, but that wasn't too bad because the coaches did a lot of talking. The second practice of the day, however, was all business. By the time five o'clock rolled around, we were all totally wasted. Of course, that was when Coach Saunders thought some six-count bends and thrusts were in order to top things off. The four laps during the hottest part of the day with nothing left to go on was a nice touch.

I was in front of the shuffling, moaning, and complaining crowd when I realized that I was in front of the shuffling, moaning, and complaining crowd. I was half dead, but I was in front. I felt a renewed energy flow through my veins. My shuffling became a jog. I picked up my feet and set them down, pulling away from the body of misery that represented the Washington junior varsity football team. After about two laps, the team was spread out all over the track, and I began to pass the slowest of the stragglers. The last lap, I picked up the pace, sprinting the final one hundred yards. I felt like I could die any second, but I didn't, and I headed for the showers. It was a very good first day.

In my basement retreat that night, I thought that I would be too weak and too tired for much of a workout, but actually, I felt pretty good and did all right. I guess the hard work was paying off.

After three days of nothing but gut-wrenching killer workouts, we were divided into position groups.

"When you hear your name, fall in with Coach Saunders," Coach Wurthlin barked.

The first day of practice, we all signed up for the position or positions we would like to play. I signed up for wide receiver and linebacker. My speed had increased considerably, but I was still one of the bigger guys, and that probably meant lineman.

"Levitz, Johnson, Carlton, Mitchell." Four big obvious lineman-types went over and stood next to Coach Saunders. "Laughton, Homestead, and Smith." There it was. I was a lineman with Fred and Gary. Gary was working out with the JV team, but the Coach had told him that he would be playing with the varsity if he was able to get up to speed.

I stood with the linemen. The next smallest guy to me was Fred. He had grown a couple of inches and was now a good two hundred and twenty-five pounds. I was the smallest of the lineman at one ninety-four. Hopefully I could show the coaches some speed and athletic ability and they'd let me play receiver or linebacker as I had hoped. Whatever the position, I was determined to give it my all.

Now that we were assigned our place on the team, we would work with our group in the morning, on technique and drills designed for our position. In the afternoon, we started scrimmaging with the whole team. At first, we went with just helmets, and then after a few days, we put on pads and started hitting.

"Hut one, seventy-five, three," barked our first-string quarterback. The ball was shoved into his hands by the center as I lunged forward with all my might, elbows extended, my hands groping for a little bit of legal jersey as I drove my legs into the ground, propelling myself forward. I caught the oversized high schooler who was playing defensive end just as he came up out of his three-point stance. I drove him back and down. The play went the other way, albeit unsuccessfully. The next play was a run-off tackle behind me.

I lined up in the tackle spot again, but this time, the coach had replaced Levitz, who was large but a bit slow, with a kid named Joel Kimber. Joel seemed like a pretty good guy who played fullback on offense, and it appeared that the coaches still weren't certain where to play him on defense. A lot of the kids would play both ways. I know I was hoping to.

Joel was about five foot ten, two hundred pounds, and strong. I had seen him bench two hundred.

"Hut one, two." The ball was shoved into the quarterback's hands as I did my best to explode out of my stance, hoping to stand Joel up as he was coming out of his as I had done to Levitz.

Joel, however, came up quicker than Levitz, and being shorter, he kept his shoulder pads lower, not giving me the leverage to knock him off balance. I locked up with him for a moment, and then he simply spun and left me holding air. Our little speedy running back Morris Henry was able to slip through just the same as Joel spun to the left and Morris went right. The linebacker got him as he popped through for a three-yard gain.

"Smith, you're out," Coach Wurthlin barked. "Laughton, take the right tackle spot."

Gary lumbered in, and the play went his way. Gary wasn't nearly as quick as I was, but he had worked hard all spring with Fred and I, and he continued to work over the summer. The quarterback called out the cadence, and the ball came up into his hands. Gary surged forward, pushing Joel back with his massive bulk into the linebacker as Morris followed right behind him into the backfield before making his way to the end zone.

Throughout the remaining summer practices, it became apparent that I was able to have some success against some of the slower, larger lineman and the slower, smaller guys as well, slower being the key. Guys like Gary were able to push the smaller guys around and at the same time hold their own with guys their own size. That made me a bit of a specialist to be used in certain situations, meaning I was a second-string offensive lineman. The coaches also had me penciled in as a defensive end. The problem on defense was that there were all kinds of guys who were small and quick, and not many with size. They needed all the bulk they could get on the line even though I was built more like a linebacker than a defensive lineman, and since I was a bit on the small size for the line, I would be used in special match-ups and situations. That meant I would be warming the bench on defense as well. Not for long, I promised myself.

It was the Thursday before Labor Day weekend, and the coach was giving us Friday through Monday off, with school starting on Tuesday. We showed up at eight that morning, and instead of two approximately two-hour practices, which were always more like three hours, we were going to have one four-hour practice, and the coach was supposedly turning us loose at noon.

The coaches didn't waste any time. This was our most grueling practice yet. After warming up and stretching as a team, we did our individual group drills and then went right to scrimmaging, being divided into two full teams. The coaches were yelling and screaming and driving us the whole time with short periodic breaks for water. The late-summer morning air was warming, and the two weeks of two-a-days were taking their toll, as most of the team was running on rubbery legs.

I was on defense, lined up against Levitz. We had been working on run defense, and Coach Wurthlin wanted to see what we could do in a game-like situation.

"Okay, defense, it's game time. We're going to run a series of plays. Let's see what you've got," the coach hollered.

The offense huddled up after receiving the play from the sideline. Once the play was called in the huddle, they took their positions at the line with the quarterback behind center and the running back behind him and off to one side.

There were two wide-outs on my side and one on the other along with one tight end and a lone back in the backfield. Looked like pass to me.

With nothing but Levitz in front of me and no one to his immediate left, I knew what I was going to do. It was a bit of a gamble because if it turned out to be a run to my side, I would be leaving a large unprotected hole. If the linebacker stayed home like he was supposed to, at least that was the call on defense, he would plug the hole I was leaving. Of course, if he decided to help out in pass coverage, I would be on my own.

"Hut one. Hut two." The ball was snapped, and I shot up with all the strength and energy I had left. I hit the big, slow behemoth as he began to come out of his stance and slid off him to his left, where the quarterback was faking a handoff. I drove forward as he began to roll out and away from me. I got up to speed quickly with the help of massive amounts of adrenaline. I got him clearly in my sights. My legs still felt strong, the many runs and workouts paying off. Our quarterback was quick but I knew I had him. Another three steps and he would be mine. His arm came up. He was preparing to dump off a quickie to the tight end, which had slipped off his man and was rolling to his right looking for the ball, when I hit him. I hit him good. I hit him with everything I had. Down he went and the ball popped out of his hand.

A skinny kid named Henry jumped on the loose ball for the fumble recovery as I jumped to my feet.

Tweeeeeeet! went the coach's whistle.

"Now that's the way you play football!" Coach Wurthlin shouted enthusiastically. "Good job, Smith. You keep that up and I'll have to start you!"

I helped the quarterback up, as he was having some difficulty. Man, did I feel good. The rest of practice was a little more challenging, since the coach made sure he lined me up against more worthy opponents, but as they were tiring, I seemed to be getting my second wind. I think I impressed the coaches. I got to the quarterback two more times and stopped several runs that came my way.

"Good practice," the coach sincerely stated. "You continue to work hard, and I can guarantee you that we'll have success.

See you in three days, and have some fun. And oh, yeah," he added, "Four laps."

I ran around that track as fast as I could, took off the pads, and headed for home without showering. No sense taking a shower when I was just going to run home and hop on my loaded and packed 10-speed, pedal to Sauvie Island, and pump some iron with Greg. Besides, after our workout we would go for our swim in the only slightly polluted Columbia. But it's wet, and washes off the sweat and dirt.

The air was quite warm as I stood on the pedals and churned my way over the hill and then down to the old highway that leads to Sauvie Island. There was the giant hand in front of the fortune teller's house. As I drew closer, I noticed that someone had made some alterations to her large palm-reading sign. The fingers had apparently been sawed off, leaving just the middle one, giving a whole new meaning to "Fortunes Told." I snickered as I saw the sign and wondered if maybe the Zig-Zag man ex-boyfriend had come back to extract a little revenge.

At the T, I decided once again to cruise by Sally's house, even though if she were around, she would be at Marshall Beach with her friends. I cruised past the school and Sally's farm, and again my stomach kind of sank when Sally was nowhere to be found.

Greg and I wasted no time once I arrived.

"Let's go," Greg shouted as I pulled into his driveway.

"What about our workout?" I inquired.

"We'll work out twice as hard tomorrow," Greg replied "After two weeks of two-a-days, we deserve at least a half day off."

"You're right," I agreed as we started running toward Marshall Beach.

We swam and dove off the pilings until the sun began to set and then headed for Greg's house at a slow, shuffling jog.

We compared the intensities of our individual two-a-day

practices with the second episode always topping the first. That's the way it is. The first liar never has a chance.

That night, we bedded down at our usual campsite behind the orchard on the bank of the small pond right where a little creek runs into it. You throw your line in and let it drift down the creek into the pond, and more often than not, you'll be awarded with a nice perch or crappie. At night with a sinker and properly placed line, a catfish can be had.

I had been sleeping like a baby when something drew me out of unconsciousness. I lay still in my sleeping bag, looking up at the stars, as I listened. Everything seemed normal. The fire had burned down to a glow. I could hear the small creek trickling into the pond just yards away. The crickets were chirping. An owl was hooting somewhere in the woods. There it was. A funny muffled sound came from the trees just across the pond. I lay there listening intently as thoughts of cougars, bears, wolves, and Bigfoots, lurking in the trees looking for something to eat, ran through my mind. There it was again. It had kind of a high-pitched, edgy-yet-muffled sort of sound. *It must be a cougar trying to be quiet*, I thought as my heart began to race. *A cougar trying to be quiet?* I almost said it aloud. There it was a third time. It was a muffled giggly sort of sound. A cougar with the giggles trying to be quiet? Something didn't add up here. I looked over toward Greg.

"Psst. Greg, you awake?" I whispered as quietly as I could. Greg was about five feet away, lying in his sleeping bag, obviously awake and listening, like me.

"Yeah. Do you hear what I hear?" Greg asked alertly, yet quietly.

"It's coming from the trees on the other side of the pond," I whispered, not moving. "Got your flashlight?"

"Yeah, it's here somewhere," Greg replied as he rummaged around in his sleeping bag. "Got it."

"When I give the word, let's shine our lights over there in the trees and start shouting as loud as we can," I instructed.

"Okay," Greg returned.

"Now!" I yelled as Greg and I jumped up hollering, and shining our flashlights into the darkness across the pond in the general direction of the muffled giggle noises.

We definitely startled something or some things from their hiding place, as they began screaming and running through the woods. We gave chase, jumping the small creek and running toward the sounds in the trees, but in our bare feet, we weren't able to catch them. I did, however, see enough of them in the beam of our flashlights to discern that they were not cougars, but humans. They were humans who giggled and screamed.

"Hey, those were girls," Greg shouted as he picked sharp barbs from his feet.

"They'll probably come out at Carp Pond Road. If we get our bikes, we might be able to head them off," I suggested as the excitement of the situation took hold.

The woods behind the orchard were dense and about quarter of a mile deep, with several ponds and brambles surrounding the area. On the other side of the woods is an opening and a pond jammed full of carp. They often sun themselves in the shallow water along the banks. If you walk up to the pond, they will hear your footsteps, and the water will literally churn with hundreds, maybe thousands, of carp. There's a short dirt road that leads to the main road from the pond.

"Let's go!" Greg almost screamed.

We limped to our sleeping bags, the barbs from the blackberries in our feet. We threw on our shoes and ran through the orchard, grabbed our bikes, and headed for Carp Pond Road.

It was about a half mile or maybe a tad bit more from Greg's farm. We peddled our ten-speeds as fast as we could, the full moon giving us considerable light. As we rounded the bend, the entrance to Carp Pond Road came into view.

"We've got them for sure," I shouted. The entrance was just three hundred yards ahead.

The night air was warm, the sky was clear, and the moon was bright, yet there was a sound like rolling thunder in the distance.

"Thunder?" I asked myself, looking at the cloudless sky as we closed the gap to the dirt road.

"What's that sound?" Greg shouted as the noise became louder.

"It sounds kind of like . . ." I was going to say "thunder," but that was when I saw the opening to Carp Pond Road fill with light. A roaring three-wheeler with a single bright headlight came into view. It slowed, turned the corner on the main road, and sped away, leaving us in the dust. We hadn't been seen. We were still about a hundred yards away and didn't have our lights on.

"That's got to be Marianne Sebastian," Greg exclaimed. "She lives just down the road."

I pulled alongside Greg as we continued to pedal vigorously.

"Who's Marianne Sebastian?" I asked, huffing and puffing.

"She's a new girl at school from California. Her folks bought the Jorgensen farm. They raise horses. Her dad's a big-shot banker in Portland," Greg replied as he huffed and puffed too.

"You sure seem to know a lot about her. She must be a babe," I suggested.

"Yeah," Greg replied simply, not volunteering anything more.

"Who's the other girl?"

"Well, Marianne's been hanging around with Sally Rayfield mostly," Greg replied, not realizing the impact of his answer.

I didn't say anything. I just pedaled harder.

About a mile or so later, Greg cautioned me with a raised hand, slowing as he did so. I followed his lead and eased up on my pedaling as we approached a driveway, where we came to a stop. About five hundred yards down the gravel drive, we could see a large old farmhouse. It was the old Jorgensen home. It had been completely renovated inside and out. I had observed the construction work going on all summer, but hadn't given it much thought. Who knew that an attractive female specimen would be living within those walls and would be friends with Sally?

We peered down the long, straight driveway surrounded by a huge manicured lawn lined with maple trees. We could see something about halfway down. We got off our bikes and looked intently.

"Hey, that's the girls pushing the three-wheeler." Greg chuckled. "Let's get a little closer."

We crept silently, yet quickly, from tree to tree down the driveway. The two girls were so preoccupied with their task of pushing the off road vehicle home that they didn't see or hear us as we got within thirty feet or so of them. We could hear them talking as they struggled with the three wheeled machine.

"This thing sure is a lot heavier than it looks," breathed out one of the girls.

"Shhh," replied the other. "We don't want to wake my dad. He'll kill me if he knew we were out running all over with it."

We watched as the two girls worked to complete their task and then followed them at a discreet distance as they went around back. The girls had set up a tent and were apparently camping out in the backyard. We kept to the shadows behind some nearby bushes and waited. The two of them went into the house, but were soon back with supplies in the form of snacks and entered the tent.

We cautiously slipped around behind the tent and lay on

the cool lawn with our ears perked. Sure enough, Sally was the other girl. I would recognize that sweet feminine voice anywhere.

Greg and I continued to eavesdrop as the girls reveled in their great adventure. They were convinced that they had really put one over on us and that we would be spending the rest of the night wondering who or what it was stalking them in the woods. Greg and I just smiled at each other as we listened.

The next subject of discussion took both Greg and I completely by surprise.

"Greg sure is cute. You know, the way his one eyebrow lifts up and his other eye kind of squints when he talks to you," the voice on the other side of the tent wall was saying.

"Greg is a nice guy, but I'll take that hunk, John. He's so sweet. I love how he gets all flustered when he's trying to talk to me," the second voice added.

My jaw dropped, and for a moment or so there, I wasn't sure I'd heard right. I looked at Greg, and he had the same dumbfounded expression on his face that must have been on mine.

The girls started talking about clothes and makeup, so we headed for our bikes. Once we were on the road, we started to discuss this new information.

"Well, I guess the girls think we're pretty hot," I said.

"Yeah, well, why wouldn't they?" Greg wanted to know.

"You got me there. But what are we going to do about it?"

Greg looked at me kind of funny as we peddled in the moonlight. "You really do like Sally, don't you?"

"Well, why wouldn't I?" I replied defiantly.

"No reason," Greg answered, smiling.

"She's nice and she's cute. What else is there?"

"Well, she's smart too," Greg added diplomatically.

"That's right. She has to be smart. She thinks I'm a hunk, doesn't she?"

"Well, there you go."

We continued to discuss the girls, and their obvious good taste and gifts of discernment as we rode back to Greg's house. Once we were behind the barn, we dismounted and headed back through the orchard to our sleeping bags.

We were kind of on edge, but sleep did come. It was late in the morning before we stirred. The bright light of the sun was delayed by all the trees surrounding us. We broke camp, got some breakfast, and then hit the weights.

Coach Wurthlin had changed our workout regimen. For the duration of football season, we were to continue our weight lifting, only we were to go lighter with more repetitions. We were to do more of a "maintenance work out," the coach informed us the first day of practice.

"For the next three months, I want you to lighten up on your weights and do more reps. Do your strength and power conditioning during the off season. Now is time for football. I want your bodies as well as your minds focused on playing better football. I have a small booklet that I will pass out outlining your workout." With that, Coach Wurthlin saw to it that each of us had a booklet in hand.

In the booklet, the coach expressed the importance of flexibility and endurance. Greg and I zipped through our workout. Greg's coach hadn't made any alterations to his workout, but Greg liked the sound of Coach Wurthlin's, so that's what we did.

CHAPTER SEVENTEEN

The reflection in the mirror wasn't really me, was it? I stood there with a towel wrapped around my lower extremities. Looking back was not the same butterball I usually avoided. There were lines and indentations here and there where bulges had normally resided. My shoulders seemed broader than I remembered, and my arms had definition. I could see muscles without flexing.

Summer was over. I was now a sophomore on the junior varsity football team, and I was looking forward to being one of Washington High School's elite. I had worked hard, and I was finally getting somewhere.

"Maybe Bunny is ready for a real man," I said to my reflection with all thoughts of Sally Rayfield lost in the adolescent recesses of my mind.

I reluctantly pulled my brand-new white jersey over my head, hiding my evolving torso from my appreciative view. My hair was bleached blond again from the sun, and my skin had a reddish-brown hue with a few freckles thrown in here and there to remind me of my mortality.

Once fully dressed in my new Levi's and jersey ensemble, I was out the door. The sun was shining and I felt good, really good. I had worked hard all spring and summer. Actually, I had been working hard for a few years now, and the results were beginning to show. Not only was my big ol' belly flattening out nicely and muscles were beginning to appear, but I was probably going to earn a starting spot on defense. As far as I could tell, there wasn't anyone who had been nearly as effective at the defensive end spot as I had. It wasn't the wide receiver position I had hoped for, but . . .

"There are still two more years after this one," I said to myself, fully believing. I felt like I could accomplish anything I put my mind to, including winning Bunny over. There was one problem, however, that just would not go away.

Bunny was standing at her locker looking lovelier than ever as I came through the northeast entrance to Washington High School.

"Hi, Bunny," I said boldly, making eye contact as she looked up from whatever she was doing inside her locker.

Bunny's eyes lit up, and that patented smile that make guys crazy appeared on her pretty face. "Hi," she replied ever-so-sweetly as I continued past her locker, not taking my eyes from hers and bumping into someone in the congested hallway.

I clumsily came to an abrupt halt and looked to see to whom I should direct my apologies. A familiar feeling quickly spread through my being at the realization of who was standing before me.

Rodney Skylark looked taller than I remembered as I looked up into his face. His eyes were almost jet black, and boring into me with the intensity of lasers powered by a power plant of anger emanating from his dark soul.

"Hi, Rod," I squeaked.

After all the work I had done to make myself into something just short of a Greek god, I was still unable to get past the fear and function like a man—at least, how I thought a man was supposed to function.

"Hi, punk," Rodney returned as he gave me a two-handed

push to the chest. "What do you think you're doing, talking to Bunny?"

"I, uh, was just saying hi," I stammered.

Rodney grabbed a handful of jersey and pushed me up against the lockers. "Keep away from Bunny. You don't even look at her if you want to live a long and natural life."

I did not know what Rodney meant by "a long and natural life," but I was sure I didn't want to find out.

I didn't say anything. I just stood against the locker, shaking. Rodney gave me a shove as he released his grip from my jersey. With one last glare, he turned and took Bunny by the hand as she closed her locker, and the two of them walked down the hall.

After all that time, I thought that the fear was gone and the days of terror were behind me. Wrong. Nothing had changed. I was still the same big good-for-nothing chicken-livered coward I'd always been.

I tried to gather my composure as I headed for my first class of the new school year as a sophomore at Washington High School.

For the next couple of days, I just went through the motions as the reality of my lack of progression sank in. School held no particular interest for me. Football practice was a chore. With one little experience in the hall, all that I cared about was gone. I had no respect for myself, and I couldn't see how anyone else could have any respect for me either.

"Smith!" Coach Saunders barked. "What in the blazes is wrong with you?"

I picked myself off the ground after being leveled by Levitz, allowing the running back to get into the secondary unmolested.

"Get over here, Smith," Coach Saunders demanded as he waved in my replacement and blew his whistle to get the scrimmage back underway.

"Coach Wurthlin wants to see you in his office after practice," the mystified assistant coach said without emotion as I reached his side at the edge of the practice field.

Great. Now I'm off the team, I deduced as I stood there dejectedly, looking at the ground as my throat tightened and my stomach began to ache. My life was over. I started thinking about Moon Pies and Twinkies.

After practice, I found myself freshly showered and changed back into street clothes, standing tall in front of the coach's cubicle. I knocked twice on the wall locker.

"Yo," came the upbeat voice of the coach of our junior varsity football team. "Enter."

I pulled back the curtain, slipped into Coach Wurthlin's office, stood in front of his desk, and waited as he finished putting some files away. He looked up.

"Smith." He greeted me with a somber smile. "Take a seat." The coach gestured toward the chair as he swept pencil shavings off his desk into his hand and then brushed them into the waste basket.

Coach Wurthlin looked deep into my eyes as I sat in front of him. "What's wrong?" he asked, not wasting any time.

I couldn't speak. My throat got tight, my stomach was churning, and I just wanted to hide.

The coach sat back in his chair, his countenance softening, and waited for my reply.

I tried to speak, but what was I going to say? That I was afraid of my own shadow and didn't want to live and that for the last year or more, I'd been living a lie? My throat got even tighter, and I could feel all the same old pain and frustrations welling up inside me like some kind of alien that had possessed my body and was trying to get out. I gasped for air, and then the dam broke. I sat there sobbing like a little baby, totally out of control.

The coach just let me be for a few moments and then pushed a box of tissues over in my direction. He assumed his relaxed position in his chair, waiting for me to regain my composure.

I grabbed a couple of tissues and quickly wiped my eyes and nose, feeling like a complete good-for-nothing piece-of-garbage wimp. I was starting to get angry with myself.

My sobbing under control, I just looked at the floor.

"What's wrong, John?" The coach was speaking softly.

I looked up, and I told him. "I'm a coward."

"Care to explain?"

I told him everything, from my early experiences with bullies and how I worked hard to get in shape and how badly I wanted to play football and how I was still terror-stricken whenever I was confronted by Rodney Skylark.

The coach listened intently as I babbled on about what a loser I was.

"You know, John, you're not the only one who's had to deal with fear," Coach Wurthlin began once I had finished my sad tale. "Fear is an emotion that warns of possible danger. Fear lets us know that we need to use our best judgment before advancing or retreating. Fear shouldn't control us. It can be a powerful tool, and as with all powerful tools, we must be in control of it." He paused for a moment. "If we let fear control us, we will always be the victim. As hard as it may sound, you must push through the fear. You must do whatever is needed, or right, no matter what the fear may be telling you. Fear will always tell you to run. That's its job. It's our duty to ourselves to use our brains to determine whether fear should be heeded or simply noted before doing what we have to do. We should never dismiss the fear, but we shouldn't let it rule us, either." Coach paused again. "Any of this making sense?" he wanted to know as he gave me a hard look.

I managed a nod.

"Let me tell you a story," the coach continued again. "When I was over in 'Nam there was this guy in our platoon who was really mean. In fact, he was more than just mean. He was an evil kind of mean, and he was big—strong, too. We called him Kong. I once saw him tip over a jeep. All of us were afraid of him. He was always bullying someone. He especially liked to pick on me because he knew I was scared to death of him. Whenever he would come around, I would freeze up. One day, we were out in town and Kong had a few too many drinks. He wandered into a small school building and began terrorizing the place. The children were screaming, and I could hear him smashing things. I stuck my head through the door and saw him begin to lock and load his M-16. I was never more scared in my life, but I knew I couldn't let Kong do whatever it was he was going to do. Somehow I managed to push the fear aside. I ran into the room and tackled him before he was able to fire his weapon. He beat the daylights out of me, but he left the kids alone. After that, I made it a point never to let fear rule over me again. No telling what might have happened to those kids if I had caved in to the fear."

Coach Wurthlin sat back again in his chair, pausing a moment for his story to sink in.

"What about Kong?" I asked. "Did he still pick on you?"

"Some," the coach replied. "But it didn't bother me like it did before. I was still afraid, but I made it a point to stand up to him. After a while, he left me alone."

"I stood up to Rodney Skylark once."

"What happened?" the coach wanted to know as his eyes squinted slightly.

"I punched him in the nose, and then he beat me silly." I replied.

"How did you feel?"

I stopped to think for a moment. "It felt really good," I answered sincerely. "But then I was scared to death again."

The coached sat quietly for a moment or two before speaking again. "John, fear is something you have to deal with each and every time it shows itself. It's like a fire. If you continue to throw logs on it, it will get bigger and bigger until it's completely out of control. You have to stop throwing logs on the fire. You have to stand up to the fear. You have to gain control."

"You mean I need to stand up to Rodney Skylark?" I asked in a small, husky voice as my throat began to tighten again.

"Now don't get me wrong," Coach Wurthlin quickly tried to explain. "Standing up to the fear does not mean that you have to take Rodney Skylark on and get your butt kicked. It means you get the fear under control and do what you need to do."

I left the coach's office still a bit confused. Standing up to the fear made sense, but didn't that mean I needed to stand up to Rodney too? I wasn't sure how I was going to handle the Rodney Skylark situation, but I was determined to stop letting my fears run my life.

CHAPTER EIGHTEEN

That very next morning, I awoke from a dream. I had scored the winning touchdown. It had been a few days since my subconscious mind allowed me to believe in myself enough to dream again.

I kicked my feet over the side of my bed and sat up, trying to get my bearings. The euphoria of being the hero in my dream quickly slipped away with the realization of what the day's agenda held. I had made the decision that no matter what the consequence, I was not going to let anyone, including Rodney Skylark, push me around any longer. I gritted my teeth and got ready for school. I was still afraid, but I was even more fed up and tired of hating myself for my lack of courage. I knew that Rodney could hurt me, but was it so much different from getting creamed by a headhunting offensive lineman almost twice my size?

The last couple of days, ever since the incident with Rodney, I entered school at the south entrance to avoid confrontation. Not this time I decided. I headed straight for the northeast entrance, where Rodney would meet Bunny at her locker and then walk her to class. I figured if I was going to lick this fear thing and since Rodney wasn't going to go away, I might as well not prolong the inevitable.

The fear was raging through my body, but the self-loathing that came with listening to it wouldn't let me turn away. I took a deep breath, pulled the door open, and entered the building. No Bunny, and no Rodney Skylark lurking around her locker.

"Rodney must have gotten the word that I was looking for him," I said to myself as I sauntered past Bunny's locker and turned the corner, heading for algebra class. Relief flooded through my body.

The feelings of relief were stopped short. Right there in the middle of the hall was Rodney, with several of the varsity football players playing keep-away with some poor freshman's briefcase. Briefcases may be an organized, as well as convenient way of dealing with all of a guy's papers and books and things, but it's like carrying a big neon sign that's says "I'm a nerd! Come beat me up and have some fun at my expense."

I tried to slip around Rodney and his friends, but the flying briefcase was deflected and landed at my feet. I instinctively bent over and picked it up. The freshman was standing within a few feet of me with a pitiful, scared, and forlorn expression on his face. I looked at Rodney Skylark and then tossed the briefcase to the freshman, who caught it and ran for all he was worth down the hall.

I could have run too. The fear in my stomach said I should. But I wasn't listening. I stood there, looking Rodney Skylark right in the eye. I didn't glare at him. I didn't try to embellish some sort of false bravado. I just stood there, looking at Rodney, waiting for him to make his move.

"I can't believe you just did that," Rodney exclaimed as anger flashed in his eyes.

I was shaking like a leaf, and I don't think I've ever felt more fear than I did right at that moment.

Rodney walked over to where I was standing, looking me

over carefully. "You must have had your Wheaties today," he said as he reached up to grab my shirt.

I roughly pushed his hand away, still looking him right in the eye as every fiber of my body was telling me to run. Run like the wind. After all the exercise I'd been getting, it just might have been possible to outrun these guys, especially with the massive amounts of adrenaline that was being pumped through my veins.

Rodney's eyes grew large in disbelief, and then the anger was back. He tore into me like a whirlwind, and I fought back with all my might and strength. I don't know what happened next exactly except the two of us ended up rolling around on the shiny hallway floor. Rodney was strong, but not so strong that he overpowered me. I was surprised to find that I was holding my own fairly well. Hands grabbed me and pulled me to my feet. Rodney's varsity football buds were holding me. Rodney jumped to his feet and hit me square in the gut. I saw it coming and flexed my stomach muscles as hard as I could. The blow hurt, but it didn't knock my wind out. All those hours of sit-ups and leg lifts had paid off. Rodney stepped back after he hit me. As he did so, I brought my foot up and planted the toe of my Converse low-cut white tenny runners, that were all the rage, right up into his private parts.

Washington High's star quarterback keeled over, grabbing his knees in obvious discomfort. I kicked again, hitting him in the chest, catching him off balance, and down to the floor he went. After that, it got kind of hazy. Something hit me over the head, and then the rest of Rodney's buddies worked me over pretty good. Some teachers came and broke it up. I got to my feet and was directed to the office for a visit with the principal. I sat just outside the principal's domain in an area reserved for unruly students such as myself and Rodney and his six buddies, waiting for a turn with Mrs. Kingston.

"John, what the heck was going on out there?" Mrs. Kingston asked, obviously distressed about the situation.

"Just a little misunderstanding," I said as I continued to dab the blood from my nose and mouth. I didn't tell Mrs. Kingston anything. It wouldn't have done any good.

"Go to class," she commanded, exasperated at my lack of cooperation.

I walked out of the office past Rodney and his friends, who sputtered threats under their breaths. The fear was still there.

My classes were uneventful for the most part other than chemistry class. Fred slipped a lit Bunsen burner under Mr. Chemstock's metal chair. Got a lot of laughs and we learned a few new words, but I didn't enjoy it like I might have. My stomach was tied in knots all day.

Practice was better. I was determined to get on with my life. I would deal with my problems when they presented themselves and not let them deter me from what I wanted—football and Bunny. Besides, if I really wanted Bunny, I was going to have to deal with Rodney sometime.

The rest of the week was fairly uneventful. I came in contact with Rodney twice, and both times, he merely sneered at me in passing. Practices went well, and I was assigned a starting position as defensive end. I was pumped.

"Okay, load up," Coach Saunders bellowed in his good-natured way.

All fifty of us scrambled aboard the large yellow bus with most of our gear, wearing our uniforms. We were playing Cleveland High just a couple of miles south. Cleveland was a lot like Washington. The neighborhood was old, and most of the kids were lower-to low-middle-income types.

I sat with Fred and Gary and most of the linemen at the back of the bus. We had a great time on the short trip over, with Fred telling us jokes and singing his rendition of Cleveland's fight song.

"Oh, I'm a stinking Bronco,
I hang out in the bars,
I wear my father's dresses,

And smoke my mom's cigars."

Everybody was fit to be tied with laughter. Fred had a couple of more verses that were a tad bit colorful, so I won't repeat them. They were very funny, though, and most appreciated by our team.

Once at Cleveland's stadium, it was all business. The coaches had us doing our stretching and warm-ups as soon as we were off the bus and on the field. We were all excited, especially me. I'd always hoped I would play football, but part of me didn't think it would ever happen. But it was happening. I was in uniform, getting ready for my first game, and I was starting.

We did our warm-ups and stretches down at one end of the field while the Cleveland players occupied the other.

Parents and a few students began to find seats in the stands under the roof on the east side. Cleveland's cheerleaders were already hard at it, jumping and gyrating to the sounds of their pep band. Our junior varsity cheerleading squad was practicing some of their moves while our intermediate pep band tuned their instruments on the opposite side of the field. Our fans were relegated to a set of worn-out bleachers with no roof. The game was to start at four thirty and be over by about seven. The varsity would play at seven thirty on the same field. The sun was still shining, the air was warm, and we were ready for football.

The captains from each team were summoned to the field, and the coin was flipped. Heads was our call, and heads it was. We chose to go on offense first, and our receiving team took the field. I nervously found my spot. Morris Henry, the fastest guy on the team, positioned himself on the fifteen-yard line to receive the kickoff. The pep band was making a lot of racket while the cheerleaders were attempting a cheer. The kicker's hand went up, signaling to the refs that he was ready. The whistle blew, and the kicker approached the ball as the line of Cleveland defenders surged forward.

The kick was a bit of a line drive that bounced once before Morris gathered it in at the twenty-yard line. I quickly moved into position with my comrades to help create a wedge for Morris to run into. Number Forty-Three was coming up fast with his sights on Morris as our speedy ball carrier came up the middle of the field. I made a slight adjustment in my angle, turned on my afterburners, lowered my head, and drove into Forty-Three with all my might. Down we went. I looked up to see Morris being pummeled by several Cleveland players on about the thirty-six. A sixteen-yard return. Not bad, but not really great, either. But man, what a rush.

I jumped up and ran off the field as the offense came in. After a brief huddle, they lined up at the line of scrimmage. "Twenty-two, thirty-one, hut, hut!" shouted Ryan Long, our steady but unspectacular quarterback. The ball was shoved into his hands, and he turned to his right and handed the ball to Morris, who slipped through a crease in the line and was met by a linebacker for a three-yard gain. Next, Ryan took the snap, dropped back three steps, and fired a quick one to Bill Wringley on the flank for another three-yard pickup. It was third and four. Ryan rolled out like he was going to pass, and then turned it up the middle for the first down. We continued to nickel-and-dime it down the field until our drive stalled on their thirty-three-yard line. Our field goal kicker was not overly talented, so a punt was called, and our punting team took the field, which included me. I lined up in the tight-end position. My job was to hold off their linebacker or whoever it was who lined up opposite me until the ball had been successfully punted and then get down field and hurt someone. The punt was short and fielded on the twelve. I let my man slip away once I sensed the punt had occurred and started toward the ball carrier. Before I could get to him, the second-to-fastest guy on our team, a safety named George Simmons, had nailed him. George was fast, but he couldn't catch a football to save his soul. Hence, he was a safety, and a pretty good one too. The ball was placed on the sixteen.

I stayed on the field as players were shuffled in and out. We took our positions on defense as the other team huddled.

"Ready, break." Eleven players broke their huddle and quickly assumed their positions at the line of scrimmage.

"Hut one," called out their tall skinny quarterback as I sized up the guy facing me.

Number Seventy-Six was a big kid, probably going two hundred and twenty. But he wasn't very tall for that much weight, and most of it was around his middle.

"Seventy-three," the Cleveland quarterback continued.

We were expecting a run-off tackle for the first play, so I was to simply tie up my man and allow the linebackers and safeties to fill the gaps and make the tackle.

"Red fifty-three," barked the quarterback.

Something was up. I could see it in the eyes of my man.

"Two." The center snapped the ball back to the quarterback as the whole line pulled to their right, my left. I leaped from my stance, but Seventy-Six wasn't in position for me to lock him up. In fact, if I were to make contact, it could be called a block in the back, as he was moving sideways away from me. The quarterback was moving behind a wall of blockers laterally with the running back slightly ahead to either take the pitch or make a block.

I was now in the backfield, but being several yards behind the play, I didn't have much of a chance to help out. I ran hard just the same, as I was coached to do. "You never quit on a play," Coach Wurthlin had beaten into our heads. "You never know how a play might go."

Our outside line moved laterally with theirs as our linebacker and safety were stringing the play out, not allowing a gap for the quarterback to slip through. At the last instant, he pitched the ball to the running back as he attempted to duck into the wall of defenders only to bounce back a step.

The little running back, with nowhere to go, turned and began to run in the other direction.

At that very instant, I realized why it was so important to never quit on a play, even though it might appear to be out of reach, as I met their ball carrier head-on at full speed. I don't think he realized I was there. I hit him hard and square, and the two of us went down in a heap. He managed to hang on to the ball, but he was a bit slow getting up. I ran over to our side for a brief defensive huddle amid excited pats on the back and "atta boys" from our pumped-up defense. A defensive alignment was called, and we took our places. We were to stay home again, but be ready for a pass.

Again the ball was placed into their quarterback's hands, and this time, he handed it to their running back, who attempted to go up the middle, but was met by Gary for no gain. Gary had worked hard and was really starting to look like a football player.

It was now third and fourteen on their own twelve. They had to get at least five yards to give their punter some room. They lined up with two tight ends. It looked as if they would try to power it forward for whatever they could get and then punt, but I just had a funny feeling again that something was up. My responsibility in this situation was to try to drive my man back, or at least hold him steady so the linebackers could stop the run through the creases. On a pass play, I was supposed to go after the quarterback. But if I went for the quarterback and it turned out to be a run, there would be a huge hole for the ball carrier to go through.

"Hut, hut." The ball was placed firmly into the hands of the Cleveland quarterback, who turned to hand it to their running back, who was surging forward. I couldn't see exactly what happened next since I was tied up with my man and there were a lot of bodies all around, but I still sensed that something was up. The linebacker who should have been plugging the gap between Levitz and me wasn't there. I looked to my left, still fighting with the large, portly lineman, and could see a surge of bodies going in that direction. I was able to slip off my opponent and found myself in the backfield in time to see the football floating directly in front of me. I instinctively threw myself headlong toward the falling ball with out stretched hands. The football fell gently into my mitts, and somehow I managed to hang on to it as I hit the ground and then curled up into a ball to protect myself as a half a dozen bodies plopped all over me.

Our ball. Man, I never felt so good in all my life as the ref placed the ball on the nine-yard line and pointed in the direction of the Cleveland goal posts. I wasn't sure what had happened. The quarterback, I guess, had rolled to his right after pulling the ball and was trying to get off a pass, but someone got a hand on it and deflected it my direction. I jogged off the field to the cheers of our little crowd and enthusiastic cheerleaders, one of which was Bunny. I caught her eye before being enveloped by my teammates and coaches, who all had to hug me and slam me around. She was smiling, and her eyes had that twinkle grown men would die for.

We ran the ball to the outside twice, setting up a three-yard hammer play up the middle by our stout fullback Joel Kimber for the score. Joel was strong as an ox, with good quickness. The rest of the game was a bit of a defensive struggle. That chubby Cleveland lineman gave me all I wanted—for the most part. He kept me from making any more spectacular plays. I did, however, manage to keep their running back from getting by me, tackling him several times, and I got into the backfield and hurried the quarterback's throw now and then, clobbering him good each time. All in all, it was a very good first game. We won 12 to 7. We scored the other touchdown on a thirty-five-yard pass to Bill Wringly.

The bus ride home was great, as all of us were pumped from our first win. The coach, however, burst our bubble somewhat once we got inside our own locker room.

"It was a win." Coach Wurthlin paused, gathering his thoughts. "And that's good. We'll take it. You played hard. Cleveland, however, isn't exactly the cream of the crop. Next week, we have Grant, and they're gonna be tough. We can beat them, but only if we play our best game. They like to throw the ball, and they're darn good at it. We'll have to play smart on defense, and we're gonna have to score more than twelve points if we want to be in this game. We'll go over all this on Monday."

Even though the coach had brought us back to reality, I still felt pretty darn good about my first game. I had played well, and there was that look from Bunny right after my interception that set up our first touchdown.

At home, I just had to share our success with someone. Mom had that glazed look in her eye that she gets whenever I try to talk to her, and gave me a "That's nice" after each pause in my animated oral report. So, I gave Greg a call, but there was no answer. Greg and his family were no doubt sticking around to watch Tom play. Tom was a senior now, and the star running back. The year before, Scappoose finished third in the state in the 2A bracket. This year, the word was that they might go all the way.

I guessed I could go to the dance. There was a dance after each game, but I never felt comfortable at those things even though I had been practicing my James Brown moves and looking pretty good if I do say so myself.

I considered hopping on my bike and heading for Sauvie Island, but I decided to start out first thing in the morning.

I went downstairs to my sanctuary, threw on the *The Animalization of the Animals* album, flopped into my big easy chair, and began to reflect. Life was good. For the first time in my entire life, I felt like my destiny was in my own hands.

CHAPTER NINETEEN

I spent that weekend swapping exaggerated stories with Greg. The river was still warm, and we took advantage of it.

Monday morning, I was back in my first-period biology class. I felt good. I felt in control. I still had to deal with Rodney and I was certain that meant another confrontation or two or three, but it wasn't bothering me nearly as much as it had. I guess I was just getting used to the idea of taking him on. Actually, the last time, I did better than hold my own against him. If it wasn't for his buddies, I would have mopped up the hall with him, eaten his lunch, kissed his girl, taken his dog home and . . .

"Hi, John," greeted an angelic-sounding voice interrupting my thoughts. It was Shirley Thompson, one of Bunny's friends. "Is it okay if I sit here?" she asked seductively as she placed her books on the desk next to mine. Shirley was a very attractive girl—maybe even more so than Bunny, if that was possible.

"Sure," I said a bit coolly. Shirley had never given me the time of day or even noticed me except for that time back in the fifth grade when I got worked over by a mob of fifth and sixth graders out on the Buckman field. It was hard for me to let that go. I had forgiven Bunny for snickering because I felt that she really didn't find it all that amusing and because, well, she was Bunny. But Shirley, on the other hand, had really seemed to enjoy herself that day.

Shirley sat down at the desk next to mine, letting her mini skirt ride up her thigh without attempting any pretense at modesty. Now, don't get me wrong—I was duly impressed by her long, shapely legs and all, but besides feeling mighty uncomfortable, I wasn't buying it. She had to want something, and I didn't think it was me.

"I saw you play Friday and was very impressed," Shirley cooed.

Maybe it *was* me she wanted. It could happen.

"Thanks," I said, starting to squirm.

"I didn't see you at the dance," Shirley purred as her big brown eyes gave me that come-hither look. "I was hoping to get a dance."

Shirley was hoping to get a dance—with me? Since when did Shirley Thompson care one whit about me?

"Why?" I asked, totally dumbfounded.

Shirley was taken aback somewhat at that simple and direct one-syllable question. "Well, John, I know that we haven't been exactly friends, but I would like to change that," she replied, recovering her composure nicely.

"Why, Shirley, do you care about me all of a sudden? Ever since the fifth grade, the most you have ever done to acknowledge my existence was an occasional smirk or sneer in my general direction."

"I know I haven't behaved very well toward you, but things are different now." Shirley's smile was strained.

"What's so different now?" I needed to know.

"Well, you have to admit that you've changed quite a bit," she said as her pretty red lips turned back into a full smile.

A lesser man would have wilted, but I was having none of it. For some strange reason, Shirley Thompson was easy to resist. Yes, she was beautiful, with just the right amount of everything in all the right places, but that was all there was. There was no twinkling mystery in her eyes like Bunny's. There was no soft, playful shine in her eyes like, well, gulp, Sally's. There was nothing, and if the eyes are the windows to the soul, Shirley Thompson was in trouble.

"I have?" I knew that I had made changes in my appearance and abilities and I guess social stature, now that I think about it, but I was still the same guy who was singled out and used by the elite of my peers for their sick amusement. Life hadn't been much fun because of people like Shirley and her friends. Yes, I had changed on the outside, but I was still that same guy she used to snicker and sneer at.

"You certainly have," Shirley continued. "Everyone is saying that you're the best player on the JV team."

My jaw dropped open. What was she talking about? The best player on the team? My head starting spinning.

"Really?" I looked into her big, beautiful brown eyes. I did have a pretty good game.

"Okay, class, open your books to chapter three," instructed Mrs. Clark, our biology teacher.

I had trouble concentrating on the lecture. Apparently, word was going around that I was the best player on the team. I sat there and analyzed the whole situation. It was hard for me to believe that I was seen as the best. Yes, I had made some nice plays and yes, I worked hard and tried to make something happen on every play. And it was true that nobody got past me on the line. And I had made life tough on the quarterback whenever he dropped back to pass. And I had started to assert myself somewhat as a vocal leader on defense as the game went on. Well, maybe Shirley did know what she was talking about.

I looked at Shirley sitting next to me, her long legs exposed. She was something to look at. She turned and smiled that award-winning smile I had seen many times over the years. This was the first time it was directed at me. She had used that same smile to rope in every boy who was at or near the top of the food chain. The first one I remember was Mike Stevens in the fifth grade. Mike was actually a nice guy. He was the first boy to have underarm hair and could whup every boy at Buckman by the time he was in the seventh grade. He was the only guy Joey Aardema and Many Garcia left alone. Then there was Tom Halsey. Tom was a good-looking guy all the girls liked. Next was Jim Bishop, the quarterback of our seventh grade flag-football team. After that it was Blaine Arson, the lead singer in the band that used to play at our dances. There were others, and everyone was sort of the happening guy for the moment. I guessed Shirley must be thinking that I was the new happening guy and wanted to stake her claim while the staking was good. Then she could dispose of me when someone better came along.

Whew—all this was new to me. On the one hand, I was flattered. No, not just flattered—overwhelmed that Shirley thought I was worthy of her attention. Then again, on the other hand, I didn't much care for her. I hadn't seen anything that told me she had changed at all. She hadn't even looked my way the first few days of school. Now I was worthy of her attention because I'd had a good game? I was worthy because I was no longer a butterball, but had transformed myself into something resembling a Greek god? I was worthy because I was the hottest commodity this side of Roman Gabriel and the Los Angeles Rams? What would happen if I had a bad game? Chances were pretty good that someone was going to whup my butt before the season was over. Then what?

The bell rang, and Mrs. Clark gave us our reading assignment as we gathered up our books.

"John, would you like to walk me to my next class?" Shirley asked, smiling sweetly.

I looked into her cool, calculating but beautiful big brown eyes.

"Sorry, Shirley. I've got to get to study hall before all the good desks are taken," I replied with a hint of a fake smile as I gathered up my stuff and turned toward the door. Not very nice, but it was the best I could do with all the hurt from the past fighting to get to the surface.

All the rest of the day, I thought about what Shirley had said. I was the best player on the team. Was I? That was very hard for me to believe. But after breaking everything down, I guess I might have had the best game and was pretty conspicuous with all the guys pounding me after each successful play. I was pumped. Whether I was the best player, which I still doubted, or not, it was true that I had come a long way. It was also true that I could go even farther. I was ready to get to work and make it happen.

Practice went well. Shirley had helped me to get reenergized and refocused. I was determined to be the best I could possibly be. I practiced as hard as I could all week long. I worked extra hard in the weight room and ran several miles after each practice and finished each workout with forty-yard sprints until I could barely walk.

Friday rolled around, and our bus rolled onto Grant's expansive campus. We piled off the bus and promptly got our butts whupped. The coach was right. Grant was good. They beat us 30 to 17. I lined up against their big tackle, and he had his way with me all game long. My legs felt like rubber, which didn't help. I learned a little something about preparing for a game—you have to be rested. I should have backed off on the extra running. Oh, well. I'm not sure it would have made that much difference. Their offensive line averaged over two-forty and were pretty good athletes. I hated to think what their varsity offensive line was like.

We sat with our heads down as the coach stood in front of us for our postgame butt-chewing.

Coach Wurthlin stood quietly for a moment or two before

beginning. He spoke calmly, without anger. It wasn't what we expected.

"Do you know how Grant was able to beat us like that?" he asked us in an almost kindly sort of way.

Most of us raised our heads ever so slightly to see what the coach was up to, as we sat in our locker room with our grass and bloodstained gear still on.

"Number one." The coach paused. "They believed. Number two, they wanted it. And number three, they were prepared. Those guys played like a machine, every part working with perfect precision. What happens to a machine when one or two parts are doing their own thing? It doesn't perform properly, does it? It might even break down completely.

"Now," the coach continued, "next week we play Lincoln. Lincoln isn't quite the team Grant is, but they are well coached, and I can guarantee you that they will be ready to play. We have the necessary components on this team to be successful." The coach was becoming somewhat animated at this point. "If we play like a machine where everyone performs his assignment with precision, I don't think there's a team left on our schedule we can't beat."

We were all listening very intently now, every eye on the coach.

"Are you with me?" the coach roared.

We all sprang to our feet, screaming our commitment to our young coach and to each other.

"Are you ready to play with precision?" the coach demanded as loudly as he could.

More yelling and fist-pumping in the affirmative.

"Are you ready to play as a team and win some football games?" He was literally screaming now.

With that, we were all completely delirious, ready to jump off a cliff if that's what it took.

Saturday morning bright and early, I pulled into Greg's

yard on my loaded-down ten-speed. Greg's mom directed me back behind the barn, where I found Greg and Tom hitting the weights.

"Hey," I hollered as I hopped off my bike, letting it fall to the ground.

"Hey," Greg responded as he spotted Tom on the bench.

Tom pushed up with all his might, forcing the air from his lungs, as he fully extended his arms. Greg guided the bar back on the rests.

"All right!" Greg congratulated. "That's two hundred and eighty pounds, a personal best."

Tom shook his arms out, acting like it was no big deal.

"How 'bout you, John? Whatcha got?" Tom looked at me in a challenging way.

"Well, let me get warmed up a little bit first," I demanded.

"Warm away," Tom said in his patented condescending way.

"What you bench?" I asked, looking at Greg as I took several plates off the bar.

Greg had been making good, steady gains since we first started lifting together back in grade school.

"One eighty even," Greg replied with pride.

"Not bad." Not bad indeed since he was still weighing under one fifty.

I loosened up some and then did a few light reps with a hundred and thirty-five pounds. I got up and shook it off as I instructed Tom to put another forty-five-pound plate on his side. I did the same. My best had been one ninety before the season started and I hadn't maxed out since, but I had kept working the bench, doing sets with one hundred and eighty-five pounds.

"Two hundred and twenty-five pounds," Tom stated as Greg looked on skeptically.

I got under the bar, feeling a bit anxious. I sucked in massive amounts of air and blew it out a couple of times as I gripped and regripped the bar. I pushed and the bar came off the rest. I let it drop fairly quickly to my chest, hoping to get a little bounce. Once the bar hit my chest, I pushed with all my might in the opposite direction. The weights went up, and I placed it back in the rests with Greg's guidance. A personal best. Two hundred and twenty-five pounds.

"That went up too easy," Tom declared. "Shake it off while I put five more on each side."

"Two hundred and twenty-five pounds isn't enough?" I asked somewhat incredulously.

"No. It's never enough," Tom woofed. "You can always do better."

"Okay," I said as I prepared myself for a go at two hundred and thirty-five pounds.

Again, I slid into place under the bar. This time, Tom positioned himself to do the spotting. As before, I gripped and regripped the bar and sucked air in and blew air out until I was ready.

"Okay," I said as I pushed up. Tom pulled and guided the bar into position over me. I paused for a moment and then let it drop. It bounced off my chest, and I pushed with all I had. The bar went up about three-fourths of the way and slowed down to almost a stop. I continued to push with all I had. The bar moved ever so slowly. I was beginning to stall as Tom reached down to the bar, touching it lightly, and shouted, "Push."

The bar went up, and Tom guided it into the rests.

I jumped up from where I had been struggling. "Did you pull it up?" I demanded, hopping around, all full of testosterone-driven fury.

Tom backed off, raising both hands and arms to half-mast in a passive manner. "No way, man. It was all yours."

"Two hundred and thirty-five pounds, you stud you!" Greg shouted.

I stopped prancing around at the realization of what I had

just done. I had just benched more than anyone on our JV team except Gary, who had been working very hard and weighed over three hundred pounds and was a year older.

"I'm a stud," I gushed, not caring how goofy I sounded.

"That's right. I told you that if you just followed my plan, you'd get there," Tom replied, taking full credit for my studly progression.

"Hey, let's weigh in," Greg suggested.

We hadn't weighed in for several months. We strolled over to the scale in the barn. Greg went first.

"One hundred and forty-nine," Tom announced as he balanced the scale.

"That's five pounds more than the last time," Greg exclaimed.

"Okay, John," Tom directed.

I hopped on the floor scale that had weighed many a steer before they went to market. Tom made the adjustments until the scale was balanced.

"One hundred and ninety-three pounds," Tom announced.

"Man," I said with disgust. "I weigh exactly the same as I did in the eighth grade."

"John, you're forgetting that you're now a couple of years older, most of the fat has been turned to muscle, and you're taller." With that, Tom ushered us over to the wall where we kept our heights recorded. We stood next to our old marks as Tom laid a board on our heads and made new ones with some chalk.

Greg was now five foot seven, which pleased him immensely. He had grown four inches in a little over two years.

"Five foot ten even," Tom declared with satisfaction. "John, you only have two inches to go to reach your goal as the ultimate stud."

It was true—I hadn't lost a single pound, but what I was

carrying was pretty firm, and there was no longer a big belly hanging over my belt. Two more inches, and I'd reach my goal. I was only fifteen and three-quarters and figured I would grow some more easy enough. Besides, I must not be looking too bad to have a girl of Shirley Thompson's stature taking an interest.

CHAPTER TWENTY

All week long, the team was on the same page. We practiced hard and we listened to the coaches. I don't know what happened exactly. I guess the loss to Grant got us thinking. Just because we were part of the Washington High School legacy didn't mean that all we had to do was show up. By the time Friday rolled around, we were more focused than I thought was possible.

It was our first home game. The student body, friends, and family would be out in force. We were ready.

"Okay," the coach said quietly once the hubbub of the locker room quieted down. "Lincoln is out there on our field right now, thinking they are gonna come in here and kick our butts." He paused for effect. "You have worked hard all week. You're playing good football. If you remember your assignments and responsibilities, stay together, work together, and give your best effort, Lincoln will learn real quick what it takes to kick our butts—and they ain't got it!"

With that, we went crazy. A rabid dog couldn't match our enthusiasm.

We took our position on the field, the captains at the front, preparing to dash through the paper banner being held by our junior varsity cheerleaders.

The signal was given, the junior band blasted our school song, and through the banner we ran to the cheers of the home crowd. We followed the team captains down around the far end zone and then back to where the coach was standing. "The Star-Spangled Banner" was played, and the coin was tossed. The kickoff team took its place on one end, and I lined up with my teammates, stretching across the width of the field, on the other. Our kicker placed the ball down and assumed the position with his hand in the air. The whistle blew, and we all surged forward, being careful to stay in line with the kicker as his foot found the ball. Then off we went.

The kick was high, giving us time to get downfield. I ran as hard as I could toward the Lincoln kick returner, who had scooped up the ball after one bounce on the twenty-five-yard line. I got downfield quickly and slipped through their wedge of blockers. Next thing I knew, I ran headlong into Lincoln's number Thirty-Five, who was attempting to help clear a path for the Lincoln running back. I was bigger than he was and had a good head of steam up. I bowled him over, but lost my balance as their speedy little return man came running through the gap that I was supposed to be filling.

I hit the ground hard, stretching out to my right, trying to grab whatever I could as he ran by. I managed to get my hand on a foot. It was enough to trip him up. Several of our guys pounced on top of him as he went down. We jumped up, pounding each other in celebration. It was Lincoln's ball on their thirty-eight-yard line.

Lincoln liked to run the ball. They had a big strong fullback and a speedy little running back they used to move the ball fairly successfully. They could pass, too, but preferred to run if it was working. We lined up, looking for their fullback to test our mettle up the middle. He was about five ten, one hundred and ninety pounds, and very physical. They had a good-sized offensive line, the smallest being the center at six feet and two hundred and ten, two guards at two fifteen and two twenty respectively, and two tackles weighing around two hundred and twenty-five or so each.

Number Eighty-Eight was my height, but about two twenty-five. He looked pretty fat as he took his position on the line in front of me, but Coach Saunders had warned that he was plenty strong and athletic. I got down in my three-point stance as the quarterback barked out the cadence. The ball shot back into his hands and I blasted out of my stance, as did Eighty-Eight. He tried to lock me up. I could see the quarterback turn to give the ball to the fullback as he rushed forward. I drove my legs with all my might, gaining some ground on my man as the fullback entered the crease between me and Levitt, who was playing next to me. I slipped off Eighty-Eight, grabbed the big fullback, and drove sideways, pushing him into Levitt, who assisted in tying him up as our linebacker drove head-on into him, stopping any momentum he may have had. They gained maybe a foot.

We lined up again, and again, it was the same call, this time to the other side for a two-yard gain. It was now third and eight. It was an obvious pass situation, but their running back was fast enough to go outside. The ball was snapped and I drove forward with all I had, fighting to get past the husky lineman as their quarterback backpedaled, looking for a target. I broke loose of Eighty-Eight's grasping hands and got the quarterback in my sights as he was looking to his right, starting to set his feet. I was still a good three or four yards away. I didn't think I had a chance to get to him in time, but our defensive backs must have been doing their job because he pulled the ball down and began to sprint out of the pocket that was quickly breaking down. By this time, I was close to full speed and closing the gap as their quarterback tried desperately to get out of danger. I don't think he saw me as I drove into his backside at full speed. We both went down in a heap. It was now fourth and thirteen, and they were forced to punt the ball away.

The ball was placed on our thirty-yard line where it had gone out of bounds. Our offense took the field and commenced to work the ball down the field with a series of short passes and a variety of running plays for the game's first touchdown. The game continued in similar fashion. I played great even by my own standards. As it turned out, Eighty-Eight couldn't match my quickness off the line, and I found he wasn't nearly as strong or athletic as the coach had claimed. I sacked the quarterback three times, and I must have hit him after or during the act of throwing another six or seven times, once resulting in an interception. I also assisted in several tackles of their running backs and got in the backfield to disrupt a reverse, and I picked up a fumble and ran it a few yards before being tackled by their running back. The final score was 44 to 6. They scored their lone touchdown in the fourth quarter after the coach ran the subs in.

We were pumped. We had worked hard all week, and we had listened to our coaches and did exactly what we were supposed to do. We played hard and we played with discipline. We learned what our individual responsibilities were and we executed them, trusting our teammates to do the same. We played team ball. We were a machine.

The next few weeks were similar. We now knew what we were capable of. We knew how to be successful. Our record was five and one, with two more games before the playoffs. We still had to play Jefferson. They had really good athletes, and like us, their only loss was to Grant. Franklin was the next team we faced and they were good too, having only lost close games to Jefferson and Grant.

We were winners, and we liked it. The hope that had driven me to work hard and endure had now been replaced by faith. Actually, it was more like faith bordering on knowledge. I knew that if I continued to work hard, I would get better, and I believed that if I worked hard enough, I could accomplish anything I set my sights on.

I did take time to notice in between football practice and school work and the like that the kids and even the teachers were treating me differently. Where just a few weeks prior, I had been just another nondescript kid without a name or a face, I was now . . . uh, what's the word? Popular?

Being suddenly popular gave me reason for reflection. Was I different? Was I somehow more interesting or funny or charismatic? Did I now have worth because I could play football? Some of the very same kids who laughed when I took a beating and shunned me and made fat jokes were the ones who were coming around wanting to be my friend. On the one hand, I was flattered, but I didn't really buy it. I had a tough time letting go of the past, to embrace a new life with new friends. In fact, I really didn't want to replace my way of life or my friends. The friends I managed to make over the years were real. They liked me when I was fat and wimpy, and they still liked me now. I still liked them, even though I was on my way to accomplishing my goals of being somebody. It didn't matter. It was easy to see through Shirley Thompson and it was easy enough to see through the rest of them too. There was, however, one exception . . .

"Hi, John," Bunny greeted, smiling that smile, as I reached for a carton of milk and placed it on my tray, side stepping through the chow line. Bunny picked up a tray and slid in line next to me.

"Hi, Bunny," I returned, my knees suddenly feeling weak.

"You sure had a great game last Friday." Bunny was still smiling. "I don't think I've ever cheered so loud."

"I, . . . uh . . ." I stammered, trying to think of something to say to the most beautiful girl in the whole world.

At that moment, Rodney Skylark appeared in line next to Bunny, giving me the scowl that usually sends shivers up and down my spine. This time, however, I believe I was almost glad to see him. I think Bunny intimidated me more than Rodney did.

"Hi, Rod," Bunny greeted her boyfriend, trying to sound casual.

Rodney didn't say anything. He just glared at me as if he wanted to rip me to shreds. Which I'm sure he did, but for some reason, he didn't. I figured I could analyze that later as I got my meal together and found a spot next to Fred and Gary on the far side of the cafeteria. The three of us were gaining in popularity, it was true, but we were still relegated to the back. The seniors and other cool guys like Rodney had the front locked up, and the likes of us younger classmen had no part in it.

"Hey, I saw Bunny talking to you," Gary informed me as I sat down. "I noticed she was smiling at you, too," he added, impressing me with his obvious keen eyesight.

"You sure are observant," I said, acting like it was no big deal.

"I'm not the only observant person in this cafeteria," Gary said with a wicked grin. "Rodney was standing behind you and Bunny and saw the whole show."

My stomach sank. "So, Rodney saw me talking to Bunny. Big deal," I retorted bravely.

"He saw you smiling at each other, too," Fred added without Gary's enthusiasm. "That's probably not a good thing."

"I'll deal with Rodney," I said a bit apprehensively but determined to do just that. Why did life have to be so complicated? All I wanted to do was sweep Bunny off her feet and take her away from Rodney Skylark. What harm was there in that?

Franklin looked big. They were warming up as we got off the bus and walked through the gate onto their field. It was their homecoming, and from the looks of the scowls that were directed our way, they were ready to go. Brand-new chalk had been laid down. This was a pretty significant game, and the bleachers were filling up.

Like I said, Franklin looked big. Number Ninety was a two-hundred and sixty-pound junior who played both junior varsity and some on varsity. The junior varsity guys are allowed to play so many quarters a week on both varsity and junior varsity, and since they had this extra behemoth hanging around, they used him here and there as needed. According to Coach Saunders, they lined him up on the other team's best lineman. "That's you," he informed me.

Sure enough, the ball was put into play and we stopped their return man on the twenty-six, where we lined up ready to take on their offense. Big number Ninety lined up in front of me.

I got down in my stance. Ninety did the same, glaring at me as he did so. My job was to tie him up and allow our linebackers and safeties to plug the gaps. Franklin was a straight-ahead power team. They had a huge offensive line and a couple of physical running backs. Their quarterback was a good runner too, but not much of a passer. He didn't need to be. No team has been able to stop their offense. Grant and Jefferson were able to outscore them, but Franklin still got their points.

The ball shot into the hands of their quarterback, and Ninety came up hard. I was surprised at his quickness. He hit me as I was coming out of my stance. I was still fairly low so he couldn't stand me up, which was a good thing. He just kind of plopped on me, and down we both went as the running back came shooting through the gap. Fortunately, our linebacker was there to meet him and stopped him for a one-yard gain. Big Ninety got off me, and I jumped up and went to our defensive huddle.

"Way to stop ol' Big Ninety," hollered Joel, our stout linebacker.

Stop him? I mused to myself. He about killed me. A few

more stops like that, and they'll have to scrape me up with a spatula.

We lined up again, expecting another run since that's what they do. Sure enough, the ball was snapped, and I came out of my stance a little quicker this time and got a hold of their big lineman as he began to surge forward. Big mistake. I was a little too tall in the saddle for this big strong kid and he simply pushed right through me, falling on top of me for good measure. That hurt. I might be slow at times, but I learned very quickly that I had to keep low or he was going to kill me. Actually, he was going to kill me regardless, but when I kept low, I was able to get to his feet, and he would just plop on top of me instead of pushing me back onto my back and *then* plopping on top of me. As long as I was able to keep him at the line of scrimmage, the linebackers and safeties should be able to stop the ball carrier.

Franklin managed to work the ball down to our eighteen-yard line before I got it all sorted out.

"Hey, I'll take Ninety to the ground. You guys just make sure you're in position and make the play on their runner," I shouted to Joel and Carl, the two guys assigned to stop the ball carriers through the gaps.

Stopping Ninety meant I was going to take a lot of abuse, but I knew I could do it. I guess I could have just locked up with him and let him push me wherever he wanted, keeping my feet under me. It wouldn't hurt nearly as much, but I couldn't let him open up any creases for their running back. So a good portion of the game I was underneath Big Ninety. Franklin still managed to score twenty-four points, most of them coming from plays to the other side. We scored twenty-six.

It was a happy but somewhat subdued bus ride home. We were all beat. Franklin was a very physical football team. I knew I would be plenty sore the next couple of days.

Coach Saunders came down the aisle of the bus and gave

me a slap on the back and an approving smile. "Great game, John."

I looked up, a bit puzzled. I thought it was my worst. I had never been more dominated. "Really?" I managed in unbelief.

"Yeah, Smith. It was probably your best." Coach Saunders continued his way down the aisle, congratulating other players.

I had to think about that one for a while.

No dance again for me. I was just too beat up. The last thing I wanted to do was try and whip into my imitation of James Brown feeling like I just got hit by a Greyhound bus. Besides, Rodney Skylark would be there with his varsity football entourage. I could wait to deal with that.

CHAPTER TWENTY-ONE

Pedaling my bike up over the hill in Northwest Portland on my way to Sauvie Island and Greg's house was especially difficult. I was reminded of Big Number Ninety with each painful turn of the pedals. I didn't remember ever being that sore.

It was a typical dark and cloudy Oregon fall morning. The cool air felt good as I strained to get to the top of the hill. Early shoppers were directing their cars into the parking lot of the large Montgomery Ward store. Once at the top, I let gravity take over, picking up speed as I hurtled down the backside of the hill. I had made better time before, but the ride was rejuvenating. The cool, moist air cleared my head and the mild exercise loosened things up, making me feel almost normal.

I rode past the large container ships being loaded and unloaded. I zipped by the fortune teller's house, which was sporting a new sign, and eventually crossed the bridge and onto the island. I took the road to the left, which had become a habit recently since I had become somewhat interested in Sally Rayfield. Sally's house was just a few miles ahead. Chances of seeing her were pretty slim. It was still fairly early, and the damp and dreary conditions would probably inspire her to catch up on her sleep or tune in to some early morning cartoon shows. Bugs Bunny and company can be hard to beat on a rainy Saturday morning.

I slowed down as I approached Sally's house. I really didn't expect to see her, and frankly, part of me didn't want to. She made me feel funny, and I could never think of anything to say in her presence.

The large farmhouse seemed pretty quiet. The porch light was the only light I could see. I felt a surge of relief. I wanted to see Sally, but . . .

"Hi there," a sweet-sounding voice called to me as I cruised slowly past a small three-sided enclosure that was next to the road. There was Sally, sitting in the little school bus shack. In Western Oregon where the rain is an everyday reality, many of the rural families build little roofed enclosures so the kids can stay dry as they wait for the bus.

"Hi," I said back as I gripped the brakes, bringing the bike to a halt. Sally sat there smiling up at me. She sure looked cute, and my stomach sure felt funny.

"Nice day for a bike ride," Sally offered, still sitting there smiling.

"Well, it's kind of wet," I returned.

"Here," she said as she patted the wooden bench next to her.

I laid my bike down and sat next to her, as instructed.

We made small talk while a light drizzle continued to fall. Actually, Sally made the small talk. I just gave one-syllable replies like "yup" and "nope" and "sure."

"How is your team doing?" Sally asked.

"We're doing very well." Finally, a subject I could talk about. "We're six and one, with one more game against Jefferson. If we beat them, we go to state."

Sally coaxed more information out of me about our team and how I was doing.

"Well, I guess I'm doing pretty well," I said, trying not to sound like I was bragging. "No one has been able to handle me yet." *That might have sounded like bragging,* I thought to myself as I continued. "I'm a quarterback's worst nightmare." *That one was bragging for sure.*

Sally just smiled as I informed her of my unconquerable spirit and physical excellence. I wasn't sure if she was buying what I was selling, but she did seem to be okay with it as long as I didn't overdo it.

". . . and I believe I just may be the best thing that has ever happened to Washington High School's football program." That time, I'm pretty sure I overdid it.

"Oh, really?" Sally returned a bit skeptically, peering at me closely from squinty eyes.

"Well, maybe the next-best thing," I said, grinning sheepishly while Sally's squinty eyes bored into my soul.

She gave me a sock to the arm, smiled that great big cute smile and said, "Boy, you must be good. I'll be looking for your picture on the cover of *Sports Illustrated.*"

I started to snicker and then kind of giggle, and then Sally started to giggle. Then I started laughing out loud. The two of us laughed together for several moments. Sally seemed to have a way of exposing the real me and making me feel good in the process.

After our laughter subsided, Sally looked at me with that big smile again.

I grinned back somewhat self-consciously.

"What?" I wanted to know.

Sally's smile got even wider.

"Would you go to the Sadie Hawkins dance with me?" she asked as her eyes sparkled.

"I, uh, well . . ." I stammered, being taken completely by surprise as the sparkle from Sally's eyes began to dull. "Sure," I said, not wanting the sparkle to go out. A guy doesn't have a chance in this world. If you don't have the nerve or motivation to ask a girl out, she just waits until the annual

Sadie Hawkins dance comes around, which makes it morally ethical for the girls to ask the boys. Then she does. Who was this Sadie Hawkins, anyhow?

With that, Sally hooked her arm in mine and slid up next to me, causing all kinds of turmoil in my stomach.

"It'll be fun. We've got a great band lined up, and lots of refreshments," Sally informed me as she began to chatter along about this and that.

It appeared that I was going to next week's Sadie Hawkins dance at Scappoose High School. Just like football and many other extracurricular activities, the dance would be at Scappoose High instead at the Sauvie Island School because of the small number of students. I just had to figure out a way to get there.

I said so long to Sally, who sat beaming on the bench of her three-sided bus stop, and headed for Greg's. Greg and Tom were working out in the barn. I could hear them grunting and shouting as I parked my bike under the tree. The rain was beginning to let up, and sunlight was starting to break through the clouds as I entered the barn.

"Hey, anybody in here?" I hollered as I found my way back to the weight room.

"Yeah," Greg shouted as he helped lift the bar off Tom's chest and placed it on the L-shaped holders.

We exchanged greetings and got each other caught up on all that was going on. Tom ran for over one hundred and seventy yards and three touchdowns against Astoria, and Greg had five receptions and one touchdown with the JV team.

"How was your game?" Greg asked after he and Tom finished their reports.

"Well, the coach said it was my best game ever, but it's kind of hard for me to concur since I spent the entire game on the ground with a two-hundred-and-sixty-pound freak of nature on top of me," I said, trying to sound casual.

"It was your best game, and you spent it on the ground

with a big lineman having his way with you?" Tom wanted to know with doubt in his eyes as he and Greg both waited for an explanation.

"Well," I began, not sure what I had done that was so great myself. "Franklin is a big physical team that likes to run, and Big Number Ninety is their best lineman. I kept him from blowing holes in the line for their running backs." It was sounding pretty good, so I continued. "We held them to their lowest score this season, and they had to get their yards on the other side of the line and through the air which isn't their strength because I . . ." I paused for effect, as I was about to take credit for the entire success of our team, "was able to stop their big mean franchise lineman."

Tom still had doubts, but that was good enough for Greg.

"Aw right!" Greg shouted. "Let's pump some iron."

With that, the three of us threw the weights around like Jack LaLanne plugged into a nuclear reactor.

I told Tom and Greg about being asked to the Sadie Hawkins dance by Sally Rayfield. After they razzed me for a while, Greg admitted that he was going with Marianne Sebastian, Sally's hot three-wheeler friend. We decided that Tom and Greg should pick me up and the three of us would go to the dance together. Since Greg's and my dates weren't sixteen and we weren't either, their folks would not let them go on an actual date, so the plan was that we would meet them at the dance. Tom, on the other hand, would drop us off and then go get his date. Greg's mom would give us a ride home after the dance. We had it all worked out.

That night, the skies cleared, and Greg and I headed out, seeking adventure.

CHAPTER TWENTY-TWO

"Hey, stud," a gruff but familiar voice rang out as I walked past the boiler room door.

It was Monday morning, and I was on my way to see Coach Wurthlin before school started. He had informed all of us JV guys that he would be in his office Monday mornings before school if any of us wanted to see him.

I stopped and turned around to see Mr. Johnson's smiling face and twinkling black eyes as he came out of his janitorial sanctuary.

"You the captain of the team yet?" he wanted to know.

"Not yet, but I'm closing in on it," I said as a big smile spread across my own face. Mr. Johnson had been to every game that year. It wasn't easy for him to get to the games since most of his work took place after school was out. In fact, I was a little curious why he was at school so early.

"You're here early," I said.

"Yup, I gotta get the boiler tuned up before the cold weather gets here," he informed me. "Are you lookin' for Coach Wurthlin?"

"Yeah."

"He went for coffee and will be right back. Just go on in and wait for him," Mr. Johnson instructed me.

I went into the athletic department and waited just outside of Coach Wurthlin's cubicle. Coach Bumwack was on the telephone in the cubicle next door.

"I don't care what it costs," I heard him bellow into the phone. "I want two extra-large cheesy anchovy and smoked-oyster pizzas delivered to the athletic department of Washington High School. And I want it now!"

Yuck. The thought of anchovy and smoked-oyster pizzas for breakfast did not make my nervous stomach feel any better. I had finally made up my mind to talk to the coach about becoming a wide receiver. I had put it off for as long as I could. The season was running down, and my opportunity for a shot was dwindling. Next year, I would probably play varsity with Rodney's dad as the coach, and I had no idea how receptive he would be to me wanting to make the switch. I figured I had better get started now with Coach Wurthlin's help if I wanted any chance at all.

"Yeah, and throw on some hot peppers too," Coach Bumwack further instructed. "And make it snappy. We're hungry over here."

I could hear the phone slam as Coach Bumwack completed his call. Coach Wurthlin entered the athletic department carrying a large mug with a golden football helmet emblazoned on the side. Notre Dame.

"Morning, Smith." Coach Wurthlin smiled as he greeted me. "You here to see me?"

"Yes, sir," I said firmly. I wanted the coach to know that I was there on serious business.

"Come on in."

I slipped through the entrance as the coach settled back in his chair, sipping his coffee while giving me an expectant eye.

"Coach, I want to try out at wide receiver," I stated, getting right to the point.

Coach Wurthlin put down his mug of coffee, his brow furrowing as he gathered his thoughts. "John," he started, using my first name. "You would probably make a decent or better wide receiver, but your strength and aggressive nature make you a very valuable commodity at defensive end."

"What would I need to do to become a wide receiver?" I asked, not listening to his argument.

The coach leaned back in his chair and smiled. "Okay, John, here's what you'll have to do. You'll need to work on your speed and maneuverability. You'll need to be light and quick on your feet. You'll need to practice running routes and catching passes, and you'll need to learn all the pass plays in the varsity playbook. If you manage to improve your speed to the point where you're one of the three or four fastest guys on the team and show some good hands and learn the playbook, you might get to play. I won't be making that decision. Coach Skylark will." The coach paused for a moment. "You might want to talk to him."

"Right," I said, running over my mind what it might be like trying to convince Coach Skylark to try me at wide receiver.

"Hey, if you're serious about playing wideout, there's a new kid who wants to play quarterback. The two of you could get together and help one another get up to speed," the coach offered. "His name is Joe Billings. He'll be coming out to practice today. I'll introduce you."

"Okay," I said, getting excited at the prospect.

Practice came quickly enough. The assembly right after lunch helped time to pass. Mr. Gamebridge, the geography teacher, showed slides of his vacation to Australia. It was actually quite interesting, especially when the main auditorium lights were turned off, leaving just a row of lights in back of the stage behind the screen revealing the silhouette of two people smooching up a storm.

"Aw, yes," Mr. Gamebridge began as the silhouette of two

young lovers appeared on the screen. "This is a very rare shot of the mating ritual of a pair of Australian Outback tailless willie-willies, very rare. In fact, to this day this is the only known slide in existence."

With that, the whole auditorium roared with laughter. The two young willie-willies realized something was up and hastily departed.

"Hi, I'm John, and you must be Joe," I offered as I extended my hand.

Joe had been throwing balls into a net from about twenty yards out as the team was finding its way onto the field for practice.

"Hi," he said as he gripped my hand.

"Coach Wurthlin tells me you have plans to be our next quarterback."

"Yeah, well, that's the plan," he said almost apologetically.

Joe was tall, about six-three and slim with brown hair, hazel eyes, and a quiet, almost shy demeanor.

"Well, I want to switch to wide receiver, and the coach says you and I should practice together in our spare time."

Joe looked at me for moment. "Sounds good. Go deep." His whole countenance seemed to change from shy to a guy in charge. Joe dropped back with the ball grasped in his hands as I ran as fast as I could. Joe let her go, and the ball fell softly into my outstretched hands. A perfect pass and reception.

Every day, we practiced with the team and then spent a good hour afterward working on pass routes and handoffs. Joe wanted to work on the running plays as well as the pass plays. That wouldn't help me since I was trying out for receiver, not running back, but Joe was in charge. He had a way of imposing his will without it being a bad thing.

The week went by quickly, and the big game with Jefferson and the Sadie Hawkins dance was upon us. I was wound up tighter than I ever remembered being. Jefferson was an athletic team with lots of speed. They gave up lots of points, but they'd score plenty too. To beat them, we'd have to slow down their offense. Jefferson, however, was not the reason for my nervous condition. It was that Sadie Hawkins dance. I had worked hard all week preparing for Jefferson, but I also had fretted and prepared for Sally, and the dance. I had even dipped into my car savings and bought some new threads. All systems were go.

We lined up to receive the ball. It was a high short kick and we quickly formed a wedge for our return man, who snagged the ball and ran right up the middle. Down he went at our forty-five-yard line. The offense took the field and promptly worked the ball into the end-zone. Like I said, Jefferson generally gave up a lot of points, and they were off to a typical start. It was up to me and the rest of the defense to slow down their offense if we wanted a shot at winning.

I lined up opposite Number Eighty-Eight, a kind of smallish offensive lineman. He looked to be about one hundred and ninety pounds and kind of flabby. I licked my chops. I was thinking MVP.

The ball was snapped, and the smallish flabby lineman sprang out of his stance very quickly and locked me up before I could get any momentum. Their ball carrier slipped by me and into the backfield where he was met by our linebacker, who was playing pass and hadn't adjusted in time, allowing Jefferson an eleven-yard run and a first down. Man, those guys were quick.

Jefferson came at us with quick running plays and quick short passing plays. Everything they did was quick. At the half, it was Jefferson 26 to our 24. They scored four touchdowns, but only managed two successful extra-point tries. We had three touchdowns with two successful two-point conversions and a safety for two points when a snap from center went over the head of the Jefferson punter into the end zone, where he fell on it before we could get to it.

I did okay the first half, but that small—well, he was

actually about my size—lineman kept me tied up most of the time. I did manage to slip by him on a passing play and sack the quarterback once, though.

The second half was more of the same. Neither defense was able to stop the other's offense. With three minutes left, it was Jefferson 46 to our 43, and they had the ball and were driving. They kept mixing it up with short passes and running plays. We were having a lot of trouble stopping them.

I lined up facing Eighty-Eight again. For most of the game, he had neutralized my effectiveness with his quickness. However, I was sensing that he was getting a bit tired. He wasn't coming up out of his stance quite as quickly. I, on the other hand, felt good. All the hard work was paying off. It was third and seven. Jefferson was on our thirty three and there was just under three minutes left. It was a passing situation. We had to stop them.

The ball was snapped into the hands of the Jefferson quarterback. I leapt out of my stance with all the strength and quickness I could muster. Eighty-Eight tried to meet me with equal energy, but it just wasn't there. I pushed him back. The quarterback was attempting to set up in the pocket just to my left. His arm was going back, preparing to pass. I continued to drive my legs as I used my hands to push Eighty-Eight to my right, trying to slip off him. The Jefferson lineman was grabbing at my jersey and my right arm. He knew he couldn't hold me much longer. He was right. I got free and threw myself into the Jefferson signal caller just as he was bringing his arm forward. The ball floated aimlessly out of his hand as I drove him into the turf. I could hear a roar coming from our side of the field. I jumped up in time to see one of our guys running toward the opposite goal line.

I never did see who had intercepted the ball and ran for a touchdown as my teammates started slamming me around in celebration. Our offense took the field and managed to score another two points on a quarterback sweep. The score was now 51 to 46. Jefferson had two minutes and twenty-eight seconds to score a touchdown to win, and our defense wasn't going to let that happen. We shut them down and got the ball back with thirty-six seconds left. Our offense ran the time off the clock. We were on our way to the state playoffs.

As nervous and apprehensive as I felt approaching the Jefferson game, it was nothing compared to the turmoil in my gut as I readied myself for the Sadie Hawkins dance. I stood in front of the full-length mirror in the hall, inspecting my new look. I had on a full-length white Nehru shirt, with paisleys around the collar that hung down about halfway to my knees. It contrasted nicely with a pair of semi-glossy charcoal-gray sharkskin slacks that were tapered down to my all-leather black Italian shoes with two-inch heels and laces on the side. The whole ensemble, including the over-the-calf black nylon socks, set me back forty-eight bucks. It was worth it, I said to myself as I sized up the image in the mirror. I was looking good.

CHAPTER TWENTY-THREE

I could hear the rumble of Tom's '64 Chevy short-box half-ton pickup outside as I grabbed my coat and threw open the door.

Greg slid over as I jumped in, and away we went. Greg and I didn't talk much on the way over to the dance. I think he must have been nervous. I know I was.

"There you go," Tom said as he brought his pickup to a stop outside the gym door of the Scappoose High School. "Come on, get going," he urged. "I gotta get my date."

I opened the door, and Greg and I found ourselves standing there in the mild evening air.

"Well, I guess we'd better get in there and find our dates," I said, trying to sound relaxed.

"Right," Greg replied grimly as he headed stiffly toward the door.

The gym was dark, with a few disco balls sending little lights all around. There were a few streamers and balloons here and there as well. We stood on the outer edge of the gym, trying to be cool as the band played some obscure rock-and-roll number. It was still early, and no one had gotten up the nerve to go out on the dance floor. There were three girls dancing with each other off to one side, and that was it.

I continued to look around nervously, hoping the girls weren't there yet. I didn't want to be the first out on the dance floor.

"Hi, John," a sweet, feminine, voice pierced my ears.

I turned to see Marianne and Sally running up to us. Both of the girls were looking very nice, causing a great commotion in my gut.

After a few one-sided pleasantries, the girls dragged us out to the very middle of the gym, much to our horror, where we began to stiffly gyrate around self-consciously. Thankfully, it wasn't long before the other kids followed suit, and Greg and I began to loosen up.

After a while Greg started to show off some of the more complex moves he had picked up from *American Bandstand*, causing the couples nearby to back off somewhat so as not to get hit by a flailing arm or leg. As for me, I just smoothly whipped into my James Brown routine by slithering all around the dance floor.

Yow! I feel good.

Sally and Marianne were quite impressed with our dancing as we continued to wow them the rest of the evening.

Then it happened. The moment that I had been secretly dreading since the day Sally asked me to the dance. The band began to play a slow song. It's one thing to slither around and gyrate to the music a good meter or more from your partner, but a slow song meant a certain amount of intimacy. It meant getting into each other's space.

I looked around wildly for something, anything I could grab hold of in the way of an out. Greg and I had both just returned from the restroom, so another trip so soon would look like I had a problem, and I couldn't go for punch because we all were standing next to the refreshments with full glasses. I needed a diversion. Oh, if only this was the Washington

High School dance and Rodney Skylark was walking by. I could provoke him into a fight. That might work. But alas, this was Scappoose, and everybody was nice.

"John, aren't you going to ask me to dance?" Sally asked sweetly as she grabbed my hand and looked me dead in the eye.

"Sure," I mumbled, setting my drink down—feeling like a condemned inmate about to walk the *last mile*.

Sally led me out into the crowd of couples on the dance floor. I placed my right hand on the small of her back and grasped her right hand in my left. I began to sway to and fro to what I hoped was the beat. I couldn't hear a thing. As I looked into her eyes and felt her hand in mine, as well as the close proximity of all the rest of her, my heart began pounding like a runaway locomotive. Sally didn't seem to notice my discomfort, and I somehow managed to survive.

The slow songs came and went, and with each one, I felt a little more relaxed. I actually started to enjoy them. Looking deep into Sally's sparkling blue eyes was a little intimidating at first, but she was so nice and unpretentious that I eventually became completely at ease.

The band was just wrapping up "You Showed Me" by the Turtles when Marianne grabbed Sally by the hand and dragged her off to powder their noses or something.

"We'll be right back," Marianne called out as the two girls scurried towards the ladies' room.

Greg and I sauntered over to the punch bowl, where a group of his buddies was hanging out.

"Hey, guys, this is John," Greg said by way of introduction. Some of them I knew from our previous football game on Marshall beach.

The guys just sort of nodded, mumbled something, and then went back to talking about football and how they were going to kill Cannon Beach in their first game of the State 2A playoffs.

The dance was very well attended, with nearly three hundred kids in the crowded old gymnasium. It was a pretty good showing for a school with just over four hundred student's total.

I continued to look over the Scappoose student body as I waited for the girls to return. A lot of the kids lived on farms in the area. There were also a lot of them whose dads worked in the woods cutting down trees or in one of the local mills cutting little boards out of big logs. Some of the kids came from very poor families. There was a group of fairly modest homes down by the docks where some of them lived. There were also some very large and fancy homes up on the hill overlooking the river. It appeared that there was a nice representation of the social classes attending Scappoose High.

As I was scanning the crowd, trying to size up the kids and determine what their backgrounds might be, I noticed Sally coming from the ladies' room. She made her way through a few dozen kids, smiling and speaking to many of them.

She sure is popular, I thought to myself as I tried to get her attention. Still not catching my eye, she stopped at the end of the refreshment table, where a scruffy-looking boy was standing. He wore ill-fitting blue jeans, a faded flannel shirt, and dirty white tennis shoes with a couple of holes in them. He also seemed to have an acne problem, and on top of it all, he looked really uncomfortable. Sally smiled a great big sparkling smile, and I could see her lips move as she spoke to the boy. After a moment or two, the boy smiled back as Sally grabbed his arm and said so long or something, and then continued her search for what I hope was me.

"Hey," I hollered as Sally was about to go in the opposite direction from where I was standing.

Sally's face lit up as she skipped over and fell in beside me, grabbing my arm.

"Who's the guy you were flirting with?" I asked, realizing how dumb I sounded.

Sally scrunched up her nose and looked at me kind of funny. "Why? You jealous?" she asked with a mischievous grin.

"Maybe," I replied, trying to make the best of it.

"Well, if you must know, he's a friend."

With that, Sally pulled me back out on the dance floor, and that's where we stayed until the lights were turned up and the band began to pack up their gear.

Holding Sally's hand we strolled out to the parking area, where Greg and Marianne joined us as we waited for our rides. Sally's mom soon pulled up, and away went the girls, and my stomach filled with butterflies, again.

CHAPTER TWENTY-FOUR

"Smith," Coach Saunders bellowed as I pulled myself off the ground. "Would you like to join us? We just happen to be preparing to take on the number-one team in the state playoffs this Friday."

"Yes, sir, Coach," I mumbled as I got back in my defensive end position on the line. I was having trouble focusing. Ever since the Sadie Hawkins dance, my mind kept going back and forth. On the one hand, there was Sally. She was cute, with a great big friendly sparkling smile. She was fun, too. Then there was Bunny, the most beautiful girl in the world. Bunny was probably fun too. It's just that I hadn't been given a chance yet to find out. Sally was also nice. The more I thought about how she went out of her way to talk to that scruffy boy at the dance with the whole world watching, the more I believed she was, or at least I thought she might be, maybe, just a little bit special. I knew that Bunny was special too by the way that she . . . I couldn't think of anything except that she smiled at me once in a while when no one was looking. Bunny never did go out of her way to say hi or even acknowledge my existence when I was a chubby grade schooler. Yeah, that's because Rodney Skylark was always around. Once he's goes off to college she will be all mine.

With that last uplifting thought, I got run over by Gary Laughton. *Time for football,* I said to myself as I struggled to my feet. For the rest of the day, I put everything out of my mind except the task at hand, which was to get ready for Lake Grove, the number-one JV team in the state.

We worked hard all week, and I was able to keep all thoughts of Sally Rayfield out of my mind. The coach had us primed and ready to play our best game of the season, and we did. It wasn't enough. Lake Grove beat us 28 to 26. They were good, and we had trouble with our two-point conversions. We were only able to get one, but they had a great little kicker who nailed all four of their extra-point tries, and that was the difference. Our season was over.

The varsity did better and won their first playoff game against Medford. Rodney Skylark threw for over three hundred yards and three touchdowns and ran for two more.

After our game, Coach Wurthlin gave us what I'm sure he thought was an inspirational speech about there not being any losers when you do your best and blah, blah, blah. I was having none of it. I wanted to win, and we didn't.

That weekend, I just stayed at home, kind of moping around the house. Finally, the phone rang, and as expected, it was Greg telling me all about their game against Cannon Beach, which they won. I tried to sound interested and happy for him, which I was, but I was having a tough time showing much enthusiasm.

Greg tried to get me to come over, but I just wasn't in the mood. There was a lot going on that weekend anyway. My mom finished nursing school a few months back and had taken a job with the Seventh-Day Adventist Hospital in town, and with the help of my sister Karen and her husband Leroy, she purchased a small home on Thirty-First and East Burnside. So we were packing and getting ready for the move.

Our modest little home was just two blocks away from the upscale Laurelhurst neighborhood, where Rodney Skylark lived. You go up Burnside one block to Thirty-Second, turn right and go one more block, and there you are in the Laurelhurst neighborhood. The first two homes you see are small mansions, probably around six to seven thousand square feet. One is a redbrick colonial with huge white columns. The other is some kind of Mediterranean sprawl. Both homes are very nice, as are most of the others in the area.

My little brother Curt and I would get our own bedrooms upstairs in our new house, and my sister Cindra would share a bedroom with Mom downstairs. There was also a basement where I could put my weights, and a garage where I was planning on parking my first car. I began mental preparations for that day. My sixteenth birthday was only two months away. I had nine hundred and twenty-two dollars left of the money I had earned over the summer. I couldn't get the new Corvette I wanted, but I could get a nice little used Chevy.

The next few weeks were uneventful except for moving and getting settled into our new house. The Washington High varsity team was beaten by South Salem in the third round of the state playoffs. Rodney Skylark didn't take it very well and got into a couple of fights with some of his teammates. The word in the halls was that Rodney blamed his offensive line for his poor play when it appeared that they had done all right since Rodney wasn't sacked, and the team had over a hundred and fifty rushing yards.

The coach called us into his office the week after the season was over to give us our off-season workout regimen and to pump us up.

"Smith," Coach Wurthlin greeted me as I stepped into his cubicle. "Have a seat."

I sat down and looked into the coach's face expectantly.

"John," he began, "you have worked very hard this past year, and I just want you to know that I appreciate it. You've been a good example for the rest of your teammates, and that's the first step toward being a good leader. If you take this workout regimen," the coach handed me a sheet with my name on it, "and continue to work hard, you will do well on varsity next year."

"What about trying out for receiver?" I asked, ignoring the reference the coach made about me playing on varsity.

The coach furrowed his brow and leaned back, attempting to find just the right words.

"John, you know that I won't be making that decision. Coach Skylark is the varsity coach. However, if you continue to work with Joe Billings and improve your speed, he may give you a shot." The coach paused for a moment. "I'll talk to him."

"Thanks, Coach." That was all I wanted—a chance.

For the next couple of months, I worked hard. Every morning at six a.m., I was in the weight room with many of the guys from both junior varsity and varsity. During the off-season, the varsity players could work out morning, lunch, or after school, and of course those of us not officially on the varsity team were slotted for the morning. Fortunately, Rodney and his friends didn't work out in the mornings. After school, I worked with the other linemen doing drills for a half hour or so, then Joe Billings and some of the other guys and I would run routes and practice handoffs and such. If we had enough guys, we would scrimmage some.

Also every Friday after our drills and scrimmages, I would hop on my bike and head over the hill to Greg's house. Greg's stepdad, Bob, had hired us to do odd jobs every Saturday for about ten hours. We would clean out stalls, feed the animals, stack and unstack the hay as it was coming and going, and many other usually physical-type jobs for which we were paid $1.50 an hour. After work, we would throw the football around if we weren't too tired, or maybe get a little workout. Usually we were too gassed for much in the way of physical activities after a full day of chores, so we would pour over the ads in the paper, looking for cars and making plans. On one such occasion, Bob came strolling through the dining room where we were hard at it with newspapers strewn all over the table.

"What are you guys up to?" he asked with a quizzical look on his face.

"Looking for cars," we both blurted at once.

"John will be sixteen in two months, and my birthday's in April," Greg informed his stepdad.

"Well," he returned thoughtfully, "what kind of car do you want, and how much do you intend to spend on it?"

"I've got Nine hundred bucks in the bank, and I'll have another hundred or so by my birthday. I figure I can get a '64 Impala with a 327. Something with a V8," I replied excitedly.

"Yeah, and by the time it's my birthday, I'll have about eleven hundred dollars, and I can get a really nice Chevy pickup," Greg said.

"Let me get this straight." Bob sat down at the table with us, grabbing a section of the paper. "You want a Chevy with a V8?"

"That's right," I answered.

"John, do you like '56 Chevys?"

"Yeah, I like them," I said. "Who doesn't?"

"Well, my brother over in Corvallis has a '56 Chevy without an engine or transmission we can get cheap. Then we find a car that's been wrecked and take the engine and transmission out of it, put it into the '56, and you're set with money left over. You keep working for me, and by the time you go back to school in the fall, you should have enough saved to buy something really nice. Say, maybe a Chevelle Super Sport.

"And for you, Greg." He turned to Greg before I had a chance to reply. "I'm going to let you have the old '53 Chevy pickup that's out in the hay barn. We'll get it running. That will give you a chance to save your money and get that four-by-four you really want."

Greg and I just sat there thinking as Greg's stepdad stood up. "I'll call my brother and see what he wants for that Chevy."

"Okay," I said as the realization of what he had been saying began to sink in. "I'll start looking for an engine and transmission."

With that, Greg and I began our individual searches through the classifieds. Greg looked for a really hot four-wheel drive Chevy truck, and I looked for a wrecked Chevy with the proper engine and transmission.

CHAPTER TWENTY-FIVE

"One hundred, twenty, forty, and ten makes one hundred and fifty dollars," I said with a very satisfied tone.

Greg, his big brother Tom, Bob, and I managed to push the '56 Chevy two-door up the ramp and onto the trailer, and we were on our way. The Chevy had the typical two-tone paint job of the day, albeit somewhat faded. The body was straight with no visible rust, and the chrome was good. The interior was worn, but Greg's stepdad assured me that we could fix that easily enough.

Two weeks after Bob had offered to help with the Chevy, I found a 1963 Impala Super Sport in the classifieds that had been rolled several times and was being parted out. Tom took me and Greg over to investigate. Sure enough, the body was completely scrunched, and the interior had already been sold. I was hoping to get the bucket seats and console, but everything else was still there. There were 38,000 miles on the 327/300 hp engine, the four speed transmission, and the Posi-Track rear end. The owner was able to start the motor and it sounded pretty good. The next day, we dragged Bob out to see the car, and we ended up purchasing the engine, four-speed manual transmission, and the differential for another $150.

Greg's stepdad had all the tools, including a cherry picker to jerk the engine and transmission out. It wasn't long before we had everything in the back of his pickup and then stored safely back at the farm. One week later, we rolled the '56 Chevy down off the trailer and pushed it into the barn, where the engine and transmission were slipped into it. After a few weeks of working here and there in our spare time with help from Bob, we had everything hooked up, including the Posi-Track rear end, and I still had a good four weeks before my birthday.

Once my Chevy was ready to go, Greg's stepdad got behind the wheel and turned the key. It turned over a couple of times and then roared. Man, was it loud. We'd forgotten to hook up the mufflers. After attaching the mufflers we tried it again. It purred like a kitten.

"If you call around, I bet you could find some cheap used headers that would give this thing a nice rumble," Bob suggested. "Probably improve your gas mileage as well as performance."

"I'll get right on it." So I did just that. I looked in the papers, but with no luck.

"Try calling some junkyards," Tom suggested.

I called several junkyards and finally found one that had just what we needed.

"Yup, got a set right here," said a gruff voice on the other end of the line.

"How much?" I asked.

"Thirty-five bucks, and if you want some mufflers and some exhaust pipe to go with 'em, another fifteen."

"Just the headers," I answered. "I'll be right there."

Tom took us over to a very large auto salvage yard out on Sandy Boulevard in Northeast Portland. It was a very exciting place. There were cars of all models and years going as far back as the forties, maybe even the thirties, stacked all over the probably ten acres or more. If a guy had a mind to, he could put together some real gems.

We went inside a very grimy little office attached to a large warehouse building just inside a tall rickety wooden fence with barbed-wire rolls at the top. We told the man what we were there for, and he produced the headers. I paid him while Tom and Greg grabbed the high performance exhaust manifolds and headed for the truck.

"Hey," the large, gruff, and somewhat greasy, owner of the junkyard called after me as I headed out the door, shoving the receipt in my pocket. "I got a real nice 650 Holley and aluminum intake manifold I can let you have cheap."

"For my 327?" I asked, getting excited. "How much?"

He scrunched one of his dark shaggy brows and replied, "Fifty bucks."

Fifty dollars wasn't in the budget, and the junkyard man seemed to sense my disappointment.

"I'll throw in a pair of chrome valve covers and air cleaner," he barked as he reached under his grimy counter and grabbed a couple of shiny chrome valve covers with the word *Chevrolet* on each one.

"It's a deal," I said quickly, succumbing to temptation. Not only would the big Holley carb make the little 327 perk up, but it would look great with the chrome valve covers and air cleaner.

We had the Chevy small block all decked out with the headers, big Holley carb, and chrome accessories a good two weeks before my sixteenth birthday. We washed and waxed the car, and Greg's stepdad produced some black vinyl to cover the seats. He had a friend in an upholstery shop who owed him a favor, so after a trip to his shop my little Chevy's interior was upgraded. The vinyl really spiffed up the interior. I wanted some Cragar wheels, but that really wasn't in the budget. The tires on the Chevy were in fair condition, and I took off the dorky hub caps. All in all, it didn't look bad, and that little 327 sure did sound good with headers accentuating the rumble. Greg's stepdad estimated it had at least 325 horsepower. That was plenty enough to get in trouble.

Greg and I couldn't resist the temptation of driving it around the island, but as we were preparing to take it for a spin, Bob intercepted us.

"Where do you guys think you're going?" he wanted to know as he stood in front of the rumbling Chevy.

We just kind of stammered and mumbled as Bob strolled over to the window to confront us.

"I'll tell you what you do," he said. "You can drive all you want as long as you don't leave the property."

Greg and I perked up. We thought he might take the keys or something. There was a long quarter-mile driveway, plus all the dirt roads in between the fields and orchards. We were hoping to break her in on the back roads of the island but the farm was better than nothing. I revved my little Chevy up and turned her loose.

"Just don't kill yourself or I'll have a lot of explaining to do," Bob hollered after us.

The next two weeks went by slowly, and I spent as much time at Greg's as possible. It was kind of tough during the week, but we ran that Chevy to death for the two weekends before I turned sixteen. Greg and Bob came and got me out of school for my birthday and hauled me out to Scappoose to take my driving test. I just barely passed by inches. I got a seventy-five, which was as good as a mile as far as I was concerned. Now I was street legal and ready to load up my hot little Chevy with hot little babes. *Maybe just one hot little babe,* I thought as a vision of Bunny flashed in front of my mind's eye.

CHAPTER TWENTY-SIX

I pulled my '56 Chevy to the curb on a downtown Portland side street just a few yards from Broadway. From Burnside, you turn onto Broadway, which is four lanes going south for a mile or so past all the old luxury theaters and restaurants and large office buildings and shops and cafes and nightspots until you get to the Portland State campus. From there, you turn left and go two blocks to 6th Avenue and turn left again. Then you go north past more office buildings and department stores and shops and more cafes and nightspots. About a mile or so, you turn left on Burnside. You go past KISN radio, where the disc jockey sits on the corner, encased by large windows facing the street. If your timing is right and if you can get his attention, he'll wave and recognize your existence over the radio. Then you do it all over again and again and again every night of the week until you either run out of gas or you get dizzy. We seldom got dizzy.

Cruising the Gut in those days is what we lived for. Sure, there was football, but hopping into your car and making a run on Broadway made life worth living. It gave us credibility. A fast car or at least a nice car went a long way in compiling data for a personal unwritten resume.

It was a Friday night and I picked up Greg. Then we stopped at Fred Homestead's and picked him up along with Gary Laughton and Joe Billings.

"You got the cigars?" I asked as Fred and the guys piled into the car.

Fred pulled a fistful of large stogies from his coat in answer to my question and asked, "You got the valve cleaner?"

"Got it," I said as I turned my Chevy loose, laying down some rubber in the process. We made one pass of Broadway before turning onto a dimly lit side street and pulled up to the curb.

I turned off the engine. Fred silently passed out the cigars that he had apparently appropriated from his father. The guys got the cigars going while I hopped out and popped the hood of my '56. I spun the wing nut off and removed the air cleaner lid, exposing the Holley carburetor. I pulled a can opener from one pocket of my lightweight Sir jacket and a small can of valve cleaner from the other. Using the can opener, I punctured a triangle-shaped opening in the can, dumped it into the carburetor, put the air cleaner lid back in place, and screwed the wing nut down tight. I got back into the car, where the guys had rolled up the windows and were puffing away vigorously.

Fred handed me a lit cigar, and I began to puff along with the rest of them. The smoke quickly filled the air and made it difficult to breathe.

"Now?" I asked.

"Now!" they all hollered in choking, gasping unison.

I fired up the 327 that had been lying dormant under the hood of my '56, pulled out into the street, and turned left onto Broadway. I kept my eyes glued to the rearview mirror. We were all choking, and tears began to well up in our eyes.

"Now!" I roared as I saw dense white smoke begin to pour from my dual tailpipes in the rear.

We rolled down our windows and began hollering at the

top of our lungs. "Fire! Fire!" Smoke poured from our windows as well as the tailpipes. The street was lined with kids and their cars, and the looks on their faces made it all worthwhile right up to the moment when I detected a bright-red light followed by a high-pitched siren directly behind us in the thick, billowy plumes of dense white smoke.

The cop was pretty nice about it, but just the same, he warned us that he would haul us all in if we tried anything like that again, since the smoke screen we'd laid down was hazardous for those following behind.

We thanked him profusely for not giving us a ticket or calling our parents and then got the heck out of there.

Got to admit that cruising the Gut every night, as fun as it was, wasn't conducive to getting good grades, but somehow I kept them up to an acceptable level, as far as the coach was concerned. My mom, on the other hand, wasn't real impressed. Neither was the sophomore student counselor. She called me into her office one day and got me thinking a little differently about school.

"John, if you ever want to go to college, you're going to have to get your grades up. From what I've been led to believe, you may have an opportunity to earn a scholarship to play football, but you never will with these grades," Mrs. Honorly explained somewhat soberly.

That was the first time anyone had mentioned college football. People were talking about me and college football in the same breath? I was shocked. Other than fantasizing, I hadn't given college any real thought at all. I hadn't thought beyond high school. From that moment on, I began to take school more seriously. I still didn't know what I wanted to do, but the idea of playing college football for a degree began to sound pretty good. Cruising became a weekend-only activity.

Once cruising was relegated to Friday and Saturday evenings, I began to work even harder at my goal of becoming a football animal. I started looking beyond high school. I began thinking how it would be to pump gas all day and then come home to Bunny at night. I didn't think she would put up with a lifestyle of beans and rice. Then there was Sally. For some reason, I didn't think I would be happy coming home to her after pumping gas all day with a meager offering of beans and rice. Some weird, undecipherable, feelings were cruising through my system. Whenever it came to Sally versus Bunny, I had trouble sorting things out. Bunny was my goal, my dream. Sally was just this cute, very nice and fun girl who kept jumbling everything up.

CHAPTER TWENTY-SEVEN

First day of summer, and I was back at Greg's shoveling manure.

"Hey, watch where you're throwing that . . . stuff," I said, wiping green splatter off my arm as I glared at a grinning freckled face.

Actually, Greg's freckles weren't as pronounced as they once were. He was sixteen going on seventeen, as was I, and there was a hint of facial hair under his nose. He called it his "stache." It had a ways to go before it could actually be considered a mustache, but it was a start.

Both Greg and I had worked very hard the last five months, and now we were gearing up for the most important summer of our lives. We were going to be juniors, and we had three months to get ready for a shot at varsity football.

Greg's stepdad was doing his part by giving us eight-plus hours of backbreaking chores six days a week until summer workouts. We'd start at six and hopefully get off the clock at two. Then we'd hit the weights for an hour. We had made plans with some of the guys from Washington and some of Greg's teammates from Scappoose. We were to meet up at the field over at the Sauvie Island school ground, where we would do drills and scrimmage and stuff. Joe Billings would be there. He was as dead serious about playing quarterback as I was about playing receiver, and over the last five months, he'd really made some progress, as had I. I'd worked on running routes and I got so I could catch pretty much anything Joe threw at me. My speed had improved, too. I didn't know if it had improved enough, but I was still working on it. And Joe could hit me from anywhere on the field blindfolded. I was confident that he could play. The problem for him was Rodney Skylark. Rodney was the quarterback, and that was it. Of course, Rodney would be gone after next year.

The thought of playing on the same team and sharing the same locker room with Rodney Skylark every day was something that had caused me considerable anguish. And what if I did become a wide receiver? Would Rodney throw me the ball? *Maybe I should just stay on defense,* I thought.

"No," I said aloud, practically shouting.

Greg took a step back, startled. "You okay?"

"Yeah," I said sheepishly. "I was just thinking about something."

With that, I flipped a shovel full of . . . . stuff over in Greg's general direction, and it was on. Greg's mom wouldn't let us anywhere near the house for lunch until we had hosed each other off—even then we had to eat outside.

Greg's older brother, Tom, was still around, but we seldom saw him, as he was spending most of his time getting ready for college. He had managed to get a small financial grant from Linfield College in McMinnville, Oregon, to play football. They were an NAIA Division Three school. Not exactly big time, but Tom was excited. They wanted him to play defensive back and to run back kickoffs. So Tom got together with a couple of other freshman and rented an apartment close to campus so they could get ready. That meant that Greg and I would be on our own.

Once the chores were done, Greg and I started getting

hungry for a little action. The guys wouldn't meet up till the next day for the first of our summer workouts, so the night was ours.

"Hey, let's go over to the Spinner and get a milkshake or something," I suggested, knowing that Sally Rayfield would probably be there behind the counter. The Spinner was a drive-in burger joint in Scappoose. It had a roof that looked like a beanie with a large, slow moving, spinning propeller on top. The local kids hung out there with their cars and Sally had just turned sixteen and was now working under the spinning top as a counter girl for the summer. I hadn't seen her since uh . . . the dance? The Sadie Hawkins dance was last October. I guess maybe I should've kept in touch.

"Okay," Greg returned. "But we're taking my truck."

"Hey, we gotta be cool now, and besides, I just got my Cragars." It was true. A kid from Washington High needed money, so I gave him a hundred bucks for his Cragar wheels and practically brand-new wide oval tires with raised white lettering. The chrome exhaust extensions out the back completed the look.

Greg was still driving the beat-up old '53 Chevy farm truck. He didn't quite have the money for the four-wheel drive rig he wanted.

"Okay," Greg quickly relented. "But when I get my four-by-four, we'll be taking it."

We got cleaned up and threw on some suitable duds consisting of washed-out Levi's, white T-shirts, and Converse low-cut tenny runners—we could have been twins—and piled into my '56 Chevy two-door. It was looking pretty good with the practically new Cragars and the large white-lettered wide oval tires. The paint was still a bit faded, but it was nice and shiny with several coats of Turtle Wax. I fired that bad boy 327 up and with a couple of gratuitous revs, I pulled out of Greg's driveway, laying down just a little bit of rubber. I had to be careful not to leave tire marks or squeal the tires more than what was tolerable to Greg's mom. I smoked them off really good one day, and boy, did I hear about it. Greg's mom is nice, but you don't want to get her riled.

I smoothly guided the floor-mounted four-speed shifter through the gears as the exhaust echoed out the back while keeping an eye on the eight-grand tachometer that was attached to the steering column. The tach, along with several gauges now adorning the dash, helped make the whole interior of my '56 look legit. I loved my car.

Scappoose wasn't far, and it didn't take my Chevy long before we were pulling into the Spinner. I guided the rumbling '56 into a vacant spot that just happened to be right next to this brand spanking new '69 Roadrunner. It was burnt orange with factory-custom black trim and rally wheels. That was one sharp car. As I looked it over, not without a bit of envy rearing its ugly head, my heart came to a complete stop. On the fender of the shiny new Roadrunner was a small rectangular badge that simply said *HEMI*.

I got out of the '56 feeling a little bit more humble than I had just a minute prior. My Chevy was a cool car—at least, *I* thought it was. But as cool as my car may have been, it was not even close to being worthy, to even be in the presence of that beautiful Hemi Roadrunner.

"Cool car," Greg gushed as I kept silent.

I've never been one to care about status symbols or showy examples of decadence, but that car bothered me. A Hemi Roadrunner isn't about "Look at me. Aren't I special?" No, a Hemi Roadrunner says, "I can kick your butt anytime I want and I'm going to look good doing it, and there ain't a thing you can do about it."

Feeling just a little less macho, Greg and I strolled toward the window to place our order with Sally Rayfield. She was waiting on some tall, good-looking guy. I guess he was good-looking. He had classic Hollywood chiseled-type features and dark wavy hair that was being tossed around by the wind. He kept smiling at Sally, who was smiling back at him. I don't know—maybe he wasn't that good-looking after all. All I did know was that I wanted to tear his head off.

Sally managed to catch our eye, preoccupied as she was, and motioned us closer to the window.

"Hi," she said, still smiling brightly. "I want you guys to meet James. He's new around here. James, these are my friends John and Greg."

He offered his hand, and we shook. You can tell a lot by a guy's handshake. If it's wimpy and soft, it would say he doesn't care, that maybe he doesn't think you matter in the scheme of things, or that you're no threat to him. If his handshake is overly firm, he might be trying to send a message like, "She's *mine*, and you had better back off or else." Or, "I really feel threatened by you, so I'm going to show you I mean business." If his handshake is firm, but not overly, and he looks you in the eye with a hint of a smile, not a smirk, it means he just might be sincere and gracious. James' handshake was firm, and he smiled politely and sincerely. He seemed like a great guy.

"James will be a senior this year at Scappoose High," Sally informed us as she handed a white paper bag to James with his order, still smiling brightly—too brightly.

James took his order, thanked Sally, nodded toward me and Greg, saying something about it being nice to meet us or some such drivel, and headed toward his car—of course, the '69 Hemi Roadrunner.

I watched him get into his rig, fire it up, and slowly pull away from the Spinner, gaining speed while that darned Hemi purred effortlessly.

I turned back to Sally, who had been watching him as well.

"I haven't seen you for quite a while," Sally stated without much enthusiasm, her smile beginning to fade.

"You're right. I've been really busy," I replied lamely.

"John's been hitting the books trying to get his grades up

for college," Greg exclaimed, trying to excuse my seven-month hiatus.

"Oh?" Sally seemed interested. "I thought you were going straight to the NFL," she added with just a hint of wickedness in her smile. I might be a little slow at times, but I was having no problem picking up on Sally's acidic sarcasm.

"Right," I said in a somewhat subdued voice.

I stood there feeling myself turning red, not knowing how to recover from her obvious jab. It was true that I had totally blown Sally off after the Sadie Hawkins dance. I had been so wrapped up in myself, what with getting my car ready for the road and then getting my license and trying to get ready to play wide receiver and then cruising with the guys and then realizing that I might have a shot at going to college if I got my grades up and if I could continue to work hard and even harder to improve in football and become more and more of a stud and . . .

My discomfort and my self-absorbed thoughts were interrupted by giggles coming from inside the drive-in window. Sally was beaming again as she tried to keep her obvious amusement under control.

I really didn't know what to say now and just continued to stand there as red as a beet. Man, girls make me feel funny.

Greg, not under Sally's power to any degree, saved the day by pushing past me and simply saying, "How about a couple of large chocolate shakes?" to Sally through the service window.

"Coming right up," Sally replied, smiling sweetly, and off she went to get us our order.

By the time Sally returned with our shakes, I had regained my composure and remembered the tall dark-haired Hemi guy who just moments before had Sally smiling like she had just won the lottery.

"What's with James?" I asked, trying to sound indifferent. "Does he live around here?"

Sally looked at me like she knew exactly what I was thinking. "Why do you ask, John?" she asked innocently, and then after a little pause, she continued with just a hint of that same wickedness as moments before in her pretty smile. "Afraid of a little competition?"

That did it. At that very instant, I wanted to kill that guy.

Sally was giggling again, which helped deflate the crazy burst of emotions in my head. Or was it my heart? I was obviously confused. Sally was like a giant wrench that had been forcefully thrown into the works. Since the first time I had laid eyes on Bunny back in the fifth grade, I could think of no other. Bunny was what motivated me to turn my life around. She was the one image in my head every day that kept me going. But then Sally came around and I didn't know which way was up. Right then and there, I decided it was Bunny I really wanted.

Sally handed me the shakes and took the money from my hand, making contact with her slim fingers, skin on skin, while giving me a big sparkling smile. She tossed her strawberry-blonde hair out of her eyes, turning toward the cash register to get me my change.

"You wanna go to the movies?" I heard myself asking as she turned back.

"Well, I'll have to ask James if it's okay," she replied innocently.

I knew she was teasing, but my blood began boiling again anyway.

Sally did agree, and the time was set for Saturday night. Greg said he would ask Marianne Sebastian—or I should say that Sally agreed to ask Marianne, her best friend, if she would be Greg's date. Apparently, Greg was having some nerve issues concerning certain girls himself.

CHAPTER TWENTY-EIGHT

The week went by quickly, and I wanted to kick myself every time I thought about my date with Sally. I don't know what came over me. I felt like I was cheating on Bunny. I know that sounds silly, but Bunny was my girl, at least in my head.

The week did go by quickly, what with Greg's unrelenting taskmaster of a stepdad trying to work us to death and the guys showing up every afternoon for our scrimmaging and drills.

The date with Sally, Greg, and Marianne came and went. We had a nice time, if that's what you call trying to act nonchalant and cool with clammy hands clenched tightly to the armrests of the movie theater seats for nearly-two-and-a-half hours as we watched *Paint Your Wagon*, a movie about two guys, Clint Eastwood and Lee Marvin, sharing the same girl. Pretty sick movie, which made me feel even guiltier for going out with Sally when it was Bunny I was determined to be with. I made up my mind right then and there. It was Bunny I wanted, I think.

After the date, Greg and I focused on football. At least, we *tried* to focus on football, but by the time we got done bucking hay bales all day and then hitting the weights, we were pretty worn out. Greg's dad's hay business had continued to grow. Pretty much every day, a semi-truckload of hay bales of some kind would need to be unloaded and stacked. Then customers would come with their flatbeds and pickup trucks that needed to be loaded. The bales ranged in size from about fifty pounds of regular old grass hay to one hundred and twenty-pound bales of alfalfa and every variety of grass and size of bale in between. Horse breeders, goat milkers, and cow raisers from all over were coming for a few bales of hay for their small enterprises. The hay biz, which had been just a sideline for Bob, was becoming a real concern, and Greg and I were the muscle.

Although our bodies were pretty much spent by the time we hit the weights, Greg and I did our best. When the guys showed up for football, it was pure agony. We hung in there, though, knowing that it would be for our good. After dragging ourselves through the drills, we would all go over to Marshall Beach for a few hours of diving off the pilings and such. The water reinvigorated our bodies.

Sally and Marianne would often be there, sunbathing with some of the other girls from around the area. Once the word got out that there were several of us football hunks on the beach every afternoon, the babes started showing up.

Of course, we would try to give them their money's worth by strutting around and being cool and doing fancy dives off the pilings. The girls pretended like they didn't know we were there by applying lots of suntan lotion and shaking their hair out of their eyes in an exaggerated fashion.

Our days were full, and we didn't have much time or energy for any extracurriculars. I tried to steer clear of Sally, which wasn't easy since she was at the beach most every day with her friends, but I did manage for a while. It wasn't long, however, before we found ourselves mingling with the girls. We were keeping to ourselves, pretty much just going through our manly motions, and the next thing we knew, our ranks had been totally infiltrated. Once the guys started getting chummy with the girls, it was over. All they wanted to do was hang around them all afternoon. It was getting hard to stay focused.

Of course I ended up spending time on the beach with Sally. I had to admit, she was fun to talk to. We still managed to get some good swimming in, even with all the distractions.

The summer went by fast, and before I knew it, I was in the equipment line with Washington High School varsity football team hopefuls. Assistant Coach Moreraz was attempting to make us feel welcome.

"Okay, ladies, keep moving. Grab your gear. Put it on and hit the field. We don't have all day," he growled as he looked us over somewhat painfully.

That's just what we did. There were about forty-five of us trying out for varsity. They were looking for twenty-one to replace the seniors who had graduated. I was determined not to be left off the varsity roster, even though the thought of playing on the same team as Rodney Skylark and sharing the same locker room and basically being around him for several hours every day concerned the heck out of me. I would have said he scared the heck out of me except I had made a vow that I would never ever be afraid of him again.

It was hot. It was still August, and we were doing two-a-days. We had bucked hay right up to the first day of practice, and I was pretty worn out. So was the rest of the team, as we were all having trouble getting off the ground. We were doing six-count bends and thrusts in full gear during our second practice of the day and the tenth of the week. That first week was brutal. Those of us trying out for the team were kept separate from veteran varsity squad members as Coach Moreraz worked us to death. I suppose he was trying to determine who could take it. I had a little trouble the first couple of days being worn down from close to two-and-a-half months of stacking and unstacking hay bales, jacking weights around, doing drills with the guys and swimming and flirting with the girls until dark. After a couple of days, I started to get used to it and realized that football practice wasn't that bad. I was in shape. But that last six-count bend and thrust ended up a couple counts short as we all collapsed in the hot sun.

"Get up, you bunch of pansies," hollered Coach Moreraz, "and give me six laps around the field. Then hit the showers."

We all managed to get up and shuffle around the track. There were no heroes. We stayed in a tight bunch and completed the six laps together. There were a few stragglers, but nobody sprinted ahead. Our legs were like rubber, and there was no desire in any of us to do more than an exaggerated walk.

That night I slept like a rock. The next morning, I got up and realized that I wasn't sore. My legs were a little stiff, but after a night's rest, I felt pretty good. It had been a long time since that day when I sat down on the corner and determined I had to do something with my life. Back then, I was fat and weak, with no confidence or self-esteem. The hard work was paying off. I still had a ways to go in the confidence department, but I was determined to fake it till I made it. Physically, however . . . I checked my shirtless self out in the mirror of our bathroom. I hadn't really been paying that much attention over the course of spring and summer, but I had changed. The spare tire was gone. What I saw in the mirror was the torso of what appeared to be a man. I had worked hard now for a number of years, and it showed.

Tears welled up in my eyes as I realized—no, not realized, but for the first time I *believed* completely that I could do it. I had gone on faith, being driven by the hope of becoming something reassembling someone of worth, someone who counted and who could be counted on. I knew at that moment that I could do whatever I set my mind to. Sure, I'd had success with the junior varsity, but for some reason I hadn't—

even though I had told myself otherwise—fully believed, until now.

My first week of varsity two-a-days was behind me, and I felt great. Monday, we would start trying out for positions and the cuts would start. Half of the guys would be playing junior varsity again. I was not going to be one of them.

I hopped in my '56 and headed for the island. Greg's stepdad had hired a full-time guy to load and unload the bales of hay, so Greg and I were off the hook and could concentrate on football. We exchanged exaggerated reports of our first days of practice, with the second bragger always outdoing the first. After tiring of trying to out-lie the other, we got busy on the weights.

We worked hard, with both of us showing some nice gains. After a week off from tossing bales of hay, our strength had returned. The two-a-days were tough, but our muscles had actually recuperated from our summer chores. We were banging the weights around like King Kong on steroids.

After a good long workout, we jogged over to Marshall Beach for a swim. My muscles were totally pumped, and I was ready to flash them around a bit. It was about noon with the sun straight up in the sky when we strolled onto the beach, fully expecting to see some of the girls there as they had been all summer. The beach was virtually empty except for a few kids jumping off the log pilings and an older couple sunbathing. We swam around for a while, and still no girls. We decided that we would go over to the Spinner and see what was going on.

After getting dressed, we anxiously drove over to the Spinner—or at least, I was feeling a little apprehensive. Greg seemed fine. He never got too worked up about girls, except maybe the ones named Marianne Sebastian.

At the Spinner, Judy, the day manager, informed us that a bunch of the girls, including Sally, were over at James' house playing tennis and hanging around the pool. My blood began to rise in temperature.

James' dad was some big-shot guy who owned one of the shipping companies that operated cargo ships out of the docks in the Columbia, and from what I heard, in Seattle as well. He had a big house on the side of the hill overlooking the river.

I was still having some difficulty letting Sally go even though I was supposed to be with Bunny. Of course, there was still Rodney Skylark, who I would be spending a lot of time with once I made varsity, and who would have something to say about me moving in on Bunny. The thought of facing Rodney didn't lift my spirits as I fumed over James stealing my non-girlfriend. Trying to compete with Rodney for Bunny and now James for Sally was messing with my psyche.

CHAPTER TWENTY-NINE

The first week of two-a-days was behind me, and I didn't encounter Rodney Skylark—not even in passing. He was practicing with the varsity, and I was practicing with the varsity hopefuls. However, it was now Monday, the first day of the second week of practice, and those of us who made varsity would be practicing with the whole team.

"Smith," Coach Moreraz barked, along with twenty other names. "You men report to Coach Skylark. The rest of you boys, see Coach Wurthlin." With that, Coach Moreraz tucked his clipboard under his arm and headed over to the varsity side of the field while the twenty-one of us ran as hard as we could to where the head coach of the varsity team was hanging around with a clipboard of his own. The rest of the varsity team was doing loosening-up exercises in formation as Coach Wunderman barked out a cadence.

"All right, listen up," Coach Skylark, Rodney's dad, said sternly, looking intently at his clipboard and then at us newbies. He read off ten names, including mine, and instructed us to fall in with the defense after the warm-ups. The rest of the guys were instructed to fall in with the offense after warm-ups as well. "Now fall in behind the rest of the team in formation and then meet with your respective assigned coaches after the warm-ups."

Fred Homestead, Gary Laughton, Joel Kimber, Bill Wringly, and Joe Billings were with our group initially, but Joe was assigned to the JV team because we had two senior quarterbacks on varsity. Fred and Gary, because of their size, were a lock for offense and it looked like they would play some defense as well. The rest of us? Who knew, except I was pretty sure that I was on the defensive line. I wasn't as big as what they wanted for a lineman, but I made up for it with my quickness and aggressive play. Maybe I would get a shot at linebacker. I felt pretty certain, however, that wide receiver was out. I would have to ask the coach, and the thought of doing that was a bit unnerving. I was determined, however, to do it. I just needed to pick the right time.

Sure enough, after the warm-ups, we split into groups, and I was instructed to join the defensive linemen. I liked playing defensive end, but I could do other things. My speed had improved, and I was sure I could play linebacker. The problem was that there were plenty of smaller guys to play linebacker and not that many who could hold their own on the line.

The next two days practicing with the varsity was uneventful except for a sneer or two from Rodney in passing. The third day, however, was another story. We were doing this drill where the defensive line guys would line up against the offensive line guys and try to get to the quarterback before he got rid of the ball to one of the wide receivers. I guess it was kind of a scrimmage except that the same play was called every time, and the coaches were rotating players around, trying to get a look at us to see what we could do. I was inserted into the mix and had to go against one of the senior offensive linemen. He was big and kind of soft-looking. I saw him struggling with some of the drills and huffing and puffing around. I don't think he was in very good shape. He looked like he had spent the summer watching TV with a box of Twinkies close by. Here was my chance to show the coaches what I could do.

I got down in my stance. When the ball was snapped, I came shooting up. With the use of my hands and all my bale-bucking strength, I pushed past the big slow out-of-shape lineman, and before I knew what I was doing, I launched myself right into Rodney Skylark, the pride and joy of the Washington High School varsity football team, triple sport legend and local darling of all sports-minded people of the entire state of Oregon, slamming him to the ground and causing the ball to pop loose.

I jumped to my feet in excitement and looked around. Everyone had grown quiet. Rodney lay on the grass, gasping for air. I stopped hopping around, realizing what I had done. The coaches quickly went to Rodney's aid as they scowled at me. *Am I in trouble?* I asked myself.

Yep, I was in trouble. Nothing was said to me, however. The coaches totally ignored me as they attended to Rodney. There had been no instructions to go easy on the quarterback. Was there some kind of unwritten rule that I wasn't aware of?

Rodney was okay. He'd just had the wind knocked out of him. But if looks were any indication of what was to come, I wasn't just in trouble—I was dead meat.

The rest of practice was kind of a nightmare with the coaches now paying particular attention to me, finding fault with everything I did and making me pay. I ran a lot of laps. Coach Skylark didn't say a word—never even looked my way. I didn't think he would welcome a visit from me right about then asking to switch to wide receiver. I doubted Rodney would be too keen on the idea either.

Rodney ignored me in the locker room, which made me nervous. I was sure that he was going to do something to get even. The rest of the week went by, and the coaches seemed to forget the Rodney incident. School was starting that Monday, and our first game would be the following Friday. Not a peep from Rodney.

That Friday after practice, even though I was totally spent and beat up from two weeks of 'two-a-days, I fired up the '56 and headed for Greg's. I hadn't seen him for fourteen days. I talked to him on the phone a couple of times and his practices seemed to be taking their toll, same as mine. I got to Greg's and found the place empty. Must be something going on somewhere, I surmised, and headed for the Spinner. *Maybe Sally's working,* I thought as I peeled out of Greg's driveway. Good thing Greg's mom wasn't home. I could blame the two new sets of tire marks on the new hay guy. Yeah, like his Rambler could lay down a patch of rubber like I just did with my big bad 327. No, Greg's mom was no dummy. She'd know it was me, and I was sure I'd hear about it.

I pulled into my customary spot at the Spinner, which happened to be right next to James' truly big and bad Hemi Roadrunner. I hated that car. It made me feel small and insignificant in my little '56 Chevy. "What's James doing here anyway?" I grumbled to myself as I headed to the service window where I could see him bent over, talking to Sally.

And what's with his hair always blowing in the wind like some kind of model in a photo shoot with fans placed just so, to get the right effect? I wondered to myself in disgust. *Whose side is the wind on, anyway? When it blows my hair, all it does is mess it up.* I continued my jealous mental rant as I came right up behind the ever-popular man of the hour, the Hemi-driving, hair-blown rich kid from up on the hill.

James turned to see who was approaching. He immediately smiled in recognition and stuck out his hand in a friendly welcoming gesture.

Oh, he's slick, I thought as I took his hand. An honest smile of my own reluctantly appeared on my face. Something about James was very disarming. If I didn't know better, he might be some kind of a great guy. I was beginning to wonder if I did.

Sally was beaming behind the window. Scenes from *Paint Your Wagon* came to mind, and I was determined not to share Sally or anybody else with James or Clint Eastwood or whoever. Of course, Bunny was the one I wanted anyway, right?

"Right," I said out loud, followed by a quick, "What are you guys up to?"

"Oh, nothing," Sally said innocently as she stuck her head out the window, her strawberry-blonde hair blowing in the breeze the same as James'. She smiled just a bit mischievously in my general direction, causing butterflies to take to a frenzied flight in my gut.

"Hey, Sally, John, I gotta go. Me and some of the guys have a court reserved for seven. We're trying to get up to speed before the season starts. See ya later," he said to Sally, smiling at her and then nodding to me as he headed for his big bad Hemi.

"The season?" I asked out loud to no one in particular. "What season?"

Sally, with her pretty head still out of the window, replied, "The tennis season. James is the captain of the tennis team."

Of course he is, I reasoned to myself. "Well, that's nice," I managed, not all that impressed. "Doesn't he like football?" *Like the rest of us real men.* I finally had something on him.

"He's never played. He's lived in Japan the last five years, where he competed in martial arts instead. I think he said something about a third-degree black belt or some such thing," Sally informed me.

Oh, sure. Rich, looks like a movie star, drives a brand-new Hemi Roadrunner, and is a third-degree black belt in karate.

"Did I tell you he's going to Stanford? It looks like he may get a full-ride academic scholarship," Sally added as she ran a damp cloth over the counter in the window that framed her.

"No, no, you didn't." That was it. Somebody shoot me.

I talked with Sally for a few more minutes, wondering how

much more I could take. Thankfully, she changed the subject, and instead rattled on about school and I don't really know what all. I wasn't really listening. All I could do was think about James. How was I ever going to measure up to him? Actually, I didn't really need to since Bunny was my girl. That was, if Rodney Skylark would cooperate. A cold chill made me shiver. *Winter must be coming*, I thought as my guts began to tighten. Something was up with Rodney. I just knew it.

CHAPTER THIRTY

I walked into the northeast corner doorway of Washington High on the first day of school. I was now a junior, and a member of the varsity football team. I had come a long way and had worked hard for several years now, dating back to Mr. Lawnboy's early morning fitness class. My goals were in sight. First thing on the agenda was a short trip over to the varsity football bulletin board right outside of the coach's office. Coach Skylark said the starting lineup, as well as the second string, would be listed. I felt pretty confident that I would at least be a number-two. There was one senior who started last year at defensive end, and he probably had one spot locked up. The other starting defensive end position was wide open. As far as I was concerned, I was the best man for the job. There were three other guys who had been competing with me throughout summer practices, but none of them had my ability. I was stronger and quicker than any of them. In fact, I thought I could give Mark Rosenbloom, the senior returning starting defensive end, a run for his money.

Once outside the coaches' room that housed their collective makeshift offices, I found the list on the bulletin board along with several of my teammates. I waited my turn.

After looking at the posted names, they either celebrated or turned and quickly walked away. At last, it was my turn. I stood there staring in disbelief. My name was not listed.

Just then, a familiar voice behind me asked, "What's the matter, Smith? Something wrong?"

Rodney Skylark and three senior offensive linemen were there as I turned around. I really wasn't all that surprised to see Rodney. I was surprised that he would do something that could be detrimental to the team, though. It didn't make sense for him to use his influence with his dad to keep me from playing if I could help win ball games. He probably thought the team didn't need me. He could do it all himself. Maybe he could.

"It's too bad you didn't make the playing roster. Maybe the JV team could use some help," he said with a sneer as he closed the gap between us.

I stood there waiting as the three linemen spread out, narrowing any chance at freedom. I wasn't looking to escape. It wouldn't have done any good, and only prolong the inevitable. I was scared to death, but I was determined to give those guys all I had.

I really don't exactly know what happened next, except that Rodney made some kind of move, and I exploded. I kicked and spun and hammered and twisted and punched and clawed. I fought with all the rage and strength and energy at my disposal. All those push-ups, and sit-ups, bench presses, curls, bales of hay that I bucked, and stalls I mucked, and the running when I felt too tired to move, and the swimming at the end of every summer day, and every squeeze of my gut when I bent over for a drink at the fountain, and every stroke of the pedal of my bike as I climbed up a thousand feet to get to the top of the Montgomery Ward hill on the way to Greg's, along with the motivation provided by every bully who had ever hurt and shamed me, and every unkind word and snicker directed at me because I was fat and weak of spirit and body and therefore vulnerable, which made me a target for anybody with a desire to hurt someone more than what they hurt themselves, was unleashed on those four football players. It was over quickly. I thought I was doing quite well when the lights went out. Something had crashed down on the top of my head. I was momentarily stunned. Then I got the beating they must have figured I had coming.

When my head began to clear, I noticed that I was propped up against the wall, and Fred Homestead was asking me "How many fingers?" as he held up several of his thick digits.

"I don't know. Is this going to be on the test?" I asked, still dazed. I looked around and saw Fred and Gary and no one else.

"What happened to Rodney and his buddies?" I asked.

"Don't know. You were lying out here by yourself," Fred replied.

"I must have run them off."

"Right," Gary agreed as he and Fred helped me to my feet. I hurt all over, and there was blood coming from somewhere on my face. I think it was my nose, and it was dripping onto my brand-new Johnny Unitas Baltimore Colts jersey.

My head cleared quickly enough. I got myself cleaned up and did a quick evaluation of the damage done as I looked into the bathroom mirror. Nothing permanent other than the bloodstains on my jersey. Now that ticked me off. Maybe some of the blood was Rodney's, I wondered hopefully. *Maybe I should save the bloodstained jersey until Rodney is a rich and famous NFL quarterback and then see if I could get a few bucks for it. Or maybe I should frame it to show my kids and grandkids, and tell them how I beat the crap out of the famous Rodney Skylark and the entire offensive line and . . . and . . .* whatever. Even I wasn't buying it. I dragged my battered carcass to class.

Of course, the bloodstains on my jersey didn't go

unnoticed. I tried to play the whole thing down. I didn't want Rodney to hear how I beat him to a pulp, but that was exactly what the student body was spreading around. I think Fred Homestead had something to do with it.

"Oh, yeah, it's a good thing I showed up when I did," I heard Fred say as I entered math class. "Look at his jersey. That's Rodney's blood all over it."

Oh, boy. It was not over between me and Rodney.

The rest of the day, I tried to explain that I didn't really beat up Rodney Skylark, that we just had a little misunderstanding. I wasn't very convincing. It was hard for me to explain Rodney's black eye and bruised and puffy lip while my face was pretty much intact. They couldn't see my bruised-up body or the bump on the back of my head.

I ran into Bunny during social studies. She was all smiles. Shouldn't she be mad at me for fighting with her boyfriend? *Why is she hanging around with that guy? Does she even like him?* I pushed all those thoughts out of my head. Bunny was smiling at me.

"Hi, Bunny," I managed.

"Hi," she said back, her green eyes sparkling.

I kind of stuttered and stammered around for a moment and then she was gone. She was off to her next class, and I was left standing there feeling rather stupid.

The rest of the school day went by, and I had little luck convincing anyone that I had not beaten up Rodney Skylark.

"So you gave old Rodney a good going over, eh?" Even Mrs. Raven, soon to be retired after forty-five years of service and my last period English teacher, had obviously gotten the word on my exchange with Rodney. "I'm sure he deserved it," I heard her say.

Did anybody like Rodney?

I dressed down and got into my gear as quickly as I could. I didn't want to be in the locker room any longer than I needed to with Rodney lurking around.

Practice was mostly scrimmaging. We were getting ready for our first game, and it was against Jefferson. Jefferson's varsity was a lot like their junior varsity in that they were fast and athletic. They won all but two of their games last year, only losing to Grant, who was always good, and Cleveland who was very physical. Our varsity didn't play them last year, but the year before they handed us our only regular season loss. They were tough.

Since I wasn't expected to play, I was lined up against our offense, mimicking the Jefferson defense. Along with me, there were ten other defensive guys who were not expected to play. The offense gleefully had their way with us for the most part. I was going up against Washington's number-one offensive lineman, Jim Leghorn, who I had met just that morning in the hallway outside the coach's office with Rodney and his other pals. He was six foot three and listed at two-sixty. He looked bigger. I was having a tough time keeping myself on my feet. In all honesty, though, Jim wasn't clearing out any room for a running back to drive through, either. My quickness off the ball was making it hard for him to make a hole soon enough to be effective. I kept coming at the big lineman as hard as I could, and the running plays started going to the other side. On passing plays, the big lineman would tie me up pretty good, but I noticed that he was getting a little slower as the scrimmage went on. I sensed a pass play coming. I shot out of my stance and used my hands to push past Leghorn, who was coming out of his stance a bit too slow. Rodney was rolling out of the pocket looking downfield. I didn't think about the repercussions of hitting the famous Rodney Skylark again. It was football. I don't usually think a whole lot about anything. I wasn't thinking about the beatings before or the ones that may have been in my future. I wasn't thinking about Rodney's dad, who had all power over me and could keep me from ever playing high school football again. I wasn't thinking about the team and the season ahead and the possibility of playing without our star quarterback, if he should get hurt in practice. I was like a wild dog with his prey, running, trying to get away. I turned on the afterburners and hit him as he was bringing his arm up to throw. I got him again.

Rodney hit the turf, and the ball had already come loose. This time, however, Rodney did not lay there gasping for air. He shot to his feet before I could get to mine and began kicking and stomping me with his cleated Converse football shoes that I supposed he'd be endorsing one day for a ton of money.

I guess I should have felt honored to have the soon-to-be nationally and possibly world-famous athlete, the great Rodney Skylark, who could do no wrong, stomping the stuffing out of me. But I didn't.

I tried to roll away, but I felt a big foot come down, holding me in check as Rodney continued his stomping. Eventually, I heard a whistle blowing, and someone must have grabbed Rodney because the stomping ceased, and the big foot that belonged to one of his linemen buddies lifted off of me.

I got to my feet somehow and looked right smack-dab into the face of Coach Skylark. He was not too happy.

"Are you trying to kill my star quarterback?" he snarled, his lips turning up at the corners. "You're done. Hit the showers."

I dragged my sorry butt across the field and into the locker room. I blew it. All I ever wanted to do was to play football, and of course take Bunny away from Rodney.

I took a long shower, running the warm water over the welts left by our star quarterback's cleats as well as the other assorted sore spots from that morning's encounter. The varsity would be practicing for a while yet. There was no danger of them showing up anytime soon. The junior varsity was another matter. Their practices ended thirty minutes before the varsity in order for them to shower and make their exit before the big bad heroes of Washington High showed up.

I was getting dressed as the tired mob of JV guys shuffled in. Coach Wurthlin came strolling in with them, clipboard in hand, looking very stern.

"If that's the best you can give me, then Jefferson is going to mop up the field with us." The Coach sounded pretty upset. He paused a moment to let that sink in and then continued. "If we take the field against Jefferson with the kind of energy you showed me today, we're going to be in big trouble. You'd better be ready to practice tomorrow or we'll just run laps the rest of the week and take our lumps on Friday." He slammed his clipboard down on the tiled floor of the locker room for emphasis and then began looking intensely over each young man, his burning eyes resting on me.

"Smith," he said as I was getting my books, hoping to slip out unnoticed. "Come with me." Coach Wurthlin turned and headed for his office without looking to see if I was complying. Up the stairs he marched with me dutifully behind. The coaches' offices were just up the stairs and at the end of the hallway in the south wing. He pulled aside the curtain hanging in front of his office and waited for me to enter.

"Have a seat," he said simply without the intensity of a minute ago. "What are you doing, getting dressed before practice is over?" He found his own seat behind his desk. Wouldn't take a genius to know something was up. Besides, he probably heard about my fight with Rodney and his three goons that morning.

I stammered around a bit and then just said, "The coach thinks I'm trying to kill his quarterback."

Coach Wurthlin leaned back in his chair, and his eyebrows rose slightly as he processed this information. "Are you?"

"I'm just playing football. Nobody told me to go easy on anybody," I replied emphatically, avoiding the question. Did I want to hurt Rodney? I hadn't considered that. I thought I was just playing football. I had to admit, though, it didn't look good.

"What did Coach Skylark say?"

"He told me I was done and then sent me to the showers," I said with my head drooping, my eyes on the floor.

The coach sat quietly for a moment. "I'll ask him about it." He then asked how everything else was, and I gave him a vague picture of my current life at Washington High. He seemed satisfied. He didn't ask about the fight, and I didn't share. I stood and retreated. My life as I knew it was over, again. I started thinking about Twinkies and cream sodas.

CHAPTER THIRTY-ONE

The next day, school went excruciatingly slow. Coach Skylark hadn't said whether I was still part of the varsity team. I had a sinking feeling, though, that regardless of my status with the varsity, I might never see the field again. I moped around school, shuffling from one classroom, to another. Bunny and her sparkling green eyes avoided me. When I did run into her, the sparkle wasn't there. She didn't seem to like losers. Can't blame her, I wasn't liking myself much at this point either.

I showed up for practice, and before I could get my Converse tenny runners untied, our team manager, Oliver Gonutz, came over to my locker.

"Coach Skylark wants to see you," he said with a bit of a satisfied sneer on his pimpled face.

"Great," I mumbled, tying my shoe back up. *This is not going to be good.*

"Smith, you're suspended indefinitely. You will not participate in any team functions until further notice. That means no JV as well." Coach Skylark stood and glared. I took the hint and removed myself from his saintly cubicle.

I was in shock. All those years of working hard—for what? Nothing. I don't know how, but I managed to get home, plopped myself down in front of the TV until I was sleepy, and then went to bed.

The rest of the week was similar. I didn't do anything. I would stop off at the B&M Market on the corner of 18th and Burnside and load up on goodies. Then I would go home and watch TV until it was time for bed.

Friday was game day, and the school was excited. You could feel it in the air. Our first game was against Jefferson, who was expected to be one of the teams in our conference to compete for the title. This first game could set the tone for the season. Nothing but a state championship would be acceptable. Everyone was pumped and would be at the game, except for me.

As soon as school was out, I ran into Bunny as I was heading out the door for the B&M Market to get my fix.

"Hi, Bunny," I heard myself say in greeting. She was fumbling around in her locker.

"Hi," she managed without much enthusiasm and no sparkle. She grabbed whatever she was looking for, slammed her locker, locked it, and scampered away before any more words might be spoken.

One minute she was friendly, her green eyes sparkling, and the next minute, nothing.

What? Did I suddenly have the plague? Was I a leper? I began to get angry. I headed toward the parking lot, got into my Chevy, and went right home. I changed into my running gear, and out the door I went. I ran. I ran hard. I ran fast and I ran long. The anger didn't go away. I returned home and went out to our one-car garage, where I kept my weights. I turned up my stereo as loud as it would go and started pumping iron. I jacked my dumbbells and assorted barbells around until I had nothing left. My arms and chest were so pumped full of blood that I felt a little lightheaded. I collapsed into my old beat-up easy chair in the corner as "Born to Be

Wild" blasted out of my speakers. The tears came, and I let them.

After a while, I got tired of wallowing in self pity and dragged myself into the house. My little brother and sister were watching TV while Mom was in the kitchen, cleaning up after dinner.

"You missed dinner," Mom said as I came into the kitchen through our back door.

"I had something at the office," I told her.

"You need more than Twinkies and cream sodas."

"Right," was all I could manage, quickly moving through the kitchen. I took a shower, threw on some Levi's, a T-shirt, my Converse low-tops, grabbed my Sir jacket, and was out the door. I needed to be with someone. Greg had a game, so he wouldn't be around for a while. I found myself heading for the Spinner.

I pulled into my customary spot with my '56 and this time, thankfully, no Hemi Roadrunner. In fact, my Chevy was the only car there. The employees parked out back, but in front, nothing. Everybody's at the game, I figured as I climbed out of my car and headed toward the window.

Sally's strawberry-colored head popped out. Her pretty face had a big smile. She was glad to see me.

When did Sally go from cute to pretty? I wondered as a big sheepish smile began to stretch across my own face.

"Hey, I'm off in five minutes if you want to hang out a bit," she informed me expectantly.

"Okay," I said, starting to get nervous. Sally still made the butterflies churn in my guts. *What is it with girls, anyway? Do they have some kind of special power given to them?* All my push-ups and the bales of hay I'd bucked might have given me a shot of holding my own with Rodney Skylark, but not with Sally. She had complete control over me. I felt weak as a baby.

I sat down at one of the picnic-type tables in front of the service window and waited for Sally. She didn't make me wait long, practically skipping out to where I sat. She sure was perky.

We talked for a moment or two—or I should say that Sally talked and I nodded or grunted now and then until I noticed her shiver.

"Hey, you're cold. Let's sit in my car," I suggested

"Okay." We climbed into my Chevy. I fired it up and turned on the heater.

"Let's cruise," Sally suggested.

I directed my rumbling Chevy toward Broadway in downtown Portland, where we did just that. The traffic was light for a Friday. A lot of the kids were still at games and wouldn't be hitting the streets for another hour or so.

Sally had been talking most of the time, telling me about school and this and that like girls do, when she suddenly stopped. She was looking at me kind of funny.

"What?" I asked, glancing over at her as I made the left turn at the end of the cruising route.

"What's wrong?" she asked intuitively.

That question caught me completely off guard. "Uh," I stammered. "Wrong? Nothing's wrong," I said without much conviction.

She just looked at me for a moment as I squirmed. "How's everything at school? Football going okay?"

The light was red. I brought my Chevy to a halt and looked straight into her always-sparkling blue eyes. Unlike Bunny, I didn't have to be anything other than who I was to fuel the sparkle in Sally's eyes. Right then, those sparkling blue eyes were boring right into mine.

I felt like a balloon that had just lost all of its air. With one look, Sally had shattered my protective barrier, and I was now, totally exposed.

"I . . . uh . . . got kicked off the team," I confessed weakly as my throat tightened. Thankfully, the light turned green and

I directed my Chevy through the intersection, keeping my eyes straight ahead.

Sally didn't speak for a moment as she processed this information. "Why?" she asked simply.

Haltingly, and not without some difficulty, I told her the whole story of my problem with Rodney and now with his dad thinking I was trying to hurt his star quarterback.

I turned left at Burnside as I finished my story and headed back to Broadway from 6th to complete our first loop of the Gut.

"So, what are you going to do about it?" Sally asked with a bit of an edge to her normally sweet-sounding voice.

Surprised at her lack of sensitivity, I looked in her direction to get a read as I headed the two blocks to Broadway. Shouldn't she be consoling me with soft, kind words from her tender heart? Whose side was she on, anyway? I was starting to get a little angry.

"What *can* I do about it?" I asked, trying to keep my voice under control.

Sally looked at me, and I could see the wheels whirling around in her strawberry-blonde head.

I turned left at the light and headed back up Broadway, squealing the tires as I was feeling a bit aggressive all of a sudden. I slowed the beast down and stopped at the next light. There's a light at every single intersection hindering the flow of through traffic, but makes for great little races amongst the cruising participants. A '65 Mustang GT pulled alongside me, and I was tempted.

"The way I see it, you have two choices." Sally was speaking kindly now, causing me to momentarily forget my interest in the Mustang. "You can either give up, or you can fight. Or like my dad says, you can either take it like a man or you can *be* a man."

"What the heck is that supposed to mean?" The anger was

coming back. The light turned green and the Mustang got the jump on me, as I was being distracted.

"I mean you can either quit without a fight, or you can show Coach Skylark that you won't give up and you'll do whatever it takes to be a part of the team."

I wasn't following her logic. After all, I got kicked *off* the team.

"What could I possibly do to get the coach to put me back on the team?" I wanted to know.

"Well," Sally started, her mind formulating a plan as she was speaking, "you could show him you mean business. First, be on the field every day running and doing drills and exercises during practice. And then be in the weight room whenever the team is in there. Show everybody that you'll do whatever it takes and work harder than anyone else. Be on the field or in the weight room before the team, and stay after they all leave."

Sally was making sense. If the coaches saw how hard I was willing to work and what I had to offer, they'd have to play me.

"You're right, Sally. I'm done taking it like a man. I'm going to start *being* a man." I couldn't wait for Monday.

CHAPTER THIRTY-TWO

I spent Sunday afternoon with Greg. Greg and his mom and Bob attended church in Scappoose on Sunday mornings. I sometimes went with my mom to Hinson Memorial Baptist Church in Southeast Portland. President Ford once attended there on a visit to Portland. It's one of those cool old churches built with large stones and a bell tower. During church services, some of us guys would sometimes sneak out of the main chapel and creep up the narrow staircase to the tiny little room at the top of the tower. The kids said it was haunted, but I never saw any ghosts. Anyhow, Greg and I spent the afternoon catching up. The Scappoose varsity football team was doing well, and so was Greg. I had trouble showing much enthusiasm, what with all that I was going through.

Upon entering the halls of Washington High on Monday morning, I was greeted by a huge banner that read *Congratulations, Washington Colonials*. Apparently, the varsity had prevailed. As I learned later from Fred Homestead, the score was 47 to 44.

"Thank goodness I was on my A game," Fred offered for any who cared to listen. "They gave us all we could handle." Apparently, Washington's offense with Rodney at the helm did fine, but the defense struggled to keep Jefferson from scoring. Fortunately for us, Fred Homestead was there to give us the edge that we needed for the win. At least, that's what I gathered after listening to his dialogue for a minute or two.

"Right," was all I could manage, my mind on other things. I couldn't wait for practice. I was going to show everybody that I wasn't going to lie down. I had worked too long, and too hard to quit now.

As soon as my last-period English class was over, I headed to the locker room as fast as I could to get dressed down into my sweats and be on the field before the varsity showed up. I started my workout with stretches. Once warmed up, I began to do all the same exercises that the team would do. Players began to shuffle out to the field in their practice armor, and I continued doing my routine. The coaches soon followed, and practice commenced. I tried to emulate everything that the team was doing off to the side a good hundred feet or so. It wasn't long before I began to get noticed. Rodney and some of his buddies began to make fun and holler insults my way. I ignored them and kept working hard. When the team broke up into groups to work on drills and such, I did wind sprints and practiced coming out of my stance. When there was a blocking sled not being used, I practiced on it until one of the assistant coaches took notice.

"Smith, what are you doing? Get away from that thing. That's for the use of the members of the team only," Coach Moreraz hollered, sounding irritated. "Now get out of here," he added.

I got away from the sled, but I didn't leave the field. I simply took myself to the other side and continued my exercise regimen.

"It's a free country," I said aloud with no one within earshot. I was getting a bit of an attitude.

I worked hard nonstop all during practice, and then when the team ran laps, I ran with them. I ran as hard as I could, lapping most of them, and continued running when the team dragged themselves into the locker room. Joe Billings met me after the laps were finished and we worked on passing routes and taking handoffs like we had for the previous year or so. In the morning, before school, when the football team was supposed to be in the weight room, I was there. I jacked those weights around like I was on a mission, which I was. I took a lot of ribbing, and Rodney wanted to kill me, but I stayed true to the course.

The week went by and the varsity won again, 44 to 29, beating the hapless Madison Squad who had only one win to their name in the last two years. Again, Rodney and company managed to do fine on offense, but giving up 29 points to Madison was nothing to brag about.

From what I could gather from Gary Laughton and Fred Homestead, they needed some help on the defensive line.

"The coach has me and Gary filling in on the d-line, but if we aren't in the game, they're running all over on us." Fred was being serious for once. "And," he continued, "by the time the fourth quarter comes around, we're pretty tired from playing offense *and* defense, and then, if they're any good at all, they pretty much have their way with us. Even Madison was blasting through our line in the fourth quarter."

"We need your help," Gary stated when he could squeeze a word in.

"Yeah," Fred agreed. "We've got some big games ahead."

"I'm ready, but it's up to Coach Skylark." I had no control other than to keep working hard and hope that the coach would come around.

Before I knew it, Friday had come. I had been working hard every day in the weight room and on the field. I was showing up in both places before the team arrived, and I stayed until after the team left. Joe Billings and I continued to work together after practice as well. Joe was still relegated to the JV team because we had two senior quarterbacks and he wasn't needed. He was tearing it up on JV, though. They had won their first two games by an average of three touchdowns, and there was some talk of him being the next Rodney Skylark. Joe was nothing like Rodney. Joe was a good guy.

It was Friday night and I had nothing to do, since everybody would be at the game. I guessed I could go visit Sally, but I really wanted to see how Washington was going to do against Cleveland. Cleveland liked to run the ball, and they were good at it. They had a big physical offensive line, and they liked to pound away. This would be the first real test for the Washington High varsity. As wrong as it may have been, part of me wanted to see Washington struggle against Cleveland.

I strolled into Cleveland's stadium, trying to go unnoticed, and sat down on the Cleveland side next to an older couple wrapped in blankets. It wasn't that cold, but I wished I had a blanket to hide in as well.

No one on the Cleveland side paid me any mind, and the game got under way. It wasn't long before I knew that Cleveland wasn't going to lie down in the presence of the great one. No, Rodney was not going to win this one by himself. Cleveland was big and they were physical, just as they always were, and our offense was struggling to get any momentum going. Cleveland, on the other hand, pounded away at our line with two thick-looking running backs. They drove down the field on their first possession. They didn't do anything fancy, just pounded away until I saw the ref's hands go up in the air after a two-yard run up the middle. Touchdown. They ran a play-off tackle and picked up two more to make it 8 to 0.

Our defense managed to keep them from scoring again until the last minute of the second quarter. Gary and Fred both were playing extended minutes on defense, as well as offense. They were getting a little tired and Washington's other defensive linemen were having no luck at all. Cleveland scored again, and this time didn't pick up the extra points. The score was 14 to 0 at the half.

Rodney and company came out on fire in the second half, picking up two quick touchdowns and tying the score. For some reason, Cleveland got away from what they were doing in the first half and let Rodney out of the pocket. He was a virtual magician when flushed from the pocket. He could run and he could scramble, and when things broke down, he would make things happen. He could be deadly. Cleveland regrouped and got Rodney contained in the pocket where they applied pressure, keeping him human.

Cleveland's offense kept pounding away, and Gary and Fred were tired from their extended play on both offense and defense. The other defensive linemen were ineffective against Cleveland's brutish offense. They scored twice more, making the final score 26 to 14.

I watched as the Washington varsity left the field with their heads hanging down. I didn't get much pleasure from their failure, like I thought I would. They were my team. I shuffled out of the stadium, keeping to the shadows.

There was a real and tangible fog of funk hanging over the student body of Washington High School on Monday morning. Our undefeated season was not going to happen, and our chances of winning state didn't look all that bright either. We still had a couple of huge games. One more loss and we wouldn't even go to districts, let alone the state playoffs. And if we did manage to win the rest of the way, we would more than likely face Cleveland again.

I kept up my regimen of hitting the weights and practicing by myself on the field all that week. Washington was going up against Franklin. They were okay, but we shouldn't have a problem beating them. They were nothing like Cleveland. Our next real test would be the following week against Grant. Grant High School was in a nice upper-middle-class neighborhood in Northeast Portland. They must have plenty of money because their teams were huge. They would suit up what looked like a hundred or more players for home games and they went to state almost every year, winning more than their share of titles. We needed every man to be on his A game for this one. I caught a couple of the assistant coaches watching me as I did my thing during practice. My plan might have been working. At the very least, I got them thinking.

The week was pretty uneventful. Rodney was in a foul mood, but ignored me other than a hateful glare in passing now and then. Thursday evening, I found myself with Greg, hanging out at the Spinner.

Things were going well for Scappoose. They won their first three games, and Greg was getting a lot of playing time as a defensive back and running back punts and kickoffs.

Sally strolled out to where we were sitting at the picnic table, having clocked out for the night.

"Hello, boys." She had a big honest smile on her pretty face.

The butterflies began churning and I got that flight or fight feeling—mostly flight. I didn't know what it was about Sally. She just made me goofy.

We made small talk for a while, and then Sally could hold back no longer. "So, how's your plan going?" she wanted to know.

"Good, I'm catching the coaches watching me when they think I'm not looking," I answered. "They might be getting a little nervous now with some big games coming up. Our defense didn't get the job done last Friday."

"Do you think they'll play you this Friday?" Sally asked.

"Probably not this Friday, since we should beat Franklin without any problem, but the following week, we've got Grant, the number-one team in the state. We can't afford to lose another game, and that will be a tough one."

Sally was sitting next to me on the picnic table. She closed the gap between us, and pushed her petite shoulder into my arm in an intimate sort of way. She leaned forward slightly, turned her head, looked intently into my eyes, and said softly, "Keep it up. I know the coach will play you."

There was nothing profound in her words, but I could feel her faith in me. At that very moment, I would climb a mountain for her.

CHAPTER THIRTY-THREE

The game with Franklin came and went. As expected, Washington's varsity won. The score was 38 to 31. Again, Rodney and the offense did fine, but giving up 31 points to an average Franklin team was a bit unnerving for the Washington faithful, which included the coaching staff.

"Smith, report to Coach Moreraz in his office now," barked Oliver Gonutz, the pimple-faced manager of the varsity football team.

This might be it, I thought as I piled my books and stuff into my locker, not giving Oliver Gonutz and his superior attitude any thought. I practically ran to the classroom that housed the coaches' offices. I knocked on the locker to the right of the crimson sheet with a big W hanging from a rod over the entryway.

"Enter," a big voice commanded from within.

I pushed the sheet to one side, stepped into Coach Moreraz's office, and stood in front of his desk. The assistant varsity coach was seated, going over some papers.

He pushed himself back in his chair and looked up at me sternly, with brows knitted together.

"Do you want to play football?" he asked very seriously.

"Yes, sir," I said determinedly.

"Here's the deal, Smith," he said after a short pause for effect. "We've seen how hard you've been working and are willing to reward you with a spot on the team—if you can tell me that your feud with Rodney is behind you." With that, he leaned back the rest of the way in his chair, waiting for my reply.

Oh, so out of the goodness of your heart, as well as the generous heart of Coach Skylark, and the entire kind-hearted coaching staff, you're going to give me a chance to be on the team—if I behave myself, ran through my brain along with a generous amount of anger and repulsion.

"All I want is to be a part of the team, and in no way do I want to be considered a problem for Rodney or anyone else," I said with conviction, keeping my anger in check while at the same time keeping my options open. *If Rodney behaves himself, there won't be a problem.* That much was true.

"Okay, suit up, and fall in with the defense. We've got a lot of work to do to get ready for Grant," the coach said and turned his attention to a pile of papers on his desk. I took the hint.

The guys were more than happy to see me suiting up. They knew full well that Grant posed a very difficult challenge, and they also knew that I could help.

"We're going to rip their spleens out," Fred hollered, hopping around in excitement and joy upon learning of my return.

Gary just grabbed me in a huge embrace, nearly crushing my rib cage. I felt moisture well up in my eyes and started hopping around and yelling with Fred to try to cover up my show of emotion. They were good friends.

The rest of the week went by fast, and I worked hard to shake off the rust. Ready or not, Friday came, and we found ourselves on the field looking at about a hundred Grant football players in full battle gear. Approximately five thousand of their rabid fans were seated behind them. It was an imposing sight.

We were as nervous as all get-out. Grant was undefeated, and was expected to remain that way. And if looking across the field at one hundred Grant High Generals scowling back at us, knowing that they would like nothing more than to rip our lungs out and cram them down our throats, wasn't enough to make us nervous, the word was that there were several college scouts in attendance. For most of us, that shouldn't matter, but we all had visions of playing at the next level, warranted or not.

I wasn't starting. In fact, I wasn't listed on the two-deep roster. However, they did bring me along. I didn't know what the coach's plan for me might be, but I was ready to go.

We won the toss and elected to go on offense. Rodney quickly directed the team down the field and threw a short pass to our tight end, who pushed through a couple of defenders from the five and scored. We were looking good.

Grant received the kickoff, and in three plays scored as well. Looked like we had ourselves a game.

It went back and forth for a while with both teams scoring once more, and then Grant jumped on a fumble at our thirty-five and promptly punched it in to go ahead. Our offense started driving again, but Grant stopped us on their thirty-two. It was fourth and six. Our field goal kicker struggled with extra points, let alone a kick from the thirty-two, and we were kind of close in for a punt, so the coach decided to go for it. Grant nailed Rodney in the backfield for a loss of five as he was dropping back to pass. They were in there so fast, Rodney didn't have a prayer.

Grant then went down the field in an effortless manner, scoring the last touchdown and extra point of the half going ahead 28 to 13. We were in big trouble, and I had yet to take the field.

In the locker room, Coach Skylark was a madman. Every

other word was one that could not be found in the Webster dictionary. Suffice it to say, we got our butts chewed. After several minutes of the coach's motivational rant, we headed for the field.

"Smith," Coach Skylark growled as I passed by with my clean uniform. He grabbed me, put his face within millimeters of mine, and said, "I want you to stop that Grant quarterback."

The look in Coach Skylark's eyes was a little unnerving, but I got the message and was absolutely determined to do just that.

"Yes, sir," I said simply, gritting my teeth as every molecule of my body came alive. I was never more ready.

I didn't take the field for the kickoff since I hadn't practiced with special teams much. We kicked off and managed to get to the return man on the thirty. Coach Moreraz gave me a look that said "kill someone," and I took the field with my teammates. There were a lot of pats on the back as we took our spots. I lined up in my customary defensive end position on the line across from a big ugly who wanted to plant roses on my grave.

"Fresh meat," Eighty-Six said with a sneer.

I knew who he was. I had heard all about Eighty-Six, and I had seen him in action in the first half as I sized him up. I figured if I got a chance to play, I would probably line up against him since he was their best lineman, and that's where we would need the most help. He was six foot three, two hundred and sixty-five pounds, and mean, dirty mean. He would do whatever he could to hurt you. The scouts were there to see Rodney, but this guy was getting some looks from them as well.

The ball was snapped. I surged forward with every ounce of energy, passion, frustration, and pain that I had been storing up for my entire life. I hit that dude and drove my legs as he was coming up out of his stance. I caught him off balance just a bit and pushed. Down he went, clogging the hole where the running back was hoping to go through. The running back tried to change direction, but I had him and drove him into the ground. A three-yard loss and the guys went nuts, pounding my back and slapping my helmet.

We lined back up and I knew that, Eighty-Six would be ready for me. Again, I came out of my stance quickly, but he was ready, and we fought to a standstill as the running back tried to find the same hole where this time our linebacker was waiting. One-yard gain. It was third and twelve, and an obvious passing situation. Their quarterback was good, if given time. From what I had seen in the first half, he didn't like pressure, although we hadn't put much on him to that point. So far, he had picked us apart.

Eighty-Six would be expecting me to try to get around him, knowing that I was thinking they would pass. He was right, and I shot out of my stance as quickly as I could, anticipating the snap count. I figured I could get away with jumping early at least once. Since they had twelve yards to go, a five-yard penalty for offsides wouldn't be disastrous, especially so early in the drive. The ball was snapped, and I was already up out of my stance, beating my opponent. I shoved eighty-six as hard as I could as I attempted to get around him. I managed to push away from the big lineman as he was flailing with his arms, trying to grab some part of me. I took aim at their six-foot-two slight-of-build, finesse-type quarterback. He didn't know what hit him, as he was looking the other way. The ball popped out, and my good buddy Fred Homestead picked it up on the bounce and rumbled twenty-eight yards untouched for a score. While we had their whole team discombobulated, Rodney faked a pitch to our running back and waltzed into the end zone for two. The score was now 28 to 21. One more to tie it up.

We kicked off, and again our special teams got downfield quickly, and creamed the return guy. The ball was placed on the twenty-nine. Coach Moreraz was screaming at us as we took the field. I didn't know what he was saying, but the sentiment didn't go unnoticed. We were fired up.

We took our places on defense, and Grant came at us. They must have gotten their butts chewed good. They ripped off two consecutive first downs, running option plays around the end before we knew what hit us. Our defensive backs lined up closer, and I got a bad feeling. They were baiting us. They snapped the ball, and I came out of my stance as I realized what was happening. Sure enough, Eighty-Six took a step back to pass block instead of coming right at me. I did my best and managed to get past him, but not in time. Their lanky quarterback tossed a quick one over the top where the defensive backs should have been and their receiver was gone. They kicked the extra point, making the score 35-21.

Our offense took the field, but they looked like they were pressing, three and out. We punted, and Grant was sitting pretty on the fifty-yard line up by two touchdowns. Coach Moreraz was going crazy. Me and the guys on defense took over, and I began yelling. I had never been much of a vocal leader, but for some reason, I was not going to let my teammates lie down. I had worked too hard and taken too much crap to accept another butt-whuppin'. I was done taking it. It was time to dish it out.

I hollered and directed, pointed and freaked, frothing at the mouth like a rabid dog as I lined up in front of their star offensive lineman. My teammates followed my example. We shredded them. It was a running play that never materialized. There were several of us in the backfield gang tackling the quarterback as he was attempting to hand the ball to his running back on a draw play. We collectively hit the two of them so hard and fast that the ball came loose, and again, Fred corralled the fumble. This time he just hopped on it. Our ball on Grant's forty-six-yard line.

We left the field as our offense was taking it, exchanging

high fives and atta boys. I walked by Rodney, and he gave me a look that said *I still hate your guts, but way to go*. The offense was fired up, and three plays later, they were in the end zone. Rodney and company went for two on a quick pass to the tight end over the middle, and scored. Our fans sitting on the cold aluminum bleachers, opposite of the Grant faithful in their covered portion of the stadium, went nuts. The score was now 35-29. The third quarter ended.

We gathered around Coach Skylark for some words of wisdom during the time-out between quarters. Our Washington cheerleaders were out on the field in front of us, leading our fans in a cheer. I caught Bunny's eye as she hopped around in her cute little outfit with the other girls. I could have sworn the sparkle was back.

The fourth quarter began as we kicked off to Grant, stopping their return man on the thirty-six. Again, our defense took the field. Grant ran a couple of safe running plays up the middle. I sensed Eighty-Six was getting a little tired. I, on the other hand, having only played one quarter of football, felt great.

It was third and eight, normally a passing down. It was too early for Grant to play it too safe. After all, we had Rodney Skylark and were capable of scoring at any time. They really needed to keep the drive going and score if they wanted to beat us. A high-percentage short pass was probably the best choice.

The ball was snapped and I quickly dealt with the big lineman, who was now struggling to match my energy. I saw their quarterback take the snap from under center and begin to drop back as I pushed around big Eighty-Six. The Grant quarterback was taking a three-step drop and his arm was coming up. As he was attempting to set his feet, and as his arm was not quite fully cocked, I hit him. I hit him hard. The ball came loose. I could hear our side of the field hollering as the other side went quiet. Our ball, thanks to Fred's quick reflexes. Actually, I think he tripped and fell on the loose ball. Either way, it was ours.

The Washington High varsity offense lined up on the Grant thirty-five-yard line. Rodney in the shotgun received the ball on the snap and rolled to his left, looking downfield. Rodney, as I have mentioned before, was deadly on the run. He hit his receiver in full stride. Touchdown. Our kicker, for once, hit the extra-point try, and just like that, we were ahead by one, 36-35.

We had the momentum, and our defense was not going to let up. Momentum is a funny and at times a fleeting thing. Once you lose it, it can be almost impossible to get back, especially if the other team has anything to say about it. Our defense stopped Grant cold, and our offense, with Rodney running and passing all over the place, led the team to two more scores. We won convincingly 47 to 36. The scouts must have been drooling.

There were a lot of happy campers on the bus ride home. Rodney Skylark strolled down the aisle of the bus, and stopped where I was sitting. He stood looking down at me with his patented "It's great to be me" look on his face. He didn't say anything, but gave me a nod and moved on.

That was a shocker. The great Rodney Skylark who hated my guts had just acknowledged my existence. In the past—not too distant past, for that matter—an acknowledgement from him meant a trip to the nurse's office. I wasn't sure how I felt about Rodney treating me with an element of respect, but I had to admit, it was better than the alternative.

CHAPTER THIRTY-FOUR

"John, you have to go to the dance tonight," Fred Homestead was pleading with me. "You and I are the stars of the team, and our public wants a little interaction."

"What about Rodney? I think he might have something to say about who the star of the team is," I replied, not getting caught up in Fred's delusions. Actually, Fred was partly right. We both had great games. I did get to the quarterback several times and caused three fumbles, all of which Fred was able to grab, one for a touchdown. But the rest of the defense as well as the offense certainly deserved credit.

"Fred's right," an angelic voice replied just behind me.

We were standing just outside the Washington locker room, waiting for Gary. There were a lot of kids, parents, and faculty excitedly coming and going. We had just whupped the number-one team in the state. I turned to see Bunny in her cheerleader outfit smiling the biggest smile I had ever seen, and it was directed at me.

I gulped down some air and looked into her pretty sparkling green eyes. "I . . . uh . . ." I stammered.

"If it hadn't been for you, we might have lost that game." Bunny was serious, her perfect brows knitted together. "Before you went in, the defense couldn't do anything. In fact, the offense was even struggling until you got them the ball in easy scoring range and gave them some hope."

Apparently, Bunny did more at the games than just jump up and down. She seemed to know her football.

"Can't argue with that," Gary Laughton agreed as he came out of the locker room.

"If you guys insist, I guess. But I do know that if we didn't have Rodney, we wouldn't have won that game." No one could argue with that logic. After all, it takes a team, and a team with a stud quarterback is even better.

"Are you going to the dance?" Bunny asked her green eyes boring into mine. "I'd sure like a dance."

That stunned me. Bunny wanted a dance? What about Rodney? Something monumental just took place between me and Rodney, and now Bunny wanted me to risk my life and ruin what might be the beginning of a beautiful relationship where I wouldn't get beat to a pulp any longer?

"What about Rodney? Won't he have something to say about who dances with you?" I wanted to know.

"Oh, Rodney won't be around. He's going to LA tonight for an unofficial visit to USC. Besides," Bunny added, her green eyes sparkling again and her most kissable lips beginning to form that smile that makes all of us guys crazy, "he hasn't been all that attentive of late. I think he's seeing one of the Trojan cheerleaders he met on his last visit down there."

My head felt like it was going to explode from the possibilities and opportunities that instantly began to make themselves clear in my mind. My life was coming together. Bunny was almost mine.

"Okay. I guess I'll see you there, then," I said, trying to keep my excitement in check.

With that, Bunny gave me a little hug and a huge smile, and off she went.

Fred and Gary slapped me on the back and acted as if I had just scored the winning touchdown for the state championship. Actually, it was bigger than that. Bunny wanted me.

I quickly washed my Chevy and gave the interior a good going-over. You never know—Bunny might want to go cruising or get a shake or something. Thinking about getting a shake jolted my brain, causing me to do a one-eighty. Thoughts of the Spinner and Sally Rayfield began to pry their way into my mind, disrupting my visions of me and Bunny.

Somehow the thought of Sally—ever sensible, kind, and loyal Sally—seemed to clear my head. As much as I wanted Bunny, I had to ask myself, why all of a sudden did she want me? Now that I was back on the team and I'd had a good game against Grant and now that Rodney was apparently cheating on her, she wanted some fresh meat. It looked like I just happened to be the freshest hunk of meat available at the moment. *What happens next year when Joe Billings shows everybody how good he is as varsity quarterback? Is she going to trade me in for him? Will she be there for me when I go off to college?* For some reason, as flattering as it was to have Bunny suddenly take an interest, I wasn't feeling real secure about it.

I finished wiping down the interior of my '56 and went into the house. My excitement level had dropped several notches as I thoughtfully showered, shaved off the peach fuzz that I had been proudly accumulating over the past week, and dressed in my best everyday duds. Our dances after the games were casual affairs. Blue jeans, T-shirts, and Converse tennis shoes were acceptable. Besides, the little white T-shirt showed off all my hard work and contrasted nicely with the tan that had not faded completely yet from my Greek-godlike physique. *No wonder Bunny wants me,* I said to myself as I admired my reflection in the hall mirror on the way out the door.

Thoughts of Sally lingered as I went through the gym

doors. I was met by sound waves of what was being passed off as music coming from a shaggy four-piece band against the far wall. The gym was dark, with a large disco ball hanging from the ceiling sending little lights over the entire area. It was after nine, and the place was packed. Apparently, beating Grant got everybody in the mood for dancing.

I looked around, letting my eyes adjust to the light, and there were Fred and Gary over at the refreshment table. I joined them. We exchanged greetings and collectively sloshed down several glasses of punch, trying to avoid the inevitable first dance. I hated that interval between arriving and getting up the nerve to ask someone to dance. Then comes the dreaded moment when you actually go out there and start gyrating around on wooden legs until, hopefully, you get used to it. I decided I would jump right in. Now, who should I ask?

"Hey, John."

I turned, and there was Bunny. All thoughts of Sally Rayfield were gone as I gazed into Bunny's bright green eyes. She pushed her golden-brown locks with blonde streaks away from her face, revealing even more of her wonderful sparkling green eyes while smiling that dismantling smile.

"Are you going to ask me to dance?"

Bravely, I took her hand in mine and led the most gorgeous woman in the entire world—my world, anyway—out into the throng of Washington High School kids and began to slowly sway and jerk around to the music. Every day since the fifth grade, I had thought of this moment. Actually, I had practically killed myself for this moment. We danced most of the dances together, and I realized something right away. We didn't seem to have much in common. Besides Bunny being beautiful, and having the ability to make a guy feel crazy, there didn't seem to be much else going on. There were no funny little intimate moments where we would laugh or smile together. There wasn't really much in the way of meaningful conversation, not counting the moments we shared talking about her hair and nails. It became very clear that she was no Sally Rayfield.

"John?" Bunny paused with a question hanging in the air, her face turned toward me as I guided her around the dance floor. "Do you like me?" she asked.

I looked into her warm and glowing green eyes as the band was doing a passable rendition of the Temptations' "My Girl."

As the lyrics about the month of May, sunshine, and my girl wafted through the air, I just about lost it.

The reality of the moment made it hard to talk. After all this time, after all this work to be someone, to be a tough guy who could take on the world, to be a real person who mattered and who might dare to think that someone like Bunny would care to know if I liked her or not was stirring up a storm of the century in my gut. Maybe it was my heart.

I simply nodded my head to the affirmative, my throat too tight to utter. Bunny let out a little sigh and hugged me tight, laying her world-class head on my chest. Sally who?

The rest of the evening, my brain was in some kind of cloud. As the dance was winding down, Bunny gave me a kiss on the cheek and another quick hug and ran off with the group of girls she'd come with. I gathered myself together, and joined Fred and Gary. Moments later, we were cruising the Gut with hundreds of other kids and their jalopies.

Fred and Gary both were oblivious to the milestone that I had reached that evening. Fred was riding shotgun, and Gary was in the back. They both had their heads out the window like a couple of Labrador Retrievers, as we cruised down Broadway, hollering things like "Number One!" and "Mothers, hide your daughters!" and "Washington's coming and there's nothing you can do about it!" and other such prophetic words of warning.

I wasn't paying attention. My mind was on Bunny.

CHAPTER THIRTY-FIVE

Saturday morning, I was up early and heading for Sauvie Island. I couldn't wait to tell Greg all that had happened. I hadn't seen him for a while. We'd been caught up in our own lives and hadn't spent much time together since school started. It was time to catch up.

I got there just as he was getting ready to throw some weights around. Tom was there too. The three of us went out to the barn, just like old times.

"You're looking mighty studly," Tom exclaimed, looking me up and down as I was doing some curls with forty-pound dumbbells. "What are you benching these days?"

I set the dumbbells down after doing a dozen or so reps and replied, "I don't really know. We haven't been doing any maxing out or heavy stuff since football started. The coach wants us loose for the games."

"Well, let's find out." Tom, ever the wise steward, directed me and Greg over to the bench for a test of maximum strength. "Greg, let's see what you got first."

Greg was looking really good. He had grown and was now about five foot ten and probably one hundred and sixty-five pounds. You could definitely see some serious definition in his arms and chest through his tight-fitting T-shirt.

"Just give me the bar with a couple of forty-fives to get warmed up with," Greg ordered us nonchalantly as if it was no big deal. The Olympic-style bar, we had purchased somewhere along the way, and two forty-five-pound plates without collars, was one hundred and thirty-five pounds. It wasn't all that long ago that Greg couldn't bench anywhere near that, and now he wanted it for a warm-up. Over the summer, our muscles were always tired from throwing bales of hay all day long, and we never really got a good gauge of where we were.

We put the plates on as instructed and stood back as Greg pumped out ten reps. I was impressed.

"Hey, don't burn yourself out on your warm-up," Tom demanded, not really buying what Greg was selling. "Now shake it off."

"How much more do you want?" I asked Greg as he began to shake his arms out.

"Two more forty-fives," Greg replied in a confident manner.

"That's two twenty-five," Tom said as we slipped a large plate on either side.

"Right," Greg grunted as he took his position under the bar with Tom hovering over him as his spotter.

Greg pushed the bar into position over his chest and promptly pumped out three reps.

"Give me fifteen on each side," Greg demanded.

We did as instructed. Greg got into position, and this time, Tom helped place the bar over his chest. Tom let go, and Greg lowered the bar with two hundred and fifty-five pounds down to his chest. He pushed with everything he had, and up it went. He struggled the last few inches, but managed to get his arms fully extended. Tom helped him get the bar back into its resting spot.

Greg couldn't contain his excitement and started hopping around like a madman. It was a personal best. Tom and I were both impressed as well, pounding Greg on the back, joining him in hollering and hopping around the barn.

"Hey, what can you do?" Greg wanted to know, looking at Tom as our hopping and hollering began to taper off.

"I don't know," Tom said as he began to take some of the weight off the bar. He was looking pretty stout, even for him. Playing college ball had beefed him up. We stripped the bar back down to one hundred and thirty-five pounds, and Tom did a few reps to warm up. Then we slapped on two more forty-fives. Tom did a few more reps.

"Give me a thirty-five on each side," Tom demanded stoically. "How much is that?"

I ran the numbers through my brain and replied, "Two ninety-five."

Tom shook out his arms as cool as a cucumber, as if he did this every day, and slid under the bar.

"Wait a minute. Don't half step," Greg shouted as he grabbed two tiny little weights. "Here, put this on," he instructed, handing me one of the two-and-a-half-pound plates. I complied.

"Now you've got three hundred pounds!"

Three hundred pounds was a milestone. Three hundred pounds was where the men left the boys behind. Tom was now going to attempt to make that transition.

I was Tom's spotter. With a nod from Tom, I pulled the bar out as he pushed it up and helped him place it in position over his chest. Without any to-do, he let it fall, and the instant the bar touched his chest, he pushed it back up with everything he had. Not without some difficulty, the bar went up. I grabbed it and helped place it back to rest on the iron stand. A personal best.

Tom, ever the cool one, stood and shook out his arms like

it was no big deal. Greg and I, on the other hand, went nuts again.

"Okay, John, assume the position," Tom instructed. "How much do you want?"

"Just give me the bar and two forty-fives."

Once the weights were in place and properly loaded, I knocked out about ten reps. I didn't count—I just did them until I felt a little strain. I hopped up and shook out my arms.

"Give me two more forty-fives." I demanded, mimicking some of Tom's coolness. I felt good. I was sore from the game, but it was just bruising that didn't seem to take anything away from my strength.

I pumped about five reps with two twenty-five and shook myself out again. The most I had ever benched was two sixty-five, but that was during the summer when we were working hard every day.

"Give me some of what Tom had," I said, getting cocky.

"Are you ready for three hundred pounds?" Tom wanted to know with a serious look on his face.

"Yeah, what the heck," I replied, throwing caution to the wind. I hopped around, did a couple of bends and thrusts, shook my arms some more, and made good and sure that I was warmed up thoroughly. I placed myself on the bench, where three hundred pounds awaited me.

It seemed like just yesterday when Greg and I had finally gathered enough weights to load up the bar with three hundred pounds. I didn't really think that one day, I would actually be sliding under a bar with three hundred pounds for a realistic bench-press attempt. But there I was.

It had been close to four years since I sat down on the corner of 18th and Pine and took a personal inventory. I had worked hard, and it was paying off. Whether I managed to bench three hundred pounds suddenly didn't seem all that important. I was beginning to feel like I was somebody, whether I could bench-press a bunch of weights or not.

Something else occurred to me. Bunny wanted me, but that really wasn't as important as it once was either.

As I took my position under the bar with a three-hundred-pound milestone above, I realized that I really *was* somebody. I felt good about myself. I didn't need Bunny to pump me up, and I didn't need to bench-press three hundred pounds to show my worth either. For some reason, and I didn't have time to analyze it, anger began to swell within me. *I am me*, I said to myself. *I certainly don't need to prove anything to anybody. If people can't see my worth, that's their problem, not mine.*

All my life, I had felt like less than a person. I was done with that kind of thinking. Fierce anger, almost rage, rushed through my body as I grabbed that bar. Without thinking, I pushed while Tom helped pull it into position. I dropped the loaded barbell to my chest and then pushed it back up.

Greg and Tom were speechless.

Tom helped me place the loaded bar back in its secure resting place, and I stood. I didn't hop around and I didn't pretend to be cool. I just stood there, feeling like I could take on the world.

CHAPTER THIRTY-SIX

Monday morning, I pulled into my customary parking spot at Washington High School. I liked to park in the corner at the far end of the lot where my little Chevy would be the safest from car doors flying open into its vulnerable sides. I was thinking that it might be a good day to ask Coach Skylark for a try at wide receiver. After all, I'd had a pretty good game Friday. As I was getting out of my car, a sleek black Jaguar XKE pulled directly behind me, and a '63 Chevy Impala, with loud pipes, pulled into the spot next to mine. Several large bodies poured from the Chevy and took positions around the perimeter. Rodney Skylark stepped out of his very expensive Jag. Rumors had it that he came home from LA with it after his first recruiting visit down there over the summer. Rumors further implied that a booster purchased it for him. Purely uninformed speculation. That kind of thing was, as we all know, illegal.

My gut sank. I knew instantly what this was all about. I probably should have waited until Rodney was off to USC for good before moving in on his girl. It was a little late for that kind of wisdom to do me any good.

Rodney moved slowly toward me. I couldn't get a read from his expression. If anything, I thought he looked tired. Probably a tough weekend partying and chasing world-class cheerleaders around.

"Smith, what is your problem?" Rodney asked, his tired look even more pronounced. "Every time I turn around, there you are. Do you have a death wish or something?"

He moved a little closer, as did the five offensive linemen. Two of them were behind Rodney, and three had slipped around to the gap at the front of the two cars parked side by side.

I readied myself. There was no place to run, which was my first inclination. They had blocked all areas of retreat. Only one thing to do. Sometimes the best defense is a good offense. Or, as I imagined the Japanese kamikaze suicide pilots of World War II were possibly thinking as they decided to dive-bomb the American warships, killing themselves in the process, *What the heck.*

I lowered my head and charged Rodney with all my might, catching him in the midsection. I drove my legs, pushing him back into his two big buddies. From there, it got a little hazy, as I imagined it did as well for the kamikaze pilots.

The next thing I knew, from the bottom of a pile of bodies that instantly formed over my person, I heard a whistle. At that point, I really wasn't taking all that much punishment because of the confined space I found myself in. I was actually being protected from the same people who were trying to rip me a new one.

The whistle blew even louder, and I heard shouting as the bodies began to lift off the pile. The last body was that of Rodney. He pushed my face into the blacktop as he stood. Several strong hands grabbed me and pulled me to my feet— the shouting subsided. As I stood uneasily, I looked into the strained face of the head coach of Washington High School's varsity football team, Coach Madder-Than-a-Hornet Skylark.

This was probably not a good time to ask the coach about playing wide receiver.

"It's always you, isn't it, Smith?" Coach Skylark was beside himself. "Rodney, you and Smith in my office in ten minutes." The coach stormed off as his two assistant coaches sent the offensive linemen and the onlookers who had gathered off to their classes.

Rodney parked his car, and I headed for the coach's cubicle. I got there first. Rodney wasn't far behind, sneering at me as he came into the converted office space. I noticed with satisfaction that Rodney had blood running from his nose. I smiled. Rodney didn't scare me anymore.

"Smith, Skylark, enter," a gravelly voice boomed from the head coach's makeshift office. We entered and stood there, waiting.

The coach glared at the two of us for a moment, apparently collecting his thoughts. He was faced with a predicament.

"Here's the deal," he began, the anger still apparent in his voice. "If we are to win a state championship, the two of you need to get along. You don't have to like each other. You don't have to take each other to the prom. Just leave each other alone. Smith, you are on defense, and Rodney, you are on offense. It shouldn't be too hard to stay away from each other and play football. You are both gambling with your futures. USC does not want a quarterback leading their team who can't keep from fighting with his teammates, and Smith, if you even want to think about playing football after high school, you had better get focused. Now get out of my office."

Rodney and I turned and pushed through the makeshift door, neither one of us giving ground, grinding our shoulders into one another. For a moment, I thought we might go at it right there, but Rodney simply pushed through, scowled at me, and kept going. The coach was right. There was a lot at stake.

All day, I thought about the coach's words. He had made reference to the possibility of me playing after high school. The seed had been planted in my head while playing on the JV team when Mrs. Honorly, the school counselor, had said something about college football in my future. Having Coach Skylark, who didn't seem to care for me much, mention college football and me in the same breath carried a lot of weight. I had always dreamed of playing big-time college ball. I had kept it to myself, though, not fully believing. Now the dream began to take on a whole new light.

I didn't see Bunny until third-period social studies. I entered the room a few minutes early, and there she was. She was sitting on her desk, leaning back on her hands as she talked with a couple of her friends. She was beautiful. Her long wavy hair covered her petite shoulders, and of course she was smiling that angelic "come hither, but don't touch" smile that made guys crazy. Fortunately for me, I was no longer under her spell.

"Hi, John," she purred as she straightened up and came gracefully to her feet. She walked directly over to me and locked her arm in mine.

My head began to spin, my breathing became irregular, and my knees suddenly felt weak.

"What happened to your face?" Bunny asked, sounding sincere as she looked me over.

"Rodney." I answered. I was actually in pretty good shape for having the entire offensive line plus our all-star quarterback work me over. Just a couple of scratches from the blacktop to show for it.

"Oh," Bunny replied, her grip on my arm beginning to weaken.

"Don't worry about Rodney," I said, trying to ease her mind. "I'll take care of him." Her grip on my arm regained its strength. I was feeling a little cocky. My words, however, seemed to trigger, in my brain, a more reasonable approach as my newly formed courage began to wane. *Maybe I should bake him a cake . . .*

Apparently, Bunny hadn't met up with Rodney since his return from LA over the weekend. I could only imagine what their encounter might be like, and I didn't like what I was thinking. Rodney was not a reasonable guy.

I sat down in the desk next to Bunny's as the teacher came in. I could tell that Bunny was distracted. She was probably thinking about Rodney. I felt scared for her, and for some reason, I was back under her spell. Maybe it was her vulnerability. I hated the thought of her facing Rodney.

Rodney and Bunny had study hall together next period. I planned to be there.

I followed Bunny at a discreet distance, intending to be nearby when Rodney showed up. I didn't know what I was going to do. But if he even looked like he might hurt her, I was prepared to tear his ever-loving all-star head from his body.

Bunny turned right instead of left and walked out of school. She had no intention of seeing Rodney anytime soon. Probably a good decision. Maybe he'd cool off with a little time.

I continued to ponder the situation between Bunny, Rodney, and me. Rodney didn't have any right to think that Bunny was his girl. It was obvious that Bunny didn't think they were an item any longer. Of course, Rodney seemed to be a bit on the possessive side, apparently influenced by his huge ego. He'd probably think he owned her until he went away to college. It's just possible that I might have acted a bit prematurely by meeting up with Bunny at the dance in front of practically the entire student body. Of *course* Rodney would find out. Did I really think that he would be okay with it? And what about Bunny? She knew him better than anybody. She must have known Rodney wouldn't like it. Pretty reckless of her to throw caution to the wind like that. Unless—my stomach in the vicinity of my heart began to ache—she's just using me to break up with Rodney. I was the in-your-face new boyfriend provocateur/protective barrier. It felt like there might be something to this line of speculation. Something to think about.

CHAPTER THIRTY-SEVEN

Monday's practice went without any problems. The coaches managed to get us, meaning Rodney and myself, focused on Friday's game without us tearing each other's gizzards out. We were playing Roosevelt at their place. They were an athletic team with an explosive offense. Their defense wasn't much, but they could score. We needed to be ready.

The week went by, and football was all I cared about. Bunny was around, but I didn't pay much attention to her. I couldn't tell if she was working an angle to dispose of Rodney, but she was pretty friendly.

Friday rolled around, and I found myself on the bus crammed into a seat next to Fred. We were headed for Roosevelt High in the St. Johns area of North Portland. Gary and Joel Kimber were jammed into a seat in front of us. Rodney was in the back with his entourage. Everybody was pumped and ready to kick some serious red-colored booty. Roosevelt's uniforms were red with white trim.

"Roses are red, and Roosevelt is too. We're gonna rip out their hearts and shove 'em down their throats." Fred's poem didn't rhyme, but no one cared as the busload of Warriors went nuts.

The game wasn't especially difficult. For the most part, I lined up across from a good-sized slow and not very strong lineman. I had my way with him most of the game. I sacked the quarterback several times and got into the backfield most every play, disrupting their offense. Rodney went wild, and we won 55 to 12.

There would be no dance for me that night. Rodney would be there, and I wasn't in the mood to mix it up with him. Instead, I found myself heading toward the Spinner as soon I could get showered and changed back into my duds. Sally usually got off at eight, but Greg and the guys would probably be showing up by the time I got there.

Me and my '56 rumbled on into the Spinner parking lot and sure enough, there were several cars already there. I pulled in next to a '63 Ford Fairlane. Robert Bowling, or Bobby B, as the guys were now calling him, owned the Fairlane. Robert was the same tall, lanky kid who took exception to me dominating him during a football game on Marshall Beach a couple of years before. He was even taller now, and just as skinny. He was kind of a hothead then, and he still was. Worse than that, he thought his car was the fastest thing on the planet.

"Anybody die in that wreck?" I hollered out the window of my '56 as I shut down the bad boy 327 under the hood. I knew my little Chevy had its limitations and was reminded of them every time James and his Hemi Roadrunner were around, but Robert's little stock 289 Fairlane was no match for it.

Robert was sitting in his pride and joy with a tray of goodies from the Spinner hooked to his open window, making it hard for him to jump out and face his antagonist. So he just stuck his head out the window and hollered back. "Yeah, you wanna go? Right now. Me and my Fairlane will mop up the street with you."

"Just kidding, Robert. Everybody knows you've got the

fastest car on the island," I said, trying to defuse the situation I had just instigated. It was true, though. Since Tom left for college with his somewhat souped-up pickup truck, Robert's 289 Fairlane was king. Of course, the Scappoose guys were another story.

"That's right, and I'm ready any time you say," Robert added, cooling off somewhat.

I strolled over to where Greg and a couple of his buddies were sitting around a picnic table that was covered with bags of burgers and fries and such.

"How was the game?" I asked as Greg looked up from his burger.

"Hey," Greg said loudly, glad to see me. "We beat the stink out of them. We're undefeated." He began telling me all about it. The rest of the guys chimed in, and even Robert got out of his car to help paint the picture of their collective winning ways.

"How was *your* game?" Greg asked as the guys began to wind down.

"Good. We whupped Roosevelt. We're five and one with two games left before the division championship." I heard an unmistakable rumble approaching the Spinner. I knew without looking who it was. James and his big bad boy Hemi, rolled into the parking lot.

"Hey, Robert, there's a car you haven't beaten yet," someone hollered over the distinct exhaust tones of the Hemi. Everybody except Robert laughed.

I noticed right away that James was not alone. My stomach tightened and my heart began to ache as I recognized who it was. Sally Rayfield was looking in our general direction with a big smile on her pretty face. She sure seemed happy when she was with James.

James brought his beast to a stop and shut her down. He and Sally got out and joined us at the table.

"Hey, guys," James said by way of salutation. He smiled.

James had a way of smiling that was very disarming. His smile was one of quiet confidence tempered with sincere humility with a touch of kindness and a dash of good-natured energy. He was very hard to dislike, even though I was doing my best.

"Hey, you two," I greeted them, emphasizing the word *two*. They both just smiled. Sally was especially smiley. My heart ached even more.

We shot the breeze for a bit. Sally wanted to know how football was going. I told her it was great, and she seemed pleased. Then she hopped into Marianne Sebastian's hot-pink VW Bug when it rolled up a few minutes later. I didn't get Sally alone, as I'd hoped. I hung in there as long as I could, but seeing Sally and James together, and seeing her so happy, was taking its toll. I split.

As I rolled down the highway heading back to town, I began to weigh the situation. On one hand, I shouldn't be concerned about who Sally was going out with since I was trying to move in on Bunny. I just couldn't get her out of my head, though. I wanted her, but I wasn't ready to let Bunny go. I wanted her too. With my heart being pulled in two directions, my brain was having trouble. I needed some clarity.

Sunday after church, I cruised over to Greg's house. I needed to share my dilemma with someone who might help me see clearly. Greg was never one to shy away from the truth as he understood it.

"You're crazy," was Greg's reaction as I unloaded on him. "First of all, this Bunny sounds like she's just a user. Dump her. Problem solved." He leaned back in the easy chair facing the TV, as we were watching the Rams play the Colts.

"What about Sally and . . .?" I never got James' name out. Roman Gabriel dropped back to pass as the entire Colt defense poured in on him. At the last second, he flipped a pass downfield for a big play. Greg went nuts. After he settled down, he turned to me and said,

"I never got this attraction-to-Sally thing. Probably because we've known each other since we were pretty young. I'll always see her as kind of a little sister, I guess. But I do know that she's a nice person. What you see with Sally is what you get. There isn't a phony bone in her body. Now, this Bunny chick sounds like she's anything but real. Lose the phony troublemaker, and grab Sally, if she's what you want." With that, Greg turned his full attention back to the Rams, as they were getting ready to punch it in from the two.

I sat there pondering what he had said. But what about James? Sally seemed to like him. *What's not to like? I even like him.* It just didn't seem to be as easy as Greg made it out to be.

CHAPTER THIRTY-EIGHT

Monday morning, I found myself back in school, and my mind was still in turmoil. Greg's wisdom hadn't helped. I was still confused. I got through my classes somehow. Bunny was attentive, as usual, and she still seemed to have some kind of power over me. Nothing had changed. What I needed was some hard-hitting, mind-numbing football.

Practice was especially, and blessedly, hard. The coaches were all over us, and we responded by beating the crap out of each other. It was just what I needed. Thoughts of Bunny and Sally went away as I received, and delivered, massive amounts of punishment.

We had two more games before districts. First up was Lincoln. They were okay. We should beat them without too much trouble. The last game was Benson. One never knew what kind of team they would put on the field from one year to the next. They had over two thousand boys at their disposal.

As it turned out, we rolled over both Lincoln and Benson. We were playing our best football. Our team was like a machine. The defense was high energy, and the offense was unstoppable. We were ready for districts.

Rodney and I did as Coach Skylark ordered. If we wanted to win state, we needed each other, and we knew it. Everyone knew it. So, when Bunny started to display her affections toward me in what seemed to be an exaggerated sort of way, with lots of witnesses, I became suspicious.

"What are you doing, Bunny?" I asked, not buying her shtick. She was nuzzling my neck in the cafeteria where everybody could see, including Rodney. I pushed her away and turned to put some distance between us, but stopped. There was Rodney, standing just two feet in front of me. *Here we go*, I thought. Rodney looked me straight in the eye and jerked his head toward the cafeteria door.

"We need to talk. Come on," he said as he started toward the door, apparently expecting me to follow. So I did. I followed Rodney out of the cafeteria and out the front door of the school, where he stopped and turned toward me. I fully expected him to let me have it with a sucker punch. I was ready, but he didn't do anything. He stood there for a moment, collecting his thoughts.

"Here's the deal," he started, sounding a lot like his dad. "You can have Bunny. I'm done with her and her games." He paused for effect and then continued, "I would appreciate it, though, if you would at least wait until the season is over before you stake your claim. I'd like to leave here in January with a little dignity."

I was shocked. Rodney was seceding, and somewhat gracefully, too. All I had ever wanted was being presented to me on a silver platter. However, I wasn't feeling very excited about it.

"You're leaving in January?" I heard myself ask, practically missing the point about Bunny being mine.

"Yeah, I'm finishing up school in LA and joining USC for spring practice. My dad's going, too. He got a coaching job at the same high school. So, Bunny's yours."

I looked at Rodney, and for the first time, I realized that he was a real person. I had always seen him as some kind of evil superhero. I hadn't thought, that maybe, he had feelings. I just thought he was a giant ego with chiseled good looks and muscles. I looked straight into his eyes and said with sincerity, "I hope things work out for you down there."

"Thanks," he said almost humbly as we looked at one another with just a hint of mutual respect.

I think we might have just had a moment. You know, like a Hallmark kind of thing, except, more manly, of course. Rodney walked away. Nothing more was said. I quickly weighed the situation and decided right then and there to stay away from Bunny. Hearing that I *could* have her, the attraction wasn't quite the same. Plus, I was starting to see a side of her that I didn't care for.

No more time to analyze the various complications of my love life—we had to get ready for the division championship game. Cleveland, the only team to beat us, was up next. It was us or them, and then the winner would go on to state.

Friday came before we knew it, and I had managed to do as Rodney had requested. I stayed away from Bunny. The game was being played at Civic Stadium in downtown Portland. We took the far end of the field and began to warm up. Cleveland took the other end. They were confident, even cocky. They had beaten us once, and I knew they were thinking they would do it again.

Cleveland won the toss and elected to kick off, and so they did. They got our return guy on the thirty-five. Rodney and our offense quickly got the ball down inside the Cleveland thirty-yard line, where the Cleveland defense stiffened and held. Our field goal kicker hadn't gotten any better, so trying for a field goal wasn't an option. We went for it on fourth and six. Joel Kimber blasted through the line for about three, and it was Cleveland's ball on the twenty-six-yard line.

I was pumped out of my mind when I lined up against Number Eighty-Three. He was about six feet and maybe two thirty. The ball was snapped, and I shot out of my stance like a rocket and rammed Eighty-Three with all my might, driving him toward the running back, who was receiving the ball on a quick hand-off, clogging up the hole that he was to go through. Fred was there as well, and the two of us got the runner down for a loss of one. The next play was similar, except to the other side where Gary stopped the same running back for no gain. It was third and eleven. Normally, Cleveland didn't pass much, but third and long deep in their own territory, they were feeling the pressure. I sensed a pass.

I came out of my stance and pushed off the slower lineman, and there he was—Cleveland's quarterback was dropping back to pass. I had nothing but eight feet of turf between me and him as he backpedaled, looking in the other direction for his receiver. I was getting up to full speed. He had set his feet and looked in my direction, his arm cocked, ready to throw. I instinctively raised my hands as he was attempting to bring his arm forward—making contact with the ball before it left his fingers. My momentum knocked him to the ground. I looked up, and there was twenty two yards of nothing but turf, and the ball was in my hands. Nobody could catch me. Carl Lewis himself could not have caught me.

That one play, that one huge magnificent play, set the tone for the rest of the game. We slaughtered them. The final score was 53 to 13. It shouldn't have been that close, but they managed to score a couple of touchdowns against our scrubs. We were going on to state.

CHAPTER THIRTY-NINE

I talked with Greg over the phone, exchanging grandiose versions of our individual games. The second liar, as was our custom, topping the first. Apparently, Greg and his Scappoose buddies were going to state too. Greg was doing well. The two of us had stayed focused and worked really hard. I was happy for him, as he was for me. He was a good friend. Greg had a problem, though.

"I kind of met someone I think I like more than Marianne Sebastian," Greg confessed almost sheepishly over the phone.

"What?" I was shocked. Greg was crazy about Marianne. "Who?"

"Georgia Rayfield," Greg answered.

"Rayfield?" I asked.

"Sally's cousin. She's the same age as Sally and Marianne, and she's been hanging around with them lately."

"What about Marianne?"

"I don't know," Greg replied in a dejected sort of way.

"What are you going to do?"

"I was hoping you might have an answer." Greg sounded hopeful.

"Uh," I stammered while I was trying to think. "Find her

someone else," I finally blurted out. "She's super cute. It shouldn't be too hard to find someone to take her off your hands."

"Right." I could practically hear the cogs turning in Greg's brain over the phone as he processed my suggestion.

With that, we said our goodbyes and hung up.

I didn't know that Sally had a cousin in the area.

That week, we prepared for our first state playoff victim. Pendleton High—from Pendleton, Oregon, of course. They were a small-town school and were undefeated. Those country schools are often tough. The game was at Civic Stadium in downtown Portland again, and we didn't have any problem with them. We won 41 to 17. Rodney was getting a lot of attention. He had verbally committed to USC, but that didn't stop other schools from trying. Scouts were everywhere.

Next up was Lake Grove, our second game of the state playoffs. They were rich kids in the Lake Oswego area. Nice school, with plenty of money. They went to state almost every year. We put the hurt on them. The final score was 47 to 20. The win was costly, however. Joel Kimber, our number-one running back, broke his ankle when a big lineman hopped on it after the whistle. Joel wouldn't be ready to play for some time. Our number-two running back hadn't played much, for good reason. It looked like Rodney was going to have his hands full without a running game.

I drove out to the Spinner after the game against Lake Grove. I'd had another good game, nothing spectacular. I just kept their big tackle from blasting holes in the line like he was accustomed to doing.

I pulled into the Spinner parking lot, and there was James talking to Sally through the window, again. Was I ever going to get a break?

I walked up to the window in time to hear James say, "I'll pick you up at eight."

James, and his all-star Hollywood smile, turned and began

to walk right toward me. I saw myself in my mind's eye letting him have it with a right to the gut and a knee to the head and then a stomp to the groin. Instead, I made eye contact and returned his heartfelt smile. You couldn't stay mad at James. He was just a really good guy, which made my heart hurt. I knew Sally knew he was a really good guy too.

I said hi to Sally, who seemed really glad to see me. I, however, was not feeling the same. The reality of James being in the picture was more than my fragile constitution could take. I ordered a shake, made some small talk, and split when another customer came to the window. Before, when I was faced with the possibility of Sally being with someone else, I had Bunny to fall back on. Now I wasn't sure I wanted Bunny. I might be left with nothing.

Coach Skylark did his best to keep us focused on one game at a time, but we couldn't help but see the big picture. Two more games, and we'd play for the state title. After practice, as we had practically every day since Joe Billings showed up, the two of us got together for a little extra work. Mostly I ran pass patterns, and then we would work for about fifteen minutes on handoffs. Joe didn't need the practice, as far as I could see. He was tearing it up on the JV team. Some were saying he had a better arm than Rodney. Of course, I still harbored the desire to be a wide receiver. My speed had increased, and I could catch pretty much any pass, I could get my hands on but I didn't look like a wide receiver. I had leaned up considerably. There wasn't any fat to speak of on my body anymore, but I was still a little thick compared to the waifs who generally hold down the receiver positions. The coach still saw me as a lineman—a small lineman, but a lineman. I was now just barely a fraction under six feet, and I weighed one hundred and ninety pounds. My speed and strength made up for my lack of size on the line. If I was to play at the next level, I would have to play a different position.

"Smith," Coach Skylark hollered as if his house was on

fire, and I was standing there with a handful of matches and a can of gasoline. "What the bleep are you two doing out here every day? Are you actually expecting to accomplish something?" the coach growled. Apparently, he had wandered out to where Joe and I were practicing.

"Yes, sir," I hollered, matching the coach's intensity, but at the same time, trying to remain respectful. I couldn't, however, keep a little anger from entering my voice. "Joe here plans on being the next Washington High all-star quarterback, and I'm going to be his number-one go-to all-star wide receiver," I said with passion and conviction.

"I see," the coach said thoughtfully. "Carry on." And he walked away.

Next up was Burns, another small-town school with tough farm kids. Our defense held them in check for the most part, and Rodney was able to work enough magic for the win. The score was 27 to 17.

Scouts continued to be seen everywhere. They were at every game, and they would show up at practice. Of course, they were there mostly to see Rodney. Gary Laughton was a senior and was getting some attention from a couple of them as well. Gary, who was big as a sophomore when he and I worked out together, was even bigger now. He was six foot five, and the three hundred-plus pounds of jelly he once had, was pretty much muscle now. He was a monster, and a monster that was just beginning to show a little of his potential. The scouts were starting to drool over the possibilities.

Even Fred Homestead got some notice from the scouts. Fred had been playing very well. He had good size and had worked hard, and it was showing. An assistant coach from Montana State had pulled him aside and told him to continue to work hard because he would be watching. Of course, this went right to Fred's head.

"Oh, yeah, Montana State wants me," Fred was

explaining to a group of us at our table in the back of the cafeteria. "They'll have to get in line, though. I'm not going to just jump on their offer. I have to give everyone a fair chance. It wouldn't be right otherwise."

I smiled, and there were a couple of snickers, but I noticed that Bunny, who was sitting there at our table at the rear of the cafeteria, seemed impressed. She and Shirley Thompson had been sitting with us at lunch for a couple of weeks now. Bunny and Fred had always gotten along. She would laugh at his jokes, and Fred would tease her some, as he did most everybody. But now that I think about it, I think she liked Fred. Of course she liked Fred. Everybody liked Fred.

We had one more game to win if we wanted to get to the championship game. South Salem was huge, and our next opponent. They were a no-nonsense type of team that used their size and strength to beat you into submission. They didn't score a lot, but neither did their opponents.

As it turned out, South Salem was big and they were tough, but they were also a little slow. Rodney was able to impose his will on them. We beat them 36-12. Our defense played great. We were on to the state championship.

CHAPTER FORTY

I was really sore after our game against South Salem. We handled them okay, but it took its toll. They were tough. Our next and final opponent for all the marbles was Medford High. They had been the number-one school in the state, ever since we knocked Grant out of the picture. They were undefeated and very good. They were well balanced on offense, and their defense was stifling.

Without a solid running game, I was a bit concerned if our offense could get it done. Up to this point, Rodney had been enough. I wasn't sure if that would still be the case. I put all those thoughts out of my head as I directed my '56 to the Spinner once more. There was a big dance to celebrate our victory, but I wasn't in the mood. Bunny would be there, and I heard that Rodney wouldn't be. He was allegedly taking a recruiting visit to Ohio State, even though he'd verbally committed to USC. I heard he wanted to see what the Ohio State cheerleaders were like. So anyhow, I could go to the dance and spend a little time with Bunny if I wanted. At that point, Rodney wasn't really paying much attention to her. But I had an agreement, and I intended to honor it. Besides, we couldn't afford any distractions with the State Championship looming.

I pulled into the Spinner's practically empty parking lot. Scappoose had played their last playoff game and lost by two points. They were having a large end-of-the-season dance, and I didn't expect anyone to be there. I parked in an empty stall. I didn't know why I was there. I guess I was hoping to see Sally. I knew I couldn't have her. James had moved in and swept her away. My feelings toward Sally and Bunny were becoming clear. I didn't really want Bunny, and I couldn't have Sally.

Jeanie, another of the local teenagers, came out to get my order. "Hey there, John," she greeted me in a friendly way. "What'll it be?"

"Uh, nothing. Sally around?" I asked, knowing the answer.

"She's at the dance," Jeanie replied brightly.

"Oh. I guess I'll see you then." I fired up my Chevy and headed out. I drove around town, trying to sort things out. Really, there wasn't much to actually sort out. It looked like I was going to end up with nothing. At least I still had football. With that last thought, I pointed my '56 Chevy toward home.

Sunday afternoon, I heard my mom knocking on the door of our detached one-car garage that I had recently turned into my apartment. I was listening to "Sunshine of Your Love" being blasted through my stereo speakers, when I heard a faint knock on the door. I turned down the music.

"Telephone," my mom hollered.

I followed her back into the house. "Hello?" I said into the phone without much enthusiasm.

"Hey, John, where've you been?" Greg wanted to know, getting right to the point.

"I . . . uh . . . I've been really busy with the playoffs. We're playing Medford for the championship," I said, trying to distract Greg from his suspicions. I had been kind of scarce lately.

"Everything okay over there?" Greg was picking up on something.

"Yeah, things are great," I lied. "One more game, and we'll be the state champs," I added with false enthusiasm. I was excited about the game, but thoughts of Sally were bringing me down.

"How about you and Sally and me and my new girl get together after your big win Friday and have some fun?" Greg asked with forced nonchalance.

"Your new girl?" What new girl? "What happened to Marianne?" I wanted to know, not remembering our conversation and the advice I had shared.

"I did like you told me. I found someone else for Marianne and then moved in on Georgia Rayfield. She didn't know what hit her," Greg explained, his excitement exposed.

"Hey, that's great." I was happy for Greg.

"Okay then, you and Sally and me and Georgia on Friday night."

"I don't think that will work," I said, shooting down Greg and his enthusiasm.

"Why not?"

"Ask James," I replied simply. "I gotta go, Greg. I'll talk to you later," I managed as my throat began to tighten. I hung up the phone and went back out to the garage to wallow. Visions of Twinkies dipped in chocolate began flowing through my brain, helping to push everything else out.

The rest of the week, I focused on the game. I got up in the morning, went to class, worked hard, and then went to practice. At practice, I worked even harder. After practice, Joe and I worked on fundamentals, and then I went home, where I studied and went to bed. No extracurricular activities. No phone calls.

"Phone for you," my mom hollered from outside of my sanctuary.

I unlocked and opened the garage door.

"It's Greg. This is the third time he's called this week. He wants to talk to you."

"Tell him I'm busy and I'll get back to him," I told my mom. I just wanted to put the whole Scappoose and Sauvie Island part of my life out of the picture until after the game. I could deal with all that emotional stuff later. I needed to stay focused, I told myself. So that's what I did. No distractions— just schoolwork and football.

"Hey, John," Bunny cooed as I walked by. She stood in front of her open locker.

I slowed down and made eye contact. There it was, that same smile that I thought I was immune to. She sure looked good. My heart began to ache. Thoughts of Sally flashed before my mind's eye, and I realized that as good as Bunny was looking, it was still Sally I wanted.

"I gotta go, Bunny. Sorry, but I can't afford any distractions this week." I continued on, my heart still hurting.

CHAPTER FORTY-ONE

Time went by slowly. Every moment of the day when I wasn't ramming myself into someone in preparation for the state championship, I was thinking of Sally. I didn't know why I tortured myself so. *She's out of the picture. Got to move on.*

"Hey, John," Bunny greeted me in her special sort of way with that special sort of smile.

What the heck, I thought. I could do worse.

"Hey, Bunny," I returned. If I didn't think about it too much, Bunny was darn nice. She sure looked good. No doubt about that.

We exchanged pleasantries until the bell rang. Then we headed toward our individual classes.

It was Friday, game day. I got through my classes—how, I don't know. I didn't remember any of them.

Before we knew it, we had suited up, gotten on the bus for the short ride downtown, and found ourselves on the field at Civic Stadium, warming up. Medford was dressed in green and yellow, and we were in white.

People were slowly filling the seats. It looked like there would be a large crowd. Rodney was a big-time draw, and Medford had a pretty good quarterback of their own. It should be a competitive game, or so said the newspaper. *Not if I have anything to say about it*, I promised myself.

Finally, the coin was flipped. The anthem was sung. We were in position to kick off, having lost the toss. I was now part of the special teams unit. The instant our kicker made contact with the ball, I was off and running downfield as fast as I could along with my companions, looking for the guy with the ball with the intention of hitting him so hard, they would need to check his dental records to identify him.

Several of us got down there in time to pounce on the poor guy as he was trying to change direction. It was Medford's ball on the thirty-yard line.

We lined up against their good-sized and athletic offensive line. I was facing Eighty-Two. He was about six foot two, and he looked to weigh about two thirty—maybe two forty tops. The ball was snapped, and we collided. He let me have it good. *Maybe he was more like two fifty*, I was thinking as I picked myself off the turf. I realized right away that I would have to step it up a notch or two. Eighty-Two was good.

Medford's offense wasted little time getting the ball downfield. They scored on a quick pass to their running back coming out of the backfield from six yards out. We got the ball, and just as I had feared, without a running game, their defense was able to key on Rodney. He was having trouble. Their defense was good-sized and quick. Rodney didn't have much time, and they kept him from running wild. Three plays and we punted.

Our defense stiffened up some and slowed Medford down. They had worked it down to our thirty-nine-yard line. It was fourth and twelve. They punted the ball, and it went out of bounds at the three. On the first play of the series, Rodney managed to sprint away from several Medford defenders, who had ripped into the backfield, for a first down. That was it. We were forced to punt from our own fifteen-yard line. Medford came hard with everyone, and our punter barely got the kick away.

I was doing a little better with Eighty-Two. I realized that I needed to keep myself low to have any success with this big strong kid. We were fighting to a standstill for the most part. Our defense was struggling to hold their own. Medford scored again in the first quarter. It was now 14-0, and things weren't looking good.

During the time-out to change field position, the coach hauled us over for a little pep talk, most of which doesn't need repeating. Suffice it to say that he was not happy with our performance, and he made it clear that we had better get with the program.

We did our best, holding Medford to just one more score for the half. They kicked the extra point and were now up 21-0. Our offense was still struggling. We had no running game. As good as Rodney was, even he needed a little help at times, and this was one of those times.

We shuffled into the locker room with our heads hanging down.

"Smith, come here," a booming voice commanded.

I quickly moved toward the voice to see Coach Skylark standing there, feet spread, arms folded, looking like he was about to explode.

"Yes, sir, Coach." I reported. I was feeling more than a bit anxious and a pinch intimidated.

The coach leaned forward, closing the gap and getting into my space. "Smith, do you think you could run the football effectively?" he asked in a more subdued, yet still intense growling sort of way.

I was stunned. That was not what I was expecting. I thought he was going to chew me a new one for not getting to their quarterback.

"I . . . uh . . ." I stammered as the reality of what the coach was asking took a moment to fully register.

"Well, can you or can't you?" the coach boomed, losing all patience, his eyes bugging out and the vein in his temple looking like it would pop.

"Yes, sir, I can," I boomed back at least as fiercely after quickly collecting myself.

The coach calmed slightly, nodded, and hollered over to where Rodney was sprawled on a bench with a towel over his face.

"Rodney, get your butt over here."

Rodney did as instructed.

"Smith here is going to run the football. Grab a ball and practice handing it off. I want you two sharp and ready to go. You've got ten minutes, go! "

Rodney and I exchanged glances. I saw, what I thought, was a glimmer of hope in his eyes. Rodney wanted this game bad. I could sense it. This was it for him. I knew he didn't want to go out losing.

We quickly grabbed a ball and headed out to the field. Apparently, Rodney wasn't going to let any past experiences between us get in the way of our task at hand. As we ran through the tunnel, I realized that Rodney was not alone in his desire to win this game. I had spent what felt like my whole life waiting and hoping and working toward this very moment. I wanted it more than anything I could think of . . . *Sally who? Well almost anything.* I was however more than ready to run over somebody. *Just give me the ball.*

Rodney and I didn't speak much. We practiced almost frantically exchanging the football. The only time we spoke was when Rodney showed me how he would put the ball in my stomach and pull it out again on the read option plays. I needed to be aware of him pulling the ball back out. We couldn't afford any fumbles. The teams took the field way before either of us wanted. Ready or not, it was time for some football. Coach Skylark blew his whistle for all of us to gather around for his final little pep talk.

After a few well-chosen words, of the motivational variety, that probably shouldn't be repeated, from our head coach Rodney took the ball from my hand and said, "Let's get these guys."

We had twenty-four minutes to right the wrongs of the first half. Medford kicked the ball, and our return guy gathered it in at the twelve and managed to get to the fifteen before being pulverized by nearly their entire special team's squad. I think even the kicker was in on the tackle.

"Okay, okay," the coach hollered, swinging his arms around, trying to get the attention of the offense before sending us out. "Smith here is going to run the football this half, and he'll need your entire cooperation. You big uglies, open up some holes for him. If we can get our running game going, Medford won't know what hit them. We can do this. Let's go."

With that, the offense took the field. Gary and Fred were super excited to have me out there with them. "Let's eat their lunch," Gary shouted, pounding me on my back as we were running onto the field.

"Yeah, and kiss their girl and steal their dog," Fred added, helping Gary finish his line of thought. After a brief huddle where Rodney called a play and then explained to me, personally, that I was to run between Fred and Gary, our two best linemen, we lined up. Rodney was under center and I was just behind him and to his left. Rodney looked over the defense, called out some numbers that didn't make any sense to me, and barked out the "magic" number that sent the whole offensive machine into action. I rushed forward just like I had been doing after practice with Joe Billings for the last two years. With both hands, I grabbed the ball that Rodney slammed into my gut, and headed toward the spot between Fred and Gary. There wasn't much of a hole there, but I put my head down and rammed. Arms and hands were all over me as I pushed through the crease. I kept my legs churning, and as I looked up, all I saw was open field. Just as I was about to get up to full speed, my legs were taken out from under me, and I flew forward. I got up, and the ref took the ball and placed it on the twenty-seven-yard line. I had gained twelve yards—first down.

The guys were all over me briefly before they obeyed the angry and authoritative voice of our leader, Rodney Skylark. Rodney may have been a lot of things, but at that very moment as all of us guys obeyed and huddled up, I realized, Rodney was the man. He had complete control and I, as did the others, believed.

The next play called was similar, except Rodney explained to me that if he saw the defense collapsing, he would pull the ball out of my stomach, and find an open receiver.

The defense must have stayed put because Rodney handed the ball to me again, and again I hit the small opening provided for me and drove through hands and arms, before being dragged down after a seven-yard gain.

We huddled up, and I could almost see a smile on Rodney's lips. His eyes, however, were intense. He called the play. "Smith, be ready. I may pull the ball out on this one,"

Rodney instructed me individually as he made eye contact with each of his receivers. They knew what that meant. We lined up, Rodney under center, me to his left. He looked over the defense, and I could see that the safeties had moved in. Our ability to run the ball was leveling the playing field.

Rodney barked out some numbers and then the only one that mattered to me. I lunged forward. As expected, Rodney pushed the ball into my stomach, and with strong hands he pulled it back out as I hit the crease between Gary and Fred. Again, there were arms and hands clawing at me. I drove my legs as if everything counted on me. Down I went after about five yards, which would have been a first down if I had the ball. I didn't, though. I heard the crowd roar from under the pile of Medford's overachievers. Rodney had taken the ball from my stomach and promptly rolled out and hit our speedy little wide receiver, who apparently was wide open, and he was gone. Just like that, we scored. We failed on our two-point conversion try. The score was now 21-6.

We kicked the ball to Medford, and our team had new life. We stopped their return guy on the twenty, and our defense shredded them for a three and out. Our ball. We continued to run the ball at them. Occasionally I would line up on Rodney's right, but for the most part, we kept it simple. I ran through the hole that Gary and Fred made for me. Medford knew what we were going to do, and they managed to stop me often enough. However, using their resources to stop me allowed Rodney just enough leeway to do his thing. We scored again. This time, Rodney faked a handoff to me and took it in himself from the two. He then hit our tight end for the two-point conversion. It was now 21-14.

Our defense continued to play, inspired. We held Medford again. And again they punted. We lined up, and Rodney took several snaps from the shotgun and started running and passing the ball all over the place. Medford started to key on him, trying desperately to contain him.

We huddled up on third and three on the Medford forty-one. Rodney called another play. He would be receiving the ball from the shotgun again.

"Smith, let your man get by you, and look for the ball," Rodney instructed me in English after calling the play for everyone else.

I knew what was coming. I had seen the offense do this before. Rodney liked to sucker the defense into thinking he was going to either throw downfield or take off and run, and then once they had committed, he would dump the ball off to his running back, who would be in the area as a blocker. Because Rodney was such a threat with the ball, this little deception often went for a sizable gain. The ball was snapped, and the offensive line made, as instructed, a poor attempt at holding back the rushers. I went straight for the nearest defender, making it look good, and let him brush by as I looked in Rodney's direction. The ball came floating over the Medford assailant into my hands. I turned up-field, and there was no one there. Forty-five yards later, I was standing in the end zone. I couldn't believe it. The score was 21 to 20, and we had a chance to go ahead with a two-point conversion.

The crowd went nuts. My teammates went nuts. Rodney, however, didn't have time for celebrating. He quickly gathered the offense into a huddle and called for a run up the middle. That meant me. We lined up, the ball was snapped, I lunged forward, Rodney fed me the ball, and before I had time to think much about anything, I found myself pushing into the end zone with half of Medford's finest on my back for two. We were now ahead 22-21.

Our lead didn't last long. We had pretty much stopped Medford's running game, but we were having trouble getting to the quarterback. He was too good to give him as much time back there as we were giving him. Sure enough, he hit a wide-open receiver who had gotten loose, and they scored from fifty-five yards out. They hit their extra-point try and went ahead 28 to 22.

Medford kicked off to us and stopped our return guy on the seventeen-yard line. They were shutting us down on special teams. An official time-out was called to scrape up our kick returner from the field. He wasn't getting up on his own. As it turned out, he just got the wind knocked out of him and needed a minute.

During the time-out, I scanned the crowd. My mom and my little brother and sister were supposed to be there. My Auntie Jean was going to drive them to the game, since my mom never did own a car. I spotted them near the thirty-yard line and waved. They saw me and waved back.

My smile froze when I saw what appeared to be a familiar face. There in the crowd was a girl who looked a lot like Sally

Rayfield sitting next to another girl I didn't recognize—from that distance, anyway. A big guy sat down next to the girl, who looked like Sally, loaded down with popcorn, soda, and such. I saw the same girl, take some of his snacks from his hand. *Must be someone else.* Just the same, thoughts of Sally ripped through my guts.

I had to get her face out of my mind. She was not mine, and never would be. Football was the only thing that mattered, and we had a game to win. I turned the ache in my heart away, and anger took its place. I was boiling inside.

The coach was giving us a pep talk as our return guy was getting helped off the field. I didn't hear a word, but as his last syllable and my last thoughts ended, I let out a roar that sent the rest of the pack of blood-thirsty uniformed madmen into a collective frenzy. We took the field and huddled up.

Rodney looked into the eyes of each of us. We were ready. He called the play, and as before, told me my job. We lined up. Rodney looked over the defense and called the number that sent us into action.

I lunged forward, and Rodney slammed the ball into my stomach, and I promptly ran right into a brick wall. I bounced back and instantly realized that there was nowhere to go. I sensed something on my left, so I turned right and then cut up the middle where the center and the right guard should have been and turned on the afterburners. I got through the original line of scrimmage, where I faced Medford's middle linebacker. Lowering my head, I hit him full-on, driving my legs. Down he went, and I was off to the races. I made a good go of it, but one of their speedy corners had an angle on me and tripped me up on their thirty-five. Pretty good gain, though. The crowd went nuts. We went nuts.

Rodney got us under control again and called the play. He would fake a handoff to me and hit a hopefully wide-open receiver. The ball was snapped, and I did my job, ramming into the line without the ball. Rodney rolled out and threw to the open receiver cutting across the field. The ball hit him right in the hands and bounced off into the arms of a Medford defender, who took the ball up the field. We got him on our own thirty-five-yard line. Medford scored three plays later. Their extra-point try was good, and the score was now 35-22 Medford.

The third quarter ended, and we were in a desperate situation. They kicked off and it was our ball on our own thirty-five and down by two touchdowns. As we huddled up, Rodney again looked into each of our eyes. "We've got this," he said simply and called the play. Rodney had a confidence bordering on crazy that reached into each of our souls. We believed. With that, we lined up, each of us determined to make it happen.

Momentum is a funny thing. I remember one time when my buddies and I were playing a game over at the Girls Poly field in Southeast Portland. Our team had the athletes, and the other team was younger and smaller. In the first half, we literally ran all over them, as expected. Then, somehow, the momentum shifted. Even though we were bigger and stronger and more athletic, the other team started scoring, and we couldn't do anything. They caught up and would have won, but we called the game off before we completely lost face. Momentum—they had it, and we couldn't for the life of us get it back.

Rodney began to work his magic. With me as a threat running the ball, Rodney had room to run. Calling his own plays as he always did, Rodney directed us down the field. We scored from three yards out when Rodney pulled the ball from my stomach and took it in himself through a gap on his right. We missed on the extra-point kick. The score was now 35-28, Medford.

Medford got the ball back and seemed to go conservative. We ate them up. Three and out. Our ball on our own twenty-four-yard line with a little over seven minutes to go.

Again, Rodney mixed the plays up, giving me the ball just enough to keep them off balance. We worked the ball downfield, fairly quickly. Rodney hit a receiver, who ran down to the three where he was hit, and promptly fumbled. A Medford defender pounced on it.

Medford seemed to come alive and worked the ball down the field, using up as much clock as they could. We were running out of time. It was third and seven on our thirty-five-yard line with just over three minutes to play. Medford was having trouble running against us. Passing was what got them here, and when they went conservative before, it cost them. I was thinking they would pass.

I lined up against Eighty-Two, who had given me all I wanted all game long. I was getting tired from playing both ways. I knew we had to stop them here if we were to have a chance. I thought of all those afternoons of stacking hundred-pound bales of hay when I couldn't lift one more bale, but I did. And then I lifted another and another. I knew I could do this.

I had to get into the backfield. I hadn't been back there much in this game. I needed a little cooperation from Eighty-Two, but I didn't think he was going to come through for me. I would have to make it happen. If I could just get low and stand him up, he might just be off balance enough to push around him. Of course, I had been trying to do this all game. We were both getting a little tired, and he wasn't coming off the ball quite like he had. Neither was I, though.

I readied myself, determined to throw one last bale of alfalfa with everything I had. The ball was snapped. I came out of my stance and caught Eighty-Two as he was coming out of his and pushed. I was able to get around him just enough to get a hand in the air as the ball came whizzing over my head, deflecting it. The pass was incomplete—fourth down.

Medford punted, and the ball bounced out of bounds at

the six-yard line. We had ninety-four yards to go with two minutes and fifty-five seconds, and we were down by seven.

We were a team possessed. Rodney would not be denied, and neither would we. In just over a minute, we were in the red zone. Rodney had been running all over the place doing that for which he was famous—improvising. He handed the ball off to me a couple of times just to keep the defense honest, but it was all him.

Medford stiffened up, and we found ourselves with a third and goal on the six-yard line. Rodney called the play. We picked up three more on a quick pass to the sideline. Fourth and goal, and time was running out. Medford was not letting us run. Rodney called a pass play over the middle.

We lined up, the ball was snapped, I lunged forward, taking the fake, and Rodney dropped back as several Medford defenders came crashing in. Rodney threw the ball as a big defensive end was in his face, his hands in the air. The ball was deflected up and came down in the big mitts of Fred Homestead, who had gotten turned around, and then lunged forward with the ball, crashing through bodies—crossing the goal line.

Our offense lined up, for what would be the last time. Rodney pulled the ball from my stomach, faking the handoff, and pushed his way into the end zone, for two. The score was now 36-35, Washington.

There were thirty seconds left, and it proved to be too little for Medford.

CHAPTER FORTY-TWO

The crowd, of about twenty-five thousand, who were mostly Washington fans, went nuts. I was numb and totally spent. Shouldn't I be feeling something? We had just won the state championship. I shuffled around the field, shaking the hands of the Medford players. They were sad, but gracious. It was a great game. We had Rodney. That was the difference.

"Well, I can't take all of the credit. It is a team sport, after all," I heard Fred telling a couple of the many TV, radio, and newspaper reporters who seemed to be everywhere. Fred was getting a fair amount of attention from scoring that last touchdown.

"You the man," a little kid hollered at Fred as he was humbly explaining how he couldn't do what he does without his teammates.

"Yes, thank you," Fred replied in acknowledgment.

Fred's the man. I smiled weakly and walked by. I had no problem with that. As far as I was concerned, Fred had always been the man.

Rodney was in the center of the field, surrounded by reporters. People from the stands had poured onto the field. I got lots of pats on the back and "good game" from the fans and hugs from teammates. I was starting to feel a little something. We had just won the state championship, and I think it was beginning to sink in. But boy howdy, was I ever tired.

"Hey, Smith." A familiar voice rang out from behind me. I turned around, and there was Greg with a very cute redheaded girl on his arm.

"Great game, John. You made us all proud." Greg smiled wide.

I returned the smile the best I could and looked questioningly at his girlfriend, who obviously wasn't Marianne Sebastian.

"This is my girlfriend, Georgia Rayfield." Greg sounded kind of goofy. It was apparent that he had it bad.

I managed another smile and was about to say "pleased to meet you" or some such thing when I heard another familiar voice from behind Greg.

"Great game, John. Congratulations," James offered as he appeared from among the throng of revelers with Marianne Sebastian clutching his arm.

My mind went numb again. I didn't know what to think. I just stood there with my helmet in my hand, my uniform covered in mud, grass, and blood, with what I'm sure was a dumb look on my face.

"Hey there." Another familiar voice sounded in my ear. A strawberry-blonde head poked out from behind the smiling James.

There was Sally. She had a huge smile of her own on her pretty face, and her eyes were sparkling as I had never seen them before. My brain was still not working. James and Marianne, and Sally, talking about hogging up the whole area.

"What is this—some kind of twisted reenactment of *Paint Your Wagon?*" I asked, referring to the movie where Clint Eastwood and Lee Marvin shared the same girl.

Sally started giggling and then laughing, and then all five of them were laughing. I still didn't get it. My heart was aching.

I must have looked the way I was feeling because Sally stopped laughing. She lunged forward and threw her arms around me, squeezing me tight. I was still confused. I had left everything out on the field. I wasn't putting two and two together very well. All the hits to the head probably didn't help much either.

"Don't you know?" she asked as she looked up into my confused eyes.

"Know what?" I managed with a little break in my voice.

Sally hugged me tighter, and the tears started to well up in her eyes. "You . . . I want you."

"What about James?" I was still not seeing it.

Sally started to giggle again and then laughing as the tears ran down her cheeks. "James is my cousin," she finally managed to get out.

Instantly, everything became clear. James and Georgia Rayfield, his sister, and Greg and Marianne all took their proper places in my head.

Sally was still holding me tight as if she would never let me go as I looked up into the eyes of Bunny, who was standing just eight feet away in her cheerleader uniform. She looked lost. I realized at that moment that she didn't have anyone. Rodney, such as he was, was gone, and I was not available. A sad lonely feeling swept through me.

Just then I heard Fred, who was standing off to my left with another media professional, say, "Excuse me for a moment."

Fred walked over to Bunny. He put one of his big strong arms around her shoulders. She looked up with her sad eyes.

"It looks like it's you and me, Bunny," he said with a confident, yet kindly smile.

Bunny's face lit up, and her smile was one for the record books. I had never seen her more radiant.

Fred turned to me and said, "I've got this" He gave me a wink, gently turned Bunny, pointing her in the direction of the concession stands. Fred was indeed the man.

CHAPTER FORTY-THREE

When I was younger and getting my clocked cleaned by the local tough guys, who incidentally had not even dared to think about doing anything that might even look like an act of aggression or disrespect toward my person in some time, my life would pass before my eyes. It was a sad, short flash of memories. As I stood there on the field with Sally in my arms, my memories came flashing back again, and there was a lot more there. Every tear, every drop of sweat and at times, blood was recorded. It had been a long, hard road. But it was so worth it. I didn't end up with Bunny like I had dreamed. Instead, I ended up with more, much more.

"Smith," a strong, good-natured voice called out from behind me.

People were still on the field celebrating. There were moms and dads and cousins and friends of the players mixing with the media, and others who just couldn't tear themselves from the euphoria. I could see Curt and Cindy across the field trying to get my mom to climb over the rail so they could come over to see me. James with Marianne and Greg with Georgia were standing next to us with big smiles.

I turned with Sally still in my arms to see who was

attempting to get my attention. Coach Wurthlin was walking up to us with a man who appeared to be in his early forties. He looked a lot like Coach Wurthlin in that he appeared to be very fit and confident. He carried a clipboard and wore a green baseball cap with a large yellow O on it.

"Smith." Coach Wurthlin paused as if he was processing something. "First of all, nice game. Congratulations."

"Thanks, Coach, same to you. You had a great season." The JV team had made it to the finals and lost to Grant by two.

"Right," the coach replied, obviously not all that pleased ending up number two. "John, I want to introduce you to a good friend of mine. This is Coach Randolf Gitsum." *Known by players and the media as Gotta Gitsum.* "The running back coach of the University of Oregon. Coach, this is John Smith, my starting running back for next year. That is, if he keeps his nose clean and continues to give me everything he's got."

Starting running back? My mind went crazy processing everything that the coach had just said.

"You're our new coach?" I asked, not believing how the planets were all lining up. "And you want me to run the ball?" I'd never thought of being a running back. I always thought running backs, like quarterbacks, were positions of a political nature. Meaning the high-profile popular kids got those opportunities and the rest of us took what was left. That's partly why I strived to be a wide receiver. It wasn't quite as lofty a goal for a skill position—at least in my mind.

"That's right, John," the coach answered. Coach Gitsum extended his hand. I took it and shook it firmly. "John, great game. Your ability to run the football was the difference out there."

"I . . . uh . . . I don't know that I did all that much. I just did what the coach told me."

I really wasn't sure I had done anything all that significant. I mostly just ran the ball as a decoy for Rodney, and on defense Eighty-Two and I kind of neutralized each other. It was obvious that the media didn't think I had done all that much. None of them had stopped to talk to me.

Coach Gitsum chuckled, looked down at his clipboard, and started reciting numbers from the game.

"First of all, on defense, you kept Medford's star lineman from blasting holes in the line for their running back all game. You hurried the quarterback into errant throws three times, deflecting the ball once. You had ten solo tackles, two for a loss. You assisted on tackles another twelve times. In the second half, you played both offense and defense every single down. You ran the ball seventeen times for one hundred and six yards. You caught one pass for forty-five yards and scored one touchdown, and you also ran for a two-point conversion. All of this against the number-one team in the state."

I had to admit, that did sound pretty good.

"John, I'll be honest with you. This doesn't mean that you'll be the next great running back from the state of Oregon. It just means that if you work hard, you might be good enough to play at the University of Oregon. If you work really hard and show me more of what I saw today, then I might, just might, have a full-ride scholarship for you."

I couldn't believe what the coach was saying. Everything I had worked for and more was coming my way. Sally was crying, and I was stunned. Suddenly, my mind opened up to what the future might hold. Where I thought that my journey was ending, my goals being met, and my life being fulfilled, just the opposite was true. My life was just beginning, and the possibilities were endless.

Mr. Johnson, Washington High's beloved janitor and mentor for many of us, once told me, "It's up to you." It had always been up to me. I'd had help and encouragement and good friends, but all in all, it was up to me. I had to do the work. Now I could see the possibilities that hard work and commitment can bring. If I want it, it's there.

"You mean if I work hard, I might get a free ride at Oregon?" I asked as my emotions caught in my throat, making it difficult to speak.

"Yes, Smith. If you want it, it's there. It's up to you."

THE END

EXCERPT FROM
MR. HENRY'S EXPENDABLES

I hopped off the bus on the corner of 12th and NW Davis and was met with an image that I'll never forget. Three men were on the sidewalk, two of which were holding onto a rope that was looped through a pulley, jury rigged to a building, three stories up and attached to what looked to be a canvas apparatus with an extremely large woman wrapped inside. They had her outside the window, of what I assumed was her bedroom, and were attempting to lower her to a flatbed truck that was parked partially on the sidewalk, ready to back under the tremendous canvas wrapped package.

"Mr. Henry?" I asked of the short pudgy man with a cigar in his mouth, who was directing this captivating scene, after pushing my way through the onlookers.

"Yeah?" He grumbled, his heavy lined face and overgrown eyebrows scrunching up as he gave me a quick once over, trying to keep his attention on the task at hand.

"I was told I could come out here and talk to you about a job," I explained trying to hide my nervousness.

"Oh, you want a job?" Mr. Henry returned gruffly, again taking his eyes off the descending woman to glare at me as two men struggled with the rope.

At that moment one of the corners of the canvas contraption tore loose causing the heavy load to shift suddenly ripping the rope from the hands of one of the men. The other man held on for dear life as the huge bundle dropped about twenty feet dragging him directly under the woman breaking her fall.

Mr. Henry looked down at the man, under the exceedingly heavy woman, who was now writhing around under her in obvious pain, and then looked back up at me.

"When can you start?"

Mr. Henry runs a company called Dirty Deeds, a unique temp agency that specializes in unpleasant, often dangerous, and sometimes marginally legal jobs that regular self-respecting people won't do. John, our main character, has recently been released from the Marine Corps with a General Discharge after a stint in the brig. He is struggling to find his way. Dirty Deeds looks to be his only option. Life is about to get interesting.

Expected Release Date:
Winter 2022

ABOUT THE AUTHOR

John Mud writes because, "It's in him and it's got to come out." (John Lee Hooker-Boogie Chillen).

Former Marine, Father of ten, and grandfather of six, John Smith, writing under the pen name of John Mud, has been trying to figure out what makes people tick ever since discovering John Steinbeck's *Grapes of Wrath* and *Of Mice and Men*. He writes about life with a style, according to his college professor, that reminds her of "Mark Twain without the twang." *Makin' My Way* is John's first novel.

www.ingramcontent.com/pod-product-compliance
Lightning Source LLC
Chambersburg PA
CBHW021956130726
47903CB00014B/1480